THE BLIND KING'S WRATH

The Burnt Empire Saga

Book 3

THE BLIND KING'S WRATH

Ashok K. Banker

HARPER Voyager
An Imprint of HarperCollins*Publishers*

Map by Carly Miller

HarperCollins books may be purchased for educational, business, or sales
promotional use. For information, please email the Special Markets Department at
SPsales@harpercollins.com.

Harper Voyager and design are trademarks of HarperCollins Publishers LLC.

FIRST EDITION

Designed by David Futato

Library of Congress Cataloging-in-Publication Data has been applied for.
ISBN 978-0-358-45133-4

22 23 24 25 26 LSC 10 9 8 7 6 5 4 3 2 1

for bithika,

yashka,

ayush yoda,

helene,

and

leia.

this gift of words and swords,

this forest of stories,

this ocean of wonders,

this epic of epics.

Dramatis Personae

New Gwannland

Gwann — Ruler of Gwannland; husband of Vensera

Vensera — Queen of Gwannland; wife of Gwann

Krushni — Adoptive daughter of Gwann and Vensera, princess and heir of Gwannland; avatar of Krushita, daughter of Jarsun and Aqreen, princess and heir of Aqron, claimant and heir of Krushan empire

Drishya — Brother of Krushni, prince and heir of Gwannland; avatar of Drishya, Slayer of Tyrak

Dronasthan

Dronas — Former friend and present enemy of Gwann; legendary teacher of warcraft and guru to the Krushan heirs; king of Dronasthan

Shikari (Lady Goddick) — Betrothed of Dronas

The Reygistan Empire

Aqron (deceased) — King of Aqron; father of Aqreen

Aqreen (deceased) — Princess of Aqron; daughter of Aqron; estranged wife of Jarsun, mother of Krushita

| Jarsun | Descendant of Kr'ush; husband of Princess Aqreen; father of Krushita; God-Emperor of Reygistan |
| Ladislew | Lover to Jarsun; Maha-Maatri of Reygar; a Morgol chieftain; widow of Pradynor |

The Gods

Jeel	Goddess of water; former wife of Sha'ant; mother of Vrath
Artha	Goddess of land; the Great Mother (a.k.a. Mother Goddess); protector of the mortal realm; sister of Goddess Jeel
Shima	God of death and duty
Sharra	God of the sun
Inadran	God of storms and war
Grrud	God of winds and birds
the Asva twins	Twin gods of animalia, health, and medicine
Shaiva	God of destruction
Coldheart	Spirit of mountains and high places; forebear of Jeel; grandfather of Vrath
Brak	The Stone Father
Gnash	God of auspicious beginnings, remover of obstacles
Jaggernaut	A stone god
Lankeshva	A stone god
Vakaronus	Architect of the stone gods
Shaputi	Amsa of the stone god Shaiva

The Burnt Empire

Kr'ush (deceased)	Founder of the Krushan dynasty and the Burnt Empire
Ashalon (deceased)	A Krushan forebear
Shapaar (deceased)	Descendant of Kr'ush; emperor of the Burnt Empire; king of Hastinaga; father of Sha'ant and Vessa

Sha'ant (deceased) — Son of Shapaar; emperor of the Burnt Empire; king of Hastinaga; father of Vrath, Virya, and Gada; husband of the goddess Jeel and of Jilana; cousin of Jarsun

Vrath — Son of Sha'ant and the goddess Jeel; uncle to Adri and Shvate; prince regent of the Burnt Empire

Jilana — Dowager empress of the Burnt Empire; dowager queen of Hastinaga; wife of Sha'ant; mother of Vessa, Virya, and Gada; stepmother of Vrath

Vessa — Seer-mage; son of Jilana; biological father of Adri, Shvate, and Vida

Virya (deceased) — Son of Sha'ant and Jilana; husband of Umber

Gada (deceased) — Son of Sha'ant and Jilana; husband of Ember

Ember — Wife of Gada; mother of Adri; sister to Umber

Umber — Wife of Virya; mother of Shvate; sister to Ember

Amber (deceased) — Sister of Ember and Umber

Adri — Emperor of the Burnt Empire; son of Ember and Gada (legally) and Vessa (biologically); grandson of Jilana; nephew of Vrath; half brother of Shvate and Vida; husband to Geldry

Shvate (deceased) — Exiled prince of the Burnt Empire; son of Umber and Virya (legally) and Vessa (biologically); grandson of Jilana; nephew of Vrath; half brother of Adri and Vida; husband to Mayla and Karni

Vida — Son of Vessa; half brother to Adri and Shvate

Mayla (deceased) — Princess of Dirda; wife of Shvate; mother of Kula and Saha

Karni — Princess of Stonecastle; wife of Shvate; mother of Yudi, Brum, and Arrow

Geldry — Princess of Geldran; wife of Adri

Dhuryo — One of the Hundred; eldest son of Geldry and Adri

Dushas — One of the Hundred; son of Geldry and Adri

Kern — Foundling son (adopted) of Adran and Reeda, firstborn son of Karni by stone god Sharra and consigned by her to the river Jeel

Sauvali   Maid in the royal palace, lover of Adri, mother of his child

The Five

Yudi   Karni's son fathered by the stone god Shima

Arrow   Karni's child fathered by the stone god Inadran

Brum   Karni's daughter fathered by the stone god Grrud

Kula   Mayla's child fathered by the stone gods the Asvas; Saha's twin

Saha   Mayla's child fathered by the stone gods the Asvas; Kula's twin

ARTHALOKA

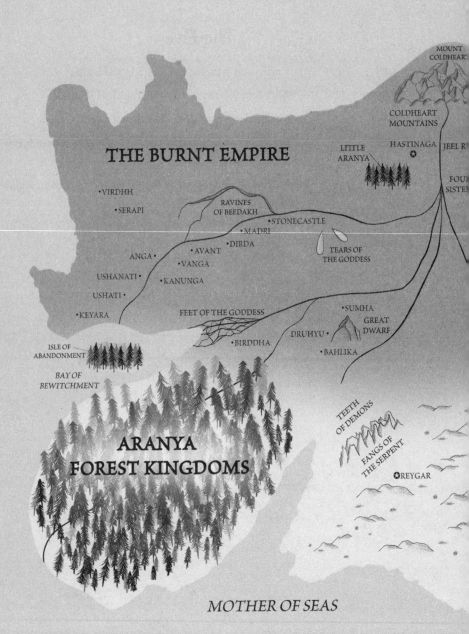

MOUNT
COLDHEART

COLDHEART
MOUNTAINS

THE BURNT EMPIRE

LITTLE
ARANYA

HASTINAGA

JEEL R'

FOUR
SISTE

•VIRDHH

•SERAPI

RAVINES
OF BEEDAKH

•STONECASTLE

•MADRI

•DIRDA

ANGA•

•AVANT

•VANGA

USHANATI•

•KANUNGA

USHATI•

•KEYARA

FEET OF THE GODDESS

TEARS OF
THE GODDESS

•SUMHA

GREAT
DWARF

DRUHYU•

ISLE OF
ABANDONMENT

•BIRDDHA

•BAHLIKA

BAY OF
BEWITCHMENT

ARANYA
FOREST KINGDOMS

TEETH
OF DEMONS

FANGS OF
THE SERPENT

✵REYGAR

MOTHER OF SEAS

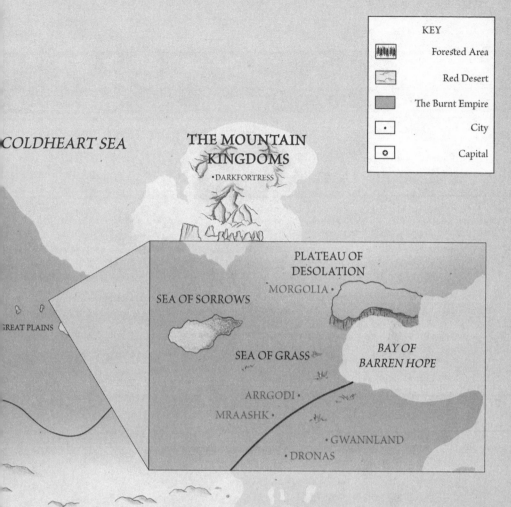

COLDHEART SEA

THE MOUNTAIN KINGDOMS

• DARKFORTRESS

PLATEAU OF DESOLATION

MORGOLIA •

SEA OF SORROWS

GREAT PLAINS

SEA OF GRASS

BAY OF BARREN HOPE

ARRGODI •

MRAASHK •

• GWANNLAND

• DRONAS

THE REYGISTAN EMPIRE

RED DESERT

AQRON ✪

PROLOGUE

A Knife in the Dark

YEAR 195 OF CHAKRA 58

(FIFTEEN YEARS AGO)

Karni

~

1

MAYLA HACKED AT THE ASSASSIN.

The sword met only air.

She screamed and swung again and yet again, but Jarsun was long gone, vanished through the portal and now a thousand miles away, or a thousand worlds distant, only a few threads of fabric from his cloak, a spot of blood, and exotic odors from a distant realm marking his passage.

Mayla sank to the floor of the hut, weeping, her sword slipping from her hands. A roar of grief tore itself from her throat, filling the hut, the clearing, the whole forest with her agony. Her children echoed her rage and grief, weeping, hitching their breaths, their little heads shaking in disbelief and denial. Only little Brum, fierce and resistant as always, clenched her fists and ground her teeth in fury, like a maddened wolf.

Karni's ears heard her sister wife's grief, but she herself felt too many strange conflicting emotions to yield to the same impulses. Instead, she watched and listened, curiously detached in this moment of devastation. An observer in her own home. Witness to her own life's ruin.

Mayla's weeping was echoed by the shrill cries and shouts of five young throats. The children of Mayla, Karni, and Shvate approached the prostrate body of their father, their little arms raised, or held out, or clasped around their chests in panic, striving to make sense of this madness.

The only other person in the hut, standing by the open doorway, a hand raised to cover half his face, the other hand outstretched against the wall to support himself, was Vida, Shvate's half brother, who had come from Has-

3

tinaga to warn them. Warn them of another attack, this one a supernatural one perpetrated by Jarsun. He had been as easily deceived as they were when Jarsun appeared in the form of Vessa and assassinated Shvate.

Never a fighter or man of action, he had watched helplessly as Jarsun slew Shvate in the blink of an eye, with just a single slash of his fingertips delivering five tiny but potent snakebites that carried instant death. Vida stared down in bewildered shock and grief at the very tragedy he had sought to warn them against, and hopefully avoid.

Karni's husband, Shvate, still lay sprawled where he had fallen, his face and neck bulging from the five snakebites received from Jarsun's fingertips, his upper body from the chest upward turning a garish blue as the poisoned blood cooled in his veins. An albino since birth, he had been named for his condition — *Shvate* meant "white-skinned or colorless one" in Ashcrit — and the toxic blue of the venom in contrast to his otherwise pale color was more shocking than blood. His eyes lay open, translucent pupils staring blankly up at the ceiling of the hut.

Karni was in shock. Frozen to the spot. She could not bring herself to think, to acknowledge, to believe. Surely this had not just happened. It was a dream, was it not? A terrible, strange, nightmarish delusion . . .

They had built this hut together, Mayla and Karni and Shvate, using only the materials of the jungle, their blades, and bare hands.

Karni looked around at her ruined life, at the rustic but clean hut and its meager items: straw pallets for beds, wooden blocks for stools, a thatched roof that leaked during the rainy season and inevitably collapsed and had to be rebuilt after the autumn storms; her sister wife, Mayla, weeping and prostrate with grief; the five children they had birthed together.

They had left Hastinaga with nothing but the clothes on their backs, and yet they had managed to find happiness here in exile, she thought.

We built a home here in the wilderness. We built a house with mud, straw, timber, and love, and made it a home. We filled it with our laughter, our despair, our hopes, our sorrows, our love.

And in a single instant, one man walked in and burned it all down.

No. Not a man.

Jarsun.

Enemy of his own kith and kin.

Shvate's own blood relative, exiled from the Burnt Empire on pain of death for his transgressions and crimes committed decades ago, in the reign of Emperor Shapar, father of Sha'ant and Vessa and, from an earlier liaison, of Jarsun himself.

Karni tried to remember the complex genealogy of her dead husband's family tree and gave up almost at once. What did it matter if Jarsun was a great-uncle or great-whatever? He was kin to Shvate, an elder of the family, a fellow Krushan, sharing the same relationship to stonefire as Shvate. Their only conflict had been as players of the game of war, back when Shvate had still served his duties as prince of Hastinaga, leading the armies of the Burnt Empire against Jarsun's forces in several clashes: the Battle of the Rebels and the Battle of Reygar being the two most notable. Shvate had left that service behind him when he abdicated his claim to the Burning Throne, handing over sole control to his brother Adri before he went into lifelong self-exile with his two wives years ago.

Why come after Shvate now? Why disguise himself as Vessa, his own half brother and Shvate's biological father? Why not as Vida, or as ... as anybody?

What did it matter?

What did *anything* matter now?

Shvate was dead.

Her husband, her lover, her friend, her wonderful, inspiring, despairing, beautiful, infuriating-at-times, but also charming-when-he-tried, Shvate, beloved Shvate, was dead.

Her mouth filled with the ashes of despair, her heart swelled with pain, her body screamed vengeance.

But first, she had work to do.

She alone, because Mayla, ever the quickest of temper and fastest of sword and foot, had already shot her arrows of endurance and emptied her quiver. She was a broken mess, weeping and wallowing in the black waters of grief.

The children were ... They were children. Babies, really. All of an age, none even three years on this earth as yet.

And Vida. Vida was a guest, a visitor, a friend; he would soon depart for Hastinaga, carrying with him the sorrow of Shvate's passing, leaving behind his commiserations and sympathy, but little more. He did not share their exile, their life, their circumstances. He would advise and help from afar, but he could not do much more at this moment of crisis.

It was all up to Karni.

She was the strong one, the pillar, the stanchion of this family.

She was the only one who could carry them through this.

"Mayla," she said softly, bending to touch her sister wife. Mayla's back shuddered beneath her fingertips, her body racked by all-consuming sobs. She was so far into her own mourning, she seemed not even to be aware of her children, wailing and crying beside her.

"Mayla," Karni repeated, louder and more firmly.

Movement by the doorway: Vida lurching outside, a darker silhouette against the dull gloam of dusk. Then the sound of his retching as he purged his belly outside their threshold. *At least he was thoughtful enough not to soil our home*, Karni thought with ice-cold clarity.

Mayla's sobbing continued unabated.

Karni bent down and took the younger woman by her shoulders. Gripping tightly, she hauled her to her feet. Mayla's knees buckled, but Karni was strong enough to hold her upright. She looked her in the eye. Mayla's face was smeared with tears, her eyes brimming, lips parted soundlessly.

"I need you to help me with the children," Karni said.

Mayla wailed. "Shvate . . ."

Karni resisted the temptation to shake or slap her. Instead, she moved her grip from Mayla's shoulders to her head, grasping it on either side, pressing her thumbs against the woman's temples.

"Listen to me," Karni said, hearing her own voice, steel-hard and sword-sharp, yet low enough that it would not alarm the children further. "There will be time to grieve later. Right now, we are all in danger. This may not be the end of Jarsun's attack. We have to protect the children and get them to safety right away."

Mayla seemed to come into herself for a moment. Her eyes focused on Karni and saw her briefly through her fog of tears and pain. "Shvate . . ." she moaned.

"Is gone, yes. I grieve for him too. But now is not the time for grief. Now is the time to survive. To protect ourselves. To stay alive."

Mayla stared at her, and Karni felt a rush of relief as she seemed to be calming down. "Alive," Mayla repeated. "Alive . . ."

Mayla looked down at the body of Shvate, now almost entirely blue from the venom, his face and throat swollen and bulging obscenely, purpling in patches. Her eyes widened at the alarming rapid deterioration. She shook her head vehemently. "I don't want to be alive," she said in a perfectly sober voice. "I don't want to live with Shvate dead. I don't want to live."

"Shut up," Karni said softly, dangerously. "Don't talk like that in front of the children. Look at them. They're devastated. They just saw their father murdered, and they're still babies. They need us. We need to act quickly and keep our heads clear. More trouble may already be coming for us. For them."

Mayla stared at her as if she were a stranger met for the first time. Her eyes drifted downward again. Karni caught her chin and forced it up, compelling her to keep looking at her.

"Get hold of yourself. You are not just a wife. You're a mother. Your children — *our* children — need you. I need you. I can't do this alone, Mayla. Those five are a handful on any given day. It will take both of us to pull them away from their father. Wake up, Mayla!"

These last three words were not spoken in a raised voice. Karni's pitch remained level, her tone urgent. She was still unwilling to pour more emotion and conflict into this already brimming home. But she could see that she was not getting through to Mayla. The younger woman was too far gone in her grief.

She's young and brash, Karni thought. *She thought she had lost Shvate before, when they were cursed by the sage. Then, again, when Shvate tried to take his own life. When he survived both times, and we continued to live together and the children were born, and then we got busy with nursing them and raising them, they filled our lives completely. She found comfort and security in our little world, our family.*

Now that world is shattered, the family broken. Of all the things that could possibly have gone wrong, this was the one thing she thought she had triumphed over. Ever a warrior, she only knows victory and defeat. She thought Shvate and she had snatched victory out of the jaws of death, not just during the battles and fights they fought shoulder to shoulder, but in these past few years of peacetime as well.

To lose him now is the one thing she was not prepared to accept, to endure. It will break her. She will never be the same again. But that doesn't matter. All that matters is the children and their survival, and for that, I need her to hold herself together, if not emotionally, then mentally and physically at least.

The instant she released Mayla, the younger woman folded into herself on the floor, like a wet cloak fallen from the clothesline. She lay in a crumpled heap, weeping the deep, desolate tears of someone who has surrendered all hope, all reason, all sense.

Karni picked up her sword and pointed it at Mayla, who seemed not to notice.

She jabbed the point of the sword into Mayla's side, fleshier since the children, even with the meager fare they had to eat in this wilderness.

A warrior born and raised, Mayla had little time to even practice her usual routines with Shvate as they had once all done together. With five little ones to manage and a forest full of potential dangers and unknown enemies abroad, they had needed to be constantly vigilant. That was apart from their never-ending daily chores and duties. It was hard to manage a household, raise little children, and survive in the forest, as well as keep up the rigorous training regime required of a master warrior. While not fat —their forest repast hardly allowed for indulgences— Mayla had softened considerably since the days when Shvate and she had gone on campaigns together.

Karni pricked that fleshy side with deliberate force, enough to draw blood and be keenly felt without causing any real damage. She might not be as veteran a warrior as Mayla or Shvate, but she had received good training during her childhood and youth at Stonecastle, and she knew basic anatomy well enough.

Mayla started at the sword prick, jerking upright. Her hair had fallen over her face, and her eyes, red-rimmed and brimful, stared up at her attacker wildly.

"You *cut* me!" she cried indignantly.

Karni raised the sword to point at Mayla's throat. "Yes, and I'll do it again, and again, until you listen."

As the point of the sword drifted upward, Mayla reacted.

Her hand shot out, slapping the flat of the blade with enough force that it jerked like a living thing in Karni's hands. Even though she had been expecting it, she still felt her wrists creak.

Mayla kicked Karni's feet out from under her.

Karni fell clumsily, banging her hip on the mud floor, catching herself in time to avoid striking the back of her head. She felt the sword snatched away and could do nothing to prevent it.

In a trice, Mayla stood over her, holding the sword to Karni's throat.

"You cut me!" Mayla said again, her eyes flashing through the folds of the curtain of disheveled hair.

Karni smiled with a twinge of bitterness, even though her hip was crying out and her husband's body lay, still warm and cooling, only a few feet away. She knew she wasn't badly hurt, just as Mayla's wound would stop bleeding in a few minutes on its own.

"That's the Mayla I need right now," she said grimly. "Now, help me up, and let's do what must be done."

2

It took surprisingly little time for the hut to burn. They watched, tears falling from their eyes as thick gouts of smoke engulfed the thatched roof. The beams crackled like dry twigs snapping underfoot and collapsed, throwing up a flurry of sparks and ash that drifted over and around them. The steady drone of Ashcrit chanting carried over the crackling and roaring of the flames.

They had decided to use the hut itself to cremate Shvate. With Vida's guidance for the specific rituals that applied to Krushan royalty, they had carried out the required formalities as best they could. The rishis and hermits from the nearby ashram had joined in to help them and were reciting them now, all chanting in unison.

Ideally, Krushan funeral rites called for stonefire to be used to cremate the bodies, but there was none readily at hand, and no time to go seeking even a chip or a pebble. Shvate would not care, Karni knew, and Vida agreed. Mayla and the kids had only gone through the motions, doing as instructed, still stupefied by shock and grief.

The five children were standing, staring, hugging themselves, sitting, and looking up at the smoke rising into the sky respectively. They had stopped the babyish wailing and were dangerously quiet now, like feral cats awaiting threat.

Mayla had tied her hair in a knot and her garment around her waist, girding her loins just like Karni had, the way they both did when washing clothes in the river or chopping firewood. Soot stains marred their sweat-shiny faces and bare arms. Mayla's eyes had a strange, lost glitter. Karni knew that although she had done as Karni requested, her actions had all been mechanical and designed to do what was needed as quickly and efficiently as possible. Her mind, her heart, the Mayla inside, had gone someplace else.

To Shvate, Karni thought sorrowfully. A part of her died with Shvate. She was too attached to him to ever separate herself. She had never anticipated a day when she would have to continue living without him, even though she knew about his curse and the fact that he was a warrior. Even when Shvate had killed a sage and his wife while out hunting, and been cursed to die should he ever lie with a woman again, Mayla, whose love for physical desire was even greater than Shvate's, had accepted celibacy and the loss of her husband's caress. When Shvate had decided to abdicate the throne as a result of the curse, because he was unable to perpetuate the Krushan bloodline, Mayla had accepted that momentous decision as well, and left the luxuries and safety of the imperial palace for this mud hut in the forest. Mayla's love for Shvate had made her believe that they could overcome anything. That they would live forever.

Karni understood that feeling. She had been young — younger, in fact, a mere girl — when she had been in love with her childhood friend. His death had shattered her. She had been so destroyed by his loss, a visiting sage had sensed her grief and granted her a boon: the God Mantra. With the recklessness of youth, she had used the mantra to summon her dead lover. He had appeared before her, not the man she had once loved but the sun god, Sharra, in the form of her late lover. She had given herself to him, consummating her unfulfilled passion, and conceived a child from that union.

And now I cremate my second lover, my husband, father of my children.

Why do all my romances end in flames? Why do the greatest loves always end in tragedy? Or is it because they ended in tragedy that we remember them as great loves?

She shook her head now, dispelling the wave of sorrow and grief that threatened to rise up like the floodwaters of a deep well. This was not the time to wallow in self-pity. Mayla was doing enough of that for the both of them.

The crackling of the fire and swirling ash and smoke helped Karni stay rooted to the moment.

I need to focus on the children.

She was worried about them. They had grown too quiet, too still.

The Five were not ordinary children.

True, they played and frolicked like any others their age, but they were far more than just mischievous tykes. They were demigods, each and every one of them, conceived from the most powerful stone gods summoned by the God Mantra. Their powers had yet to reveal themselves fully, and their extent would only be known once they came of age, but already they displayed enough talent to make them extraordinary . . . and dangerous. Karni feared how the brutal murder of their father before their eyes would affect them.

Vida stirred behind her, making a sound to attract her attention.

She turned to look at him.

The soft-featured advisor shared some features with Shvate — the broad, backward-sloping forehead for one, the perfectly shaped aquiline nose, the same eyes — but his jaw was weaker, his body softer, his shoulders narrower, and muscles undeveloped from a youth spent dedicated to the mastery of knowledge rather than warcraft. He was a good man, but unaccustomed to violence and far from a man of action.

One more life to protect and look after for now, Karni thought. She was the only one here who was mature and responsible and capable enough to make the hard decisions, at least until . . .

Until when?

She had no idea.

"Vida?" she asked simply. She had no more energy for wasted words or gestures.

He looked at her with sorrowful eyes that reflected the dancing flames. "Come to Hastinaga with me. My chariot remains at the outskirts of the jungle. It will be a challenge, but perhaps it will carry us all away from here. We can go slowly, taking our time. Once we reach the outlying villages, we can get fresh horses to continue to the city. You will be safe there under the protection of Prince Regent Vrath and Dowager Empress Jilana."

She looked at him for a moment, knowing he meant well. She reached out, touching his face lightly. "Gentle Vida, your invitation is touching and, on the face of it, logical. But Hastinaga is the last place we would be safe right now."

He blinked. "It is?"

"Yes. Think about it. Jarsun wouldn't have used subterfuge to kill Shvate unless he had a larger plan in place. Removing Shvate only makes sense if he has already set into motion other events and players that pave the way to the Burning Throne. And where is the throne, the seat of ultimate power?"

"In Hastinaga," Vida admitted. "But Vrath and Jilana —"

"Are not omnipotent or omniscient. Just as they could not prevent Shvate's assassination here, they would not be able to prevent Jarsun from striking at me or my children in some fiendish manner. You saw how easily he duped us all into believing he was Vessa today. If it had not been for you, Vida, we might not have realized the truth, and he might have simply committed the murder and vanished, leaving us bewildered. He only revealed himself because you so brilliantly observed that scar on the wrong hand. It also proved to me that even the devil makes mistakes. Stupid, tiny mistakes, but mistakes nonetheless."

She paused, recalling something else. "Besides, weren't you dispatched here by Vrath and Jilana to warn us of the next attack? And wasn't it they who sent their regrets that they could not send aid or come themselves to help us? Because of their need to avoid direct involvement in this ... epic feud, or whatever one calls it? I can't imagine they would be happy to have us turn up uninvited in Hastinaga after all they said. And it would be devastating to us to travel all the way there, only to be turned away."

Vida shook his head. "What you say about my being sent by Jilana and Vrath is true, of course. And yes, they could not send military aid to your rescue. But it would be very different in Hastinaga itself. Anyone they grant sanctuary to would be protected under Krushan law, and any attempt on your lives would be an act of treason against the throne itself, punishable by death. I can't promise that Jarsun cannot get to you there, but it is much less likely, as he will be in the enemy's den, the seat of all power. I saw how he fared against Vrath at the Battle of the Rebels. It is a victory I have never forgotten. It proved that Jarsun *can* be defeated. I believe he fears Vrath. If there is one person whom Jarsun would not dare cross, it is he. Vrath's presence alone would be your best guarantee of safety."

The fire had caught the cowshed now. They had turned loose the cow and her calf, but the shed had been full of hay, grass, and chopped wood for the coming winter, and the fire roared anew, doubling in ferocity and rage. It echoed the emotions of all those standing before it in the clearing.

"I hear all that you say, gentle Vida," Karni said. "But I would rather not return to Hastinaga just yet. I need time to think and process my grief. We all do. And my first priority is the safety and well-being of my children. So, no, I regretfully decline your invitation and offer."

Vida looked sadder still, if such a thing was possible, but he seemed to accept her decision. Unlike his half brother, he was not the kind of man who argued every point.

"In that case, sister-in-law, I would like to take your leave. It is painful and reprehensible of me to abandon you and your family at this most tragic of times. But as I said earlier, things are afoot in the palace as well, and if what you said is true — and I do believe it to be so — then surely Jarsun's plan includes working some havoc in Hastinaga as well. It is imperative that I return at once and report this sad event to the elders. Both Vrath and Jilana will be shocked and saddened by this news, but it is crucial they learn of it as quickly as possible. So long as Shvate was alive, he was still an heir to the Burning Throne, despite his abdication. Should he have chosen to return at any time, or to nominate his children to take his place, the elders would have accepted it without question. As I have said before, Dowager Empress Jilana and Prince Regent Vrath frequently encouraged me to broach the subject of return to Shvate. Even our brother Adri, though he did not say so explicitly, encouraged such an approach. The burden of empire sits heavy on his brow, and he would have welcomed Shvate coming home to rule beside him. Now that possibility has been closed off forever. Shvate's death will come as a great shock. It is a major upheaval in the chain of inheritance and changes the balance of power significantly."

It was not the first time Vida had spoken of these things; in fact, his previous visits had been centered around this very dialogue with Shvate, often attempting to recruit Karni's and Mayla's aid in convincing their husband. Mayla and Karni had even talked about it privately, together as well as with

Shvate, and had pointed out that for the sake of the children, moving back to Hastinaga would be the best way to secure their inheritance when they came of age. Karni had no idea how she alone might be accepted now that Shvate was gone. Or how their father's death might impact her children's future as Krushan heirs. But she could not dwell on such matters right now, not with her husband's corpse still warm in their hut. It was a matter to be dealt with another day.

"Safe travels, Vida."

Vida bid her farewell and then took his leave of Mayla and the children, all of whom were still too dazed to do more than mumble politely. He walked into the woods in the direction of Hastinaga. Karni wondered if she would ever see him again. The future seemed so uncertain now, a dark wall looming before her. She felt one final pang of regret at not accepting his invitation. Despite her clearly voiced — and very sensible — objections, the truth was that Hastinaga was the closest thing to a home she had left. That her children had left. But she knew in her heart she had made the right call.

And that decision was made final once Vida passed into the woods, out of her sight. Alone, he would move quickly and ride even quicker. She closed that door in her mind and turned back to more practical options.

The best place she could hope to find sanctuary in this time of crisis was her father's abode, Stonecastle. There was one more place, of course: Mraashk. Her homeland, home of her birth parents and family. But she had been adopted as a little child by the ruler of Stonecastle and raised as his own, and she regarded him as her true family. To go back to Mraashk now, after all these years, would be far too strange.

No, it must be Stonecastle, it was her last hope now. Her only port in this storm.

A break in the Ashcrit chanting distracted her from her thoughts. Then a startled yell, followed by shouts and a horrendous scream.

Karni turned back to the burning hut just in time to see a flurry of white fabric meld into the vivid yellow flames and disappear.

Her heart leaped into her mouth.

"Mayla!" she yelled, darting forward.

But several hands grasped Karni's wrists, her arms, her shoulders, stalling her motion.

The rishis and their acolytes were shouting, urging her to see sense, to think of her children.

She shook her head. She wasn't intending to jump into the fire as Mayla had just done. She had thought perhaps she might still save the younger woman.

But even as she watched, not resisting their protective hands, she saw Mayla's pale skin moving inside the well of fire, as she sought out and then found what Karni knew she had gone after.

Shvate's corpse, mounted and anointed atop the pyre they had built inside the hut.

With a final hoarse cry of despair and longing, Mayla cast herself down upon the pyre of her dead husband. *Their* dead husband.

The flames obscured the rest, rushing in greedily to feed upon their new prey.

Karni cried out in solidarity with her poor, doomed sister wife, releasing the grief, the pain, the sorrow, that she had pent up inside her, now doubled at this fresh hell.

She cried out for Mayla, who did not utter a single sound even as the flames engulfed her and fed upon her living flesh.

She cried for her ruined life, her devastated family, her murdered marriage. For the children, who were all she had left now.

The rishis released her as they saw she was not afflicted by the same passionate self-destruction that had driven Mayla to her final, desperate act.

The children came to her then, crowding around her, putting their arms around her and each other. They all wept together and called out their pain.

And across the hundred miles or more that separated it from them, the Burning Throne heard and felt their pain and anguish, and replied with the cold, emotionless glee of animate stone.

Burn, it sang. *Burn.*

Jilana

~

1

JILANA SMELLED VESSA EVEN before he materialized.

Living in the wild jungles of Aranya, the seer-mage rarely had an opportunity to bathe. She sighed, knowing that his arrival marked the end of her afternoon gossip-and-wine session, a rare moment of respite from the travails of overseeing the world's greatest empire. She was used to her son's unannounced visits. The other women, however, all mature matrons from the highest houses in Hastinaga, were not so well accustomed to wild-haired, half-naked seers appearing out of thin air. A certain amount of commotion ensued. After the serving maids hastily ushered them out, she turned to her son.

A light dusting of snow on his wild tangles, ebony face, and bony frame suggested that he might have recently departed climes more wintery than the searing heat of a Hastinaga noonday. She caught a glimpse of the portal before it irised shut behind him, seeing a mountainous peak in the teeth of a blizzard. A few snowflakes drifted around her, one landing on the back of her perfectly manicured hand, just behind the signet ring with the seal that marked her as the widow of the late Emperor Sha'ant, the last full Krushan to sit upon the throne.

"My son, if I'd known you were coming by, I might have warned my friends," she said. She had drunk a little more wine than usual, or she would have known better than to attempt to be witty. His face remained as stony in expression as ever. From his manner, she knew that something had happened.

"What is it?" she asked.

He did not look at her. Vessa's penetrating gaze, capable of seeing through walls and beyond dimensions, could also reduce a person to ashes if they provoked his volatile temper. It was a weakness of most seer-mages. Self-isolated in deep jungles for centuries of meditation, imbued with enormous powers gained through the mastery of arcane energies, they lost all social skills and most human qualities. It was worse when they were in a mood, as he clearly was at this moment. This being Vessa, she knew it meant the crisis was serious.

She tried to calm her racing pulse and braced herself for whatever he was about to reveal.

He turned his piercing gaze in her direction. Even though he avoided staring directly at her, she had to resist the impulse to hold up a warding hand. She had seen what he could do with a single look; it was a memory that even time could not erase. Fortunately, he turned his attention to the floor instead, staring at something she could not see. She frowned, then guessed the object of his scrutiny: the throne chamber two floors below, separated from him only by a few yards of solid load-bearing pillars, stone, and masonry.

"It feeds off our emotions," he said, his voice unusually bitter and tinged with a sense of tragic sadness. Jilana breathed out slowly, wondering what might have unsettled him so. The only things he cared about were his family and the eternal power struggle of which he was a small but important part; if she'd had to guess, being his mother, she would have hazarded that the issue that brought him here was something involving both. "It grows stronger when one of us experiences emotional turmoil. It feeds on our energies. Nothing pleases it more than the violent, sudden death of one of us Krushan."

She felt a chill in her bones that was deeper than the cold gust that had arrived in his wake. "You speak of the Burning Throne," she said. "Stonefire."

"I speak of the death of one of our own."

"Who?" she asked, suddenly sober, dreading the answer.

He turned to gaze at her, focusing as always slightly above her head and to the right. She saw the banked fires smoldering in his pupils, tiny flames dancing within dark pools of rage.

"Shvate."

He said no more, just the one word.

It was enough.

She felt her knees start to buckle and caught the edge of the table in time to stop herself from falling.

Time might not erase memories, but it took its toll upon the body without mercy. She had seen too many decades, too many generations, too many deaths, in this house alone. The House of Krushan, the dynasty sprung from the loins of mighty Kr'ush himself, descended from the stone gods before they departed Arthaloka, mandated to govern the mortal realm and ensure law and order through the divine writ of Krushan law.

Or so the legends said.

What the legends did not say, but should have, was that the House of Krushan was cursed. Not one generation of Krushan had ever been truly happy and content, not for more than a few seasons had the Burnt Empire been at peace ... except for the handful of years when she and Emperor Sha'ant had been man and wife. Oh, to have those happy days again. To re-live every glorious moment. She, a fisherman's daughter, already the mother of one illegitimate child, had loved and been loved for those wonderful years by the finest man she had ever known, and perhaps the one truly great liege that Hastinaga, the city-state, capital, and center of the Burnt Empire, had ever known.

But when Sha'ant's life ended, the glory days ended with it.

Both her sons, fine young men for whom her stepson Vrath, Sha'ant's son from an earlier marriage, had arranged vivacious wives, had died in their prime, childless. Faced with the threat of civil unrest and the possibility of an empire shattering into myriad shards, she had known that an heir to the throne was vital to the House's survival. And that heir could only be a Krushan, the sole bloodline capable of passing the dreaded Test of Fire and sitting upon stonefire, on the legendary Burning Throne.

So she had turned to her illegitimate son, Vessa, a half Krushan who had been fathered upon her by a wandering hermit years before she had met Sha'ant. Vessa's father had been a full Krushan, an abdicated royal who had turned his back on his legacy to embark on a spiritual quest, and with whom she had lain but a single night. Vessa had reluctantly conceded to her request after warning her of the possible consequences; she had insisted, for the sake of House Krushan, and to uphold the legacy of her beloved Sha'ant.

And thus had begun the continuing series of tragedies that would plague the House for decades.

Vessa had agreed to her request, fathering children upon the princesses Amber and Umber, the widows of her late sons. Those children had been the princes Adri and Shvate, two equal heirs to the throne and the empire. Because Adri was blind and his disability regarded as a weakness for a House that governed through threat of war and combat, Shvate had been chosen to ascend the throne. He had proven himself admirably capable, even winning his half brother's support and approval.

But then Shvate had abdicated his place unexpectedly in self-atonement following his accidental killing of a seer and his wife, and retired to the jungle with his two wives, Mayla and Karni. The last she had heard, the three of them had borne five children together, all potential heirs to the throne. She had expected them to visit soon, to pay their respects to her and Vrath and present the children to the court, the people, and most of all, the Burning Throne itself.

The throne's supernatural link with those of Krushan blood was something beyond her capacity as an ordinary human to fully understand, but she knew that they were bonded for life, and each fed off the other. Once a Krushan assumed the throne, stonefire's power became theirs to wield as they desired. The king or queen who sat upon the Burning Throne of Hastinaga decided the fate of the world. For was there any corner of this great supercontinent of Arthaloka, even those regions that resisted the dominance of the Burnt Empire, that did not live in fear of its looming shadow? It was said that when the Burning Throne spoke, even the stone gods paused to listen, wherever they might be in the vast cosmos. For the throne spoke for all mortalkind, and its flames were the fire of the Eternal River into which all souls would descend someday in order to attain the netherworld of Stone God Shima.

And now this news.

"Shvate?" she said, leaning against the table. She pressed the other hand against her face, shutting her eyes, and felt the chamber spin within her head. "Mother Jeel! Why him? He was the best of us."

"They are always the first to die."

She opened her eyes reluctantly, sliding her hips along the edge of the table until her foot found a chair. She sat heavily. "How?"

He clenched his wildwood staff. She saw his knuckles whiten. "The how is unimportant. The why is self-evident. The who is what will destroy us."

She tried to make sense of his words. "I don't understand. Who killed him?"

He turned to look at her, through her, beyond her. She had never seen him so incensed before. In that moment, she feared he might not pause to remind himself that hers was the womb that had borne him to life.

"I did," he said.

2

It was brilliantly done.

Jilana had said they must summon Vrath and Vida and Adri to hear what Vessa had to say. As family members, they would be informed of Shvate's death in any case; it was best they heard the circumstances firsthand. Vessa would permit only Vrath to be summoned. Vrath, because he was beyond reproach, being a demigod and a person who had proven himself incorruptible over a lifetime. Vrath's reputation for integrity was the stuff of legends and righteously earned. As prince regent of the empire and de facto commander in chief of its enormous armed forces, as well as administrator of the empire's day-to-day functioning, his was a crucial presence. Even had he not been Shvate and Adri's uncle and the protector of the realm, they would have been remiss had they not called him. Without him, the Burnt Empire would have fallen to pieces decades ago.

"Why not Vida and Adri?" Jilana asked. "They are your sons and Shvate's half brothers. They have a right to know."

"Shvate and Adri's relationship was once that of two brothers, but much has changed in the years since the Battle of the Rebels." Vessa shook his head decisively. "Adri is sitting emperor of the Burnt Empire, and in time, he will know all. But for the moment, I wish to discuss these matters in private with you and Prince Regent Vrath."

"I acknowledge that there was a rift between Shvate and Adri at the battle, a rift that never healed. But why not Vida? He and Shvate were close as could be."

Vida was Vessa's get as well: when the princesses Amber and Ember had reacted with shock and disgust at Vessa's appearance and unwashed physicality, one had turned pale with disbelief, the other had shut her eyes completely. The results had been an albino child and a blind child respectively, rendered thus by the peculiar mystical logic of the seer's belief system. Jilana had foolishly insisted that he cover them again to ensure they bore robust physically and mentally able offspring, but the second time round, the princesses had substituted a maidservant in their place. Vessa had fathered a third son, able and very suitable, upon the maid, but as she was not of the Krushan line by either blood or marriage, the child could not be considered suitable under Krushan law. Vida had accepted his inferior status from childhood with more grace than might have been expected, taking pride and pleasure in serving his brothers and the House in every way he could. Vida and Shvate had been very close, the one's intellectual acumen and the other's fighting prowess making them a perfect pairing.

"Indeed," Vessa agreed. "But Vida is not in Hastinaga at present. He is in the jungle, where he went to visit Shvate and his family. He was there when the assassination took place, and witnessed it firsthand."

Jilana nodded, understanding.

When Vrath arrived, Vessa gave him a longer moment's scrutiny, so much so that Jilana feared her son might be offended by some obscure aspect of Vrath's appearance or manner and be about to turn him into a squealing animal or a rock, or something far worse. On the other hand, Vrath was no ordinary man. A demigod himself, son of River Goddess and Earth Mother Jeel, he could probably deflect any curse of Vessa's as easily as he deflected a hail of arrows. He showed no reaction to Vessa's unusual scrutiny and merely stood, statuesque in marbled stillness, until the sage turned his piercing gaze away. Jilana breathed a sigh of relief.

Vessa addressed them both.

"The House of Krushan faces its most grievous crisis, both within and without this palace."

Vessa's voice was unusually quiet. There was none of the bombast or unbridled rage that Jilana had expected. Instead, he seemed almost subdued now, as if the banked fires she had glimpsed earlier had been pushed to a back corner of his capacious mind. In their place was a glacial calm. She understood that he intended to proceed with great self-control. That told her just how severe the crisis must be. This was not a passing storm that could be dealt with quickly; it was a long campaign against an unbeatable foe. Already, she glimpsed where he was heading. After all, the events he was now describing had a long history, one that she had witnessed, participated in, and indeed, precipitated at crucial times in the past.

"Jarsun."

Taciturn Vrath had spoken the name.

Vessa inclined his head, acknowledging the truth of that statement.

"He assumed my form, knowing that Shvate and his family were expecting me, and visited them in their humble forest dwelling. It got him close enough to drive venomous fingernails into Shvate's heart, killing him instantly. He was gone before Mayla and Karni even knew what had happened."

"They saw it?" Jilana asked, feeling the back of her throat prickle.

Vessa's eyes mirrored her sorrow. "The children witnessed it as well."

She shook her head, feeling tears spring up but fighting them back. "Holy Mother Jeel! Such tragedy to have befallen ones so young and tender of mind!" She raised her palms in a gesture of appeal. "Why would the Exiled One visit such pain and grief upon them? They were dwelling peacefully in the wilderness, doing no one any harm. Shvate had already abdicated his claim to the throne, departing Hastinaga forever. He had taken vows. He posed no threat, present or future, to Jarsun and his nefarious ambitions! Why kill him? Why now?"

"A good question, Mother." Vessa's tone, if not quite comforting, was sympathetic. "The answer is not reassuring, but it is the truth. Jarsun wished to achieve several things at once with the one assassination. The primary goal was to isolate and diminish Shvate's family, particularly his progeny. Under Krushan law, any child born of Shvate's wives is eligible to sit upon the Burning Throne and rule Hastinaga."

"Stonefire will not accept anyone not of Krushan blood," Jilana pointed out. "It was my understanding that not one of Princess Mayla's and Princess Karni's offspring were seeded by Shvate — Mother Goddess rest his soul — which means they are not directly of Krushan blood, though they are deemed legitimate under the law. Surely stonefire would never permit them to hold power?"

"Indeed, it would, Mother," Vessa said with rare gentleness, showing respect for his mater. "It must by Krushan law as well as by dint of their biological identities. Stonefire was the legacy of the stone gods before they departed our mortal realm, created out of Vish's own *Auma*. Each of the five children of Shvate's wives is of divine descent, and therefore each of them is a demigod like valiant Prince Regent Vrath. Since Mayla and Karni were indeed Shvate's lawfully wedded wives, joined in the presence of and by the power of stonefire, the Burning Throne must acknowledge and accept their demigod offspring as legitimate heirs of Shvate Krushan."

"All of them?" Vrath asked.

"In such an instance where there are multiple sibling claimants with seemingly equal claims, the throne uses its own discretion to choose between them."

"Choose?" asked Vrath. "But when Adri, Shvate, and Jarsun's daughter underwent the Test of Fire, it accepted all three as legitimate claimants."

"Indeed. And it may well do so again if and when the Five take the Test of Fire. But it is equally possible that it will give some preference over the others. Perhaps even just one claimant."

"How would it show this preference?" Jilana asked, looking troubled. "Surely not by —"

"Nay. It would not burn one of Krushan lineage. It cannot do so physically, since their Krushan blood — and in this case, the Five's demigod blood — protects them from such an event. But it may well choose to select one among the Five. The one it considers most suitable. Or it may accept all five and show one preference by whispering into their mind that it desires that one to rule. Thereafter, that particular claimant may draw on the throne's power, summoning stonefire anywhere they go to wield as they please — as a weapon, a tool, a means of performing great feats of sorcery, almost anything imaginable. Think of it as a rich merchant who wishes to hedge his bets by supporting all candidates with donations but one particular candidate with a much, much larger amount, secretly disbursed."

"On what basis would it select one over the others?" Jilana asked. Even after a lifetime spent in Hastinaga, she still grappled with the maddening intricacies of Krushan law.

Vessa looked at her and asked gently, "Who would the merchant favor, he being a merchant?"

"The candidate most likely to encourage trade and reduce restrictions and taxes," she replied, wondering if it was a trick question.

It was not. Vessa inclined his head.

"Just as a merchant trades in goods, the throne trades in power and violence. It would support the claimant who appears the most ruthless, ambitious, willing to go to any lengths to attain power, uncaring of how many will be slain as a result."

"Then why does it not support Jarsun?" Jilana asked. "There is none more ruthless and ambitious than he. Look at this new vileness he has committed! Murdering his own kin solely to gain some strategic advantage, the monster!"

Vessa nodded sadly. "Aye, monster he is, and more beside. Yet monsters can wreak terrible havoc when on a rampage, and are not easy to stop. The throne does not care about any particular candidate. All it cares about is encouraging war, violence, conflict, brutality, pain, and suffering. It feeds off these things. For these are the manifestations of raw, unbridled power. For all we know, Jarsun could well be drawing power from stonefire. It would account for his successes in the past years. Did I mention that he killed his own father-in-law, King Aqron of Aqron, not long after they came here to Hastinaga to attempt to claim the throne for his daughter? And more recently, he killed his own wife, mother to the same daughter, because she took the child away from him and fled across the Red Desert."

Jilana's hand went to her mouth. "Mother Goddess! Does his cruelty have no limit? So the poor child is in his clutches now?"

"No. She would not yield to his demand that she take the throne by force, with his backing. When he murdered her mother, she committed the ultimate defiance. She performed smaran."

Jilana was aghast. Even Vrath, who rarely displayed any emotion on his broad, rugged face, screwed up his eyes as if considering the implications of this news.

"Ritual suicide?" Jilana asked. She rested her elbow on the armrest of the chair and cupped her forehead. "Poor brave, desperate thing! She gave her life rather than become his pawn in the quest for power. May Mother Jeel carry her soul to the sunlit vale."

"Her soul needs no cartage, Mother," Vessa said. "The smaran was only the first step in her own strategy to thwart her father's ambition."

Vrath regarded him with renewed interest.

"The child named Krushita died that day, but her soul, her consciousness, her memories, everything that made her what she was, apart from her physical body, was reincarnated of her own volition in a new vessel."

"She took rebirth by choice?" Vrath said. "Interesting."

"As who?" Jilana asked.

Vessa's expression was guarded. "That will be known in good time. For now, let it suffice that you know that she yet lives and is very much a player in this game of empires."

Vessa looked into the distance, seeing things beyond the lacquered fittings and regal portraits on the far wall. "She may even be a key protagonist in the drama that is about to unfold. Time will tell."

"Why do I suspect that you have a part to play in her reincarnation and her strategy to combat her father?"

Vessa did not reply, but he glanced over at her, and Jilana thought his eyes might have the slightest hint of a twinkle. It was the closest to amusement or self-satisfaction she had ever seen her son display. *He's enjoying this . . . this . . . game of empires, as he calls it. Even with all the horrible things happening, he is enjoying dueling wits and pitting powers against Jarsun. And why not? After all, every victory against that vile monster deserves a cheer. I can see you are pleased that young Krushita lives on to fight another day in another form, Vessa, my son. So be it. Enjoy your victories when they come, for Holy Jeel knows this family gets far too few reasons to celebrate.*

Jilana frowned. A thought had occurred to her. "Is Jarsun still her father? I mean to say, he was in her past life, of course. But in this one?"

"That is the beauty of it," Vrath said. "She is *not* his daughter in this life, therefore he cannot use her to claim the throne for his own. But she *is* still his daughter in her mind, heart, and soul, and the daughter of the wife he slew, and that will drive her to combating him as best she is able, perhaps even to vengeance. If she survives."

"She will survive," Vessa said calmly. "It is foretold. The daughter of Jarsun in her present avatar will be the primary force in the history of the Burnt Empire and the Krushan dynasty henceforth. I, Vessa, do pronounce it so."

That had the air of a prophecy as well as an oath.

Jilana exchanged glances with Vrath, who raised a single eyebrow.

3

Jilana decided to set aside the matter of Jarsun's daughter for later discussion. Perhaps in private, Vessa might be willing to divulge a little more to her than he cared to speak of to the others. She focused instead on the immediate concern.

"What of Mayla, Karni, and the Five?" she asked. "They must be in a terrible state. We must send for them at once and bring them to Hastinaga."

Vessa looked grim. "That may not be best for them."

Jilana frowned. "Do you fear a succession struggle? Perhaps that Adri, or his wife, Geldry, may see the Five as rivals to their own children? Surely those are concerns that can be addressed at a future time. For now, they require a safe abode. Where better than under the protection of the House of Krushan?"

Vessa shook his head. "Ascension to the throne is one ambition of which Karni is not possessed, as the stone gods are witness. When Shvate and she surrendered their right to the throne and went into self-imposed exile, it was a genuine act of abdication. In all my subsequent interactions with my son Shvate, and with his wives, Mayla and Karni, I sensed not the slightest dram of residual ambition. Both women had accepted Shvate's abdication and voluntary exile and resigned themselves to a life outside of the House of Krushan. Indeed, it was I who urged Vida to go to them and impress upon them the need to return to Hastinaga solely to present the children to those here as well as the people at large, as is the custom. Whether they are eligible to pass the Test of Fire or not, they are still heirs of Krushan and, as such, deserving of all that their family can provide. I hoped at best for them to secure some inheritance or property, some faithful followers from among the many who regarded Shvate as being worthy of kingship, enough resources to found their own kingdom and rule in regal comfort."

"That would only be just and fair," Vrath said. "And could still be arranged. They deserve every comfort possible and far more." He glanced at Jilana. "With due respect to you, Mother, while we may not care about succession, and poor bereaved Karni may not either, there are still formalities to be maintained. The House of Krushan must abide by Krushan law in all doings. To take them back into the royal family would be akin to acknowledging the right of succession for the Five once again. It is not I who say this; it is the law, and we cannot ignore the law."

Jilana sighed, rubbing two fingers against her temple. She could feel a headache coming on as the last dregs of her afternoon wine abandoned her. "As always, my son, you are the ultimate upholder of *Auma*. I cannot deny the truth in your words."

She addressed Vessa once more. "Even so, they will be better off here than in the savage jungle. I urge you, my son, go to them at once and bring them here. I cannot bear the thought of those five bereaved children living in the wilderness, fatherless and unprotected."

Vessa's lined mouth creased in what might have been the faint suggestion of amusement. "Fatherless they are indeed. Unprotected, no. The Five are no ordinary children, Mother, they are the children of stone gods. If anything, they are capable of being their mother's protector. As for the savage wilderness you dread so much, that jungle is their best habitat for the nonce. Even the wild beasts of the region are their friends, and played a part in defending them against Jarsun's earlier attacks. That was why he was forced to resort to the ruse of disguising himself as me to slay Shvate. Had he approached them directly, he would have had to face Shvate and Mayla themselves in battle, as well as the Five. It came as no surprise to me that he chose the cowardly way of deceitful deception."

"Even so," Vrath said, "Mother speaks justly. They are Krushan and deserve the protection and comfort of home. With Shvate's demise, the reason for the self-imposed exile vanished as well. Karni and the Five are blameless in the slaying of the rishi and his wife, which in any case was an accident. Indeed, the very existence of the Five negates the curse by that dying sage which occasioned Shvate's remorse and decision to abdicate. Bring home my nephews and nieces and let us welcome them into the folds of our imperial hospitality. We shall order a period of empire-wide mourning and hold a grand ritual to commemorate their fallen father. He was a great warrior and a true Krushan, and his passing must be marked publicly."

Vessa held up his hand. "Stay your course, brave prince protector. Your intentions are the noblest possible, but we will come to such practical matters presently. For now, permit me to continue, as there are still more troubling matters to be discussed."

Jilana felt her pulse skip. *More troubling matters* meant that Shvate's murder was not the only bad news they were going to receive this day. She breathed in deeply and braced herself as Vessa continued.

"By assuming my form to assassinate Shvate, Jarsun drove a wedge of suspicion and doubt into both of Shvate's wives, as well as his children. To experience such a traumatic betrayal is to damage their minds forever. Even if I now convince them to trust me again, they will always doubt if I might perhaps, once again, be their worst enemy in this body and form. Perhaps someday, under suitable circumstances, I may approach them and appeal to their better senses. But right now, were I to show my face to them, they would see only the assassin of Shvate and want nothing more than to avenge his death. This is the reason why I cannot go to them with any missive, no matter how benign and beneficial to their interests."

They considered this conundrum.

"I shall send Vida," Jilana said. "Shvate and he were always close, much closer than Vida and Adri have ever been. Karni would trust him, surely?"

"She does and she would, were these normal circumstances," Vessa replied. "But Vida has in fact only just departed their company scant hours ago. He is already en route to Hastinaga and should arrive here sometime tomorrow if he rides through the night and day."

"For you to reach him on the road would be a simple enough matter, would it not?" Jilana asked. "You could turn him around and send him back to fetch them home."

Vessa looked doubtful. "So long as he was in their presence, they trusted him. They had no reason not to. After all, he was present with them when Shvate was killed by Jarsun disguised as me. But now that he has left, were he to go back with a message—that too, a missive from me—their suspicions would naturally be roused."

"Naturally," Vrath agreed. "They might fear that the Vessa who sent Vida back with the instruction to bring them here was once again Jarsun."

"It is worse than that, actually," Vessa went on. "They do not even suspect that it was Jarsun. They believe it was I who assassinated Shvate."

"You can convince them otherwise, can you not? Or rather, Vida can. He can be very persuasive."

This time Vessa did smile, but it was the sad ghost of a smile, conveying no amusement or joy. "Do you truly think Karni is of a mind to listen to logical arguments at a time like this? Or one of Vida's intellectual discussions on how the Vessa who came to him is not the same Vessa who killed her husband?"

Jilana rubbed her temple again. "I see the difficulty."

"Indeed, it is more than a difficulty. It is a major obstacle barring the path to Karni trusting me, and more importantly, trusting the House of Krushan ever again."

"I see the dilemma," Vrath said thoughtfully, gazing out the window at the tops of the trees in the imperial garden. "If Jarsun can assume your form, then surely he can assume other forms as well. He could be anyone at any time. They would never know whom to trust ever again. They would always assume that nobody from our family could be relied upon to be what they appear to be."

"Indeed, noble Vrath," Vessa replied. "Jarsun can and does assume any form at will. It is one of his many talents. Karni and the Five will go through life forever suspicious of any person, friend or family, stranger or familiar, wondering whether this person, or that one, or the one over there, might not be what they appear. In one foul act, he has condemned them to a lifetime of doubt and distrust."

Jilana shook her head. The vestiges of a headache were now a full-blown assault on her wine-deprived nerves. She decided to change the subject, her thoughts still on the children. "What happens to the children of Shvate now?"

"Karni has decided to take them to Stonecastle," Vessa said. "It is her father's house, and she believes she will be safe there."

"Will she?" Vrath asked. His impassive, marble-smooth face revealed no visible emotion, but his implication was obvious. "Surely Jarsun is not yet done with them. If he went to such lengths to assassinate Shvate, then he must intend to strike down the Five as well. Not to mention Shvate's wives, Mayla and Karni."

"Mayla is no more. Unable to endure life without her beloved Shvate, she immolated herself on his funeral pyre."

Jilana heard the exclamation of shock escape her mouth. "Mother Jeel! That is . . . I hardly know what to say. Both Shvate and Mayla . . . gone!"

Vessa inclined his head.

Vrath's eyes coalesced into some distant contemplation that also revealed hidden banks of power, the power he drew from his birth mother, Jeel, the very same Mother Goddess and river deity whom Jilana worshipped and was named after. "Jarsun Krushan must be destroyed. This time, he has gone too far."

"On that we are agreed," Vessa said. "The question is how."

They all regarded one another. The question hung in the air, unanswered.

Adri

〜

1

A ROSE OF FLAME blossomed in the void.

The bittersweet scent of jameen accompanied it: the deadliest of night-shades, more venomous than a three-headed serpent in the Red Desert. Like so many lethal flora, it was irresistibly fragrant.

To Adri, who had been born into darkness, it was as if a deeper darkness had entered his dark world. Whatever walked his chambers now, it was nei-ther mortal nor divine.

Adri sensed the gradual approach of the intruder toward his bedcham-ber. It was less the sound of footfalls and more akin to some sinuous creature slithering along the marbled floor. A wind that carried a thousand voices whispered sultry promises in one ear, rasping threats in the other. Invisi-ble tentacles hovered and wound themselves around his body, entwining, stroking, smothering . . .

"Who goes there?" he asked, hearing the terror in his voice. The taste of his last meal rose in his gorge.

No response was forthcoming.

The bed shifted beneath him, burdened by the weight of another body. Adri was light, leaner and bonier even than he had been as a pubescent boy. But the intruder was lighter still, barely as heavy as a child.

Yet he knew it was no child that sat beside him.

It was barely even human.

He knew this as certainly as he knew that death was near, as near as the satin sheet that caressed his skin. It required scarcely a wrong word or ges-

31

ture to strike. Once it struck, oblivion would fall as swiftly as a dropped curtain.

He lay there, hardly breathing, waiting for the darkness within the darkness to fall. He waited for his end.

Instead, a soft chuckle from an unseen throat.

"Why do you live in fear, Adrishya Krushan?"

Adri started at the voice, at the casual humor, the insolence. "Who are you? How dare you enter the emperor's palace uninvited? Guards! Guards!"

His words stifled in the air, going no further than a whisper's reach. He startled, then tried again, shouting at the top of his voice. It was to no avail: once again, it felt like he was shouting into a void, the darkness absorbing the volume and pitch of his voice, dampening it down. A thousand war horns trumpeting could not have produced a sound in that emptiness.

When he subsided, the voice spoke again, soothing this time, as reassuring as a wet nurse's tones. "Do not fear me, nephew. I mean you no harm . . ."

Adri listened for the hidden implication, the unspoken corollary — *this time* — but there was no indication of malice in those dulcet tones. Susurrating syllables suggested a genuine lack of hostility.

He forced himself to calm, understanding that whatever or whoever this being might be, it had immense influence over him at this moment. Not merely physical by dint of its proximity to his imperial personage, but in ways he could not fully fathom. This was a creature of power.

More.

It was a Krushan.

This he knew not merely from the word "nephew" it had used, for that could well be a lie, but from the way that its presence was acknowledged by stonefire. The Burning Throne knew this intruder and was not displeased by its presence within the palace precincts. Even from his chambers on this upper floor, Adri could sense the imperial throne glowing with anticipation in the throne chamber at the heart of his palace.

"Who are you?" Adri asked.

"I am your guru."

Adri was silent. He had had a guru when he was a young boy. His uncle Vrath, prince regent of the Burnt Empire, had taken Adri and his brother Shvate in his chariot to a distant forest gurukul. There, they had lived with other acolytes, learning to read and write, as well as mastering the arts of war and kingship.

He had hated it.

He had no desire for gurus or their teachings.

The visitor chuckled as if he had read his thoughts. "Not that kind of guru," said the slippery voice. "I understand your loathing of those who set themselves above other mortals. I loathe priests and their ilk. They seek to manipulate and shape the events of mortalkind by using pawns like your brother as tools. It was during your years at gurukul that your brother Shvate grew distant from you. You took his lack of interest as a betrayal, and so it was. He was your keeper. He should have remained by your side, guiding and showing you the way. Yet he chose to pursue his own path."

"He liked learning warcraft and how to use weapons," Adri said, his sightless eyes reflecting back on those lonely days in the forest. "He was gifted. The gurus said he was destined to be a great warrior and conqueror."

The voice sounded amused. "He betrayed you, neglected you, yet you defend him?"

Adri lowered his head. "He is my brother . . . was my brother."

"And yet it is his widow who plotted against you. You do know that it was your late brother's widow Karni who hired the mercenaries that attacked you at Pramankota, do you not? It was on her orders they abducted your beloved Sauvali and took her away from you. And she, pregnant with your unborn child!"

Adri's head rose. His limpid eyes gleamed in the hollows of his face. "My half brother Vida said as much. Though he later denied having said so."

"Vida is a diplomat and a politician. He admitted the truth to you in a moment of rare honesty. Afterward, he would have had time to regret the admission. His denial means nothing. You heard him confess the truth to you with your own ears."

"Yes, but . . ." Adri began doubtfully, then trailed off.

There had been something odd about that unexpected visit from Vida. For one thing, there had been no reports of his return from the sentries, nor had anyone else on Adri's palace staff seen Vida enter or leave the imperial bedchamber. It was as if Vida had magically materialized in Adri's bedchamber, told him that single earth-shattering revelation about Karni's part in the abduction of Sauvali, and then disappeared. Even more strangely, shortly thereafter, the sentries reported Vida's return, and the man himself had formally sought an audience with him. When Vida appeared the second time, he had behaved as if he had only just returned from his trip to the forest. On being questioned by Adri, he had denied having visited him earlier as well as any knowledge of the damning revelations about Karni.

"There are many forces abroad in Hastinaga," the intruder said. He was walking about the bedchamber now, pacing slowly. "And they are all aligned against you, emperor of the Burnt Empire."

Adri's pulse quickened. To buy himself a moment of thought, he replied by quoting almost verbatim from an old aphorism he had heard bandied about in court. "Forces are always aligned against the Burning Throne, yet no reigning Krushan will ever be unseated. Stonefire will not permit such sacrilege."

As if on cue, the living rock spoke from two floors below, responding with tongues of fire, lighting up the ceiling and the corners of the room. Adri could still feel the heat from above and around him. He heard draperies catch fire and metal objets d'art melt instantly beneath the searing heat of the alien flames. Yet he — and the visitor — remained unharmed by its supernatural power. Yes, there was no doubting it, the visitor was Krushan.

2

The visitor hissed in amusement. "You are a wily one indeed, Adrishya. But as the Krushan saying goes, even stonefire cannot protect a family from the enemies within. The court gossips always repeat that old saying like a mantra, and there is truth in it. For all our glories and accomplishments, we Krushan are a cursed lineage. Look back at your own life, for instance."

"My life?" Adri said, surprised at the sudden personal inference. His anger subsided, and with it, the flickering flames of stonefire. A few small fires burned in the corners and cornices. The chambers would require remodeling: not that such things mattered to an emperor who could not see.

"Born blind at birth, a few scant moments after your brother Shvate. Your mother disowned you, your peers shunned you, other children of the family teased and mocked and taunted you. Life was unbearable until your brother took it upon himself to become your keeper. You took his actions as love and brotherhood. Whereas he was likely just carrying you closer to the cliff from which he himself intended to drop you. Indeed, he threw you off that cliff when you needed him most: at gurukul. In that inhospitable forest hermitage, entrusted to the care of uncaring priests and unkind gurus, hemmed in on all sides by a deadly jungle filled with savage beasts, you learned the skills necessary to survive. Still, you harbored the hope that when the ultimate challenge befell you, Shvate would come to your aid. You clung to the dream that someday you would both battle foes as one warrior force, reign as one emperor. That was the lie that had been hammered into your skull from birth, the lie perpetuated by Dowager Empress Jilana and Prince Regent Vrath.

"It was a lie that had held the patchwork quilt of warring factions that made up the Burnt Empire together for another generation. What else could Jilana and Vrath have done when they were delivered two disabled heirs, neither fit to reign under Krushan law? They bent the letter of the law to suit their purpose. Their deception was understandable. Had they acknowledged the birthright of the true heir to the throne, they would have lost control of this vast empire, never to reach such lofty eminence again in their wretched lives. So they wove a lie and stitched it into the fabric of history. They brainwashed you two boys into believing that your only hope lay in sticking together through thick and thin.

"Yet what happened at the Battle of the Rebels? When your chariot was surrounded by a veritable sea of enemies, did your brother Shvate come to your aid? By doing so, he could have strengthened your hand. Together, you two could have fought on to triumph, securing a victory despite your disabilities and proving that battles are won by the spirit, not by the sword.

"Instead, what did he do? He abandoned you, abandoned his own forces, and left the Hastinaga armies at the mercy of the enemy."

Adri cleared his throat hoarsely. "He was undone by the heat of the noonday sun. It is his weakness. His albino skin —"

"Enough!" The voice thundered through the empty chambers. Not for the first time since the intrusion, Adri wondered why none of this long, strange visit had attracted the attention of his sentries. He suspected that the reason was because they all lay dead in the hallways. The visitor had taken precautions before making his presence felt. If he intended to cause harm to Adri's person, there would be nothing to stop him.

Except stonefire.

Surely the Burning Throne would not let anyone harm Adri in his own bedchambers? Even another Krushan?

Adri hoped never to have to test that assumption.

The visitor continued: "Too long have you been a silent witness to the unmaking and erosion of your own life and powers. Too long you have been marginalized by those who claim to have your well-being at heart. Too long have you been leashed by your own filial bonds from taking action. When your brother Shvate abandoned you on the battlefield and went on to pursue his own career as a military hero, you said nothing. When Dowager Empress Jilana and Prince Regent Vrath showered him with honors, parades, praises, you remained silent. When all Hastinaga and the Burnt Empire bowed and scraped before Prince Shvate, you applauded along with the rest. Yet it was your legacy he encroached upon. Your share of glory he claimed. The promise the elders of the Krushan dynasty made to the people at your birth was that two monarchs would rule the Burnt Empire jointly. Jointly and equally. Neither was to have more power than the other. Yet in the years before your brother Shvate's demise, it was he and he alone who appeared as the true heir. You were sidelined, reduced to the role of 'the emperor's blind brother.'"

"Shvate is dead," Adri said softly. Into the silence that followed, he repeated this again: "My brother is dead."

The pain of his brother's passing, he felt even now, as a prickling of needles in his unseeing eyes. He had loved his brother, despite his betrayal and distancing in the past several years. He had loved him as he had loved only one other person in his entire life. The news of Shvate's sudden death had unsettled him, shaken him to his core.

"And how was he killed?" asked the voice, just as softly, as if cognizant of Adri's emotions.

"Murdered by his own birth father. *Our* birth father. The seer-mage Vessa."

"Ask yourself, then — why?"

Adri had wrestled with this very question ever since Vida had brought the shocking news. Vida's later reappearance, and denial of his earlier visit, had confused him somewhat, but even Vida did not deny the underlying facts — that Shvate had been suddenly and brutally murdered by their own birth father, Vessa. Why had Vessa done such a thing? The question remained suspended in the air, sending shock waves through the city and palace. The elders had not spoken of it to him as yet, but he knew they were equally stunned.

"On the face of it," the voice continued, "it makes no sense. Vessa is a forest-dwelling hermit, far removed from the politics and cares of mortal governance. He fathered you and your brother, at his own birth mother Jilana's request, upon the two sister princesses, Amber and Umber, after their husbands, the sons of the last Emperor Sha'ant, expired without progeny. His mother's request fulfilled, Vessa retired to the forest. He is a pathetic, pitiful old man, living celibate and isolated in the deepest jungles, focused only on his devotion to *Auma*, the sacred source of all knowledge, wisdom, and spiritual strength. Yet, for some reason, he emerged from his reclusive existence to assassinate one of his own biological sons, the entitled heir to the Burnt Empire, in a shocking, senseless act of violence. Why?"

Why indeed. The question had haunted Adri night and day since he had heard the news. "I mean to ask him that question when he appears before my court next."

"And when might that be? I know you have petitioned your grandmother to summon him urgently, and to consider it an official summons before the imperial court. If she chose to do so, she could summon him in an instant. Weeks have passed. He has not yet appeared before you. You well know that she has chosen to defy you. She flaunts your imperial authority and prevents the assassin of your brother, a lawful heir to the Burning Throne, from being brought to justice. No, Adri, Vessa will not simply saunter into Hastinaga and offer himself up on a platter. He will abscond, obfuscate, dissemble, and use every wily ruse in his canny mind to evade accountability."

Adri thought there was something inconsistent in that argument. Was Vessa a pathetic, pitiful old man focused only on *Auma*, or was he a canny dissembler who was wily enough to evade justice? But he did not voice that thought aloud.

Instead he said, "Vessa's attack on Shvate is a shocking transgression. I mean to address that. I will order Grandmother Jilana once again to summon him as well as issue an imperial order instructing all outposts and for-ward troops to scour the jungles. But what I cannot find in my heart to truly believe is what Vida said about Shvate's widow Karni and my own wife, Geldry, and her brother Kune."

"You speak of their conspiracy and plot against your own person, ex-ecuted in the form of the attack at Riverdell, and the abduction of your beloved companion Sauvali, mother-to-be of your unborn child."

Adri knew he should no longer be surprised at anything his visitor knew or said, but he still felt a surge of emotion at the mention of Sauvali's name and her condition. "You know of this too?"

"Of course. As I said, Adrishya Krushan, I am your uncle and well-wisher. If I am not physically present by your side, it is only on account of your grandmother Jilana's and uncle Vrath's conspiracy to deny me of my rightful place in House Krushan. Yet I have watched over you from afar all your waking days. I have watched you being treated unfairly, deprived of your own lawful right to be acknowledged as the sole heir to the throne, given barely a fraction of the adulation and respect that was granted your brother, mistreated by your own wife and her politicking brother, for far too long. As if her own infidelity were not enough, Geldry neglected you, treated you with loathing, driving you into the arms of the lovely young Sauvali."

"Infidelity?" Adri asked. "Geldry *was* unfaithful, then?"

A soft chuckle with a faint hissing aftersound. "A hundred and one chil-dren born of one woman at one time? Is that usual among mortals, even if the father is Krushan?"

"No, but . . ." Adri trailed off. He had no other alternative to offer. The birth of the Hundred and One was the great unspoken scandal of his House. No one dared speak of it openly, but it was evident there was some unnat-ural agency involved. Geldry had delivered not a kicking, bawling baby but simply a large lump.

Like an egg formed of solid flesh . . .

He had heard the words whispered by an unknown servant in passing, one of the wet nurses who had been present when Vessa had been called in to intervene at the delivery, an unheard-of event in a culture where men were not permitted to be present while women gave birth. Others had heard the words, and the wet nurse and her family had vanished overnight, never to be seen or heard of again. Dowager Empress Jilana had made it known that no gossip about the royal family would be tolerated, not even among the citizenry, on pain of death.

The unwritten edict been taken seriously, as all Krushan diktats were, but it had not prevented the awkward pauses, the odd glances — these, he had sensed rather than noted — and overall sense of unease by the servants who had been close to the children of Geldry over the years.

There was also the fact that the children had not been shown to the people of Hastinaga or presented before visiting foreign and domestic dignitaries, an unprecedented departure from Krushan tradition.

"They shall be presented when the time is right," Jilana would say when asked at first, and over time, people had ceased to ask whether the time would ever be right.

"You have heard the whispers at night, the murmurs in your conscience, the fear in people's voices. You know that the world does not see the children — *your* children — as mortal children."

"They are Krushan," Adri said defensively.

Another soft chuckle. "As are you and I. As are all those of this House. Yet you are regarded with awe, respect, adoration, even fear at times. But never as *unnatural, alien, foul get of demons, spawn of* —"

"Enough!" Adri's voice rang out sharply in the midnight silence, the tone imperial for the first time since this strange dialogue had begun.

More hissing: this time it sounded pleased. "Your tone betrays your true feelings. So you admit it, then?"

"I admit it," Adri said harshly, rising from the bed on steady feet. He sensed the visitor close by his bed in the way that he sensed a cooler patch on a hot day, like the shadow of a pillar cutting a swath of sunlight. To his right, about two yards away. He addressed that direction. "I have heard the whispers and murmurs, I have harbored suspicions myself . . . If you have something to confirm or deny these, speak it now. Or . . ."

"Or what, nephew? You will confront Geldry? It would be to no avail. She would only repeat the truth as she knows it: that *you* fathered the Hundred and One upon her and any *unusual* characteristics they may possess are entirely the fruit of your loins!"

Adri raised his face toward Jarsun, searching for some subtle subtext he might have missed. "I don't understand what you are saying. Are they my get or not? Speak plainly, Uncle. If uncle indeed you are."

Jarsun laughed a throaty laugh. "Indeed I am your uncle Jarsun Krushan. And indeed it is confusing, I know. Come, then. It is time you knew the truth at last. Far too long have you been kept in the dark. And I mean that not in jest, but quite literally. For it was one man's curse that caused your lack of vision at birth, just as his curse caused your late brother, Shvate, to be born albino and susceptible to sunlight. This same being also led your Geldry astray."

Adri's face wrinkled in a frown. "You speak in riddles now. Who is this being or man you speak of?"

"Why, is it not as plain as the nose on your face? Who else have we been speaking of all this while? I speak of Vessa, of course. He is the chief architect of all your sorrows."

Adri's head swam now. "I thought you said my brother Shvate . . . no, my sister-in-law Karni . . . my grandmother Jilana . . ."

"They are all part of it, truly. But behind all these pieces upon the board of chaupat, there is a great hand that moves them in accordance with a strategy only he sees. To him, it is a great game. He does not care that this game involves the use — and destruction — of real, living, flesh-and-blood people. People such as your beloved Sauvali, your unborn son . . ."

"Vessa is behind it all? Is that what you are saying?"

Jarsun chuckled yet again. "I am done speaking. It is time I showed you. For only when you see with your own two eyes will you know the truth about your birth father, and the web of evil he has spun over the past decades. Come with me."

Adri sensed that Jarsun was holding a hand out to him. He ignored it.

"Why do you jest about a blind man's disability? You well know I cannot see with these two eyes."

"Surely, you cannot in this realm. But where I am about to take you, you will be able to see as well as any sighted person. Come with me, Jarsun Krushan. Rise up to your feet, take my hand, and let me lead you to the truth."

Adri hesitated again, but finally decided he must know what Jarsun meant. If what he was implying was true, then Adri had truly been blind, not just in the literal sense, but also in the mind and heart. He was emperor of the Burnt Empire, ruler of the greater part of Arthaloka, master of the world. To be deceived and duped in his own house, by his own family . . . to be cuckolded . . . betrayed . . . these were unacceptable transgressions.

He *must* know.

He already knew that if Jarsun had meant to kill him, he could have done so without speaking a word. He could simply have struck in the dark, silent and deadly as a serpent in the night, and disappeared whence he had come. Adri did not trust the visitor, this uncle he had not known until today, but he *had* heard of Jarsun Krushan; he had studied Krushan history as a boy and delved into it further as a prince, and knew of the Banished One, the Desolate One, and all the other names by which his exiled uncle was known. He was more than intrigued now. And the promise of being able to see was an unexpected, yet provocative one. He was provoked and incited, and agitated.

He *must* know.

He rose to his feet, took hold of the hand that was offered, and let it lead him across the room. He heard a sibilant murmur, caught a smattering of High Krushan mantras recited, and heard as well as felt and smelled the explosion of power that followed. A powerful wind began to blow, carrying with it strange, exotic odors and scents he could not easily identify. Despite his blindness, he sensed a brilliant light suffusing the room. Even through unseeing eyes, it suffused his being, bathed him in a saturation of sensation such as he had never before experienced. It continued to the point of being almost painful.

The hand guiding him led him forward, through the light and past it, into a greater darkness than any he had ever experienced.

Jarsun

‿

JARSUN WATCHED MRAASHK BURN as he waited for his assassin to attack.

People were rioting in the streets, fighting with swords in the markets, turning over the handcarts of street vendors, setting fire to wagons and shops and houses. In the high neighborhoods, the rich and powerful cowered within their palatial mansions as mobs slaughtered sentries and bodyguards, hacked down doors, pulled down iron gates, and surged inside. After the pillaging and looting — and far worse, judging from the screams and sounds — the inhabitants were dragged into the streets, paraded naked to the central courtyard, there to be trussed up and bound to stakes for the crowds to do with as they pleased before they were run through or set aflame.

All semblance of law and order had broken down days ago, once the last of the chosen people had fled the city. Those who remained were the ones who had prospered or at least thrived under Tyrak, if not served him in some capacity. There were a surprising number of them: these Mraashk and Arrgodi were so gullible and naive. Surely, they should have known that with their liege dead, a change would come in his wake.

Tyrak was nothing but hot ashes, cremated weeks ago after he was bested and killed by the Savior in a wrestling tourney watched by the entire city. The shock of his passing had stunned everyone who had thought him indomitable, none more than Tyrak himself. You would think that these fools would have seen the writing on the walls and fled the city that night itself; but instead they had stayed. Perhaps it was the shock of Tyrak's sudden death. They had truly not expected it.

Nor had Tyrak.

Jarsun had seen the look on his son-in-law's face as the life left his body. Tyrak had believed himself invincible. He had known the Savior of the people would come one day to challenge and attempt to slay him. There had been a time when he had been paralyzed by fear at the thought. But over the past several years, he had gained a false confidence. He had begun to believe that the Savior could be beaten. That he, Tyrak, had grown in power and achieved true invulnerability. He had believed this because Jarsun had wanted him to believe it.

Jarsun turned from the high window to look at the dark shape of the beautiful woman walking across the bedchamber. She poured herself more wine from the golden jug and drank thirstily, making a sound in her throat that sounded like sexual fulfillment.

"Bring me a goblet as well," Jarsun suggested.

Ladislew's mouth curled in a smirk. "Get it yourself."

She stretched out on a plush red divan, one arm draped lazily over the back. Yet he knew her pose was not intended for his viewing pleasure — or for any man. Ladislew had bedded him only because she desired to partake of him before she killed him. It was her way of asserting her superiority over him while staying close enough to strike at the opportune time. He had not given her any reason to suspect that he knew her true agenda, yet she had failed to take up several choice moments to attack. What was she waiting for? It still amused him to toy with the possibilities.

Jarsun helped himself to the jug, only to find it empty. He shook the last few drops into his mouth, his twin tongues snaking out to catch them in midair. He sensed her watching out the side of his eyes: one of the advantages of nictitating eyelids was that others could never be certain when he was watching. They ought to know by now, as should she, that Jarsun was always watching, even when he seemed not to see; *especially* when he seemed not to see.

"You seem very pleased with yourself today," she said. "Into whose lives have you struck terror this time, my lord Morgolia?"

Jarsun allowed himself a thin smile. All his smiles were thin, because his mouth had no lips, just a horizontal slash across the narrow span of his face.

"Pleased I am," he said, pouring and sipping wine. He smacked his tongues loudly, relishing the flavor. Their twin tips slithered out to catch an errant droplet or two. "I have accomplished a great deal in a very short time today, expending the minimum of effort."

She raised a bushy eyebrow. One of the things he liked about Ladislew was that she made no special effort to prettify herself the way most women of the court did. No plucking of the brows, no styling of her bouffant, no scraping off of bodily hair growth, painting of the toenails and fingernails, eyelids and lips. Her hair was a wild tangle, closer in kin to a thornbush than to the elaborate wigs and pomped-up things most noblewomen wore atop their heads in Eastern Arthaloka. Her brows, her underarms, her downy legs and arms, even her pubic thatch, were all untrimmed, unshaped. No artificial colors decorated her face or nipples or nether lips. She was as she had been born: all woman, all Ladislew.

She raised a leg at an angle to the reclining one, letting the unsashed gown fall open, revealing a long, dark, bare thigh, and a nest of dark fur where both limbs met. Her free hand stroked her own chest in slow, languorous circles, circling and trapping then releasing one nipple of one bared breast.

Even this, Jarsun knew, was not her attempt to allure him, as might be the case with most women who sought to seduce him in the hopes of currying the favor of the most powerful liege in this part of the world, if not all Arthaloka. He had seen every variation of seduction attempted, every device deployed, from any gender, to try to attract his attention, and his lust.

With Ladislew, there was no intention to seduce or attract. She was simply pleasuring herself. Her relationship with her own body was complete. She had no need of him nor desire for him and his prong or any other part of him. That was the reason why he chose to mate with her. As for why she allowed his anatomy to join with hers . . . Well, it had nothing to do with his power or his wealth.

"Tell me more," she said huskily, pausing in her self-stroking to dip her fingers in the chilled wine and apply it to the same sensitive part of her anatomy. "I like hearing of your cruelties."

He smiled thinly. "Enough about me. We shall now speak of you and your wants and needs."

She closed her long-lashed eyes as she pleasured herself, her lips parting in a soft moue. "You know what I want. You have what I need. Give it to me."

He remained standing, watching her impassively. No arousal stirred in him. The mere machinations of mortal sexuality held no special delights for him. There were far greater pleasures to be had in the dungeons and battle-fields than in boudoirs.

He considered dispatching her to the House of Pain. That was his ver-sion of the torture chamber, Morgol style. Instead of concealing the artful pursuit of body horrors in hidden subterranean chambers, he had brought it out into the open. The very heart of the capital city. After all, torture's purpose was not merely to elicit information from the incarcerated; it was also to set an example. What better way to set an example than by display-ing the agonies of the apprehended in public, in an open house in the midst of the city center? Naked bodies splayed on walls, floors, or entrapped in an inventive variety of contraptions and devices, suffering unspeakable horrors for impossible lengths of time. It served not only to humiliate the tortured themselves, but also to remind all others that this was the fate that awaited them if they defied the will of their God-Emperor.

The most useful confessions came not from the ones being tortured but from their loved ones, their families, their friends, their associates, anyone who sought to shield themselves from the same fate by offering the only thing of value they had: information. It had revolutionized espionage and intelligence gathering across the Morgol Empire, not to mention the sub-stantial elimination of rebellions, revolts, and even petty crimes. An eye for a loaf of bread was the Morgol maxim, and it was upheld regardless of miti-gating circumstances. Crime was nonexistent under his reign, and spies had become an extinct species.

But there were always exceptions. He was looking at one.

Ladislew brought herself to a climax with the usual noises and release. She seemed to have forgotten about him entirely, lost in a world of her own creation.

No, the House of Pain would not work for this one. She would suffer and die, horribly, agonizingly, but she would never talk. And she had no family, no loved ones, no relatives, friends, or even associates who would come up and tearfully confess, begging that mercy be shown to her and, most of all, to themselves. Public torture, like public executions, was most effective when the victims were active, productive members of society, integrated into a network of relationships, personal and professional, and with a lifetime of connections and contacts. Ladislew was like a rock hurtling through the cosmos that happened to have landed upon Arthaloka, an alien with no connections to this world.

In a sense, she was like Jarsun. Once he had had a family, a House, a place in society. Now, he was rootless, adrift, hurtling through history like a shooting star. It was why he had no qualms about killing, about the hundreds of thousands of lives he had already ended or taken part in ending, or the millions more he intended to end. Torturing her and expecting her to talk would be no different from doing it to himself. He had nothing to reveal except naked ambition and lust for power.

In Ladislew's case, her ambition was to slay him.

Of that, he had no doubt. It was the only reason why she would conceal her true intentions, her true identity, so effectively, embed herself in Mraashk, spend years with Tyrak, his protégé, deluding him into believing she was on his side, only to betray him at the moment of truth, and now she would spend years more with Jarsun if required.

She had not slain Tyrak with her own hands. That task was given to the cowherd boy, the Slayer, a pawn in the larger game he was playing. But Ladislew had paved the path, building up Tyrak's confidence to the point where he believed he was invulnerable, and by doing so, she made the Slayer's task a relatively simple one.

But Jarsun was no Tyrak.

He was not young, naive, or foolish enough to believe he was invulnerable. Nearly impossible to slay, certainly. But that was not the same thing as saying he could not be killed.

Perhaps that was it. Ladislew was waiting to learn his weakness, to spot the flaw in his seemingly immaculate armor.

Was that the reason she played this game?

Still, she was better than this: lying on the cushions of his boudoir, writhing in paroxysms of naked passion. Any assassin could play the seductress. Ladislew was of another grade altogether, the kind of weapon that could bring down empires, topple dynasties, threaten the reign of a stone god. Vengeance forged from stonefire itself could not be deadlier.

He tired of this exercise, of watching her, of trying to guess at her strategy, her plan. If she could not be made to talk and he could not verify it for certain, then any theory he came up with was futile. Only time would tell what her plan was. No matter what it might be, he knew that when the time came, he would be ready.

She was not the first person in his life to pretend to be his friend — or lover — in order to get close enough to him to attempt to end his life. She would probably not be the last. He would deal with her in due course.

He turned away, bored with watching her admittedly alluring nakedness, and gazed out the balcony at the night sky and a crescent moon hanging low in the east.

There was another woman about whom he ought to be more concerned, spare more thought and time to finding, whose vendetta against him was far deadlier than Ladislew's.

Krushita, his daughter.

Dead though she might be in her original form, he knew she had been reborn. No Krushan could fail to have felt the ripples in *Auma* when one of their own reincarnated, especially a reincarnation so traumatically forced, brutally quick, and blazing with rage.

Shortly after he had slain her mother, his wife, Krushita had taken her own life in the Red Desert. She had won that day, in a manner of speaking. She had doomed his quest to use her to claim the Burning Throne for his own. By killing her physical body that day, she had taken away his daughter, the only one he could use as a pawn in his attempt to wrest back the power, the empire, the throne that had been denied him when he was outcast and sent into exile by his own family.

A family saga had ended that day in the desert. But a new one had begun. Krushita had taken rebirth, he knew. But where and as whom she was reborn, he knew not.

He shut his eyes, closing both layers of his nictitating eyelids. He felt his daughter's presence in the Flow of *Auma* that connected all things. She was out there somewhere. But where? And who was she in this new avatar? The answers frustrated him despite the time he had spent questing and scouring the ends of the world.

The only thing he knew for sure was that she lived on.

And she lived on for only one purpose.

To ensure his failure, his death, and his downfall.

She was the enemy he had to watch, not Ladislew, deadly though she was, or any of the other Krushan in distant Hastinaga.

He would see her again someday, he was sure of that.

And when that day came, he would not hesitate.

Because, even if she had been his daughter in her previous life, even if his daughter's soul still lived in her new body, she was expendable. Just like her mother, and her grandfather, and so many others before her.

After all, a daughter or son who turned against their father was no different from a rabid dog that turned against its mother.

And like rabid dogs, they must be put down.

Part One

Reunion

YEAR 210 OF CHAKRA 58

Yudi

~

1

THE MOON WAS A raised scimitar poised overhead as Tshallian cursed the oarsmen with both their mouths, their two heads scanning the dark river while berating the rowers.

"Faster, whelps. Did your mothers not nurse you long enough as babes? Put your backs into it!" the Vanjhani hissed, their four arms matching action to their words as they pulled powerfully on two pairs of oars.

Even with their strength added, the boat barely moved forward. At this narrowed point, the Anusya River was still a good half mile wide, its sluggish yet vigorous current thickened by the sheer quantity of silt it would carry hundreds of miles further down south to deposit at the mangroves of the delta.

The oarsmen said nothing, grimly applying themselves to the rigorous task of rowing across the formidable river. Despite the near-moonless night that made clear vision impossible, Yudi judged they had drifted further downstream than hoped. At this rate, he estimated, they would be miles past the landing site by the time they reached the opposite shore, delaying them more on this night when every moment was precious.

"Yojanas past," Arrow corrected him. "We're already over ten miles past the landing site, and a yojana is just over —"

"Nine miles. Yes, Arrow, I know the length of a yojana, just as I'm sure you know the exact length of the ideal bowspan for a person of your height and reach. No, don't tell me what that bowspan actually is. Right now, I'm more interested in calculating how long it will take us to reach the ambush spot at this rate."

"It would take no time at all, if you had let me row to start with, Yudi." The careless drawl of Brum's lazy voice was softer than her siblings' tones, yet carried farther on the humid night air. She lay on her back in the bed of the longboat, keeping her hefty bulk low to avoid capsizing the vehicle. Even though Brum was the same age as her siblings, she outmatched them in size and weight, belying her seventeen years.

Yudi had emphasized to Tshallian that they find the most robustly constructed longboat for the crossing only because of his concern that an older, weather-worn boat might not be able to sustain Brum's weight. It wasn't just her size — at a glance, it seemed unlikely that Brum could weigh more than a Vanjhani like Tshallian, who was nine feet tall and more than half as wide at the shoulders — but her short stature and girth were not merely that of a well-fed woman. Brum weighed over half a ton, and when she lost her temper and forgot to watch herself, she could expand instantly to three or four times that weight, and at least on one occasion they had witnessed her increasing her weight to a massive three tons, just by inhaling a deep breath.

For this reason, Yudi said nothing to Brum now. She was always on a shorter fuse than usual just before a fight, and he definitely did not want to rock *this* boat.

One of the oarsmen said something in his local tongue to their captain, a heavily tattooed woman who had kept up a steady stream of curses since pushing off: without breaking the rhythm, she responded to the complainant with what sounded like even more obscene curses.

Yudi looked at Saha, who had a natural gift for languages, human as well as animal, in addition to his extraordinary speed and endurance.

Saha shrugged. "Grumbling about the weight."

Yudi supposed the oarsman was right: looking at the six of them, nobody could have guessed their combined weight would be that of a party at least twice their number. He said nothing; if the captain knew of Brum's peculiar "weight problem," she might be inclined to throw them all overboard, cursing all the while. Well, she would *try*.

He saw Arrow looking at him and shrugged. *Let her grumble. We're paying her well enough.*

His sibling's attractive face twitched in an ambiguous smile. Arrow was neither male nor female, gifted with a chameleon-like ability to shift genders at will, while presenting exclusively as no specific gender identity. This often confused lovers but proved very useful in the right circumstances, especially since Arrow's talents altered slightly yet significantly with each identity shift.

Yudi turned his attention to Kula, Saha's twin, yet about as different from his sister as twins could possibly be. He was leaning over the side of the boat, trailing his hand in the ink-black river, whispering too softly for human ears. He knew Kula was speaking with the fish, turtles, dolphins, and Jeel only knew whatever else dwelled in these waters. That was Kula's special gift, being able to speak to and secure the cooperation of animals of all species. All Yudi's siblings had the same gift in varying degrees, but the four of them combined couldn't match Kula when it came to perfect fluency and communication. He could get the most unlikely creatures to do the most unexpected things.

He looked fondly at his siblings. They were all special in their own individual ways. Empowered by their divine forebears.

Except for Yudi.

He was painfully, almost embarrassingly, powerless. He didn't possess Brum's strength, Arrow's keen aim, Saha's speed, or Kula's powers of communication. He was just . . . Yudi.

"Why am I even part of this family?" he had asked their mother more than once. "I'm not like the others."

Karni had hugged him close and asked, "Is that the voice of your heart speaking or the voices of strangers?"

"The other children in the gurukul said it," he'd admitted. "But it's true, isn't it?"

Karni had looked at him with her large, sad brown eyes. "Do you believe it's true? Is that how you feel when you are with us, like you don't belong?"

"No." He dropped his gaze. "I feel like . . . we're all parts of a single being. Like five hearts beating in a single body."

It was true. That was how it felt, not just when all five siblings were together, but even when they were far apart, as they had been in the past. Even when they fought bitterly with each other, as siblings often did, he always felt as if he was fighting only with himself. And because of their emotional and mental bond, Yudi could think and feel everything his siblings were experiencing, just as they could. Even now, he knew what each one of them was thinking and feeling, just as they knew his thoughts and emotions, sensing his sadness even in their sleep and sending back reassuring pulses of support and solidarity.

Karni had smiled then, and brushed an errant lock of hair off his forehead. "Remind me to cut your hair," she said absently.

After a moment's thought, she'd added, "You are the wise one, remember that. Even the most powerful body needs a steady, calm head that can think wisely in the most challenging circumstances. Like a commander who must see beyond the individual pains and wounds and suffering of her soldiers to view the entire army in perspective, in order to be able to direct and command its actions for success and for survival. You are the head of the body that is the Five. The head cannot carry, lift, run, or do anything physical on its own; it can only think and process what the body experiences and make decisions to ensure the body's success and survival. That is your purpose, your gift, your genius. You can command and direct your siblings to act individually to achieve a common goal, in perfect synch, with brilliant foresight, and lead them to achieve not just the improbable or the seemingly impossible, but even the unimaginable. Yours is the hand that holds the reins and the goad of a four-horse team. Without your hand and will to unite and control them, the team would run awry, or amok, and topple the chariot. You are the one who leads, and more importantly, Yudi, my eldest, my beloved, my beautiful, perfect son, you are their brother, and that itself is all in itself. Anything more that you happen to be is a gift. You yourself are enough."

He had stared at his mother, fiercely beautiful in the moonlight streaming in through the gaps in the thatched roof of their forest hut, and thought to himself, *And you, Mother, are amazing.* Unlike her children, she could not read his thoughts or feelings, so he said aloud, "I love you, Mother."

"I love you too, my son. Now go back to sleep. You have gurukul tomorrow."

2

The grinding jerk of the boat running aground drew Yudi out of his thoughts. They had reached the far shore. The captain cursed softly one last time, then finally quieted.

Tshallian turned back to look grimly at Yudi, their massive arms reaching over their shoulders to draw weapons slowly from their leather sheaths: a hammer and a sickle. Their lower pair of arms drew swords sheathed at their waist. They turned forward again and leaped from the boat's prow, landing with a dull crunch on the pebbled shore. The glint of moonlight on metal matched the sheen of their bald heads.

Arrow was next, then Brum, whose landing produced a squelching sound as the pebbles were crushed to powder and embedded a foot deep in the loamy wet soil. Yudi was next, followed by Saha and Kula. That was their standard order. Like so many other habits and rituals of the Five, it had been set from their youngest years, for reasons none of them had ever examined or questioned. They had an instinctive understanding and acceptance of their respective roles in any situation, and especially so in combat. That was as good a reason as any.

The captain cursed again softly, holding out her tattooed hands — even her palms and the webs of her fingers bore ink, Yudi noticed — in the universal gesture that meant "pay up." Yudi untied the cloth purse hanging at his waist and tossed it to the woman. He had already given her half its contents before they embarked.

She caught it deftly, despite the dim light, and her cursing ceased — but only for a moment before she turned and began cursing her oarsmen again.

Yudi heard the grinding of the boat being shoved back out onto the water and had a moment of misgiving. Perhaps he ought to ask the boat to wait, just in case they needed to cross back.

He shook his head wryly. That was not how the Five operated. They explored no escape routes, had no contingency plan. When they went into battle, they went all in.

He turned and followed his siblings into the darkness.

3

Tshallian raised the arm holding the sickle, the tip silvery wet with moonlight. Yudi made his way to the Vanjhani's side, resisting the urge to crouch. The wadi they had followed up from the riverbank was deep enough to conceal even the Vanjhani easily. If the nine-foot-tall warrior felt no need to crouch, then Yudi, who was almost two and a half feet shorter, need hardly do so.

The hand holding the hammer jabbed it forward, indicating a faintly glimpsed shape standing above the wadi.

"Ambush there, Dronas's border guards do always. Be there that one of them, lazy bastard name of Sanknart. Right proper asswipe that be! Always hang back from main force, he do, that so he not put precious neck in harm's way."

Yudi nodded and glanced back at his siblings. Four pairs of eager eyes glinted in the darkness. He could hear Brum already chuffing, drawing in breath after breath to increase her weight.

"Everyone knows what to do," he said, more for Tshallian's benefit than the others.' "Remember, quick and deadly. Hit them hard and keep moving."

Arrow's white teeth gleamed in a broad grin.

Yudi shot his sibling a sharp look. *Don't make this personal. We're not here to right wrongs tonight, we're just passing through, and they happen to be in our way, that's all. This is not about delivering justice for all the folk who were taken here.*

Arrow's eyes met Yudi's in a piercing stare. The grin widened. *It's personal to all of them, and their families, Yudi. What these bastards do to the children is unforgivable.*

Tshallian grunted softly. "Shift changes in half a watch. Finish this before that, best we do. As it is, numbers against us. No less than twenty border guards now, shift change comes, twenty more there will be."

Yudi switched to verbalizing for the Vanjhani's benefit. "Give me a minute, Tshallian. I need to make sure my siblings understand something."

He turned back to the others. "Arrow, Brum, Saha, Kula. We're not here to avenge the systemic abuse of immigrant Gwannlanders trying to escape an oppressive regime. I know those Gwanns we met in the tavern back in

New Gwann told some harrowing tales, and hearing about the way these border guards treated their group and all the other unfortunates they catch while trying to make it to the river was hard. It hit me here too," he said, pointing to his heart. "It's unacceptable what they did to those people. The way they separate the children and dare the parents to go on and cross the river without them, tormenting them with the opportunity to gain freedom for themselves at the cost of their children. Most parents refuse and are killed by these bastards. Even those desperate enough to start swimming, the Dronas border guards kill them before they go more than a few yards. It's horrible, there's no other way to see it. But that's not why we're here.

"We're here because we need to get to Gwannland, and the fastest way is through Dronasthan. We can't afford to get hung up at the border. We have the whole of Dronasthan still to cross. If we raise a ruckus here, word will go out across to every armed soldier in the kingdom — which, need I remind you, is a military state, so everybody's an armed soldier — and we'll spend the entire trip fighting our way across Dronasthan to get to Gwannland. We can avoid all that unnecessary bloodshed by dealing with this quickly and quietly, without making it personal.

"Stick to the plan. We chose this spot because it's where they wait to ambush the runners who manage to slip past the other checkpoints and head for the point where the river is narrowest and easiest to swim. We're behind them now, and we'll ambush *their* ambush. Take them by surprise. Knock them out cold, then move on. The next shift, arriving in half a clock, will assume they were somehow overcome by escapees. They'll have no reason to think we were coming *into* Dronasthan. Simple, quick, bloodless. We keep our heads down the rest of the way, keep up our cover stories, and we'll be out of Dronasthan and in Gwannland in a matter of days. Is that clear to you all?"

Yudi felt the Vanjhani's two pairs of eyes staring at him oddly. One head was looking at him like he'd lost his mind, the other was half frowning, half grinning as if wondering if he had always been crazy. "Make many more speeches, will you, then maybe you plan to bore border guards to sleep, yes?"

Yudi shrugged. "My siblings can get a bit . . . passionate."

Suddenly Brum grunted loudly. "Enough talk. Brum ready. Brum fight."

Without further warning, Brum launched herself with a standing leap from the bottom of the wadi over the top and high up in the air. She disappeared in the darkness for a moment as Yudi saw the Vanjhani's two mouths gape. Their heads went back as they tried to follow Brum's leap.

Tshallian lowered their jaws and looked at Yudi as if about to say something.

Before they could speak, the ground shook hard enough that everyone was jolted. Yudi felt the impact of Brum's landing in his bones. Even the Vanjhani's knotted muscles clenched and unclenched instinctively. It was accompanied by a burst of wind that shook dust down onto the five figures still standing in the wadi.

A succession of shouts and yells followed, accompanied by heavy thuds, crashes, and a medley of screams, choked-off cries, the sound of metal ripping, bones shattering, skulls crunching, and other assorted noises of combat.

Detritus fell all around them. Some of it appeared to be chips and splinters of weapons and armor. Some was wet and red, and might once have been attached to bodies.

"Stone Father," Yudi said, with less exasperation than he ought to have felt.

Arrow was grinning.

Saha and Kula looked angry.

Tshallian was staring.

"Brum's done it again," Kula said. "Having all the fun by herself and leaving nothing for us."

Kula ran up the side of the wadi and shot away in less time than it took Yudi to blink once.

The Vanjhani gaped.

Arrow looked back at Saha. "Sister, shall we go and see if there's any leftovers for breakfast?"

Saha winked. "Why the hell not!"

They leaped out of the wadi, not as quick as Kula, but much faster and more easily than any ordinary human.

Yudi sighed and gave Tshallian what he hoped was a reassuring smile. "It's been a while since their last brawl." Almost a day and a night, he didn't say aloud.

The Vanjhani made a sound that might have meant anything.

4

By the time Yudi and Tshallian joined the others in the clearing, there was no sign of the twenty border guards, not unless you counted bits and pieces of bloody armor and various sundries.

The Vanjhani looked around. "Vanjhani see many wars, many warriors. Proud race be us, bred of war and resistance against many enemies over many millennia. But this not like any fight Tshallian ever see. How four people eliminate twenty border guards in only few breaths? Tshallian not even hear any sound of weapons!"

"Actually, Brum did most of it," Kula griped. "Barely leaving a handful for the rest of us. You have to talk to her, Yudi!"

"You really should talk to her," Saha agreed. "She's acting selfish."

Yudi raised his hands. "I'll talk to her!"

Tshallian looked around, examining the debris that marked all that remained of the Dronasthan border guards. "What you *do* to them?" they asked no one in particular.

"Taught them a lesson," Arrow said brightly, picking up an object with the tip of their sword. It glittered in the moonlight. They took it in their hand and examined it carefully. "Never prey on the innocent and helpless."

"And if you do," Kula chimed in, "then expect a visit from the Five."

"Tell it to the world, brother!" Saha said, raising her hand high. Kula met her palm with his own in midair, slapping it. Arrow decided the glittering object was of no real value and tossed it aside.

Yudi left Tshallian still marveling aloud while he went in search of Brum.

He found her back at the river, lying face-down at the edge of the bank, drinking directly from the river with great, thirsty slurps.

"Brum," he said mildly.

She came up for air, not that she needed to — Brum could hold her breath underwater for hours if she needed to — and grinned up at him. "Thirsty!"

She always got thirsty after a fight. Yudi had once seen her drink several barrels of wine in a drinking contest, more than ten times what the other contestants — almost all men — had collectively consumed. Yet she herself hadn't even gotten truly drunk.

"We talked about this — your putting your personal feelings aside for the good of the family."

She turned over, lying on her back to look up at him. "That's exactly what I did."

Yudi raised his brows. "Tonight?"

"Of course. What I did to those border guards wasn't personal! I mean, okay, it was personal too. But that wasn't the reason I did it. I took them down because that was what the family wanted. I could feel it and see it in everyone's heart and mind and eyes. Even you, Yudi, even you wanted these border guards punished for their cruelties to the hundreds, maybe thousands, of poor, suffering innocents who only wanted to swim across to a better world. They abused, tortured, and slaughtered innocents. They had to be punished, or they would have kept doing it. We were helping all those future victims who will now be able to flee Dronasthan unmolested and alive."

Yudi rubbed his forehead with two fingers. "You might have read the will of the family correctly, Brum, but you failed to consider the consequences. Now we're going to have every border guard, maybe even every soldier in Dronasthan, after us all the way to the Gwannland border. That's not going to be very helpful to the family, sister. Next time, think family first."

Brum sat up, looking abashed. "I'm sorry if I got a little carried away, Yudi. I was just doing what I thought was right."

Yudi nodded. He knew his sister spoke the truth. Brum could be as innocent as a puppy at times. It was as if the instant she went into "justice" mode, she could see, hear, think nothing else unless her goal was accomplished.

"Very well, sister. I just hope we can still get to Gwannland as planned. Otherwise, it'll all be for nothing."

He offered her a hand without thinking.

Brum took the proffered hand.

Yudi suddenly found himself on the ground, which had risen up to meet him with surprising speed. Brum was now standing and looking down at him, laughing.

"Come on then, brother, let's get a move on. This is no time to be lolling around!"

She winked and walked away, still laughing.

Yudi joined in after a moment as he rose to his feet.

5

The tavern was crowded, which was all to the good. It was late autumn, and the brisk wind was bracing enough to drive all but the most foolhardy travelers off the road. They had walked for hours before finally stumbling across this little place, tucked away in a tiny hamlet far enough east that news of their exploits en route from the western border might not yet have reached it.

Cold winds swirled around them, raking in yellow, gold, and rust leaves to add to the inches-thick carpeting of crushed leaves, sawdust, and splintered glass that already covered the tavern's dirt floor. The odors of pipe, bowl, and hookah vied with the smells of rancid beer and burnt meat; whatever breathable air remained suffocated silently beneath the combined onslaught. The sounds of gruff laughter, tinkling ankle bells, jingling coins, thumping fists and ale mugs on boards warred with the roar of voices of every hue and color, all speaking in the slow lazy drawls of the Eastern Kingdoms.

Yudi paused in the doorway as a hundred pairs of inquisitive, mostly suspicious eyes turned to examine him and his group. Behind him, Brum and the others tramped through, still arguing about something to do with the differences between Eastern currencies and Krushan coin. They went past him and into the raftered room, neither intimidated by nor careful of the crossed brows and squinting eyes directed at them. Tshallian came last, one long arm shoving the door shut against the insistent wind.

"Ah," said the Vanjhani, rubbing all four hands together briskly. "Good it feels to be in again warm comfort."

Yudi offered no argument. Despite the strange smells and smoke-thickened atmosphere, he had to admit it did feel good to be under a real roof for the first time in days. He was accustomed to sleeping out in the wild; the night sky and stars had been his roof and night-light for all his childhood. But while he felt at home in the dense forests of the west, sleeping under a wide open Eastern sky with no cover and little tree shelter was not his idea of a restful night. He felt too . . . exposed.

He followed his siblings and their traveling companion. Tshallian was already speaking with a barhand who was pointing to an empty table on the upper level, three steps up, far at the back of the room. The presence of the Vanjhani in their group appeared to have eased the tavern's occupants somewhat; Vanjhani were perennial rovers, one of the few races found across the continent, and people everywhere were accustomed to seeing them passing through their villages. It was Yudi's presence and that of his siblings that wasn't being taken too well.

But that was why they had brought Tshallian along. The Vanjhani knew it and was deliberately drawing attention to themself, speaking loudly and boisterously, exchanging words with the barhand, offering a friendly smile, an extra coin as a tip — a habit foreign to the region but common practice in other more sociable kingdoms — and even a jest that brought a reluctant smile to the young fellow's face. The barhand leaned over and said something in one of the Vanjhani's ears, and from the way that Tshallian nodded and winked, Yudi guessed that their charm had worked its magic once again.

He nodded to himself with a hopeful sigh. Charm was good. Charm was better than another night of fighting and running through a cold, windswept wilderness with packs of howling dogs and angry soldiers on their trail. Yudi could do with a hot meal and a night spent on an actual bed in a room with a door. Preferably one that locked. His siblings lived for the fight, but as far as he was concerned, even fighting for your life wore thin after a while.

He took his seat at the table with them, still painfully aware of the curious eyes and whispering mouths all around.

The reason for the table's lack of occupancy was obvious at once: it was blocked into a corner, wedged between a long rectangular table lined with a profusion of bushy beards and battle-axes, and a round table ringed with three-eyed rake-thin warriors each with a clutch of throwing spears seemingly thicker than their wrists. Yudi recognized neither race, but then again, he was the least traveled of his siblings. The two groups appeared to be vying with each other for the title of Most Food and Drink Consumed in One Night, and the sheer quantity of ale flowing from gigantic tankards, and wine pouring from chilled bladders was enough to fill a small lake.

"Food! Ale! Keep coming them!" Tshallian shouted above the hubbub, which had resumed with full force the moment they had taken their seats. The barhand scurried off to comply. The Vanjhani placed two of their hands on the battered, stained board, while their two spare hands massaged weary shoulders and muscles.

Their table had probably once been round until the outer edge had been broken or sawed off and roughly sanded down. Yudi insisted on Brum taking the outside chair, convincing her that she would get the most space; his real reason was to avoid her making eye contact with any of the other patrons. Tshallian sat in the next seat, where they could easily rise to handle unwelcome approaches, their sheer bulk and intimidating arsenal, jutting out at all angles on their backs, helping keep any curious strangers at bay. Yudi sat in the innermost seat, exactly opposite Brum. Saha and Kula were to either side of him, and beyond Kula was Arrow.

Kula was rubbing his nose, with a pained look on his handsome face. "This place stinks."

Arrow grinned. "That's probably just the food, brother."

They slapped Kula on the back. Kula rolled his eyes. "In that case, I just might wait until we catch another braga before I eat again."

Saha shuddered. "I'll starve before I eat another braga. How can you even joke about a thing like that? They're domesticated animals. People keep them as pets."

"Not the ones that were chasing us, sis," Kula said. "Those guys would have eaten us alive. It was them or us."

"We were misdirecting them away from us," she pointed out. "They were headed miles away. The only reason that poor braga even followed us is because you guided it to yourself. And then you shot it down! I can't believe you did that."

"I love animals as much as you do," Kula said, "but we hadn't eaten in two days. We needed the food, and it was our only chance. This wretched country doesn't even have enough wildlife to live off of. Where did all the fauna go?"

"Hunted down, rounded up, and kept in stockades by King Dronas's decree," said the barhand, setting down giant tankards of frothing ale. "All livestock sales are controlled and taxed by the king's guards." Despite his lanky physique, he had somehow carried the six tankards in a single hand. In his other hand, he bore two steaming platters stacked on top of each other, both laden with an assortment of savories. Another barhand accompanied him, carrying four more platters.

Tshallian must have given the barhand a bigger tip than he'd noticed, Yudi guessed.

Saha looked at the food dubiously. "What is this?"

"Smells like roast meat to me," Arrow said, picking up an entire skewer, pulling at a knot of meat, and chewing with relish. "Yup. Definitely roast meat."

"But the meat of *what?*" Saha asked.

"Who cares!" Brum said. She picked up a skewer, stuck its entire length into her mouth, and pulled it out like a toothpick; the meat disappeared in a few quick chews. The barhands gaped at her. "It's hot, and it's meat, that's all I need to know!"

She picked up her tankard of ale and, as the amazed barhands watched, poured its entire contents down her gullet. She picked up the two remaining skewers on her platter, stuck them both into her mouth, drew them out clean as the day they were forged, and handed the empty platter and mug to the nearest barhand.

"I'm going to need at least a dozen more of each of those," she said. "To start with. What do you have in entrees?"

"We . . . we have mutton stew," said the female barhand, staring down at the empty platter and tankard that could probably have filled the bellies of an entire family.

"I'm not talking about appetizers," Brum said. "What do you have that's a real meal?"

"Um . . ." The barhand was at a loss for words.

Tshallian explained in a more cheerful tone: "A roasting haunch perhaps? Or a whole calf even? A big appetite my friend here has."

The first barhand, the one whom Tshallian had tipped, recovered from his shock and said, "The kebabs are all we have for tonight. But we do have plenty of them. I can bring you more, certainly."

Brum nodded. "That's good. It'll do for my brothers and sisters. But how about some main courses? Something big. Something *substantial.*"

Arrow added shrewdly, "You said that's all you have for tonight. Does that mean there's something you're saving for another occasion?"

The barhand exchanged a glance with his companion. "Well . . . we have a roast suckling and an entire roast calf in the kitchen. They've been slow-roasting since yesterday. But I couldn't possibly serve those. They're for Lady Goddick's betrothal tomorrow afternoon."

Brum guffawed. Arrow's eyebrows shot up to meet their hairline. Saha and Kula looked at each other with identical grins. Even Tshallian's two faces stared at the barhand. Yudi felt his own lips twitch in a smile.

"God DICK? There's someone who has to live with that name? A *lady*, no less?" Brum let go of a laugh that bubbled over the noise and exploded into the rafters. She slapped the table hard enough to make the laden platters and full tankards jump. Yudi sighed as the tankard he had barely taken a sip from spilled ale on his lap.

Heads were turning all around them.

The barhand looked nervous suddenly. "Um . . ."

"*Goddick!*" Brum said again, still laughing.

Tshallian stared at Brum with one of their heads, at the barhand with the other. "Mind her not. She's amused easily. Take the roast suckling we will."

"And the calf," Brum added quickly, wiping away tears of laughter with the backs of her hands. "And a dozen more platters of whatever you call this."

"Kebabs," said the barhand reflexively, still looking nervous. "I couldn't possibly bring you anything else. The suckling and calf, as well as the grilled ducks, are all being prepared for Lady . . . for the lady's betrothal. They were specially ordered weeks in advance, and paid for in advance too."

"We can pay," Tshallian said, taking out a purse and tossing it to the barhand. Their reach was long enough that they practically handed it to him. He took it and felt its weight, blinking rapidly. "After all, we're here now, and hungry. You could always put another suckling and calf on the flames tonight, well in time for tomorrow's function. Brum here has special needs too."

"I could eat a duck!" Kula said.

Saha slapped him on the back. "No, you won't. Not in front of me!"

"And sucklings and calves are all right?" he asked her. "That's not fair."

She shook her head and took a deep draft of the ale. "This is warm. It should be chilled."

"I'll eat my fair share too," Arrow said. "And our good Vanjhani here could probably put away a good portion of those victuals as well, I'd wager."

The barhand looked torn now. "Um . . . The lady's betrothal—"

"Proceed it still can. Nobody be able tell apart one suckling and calf, yes, no?" Tshallian said. "Now. Our coin you have. Food bring quick, boy."

"And more *ale!*" Brum said, thumping her empty tankard on the table again, before tossing it to the female barhand, who caught it with surprising ease, betraying a familiarity with boisterous patrons. "Hey, nicely done!"

The barhand winked and came around the table. She was tall, hard-looking, with deep cleavage and a skirt short enough to keep the patrons more interested in what was beneath them than what was on their plates, Yudi thought. Unfortunately, she was exactly Brum's type.

She leaned on the table and stroked Brum's cheek with the back of one calloused hand. "I'd wager there's a pretty girl under all that road dust. Will I be lucky enough to find out tonight, I wonder?"

Brum flushed deep crimson. She swallowed as the barhand deliberately twitched the folds of her too-short skirt within inches of her face. "I . . . I don't think we plan to spend the night," she stammered. "We have a long way to go yet and only stopped by for a hot meal."

"Followed by a hot dessert?" suggested the barhand.

There was laughter all around their table, as well as the neighboring ones. The barhand was popular among the regulars, clearly. Yudi only wished she wasn't quite so brazen. Was she only teasing, or did she actually like Brum that much? He could never tell. While his brothers and sisters all enjoyed a warm body shared at night, he remained mostly indifferent to the pleasures of intimacy. Besides, they were deep in enemy territory, and this was hardly the time or place to linger.

"Well," said the barhand to Brum, "if you change your mind, we do have rooms upstairs. Or you could just bunk down with me. I sleep in the back."

"If she doesn't take you up on that, I'm available, Jenesha!" cried a wit from another table.

A chorus of *aye, me too* responses rang out across the crowded room.

The barhand walked away with some more twitching of skirt and sashaying of hips, attracting all eyes, male as well as female, as she went down the stairs and into the kitchen. The male barhand followed her, still looking doubtfully at the purse, brow crinkled.

Arrow whistled. "Yudi, we will be spending the night here, won't we? It seems like a jolly enough joint."

Yudi smiled wordlessly at his sibling.

Arrow laughed.

Tshallian's heads conferred among themselves, glancing often at Brum, but neither said anything. Yudi wondered if the Vanjhani was concerned about their attracting too much attention to themselves or if they were a little shocked at the flirting; he knew Vanjhani could be quite traditional about sexual mores. Ironic, since by dint of biology, every pairing of Vanjhani was also a foursome.

His question was answered shortly thereafter.

The loud commentary and laughter had died down somewhat, and the noise around them had resumed its earlier level, but Yudi noted that the occupants of the table to his right were still silent, and were now staring at them. Or, rather, glaring would be a better description.

Tshallian leaned in his direction, and the closest head said quietly, "Table left of us, look not directly."

"I noticed," Yudi said just as quietly. "Let's hope it's nothing."

6

Everything was fine until the roast suckling and roast calf arrived. It required six of the tavern's seven barhands to carry them to their table. The barkeep, who was also the owner, accompanied them with a steady stream of admonitions, cautions, and curses. Silence fell in stages over the inn, until by the time the food arrived at the Five's table, they were the only ones still talking.

"Finally, real food!" Brum roared, rubbing her hands together briskly. She looked around their table. "I'll have the suckling and the roast calf. You all like the kebabs so much, you can feast on them!"

"You just inhaled the last platter, sis," Saha said. "What was that? Your third? Fourth? We're having the suckling *and* the calf!"

"Fight me for them!" Brum said good-naturedly, sticking out her hand in an arm-wrestling challenge.

"How about telling us where each animal came from, their life history, and how they died?" Kula said, teasing. "You get it all right, you can have them both!"

Saha and Arrow both laughed. Kula and Saha's gift for animal communication was preternatural, and unique to them, in addition to their other individual talents. Brum would easily win in any arm-wrestling match, but when it came to animals, living, dead, and even unborn, the twins were, well, a force of nature.

"We'll have equal portions around the table," Yudi said to the barhands, who had been listening to the conversation with frank curiosity. Brum made a loud noise of protest. "Two portions for my sister over there."

"Three at least, please," she pleaded. "I haven't eaten in days! You wouldn't let your sister starve while you feast, would you, Yudi?"

Arrow grinned at Saha and Kula. "You better watch out, guys. Your portions may just disappear from the plate. When Brum inhales, she sucks all the oxygen out of the room!"

The owner carved the portions, placing them on plates which his barhands distributed around the table. The female barhand—Jenesha—butted in to take Brum's plate herself. Her father, a tall, reedy fellow with a perfectly round potbelly and a round bald head to match, glared at her, then shot a glance at Brum. With a warning shake of his head, he gave Brum the plate. Janesha smiled sweetly at him, but the moment her back was to him, she winked at Brum with both eyes alternately.

Brum immediately blushed and looked down shyly. She began twisting a corner of her road-soiled garment in her hands.

Yudi was always amazed by the transformation that came over Brum when she met someone she was attracted to. The gruff, rambunctious warrior who could take on any comers in a brawl suddenly turned into a shy teenage girl, still wary of the mysteries of mating.

She is a teenager, he reminded himself. *We all are, at that. We just happened to have grown up faster than most kids do, but under all our bluster and calluses, adolescent hearts beat.*

They had barely begun tucking into the food with relish — even Yudi was impressed by the succulent meat and delicately nuanced flavors of the sauces — when two members of the group seated to their right stood up and strode over to their table. Yudi knew at once they were going to be trouble. He saw Tshallian's abdomen and chest muscles clench reflexively, as they always did when the Vanjhani prepared to fight.

They were the same diners who had been glaring at them earlier, and whom Tshallian had warned them about. Both men were hulking brutes with beards that reached down to their waists and backs bristling with criss-crossed battle-axes. Their eyes were deep set in hardened diamond-shaped faces, and almost all pupil. Underdwellers of some kind, he guessed from the eyes. That kind of dilation occurred in races who lived in subterranean caverns. The men were tall enough that they had to bend their heads down to avoid hitting the curved beams in this corner, and even then, the tip of one battle-axe drew a shaving or two of wood, which landed on their rock-like shoulders.

The men leaned down to glare at all of them in turn, but Brum in particular.

"Food there belong to Lady Goddick," said the one with darker-hued hair. He had notches cut into one ear, like he had used it to mark off important events in his calendar. His hair fell over his eyes and into his face like a stream of oil. "You got no right to eat."

Several of the siblings started to speak at once. Yudi silenced them with a mental command: *Let me handle this.*

"Good evening, sir. Are you referring to this excellent meal of which we are partaking? We have ordered and paid for this repast. I assure you it is very much the dinner we ordered, and may I say, it's quite delicious."

The first man looked at his companion. "What accent be that? Aranyan? Reygistani? Never heard nothing like that gibberish 'fore. Sounds like they gargling out of their butts while pinching their noses."

It's Krushan, actually, Yudi thought to himself, *but since Dronas is an exile from the Burnt Empire and a sworn enemy of the Krushan, I'm hoping everyone here is too foreign or too drunk, or both, to realize it, until well after we're gone.*

The second man ignored his friend and took a step forward, already looking angry. He made a fist and shook it at Yudi. "Best you stop eating the lady's betrothal feast. It's sacrilege, is what it is. Those victuals be meant for her ladyship's betrothal tomorrow. We come all the way up from Bhoomi City to attend the event. She be family."

"On the bride's side," said the first man proudly. "Our uncle's mother's cousin be third cousin to the fourth bridesmaid in the wedding party."

Arrow made a choking sound into their joint of roast. Kula slapped his sibling's back and pretended to massage it, while coughing to cover up his own burst of laughter.

Control yourselves, please. We can still talk our way out of this.

Good luck with that, Arrow sent back.

"The lady's betrothal feast is being prepared as scheduled, I assure you. This is our dinner, which we ordered and paid for, just as, I'm sure, your party ordered and paid for yours."

The two men looked at each other. "That be some of that double-talk Ben'fanwe telling us about the Northeasterners he met up in Gwannland, I be thinking."

The second man nodded, eyes narrowing as he scanned the Five's table. "I be thinking so too. Talking's useless to these lot. Only one way to deal with such likes."

Yudi sighed as both men reached for their axes. He could already sense his siblings all preparing to counter the coming attack. At the neighboring table, out the corner of his eye, he could glimpse the rest of the bearded party rising from their seats, reaching for their weapons as well. He glanced over the crowded tavern hall. This was going to get messy, unless . . .

Brum, we need to handle this without violence.

From his sister, he received images of juicy roast dripping with sauce; his palate exploded with the flavors of the meat and spices, his mind all but purred with the contentment of good, hot food, strong ale, and the warmth of family. That was so like Brum. Always ready to fight but right now completely preoccupied with the even more important task of eating.

Brum, come on!

He felt her sigh, saw her lower the ham-sized joint she was gnawing on, and look at him with one eyebrow cocked.

Arrow and Kula can handle it. Either one can handle it, actually. Let me eat! This is actually pretty good. You should try some. Put some meat on those skinny bones!

He resisted the urge to call out to her across the table. Already, the bearded men standing at their table had their axes drawn and were grinning with bearish expressions that betrayed how much they were looking forward to separating some foreign heads from bodies. The rest of their group was on their feet and approaching with weapons drawn as well.

The drawn weapons were attracting the attention of the other diners, and hands were reaching for their own weapons in anticipation. What sort of tavern allowed patrons to dine so heavily armed? A tavern in a military state, of course. There would be no question about which way the loyalties of the other patrons would turn once the fighting began. Dronasthan was notorious for its treatment of "outsiders," the euphemistic term for anyone deemed to be out of line with the community's norms. The systematic erad- ication of their own "less desirable" elements was well known, with mass graves containing thousands of slaughtered refugees — unarmed families, even — whose only crime was wanting to leave the fascist state to seek a free life elsewhere.

There would be no quarter here, no mercy. And that meant the only way to defend themselves would be fighting the entire hall, as well as being chased by whoever else came after them from the nearby town and villages, the friends and relatives of this lovely bunch of diners. Yudi could already see himself and his siblings leaving the tavern looking more like an abattoir than a dining hall.

He saw Tshallian's disappointed, grim expressions. The Vanjhani had emphasized the importance of passing through Dronasthan with as little disturbance as possible. Not only for their own safety — since Tshallian had not truly believed what the Five were capable of even after being told they could handle anything — but because, once they crossed over into Gwann- land, Dronasthan could use their troublemaking as grounds for starting an interstate dispute, as prelude to a war on their neighboring kingdom.

After all, Dronasthan itself had been carved out of the better part of what was formerly Greater Gwannland, leaving the great republic only a thin sliver of relatively hostile land on which to eke out its survival. The imbalance of power between the newly formed kingdom and the former one was so immense that there was simply no point, and no advantage to be gained, by eliminating the tiny, humiliated neighbor. But one incident such as this could easily give Dronasthan the justification it sought to wipe out the remnant of its former enemy.

So we would be responsible not only for killing a sizeable number of people here, but also causing a war that could result in the genocide of the remaining Gwann- landers. Definitely not what I had in mind when we embarked on this trip, Yudi thought dejectedly.

Brum, please.

"Foreigner scum!" one of the beards was snarling. "The likes of you aren't —"

Whatever blather he was about to spew flowed unheeded over Yudi's head. He was distracted by a pause in the noisy chewing and lip-smacking from his sister.

Brum had finally paused her feast to respond to Yudi's pleas.

Oh, all right, then. But we're not leaving until I finish my dinner. Agreed?

Agreed. Just do it before this gets out of hand, Yudi sent.

Arrow and Kula both sent together: *Aw, we could use some entertainment with our dinner. It'll be like supper theater!*

Yudi ignored his siblings' wisecracks. Tshallian, ever the gallant Vanjhani, was already rising to their feet, hammer drawn, ready to crack skulls. In a few more seconds, this would pass the point of no return.

Brum!

He felt, rather than saw, his sister smile, wiping her grease-smeared mouth with the back of one brawny forearm. She only succeeded in smearing road-dust across her cheeks in a slashing stain. The smile she gave him — and the rest of the hall — was the kind that might be expected on a stone carving of Grrud, the stone god of wind, who was in fact her forebear. It gave even Yudi, her brother and someone he knew she would never harm, reason to fear.

Then Brum took a deep breath.

7

Yudi felt a sensation he had felt before and had hoped he would never feel again. When Brum was still a precocious little child as yet unaccustomed to her own strength and powers, like all toddlers, she had poor impulse control and was prone to tantrums when she didn't get her way. He didn't recall exactly what had caused her outburst that day — he was of the same age as she, all five siblings being born within weeks of each other — and it hardly mattered. What mattered was that they had been in an ashram in a forest clearing, attending kul.

The guru instructing them that day in Vessa's absence — and as Yudi recalled quite clearly, Vessa was absent more often than present — had been intent on completing the lesson he was in the middle of. Brum was hungry: Brum was *always* hungry, but that day she was hungrier than usual. She wanted to go eat, but the guru insisted that she finish the lesson first. Brum had learned enough manners by then to know it would be rude to argue with the guru, or to yell and shout and hammer her fists on the ground. She was also clever enough to know that there were alternate ways to achieve her goals, thanks to her extraordinary gifts. All five of them knew this, but the others were patient enough to wait the few minutes longer it would take for the guru to complete his instruction. Brum, on the other hand, chose not to wait.

She had given Yudi a grin, a younger, more childish version of the same grin she gave him now. Then she had sucked in a long, deep breath.

At once, Yudi had felt a strange sensation, like everything was going silent around him. The parrots squabbling on an overhead branch, a pride of leopard cubs frolicking in the forest nearby, the wind rustling the tops of the banyan trees, the sound of the guru's droning monotone, even the sounds of his own heart beating and breath passing in and out of his nostrils. His ears, his lungs, his head, everything had felt curiously . . . empty. He had struggled to draw in breath, but his chest heaved and heaved and found no purchase. He'd felt like he was being turned inside out. As if, any minute, his insides would burst out of his mouth and nostrils and ears and other orifices, and his life as he knew it would end.

Then the day had turned mercifully dark, and he passed out.

When he'd regained consciousness, Mother was with them, admonishing Brum quietly but firmly. Brum was looking recalcitrant, but her cheeks were flushed pink, as they always became when she had done something she knew she wasn't supposed to do but that was also extraordinary: a very Brum mixture of guilt and defiant pride. The guru, poor old chap, was on his back, being attended to by his shishyas, who were fanning him, giving him water to sip from a brass pot, and generally fussing over him.

After that day, the guru had always made sure to end his lessons well before mealtime and would even ask Brum, nervously, if she was hungry yet. She would always answer smugly that she didn't mind finishing the lesson first.

Now, Yudi felt the same awful sensation. The difference was, he was older, wiser, and prepared for it. He had, after all, asked Brum to use this option. It was the quickest and most effective way to incapacitate all the enemies in their vicinity without harming them permanently. He and his siblings all knew Brum was about to do it, so had breathed deeply and were holding in their breaths when she began.

Too late, he realized that he had forgotten Tshallian. The Vanjhani was halfway to their feet, weapons in hand, faces tense with anticipation of the brawl they thought was inevitable. Yudi thumped himself for failing to warn their traveling companion. They had only first met Tshallian a day before this trip, but the Vanjhani had come highly recommended and already proved themself a loyal and trustworthy friend.

Don't fret, brother, Arrow sent. *There wasn't time to explain it enough that he would believe it anyway.*

Yudi knew that was true. But he still flinched when he saw the Vanjhani's eyes widen, then their two free hands clutch at their throats, gasping for air, before their eyes rolled back in their heads, and they collapsed in a heap. Their weapons clattered with dull thuds on the sawdust-strewn floor.

They were joined by the weapons and various items — tankards, platters, cutlery, assorted objects that happened to be held or clutched at by the other diners in the tavern hall — as the hundred-odd occupants all imitated Tshallian's choking, gasping, panicked expressions and actions before collapsing bonelessly.

Brum, her cheeks full from the deep breath she had drawn in, beamed at Yudi. She winked at him. *Will that do, brother?*

Yudi raised his forefinger and thumb in a circle. *Nicely done, sis.*

She nodded, then slowly released the breath. Even though she was careful, the sheer quantity of air she was breathing out — quite literally *all* the air in the tavern hall — created a strange effect and sound.

Yudi felt his ears pop, and the peculiar sucking, pulling sensation on his body dissipated. He inhaled cautiously and was relieved to find himself able to breathe again.

Brum could have held her breath for several minutes, or even hours — she had never actually had the patience to hold it long enough to find out if she had a limit — but that would have defeated the purpose. Long enough without air, and everyone in the hall would have died, Yudi and Tshallian included. When it came to Arrow, Kula, and Saha, while they possessed their own individual talents, each unlike Brum's, it was debatable how easily they could be killed, or by what specific means. But for Yudi and Tshallian, as well as the rest of the occupants of the tavern, the danger was as real as a dagger to the heart.

"Nicely done," he said to his sister, sucking in air eagerly. "That was perfect."

Around the tavern hall, everyone else was still lying as they had fallen. A few stirred, groaning like drunks the morning after, but didn't actually rise; they soon dropped back into unconsciousness. The effect of having all the air sucked out of the room, as well as from their lungs, usually had a stronger effect on those who had drunk too much. Yudi had barely sipped his ale, as usual, but judging by the lack of movement around them, everyone else in the hall had consumed more than their fair share.

Surprisingly, Tshallian remained unconscious, still slumped on the floor beside their table. Arrow checked their vital signs to make sure they were all right.

"Out cold," Arrow told Yudi.

Yudi frowned. "They ought to be awake."

"They did put away a fair bit," Kula pointed out.

Yudi nodded, unconvinced.

"Maybe they just need the sleep," Saha suggested.

Yudi liked that answer better. "We should get going," he told his siblings. "Before they wake up again and pick up where they left off."

"Yudi, this is the first goddamn good meal I've had in weeks. I'm not leaving till I've polished off every last bone!" Brum spoke around mouthfuls, juices running freely down her chin and throat. She picked up her tankard and drained it.

Arrow, Saha, and Kula continued eating and drinking as well.

"We may as well finish eating," Arrow said.

Yudi sighed. "I guess so. But let's not linger any longer than we need to."

8

Some time later, they found themselves on the road again, walking down a dirt track. The eastern sky was already showing signs of life. It would be dawn soon. Yudi glanced back. Brum was carrying the Vanjhani slung over her shoulder, held in place by one hand, and a small barrel of ale in the other hand. She kept guzzling ale as she walked, spilling almost as much as she consumed. Wonderful, Yudi thought, they would leave an odor trail in their wake for anyone to follow. Then again, how would anyone know who had dropped the ale?

"They're waking up," Brum said suddenly.

They stopped as Brum set the Vanjhani on their trunklike feet. Tshallian swayed a little at first, then their eyes focused and settled on the five of them. Life and confusion returned to their eyes at the same time.

"What? I . . ." They looked around at the dark fields through which they were traveling. "In Dronas still we are? How come to be here? Tavern . . . ?"

Kula clapped a hand on one of the Vanjhani's shoulders, his slender, shapely hand delicate against the complex network of muscle and sinew. "Don't worry about it, friend. Did you get a good rest?"

Tshallian blinked all four of their eyes and stared at Kula, then at the others. Their eyes found Yudi. "Master Yudi?"

"I told you before, Tshallian. Just call me Yudi. We use first names among friends."

"Yudi?" Tshallian said doubtfully.

"We ran into a little trouble back at the tavern. Brum here took care of it."

He explained the how of it. Tshallian looked simultaneously dismayed and troubled. "Not honorable is such method. To kill or render incapacitated without enemy even having chance to retaliate is not way of warrior."

"To incapacitate the enemy before they could retaliate was the whole point, my friend," Arrow said, using the tip of an arrow to remove a fleck of meat stuck between their teeth. They examined the morsel, then flicked it away.

Yudi nodded. "We thought it best to avoid a brawl."

Tshallian thought about it for a moment, then nodded. "True is. Fight in tavern cause much disturbance, attract king's guards. More difficult it would make journey our."

Kula slapped them on the back again. "Great, sport. Now, let's get on our way, shall we? I can't wait to get out of this fascist kingdom and reach Gwannland."

"Let's pick up the pace, then," Saha said. "I'm tired of this place too."

On that, they were all in agreement.

They made good time and encountered almost no further trouble all the rest of the day, taking country roads and avoiding towns and villages with the aim of reaching Gwannland the next afternoon.

At one point, Tshallian said to Yudi quietly, almost conspiratorially, "Gods are you."

There was no interrogatory uplift at the end of that statement, but Yudi took it as a question anyway.

"No," he replied. "Merely demigods."

Gwann

⌒

1

KING GWANN WAS NOT looking forward to this day.

Vensera was enjoying herself, of course. She loved such occasions. Festivals, celebrations, parades, rituals, anything that required everyone to turn out in their finest regalia, bone trumpets blaring, buffalo horns booming, conch shells reverberating, confetti in the boulevards, colorful pennants festooning the ramparts, giggling children tossing fistfuls of petals in the air, colored powders exploding from outflung fists. The louder, the more raucous, the crazier, the better.

To her, this was a chance to bring out her Beha'i side, the wild, wanton, anything-goes sword maiden who lived for the hunt, the melee, the battle by moonlight. The Beha'i regarded war as a celebration. A festival of blood and sacrifice, the necessary purging of excess population through karmic selection. Their military attire was colorful, rainbow-hued body paints — right down to their sexual organs. War was pageantry, combat a deadly dance to the death. They approached violent conflict with the joyous enthusiasm that other cultures exhibited at religious festivals.

Oh yes, Vensera was having a great time. She had been up since the stone gods knew what time, or perhaps had never slept at all, seeing to every last detail. As Gwann tied the sash of his robe, walking through the great hall which had been converted for the occasion, he had to admit he was impressed. Like everything else Vensera did, she cut no corners, accepted no compromises.

The great hall had been transformed into a space that was truly fit for royalty. Their guests would be hosted in fine style. He nodded as he took in one exquisite detail after another, from the vaulting softwood sculptures to the intricately painted pavilions, the artistically carved seating, the color-coordinated upholstery and cushions, the washbasins with petal-scented spring water, the luxurious beds that could each accommodate an orgy — and probably *would* before the week was over — and a hundred other items that contributed to the overwhelming effect of deep comfort and luxury.

He found his way to the podium and the throne intended for himself and Vensera, and sat down to observe the hall. Workers and servants bustled to and fro even now, putting last-minute touches to the masterpiece.

He stopped a serving boy and diverted him to the kitchen to fetch some repast for his breakfast. Gwann knew the dining hall would be packed with Vensera's family, most of whom had turned up days before the date mentioned in their invitation, and who turned even mealtimes into raging political debates. Gwann had no desire to listen to his brothers- and sisters-in-law bicker about the right time, strategy, and methods to defeat Dronasthan in a sustained campaign: he had heard it all before.

The boy returned surprisingly quickly with the tray of food and hot beverage, and Gwann broke his fast as he contemplated the pageant that he would be hosting within a few hours.

He had been skeptical when Krushni announced her intention to host this event. Aghast when she had spelled out in detail her plans and guest list. Shocked when she had outlined the contest she had in mind for their guests. Even after he had calmed down and finally accepted that she meant to go ahead with the event regardless of his approval, he had been mortally afraid that the whole thing might fall apart once the illustrious visitors arrived and saw New Gwannland's sparse accommodations and facilities.

There had been a time when Gwannland, the Gwannland of his youth and childhood, had been the proudest kingdom in Eastern Arthaloka. Rivaled only by Aqron in the south and, more dubiously, Mraashk in the north. That Gwannland had been lost when treacherous Dronas, his own childhood friend and fellow student, had turned against him and invaded Gwannland, carving out his own illicit kingdom, arrogantly titled Dronasthan, out of the choicest part of the former kingdom. What was left to Gwann, the thin sliver of a state he euphemistically called New Gwannland, was but a finger of the great limb that had once been a powerful Eastern

Kingdom, one of the last great independent states not beholden to the evil and seemingly omnipotent Burnt Empire.

Since the coming of Krushni and Drishya, their little kingdom had prospered greatly, it was true. Gained in wealth, prestige, influence, and even resources in a surprisingly short time. But it was still only a shadow of the powerful military state that was Dronasthan. The threat of war hung over them constantly. Even their best allies openly spoke of the inevitability of Dronas eventually taking over what he had spared the first time, assimilating New Gwannland into his growing, increasingly powerful monarchy. It was only a matter of time, it seemed.

But that time had been made more bearable thanks to the arrival of Krushni and Drishya. The few threatening advances and probing strikes from Dronas had been fended off with unexpected ease by the young pair. Yet when Gwann had broached the idea of going to war against Dronas, Krushni had firmly ruled out an open campaign, saying they must bide their time for the right opportunity.

"When will that be?" he asked his daughter.

She had smiled that enigmatic smile of hers. "When the time comes."

When that would be, she would never say.

But weeks earlier, when she tried to discuss her plan for this event, she had cut off his adamant refusals, asserting: "This is the time we have been awaiting. This is the opportunity."

He had stared at Krushni. Her coal-black face, beautiful, high-boned, inscrutable. Those burnt-sienna eyes had gazed back at him with humor and intelligence.

"For us to . . ." He swallowed, suddenly choked with emotion. "Take back Gwannland?"

That was how he had always thought of it. Not as invading Dronasthan, but as taking back Gwannland, *his* Gwannland, the land of his birth, his ancestors, his heritage and history.

She smiled. "Our time approaches, Father. This will be the start. Great things lie in store."

Now he bit into a palm fruit, the sweet, cool water spilling over his palate, filling his mouth with delicious flavor. Yes, he thought, he could see it looming. Great things indeed.

Perhaps this wasn't going to be such a bad day after all.

2

"Father?"

Gwann felt his face light up at the sight of Krushni. His daughter always brought out the brightest, cheeriest side of him. His advisors, friends, relatives, even Vensera herself, knew that the best time to ask Gwann for something was in Krushni's presence.

He knew it and didn't mind their little manipulations. Krushni had a certain effect on him. She made him feel as if there was hope in the world, that the righteous would triumph in the end, that those who did evil could not evade the consequences of their actions.

Perhaps it was a grisly way to regard one's daughter, but that was the way it was with Krushni. She had emerged from the searing blaze of stonefire fully formed, a young woman, not a mere child or even the babe he had expected and asked the stone gods for in the ritual. He had been expecting a newborn; instead he had been given Krushni. And Drishya as well. The Given Avatars, she had said when they first emerged from the sacred flames.

He had yet to learn what that meant, but it did not matter. Krushni was everything and more than he could have hoped for. An intelligent, good-humored, emotionally mature young woman who knew her mind and did not hesitate to speak it, but also chose when and where and how to express herself. She had no truck with patriarchy; if anything, she trampled over it.

That was all right with Gwann. The Kuin were a matriarchal society anyway, and Vensera was the real head of their household — or she had been until Krushni came along. It wasn't so much that Krushni had displaced her. Krushni loved her mother dearly and would never upstage or defy her. Instead, she supplemented her in ways that made even Vensera marvel.

Anything Krushni understood, she accomplished with grace and perfection. It was easy to yield to her. People asked her to take over their responsibilities, even begged her at times. Gwann had seen some of his most powerful lords plead with her to come to their castles and do for them what she had done for New Gwann City. Krushni always laughed and said she knew nothing of such matters, she was only a dutiful daughter following her parents' wise counsel, and they would do well to heed her father's and mother's advice as well.

In a single sentence, she had rebuilt their trust and respect in Gwann and Vensera, repairing the bridges that had crumbled when Dronas defeated Gwann and wrested away the lion's share of the kingdom. Now even Gwann's critics believed, if only in a dreamlike, hopeful way, that someday, somehow, Vensera and he would find a way to take back their kingdom from the invader Dronas and restore Gwannland to its former glory. They believed it because of this young woman now seated beside him. His daughter, Krushni.

"Krushni," he said to her with a smile, setting aside the cup he had just drained of tea. "This" — he gestured to the great hall — "this is magnificent. It far exceeds anything I could have imagined. How did you do it? And in just a few weeks with almost no resources or money?"

She smiled modestly. "You ought not to be surprised how much bounty there is to be had in the natural world, Father. You're the one who always says that Mother Goddess Artha gives us all we need to sustain ourselves on her loka, this great, beautiful world of Arthaloka. All we need do is respect her gifts and use them responsibly."

He shook his head in wonderment. "I meant conservation and reusing natural resources. Like salvaging wood left over from building to make furniture, turning coconut husks into footwear, burying nightsoil and refuse far from living habitats, avoiding the needless killing of animals except for actual consumption. But . . . this? This is awe-inspiring. The venue itself will be the talk of Gwannland's allies for decades to come."

She smiled in acknowledgment of his praise. "Wait until you see the contest. I have something quite special planned."

"I do not doubt it in the least," he admitted. And he truly did not. Whatever Krushni had in mind, it would be spectacular.

"One little detail I may have forgotten to mention earlier," she said.

Gwann shook his head. "You don't need to ask my opinion or permission for anything, my dear. Whatever it is, I am sure your own judgment will be far superior to my own. You have a free hand in this entire endeavor. Do as you deem appropriate."

"Yes, thank you, Father," she said, "but I would still like to inform you of this one detail."

He leaned forward expectantly. "Of course. What is it?"

She looked at him, locking gazes. "One of the invitees to the contest is King Dronas."

He stared at her. He felt the smile on his face dissipating, like a figure drawn with a stick on sand when the tide washed in. Suddenly, the hot breakfast in his belly, the good mood he was in, all turned sour. "*King Dronas?* You mean the invader who betrayed my friendship and trust, brought an invading force into our lands under cover of an invitation from my father, then illegally occupied and held our territories, committed genocide upon the Kuin people and all those who resisted his power, and went to war against me in my own homeland, slaughtering countless Kuin and driving me and your mother and our families, those who survived the invasion, to the least desirable corner of the kingdom, here to eke out a survival with barely a fifth of the lands, people, and resources we once possessed? *Dronas?*"

"Yes," she said simply.

"I see," he said after he had waited several minutes and found no further explanation forthcoming. "He is invited to this event."

"His entourage will be among the last to arrive, tomorrow in fact, a day late due to pressing matters in his capital city."

"*His* capital city?" Gwann wanted to shout the words, but restrained himself to a conversational tone. It took great effort. A word aroused dismay and rang warning bells in his mind. "Entourage? He is bringing armed soldiers into Gwannland?"

"Only the prescribed contingent as per the rules of the contest, no more."

Gwann nodded slowly, glancing around casually as if thinking about the matter. Several servants and workers bustling by glanced at him and Krushni, and smiled, bowing and nodding respectfully as they went about their business. To them, it probably seemed that father and daughter were merely discussing the arrangements or talking happily. He could have disabused them of that notion by storming to his feet and yelling and throwing things around. But that wasn't his nature. Although at this moment, he dearly wished he were that kind of man. That kind of father. It was taking every ounce of his willpower to avoid behaving like that tired old cliché of a patriarch, the way men behaved in the Burnt Empire, that bastion of toxic patriarchy.

"And what if he brings in more soldiers than prescribed in the rules?" he asked quietly. "If he brings in an entire regiment, or several regiments, or even a whole battalion, an invading force? What if he uses this invitation to make his long-anticipated move against us, finishing what he started when he killed my parents and stole my birthland?"

Krushni looked at him steadily, her eyes serious now, her gaze unwavering, her mouth firm. "You have nothing to worry about," she said simply. "This is part of my plan."

He looked at her for a long time. "I hope you know what you are doing."

"I do. I wanted you to know so you don't get upset when you see him here."

He considered that. "It will be hard. That man has caused me and so many other Kuin so much anguish . . ."

She touched his shoulder gently. "Father, please try. For my sake."

He drew in a deep breath and sighed it out. "Very well. I will be formal and polite, because I wouldn't want anyone thinking that Gwannland doesn't treat its guests hospitably, but don't ask me for any more than that."

"I wasn't expecting anything more." She leaned in and kissed him on his cheek, near the jawline. "Thank you, Father."

He nodded and rose to his feet. "Thank you for letting me know."

She rose as well, curtsying to him formally, as they were in the presence of others.

He nodded again and walked away, not trusting himself to continue the conversation much longer. He needed to consider this new development by himself, away from all this hustle and bustle and all these people. Especially away from Krushni, who he knew could get him to agree to almost anything. He needed to think it through in the minutest detail.

He walked slowly through the palace toward his private chambers, one hand toying with his beard as he did when he was contemplating deeply, the other hand bent behind his back. Several courtiers and palace staff passed him by, curtsying or bowing; the palace guards snapped to attention and sang out, "Hail the king!" but he neither heard nor saw any. His mind was ticking away like a kettle about to boil over.

He trusted Krushni completely, would trust her with his life, and in fact had done so more than once. But this was Dronas! It brought a flood of bad memories, horrible flashbacks to the worst crisis of his life, the tragedy of his family destruction and his people's genocide. He needed to look at it from every angle and think about what might happen if Krushni was wrong. However unlikely that possibility, he had to consider it, and he knew that telling Krushni to consider it would do no good. She would have done so already, in greater detail than he could ever hope to achieve. But he still needed to do so himself if only so he could get through the next few days.

Suddenly, the day didn't seem as bright and cheerful after all.

Dhuryo

~

1

DHURYO KRUSHAN GUFFAWED WITH laughter.

After a startled pause, his brothers, all ninety-nine of them, echoed him. Strictly speaking, only the eldest Krushan boys were inside the tavern with him; the rest were outside along with the contingent of guards. But all one hundred Krushan boys shared a common link, a psychic hierarchy. As the eldest and alpha leader of his siblings, whatever Dhuryo Krushan felt, thought, did, his brothers were compelled to experience as well; whatever he commanded, they had to do as well. So when he laughed at what the captain of the Dronasthan guards had just said, all the Krushan brothers laughed with him.

The Dronasthan guards stared blankly at him and his brothers, trying to make sense of their unexpected reaction. These men were not a particularly bright bunch, grown arrogant and fat after years of terrorizing the civilian populace of the lands they had stolen from what was formerly Gwannland.

Their captain, a repellent specimen notorious for his rapaciousness and willful cruelty to the emigrant children of the families seeking to leave the terrors of Dronasthan for safe asylum in the neighboring states of Gwannland or Isodinia, was very unappreciative of the irony in what he had just said. He stared at Prince Dhuryo with an expression that threatened violence. His hand was already on the hilt of his shortsword. Nobody had dared laugh at the captain of the Dronasthan guards; many screamed, cried, begged, or broke down completely and lost their sanity, but none *laughed*.

He was not used to such insolence, even from the crown prince and heir to the fabled Burning Throne.

"Enough!" he snarled. "What is so amusing?"

At his tone and volume, the platoon of armed soldiers accompanying him reached for their weapons as well, their eyes narrowing. Truth be told, they didn't give a damn if Prince Dhuryo laughed at their captain. They wouldn't have cared if he tickled him with a goose feather and danced the tandin with him on one of the tables in this tavern. They hated their captain's guts bitterly. Those among them whom he hadn't brutalized personally and intimately, or whose families he hadn't threatened — or, worse, followed through on earlier threats — he had antagonized in a dozen different ways.

Despite their hypermasculine swagger, they bore no illusions about what they did for a living. They were brutes in uniforms, armed and authorized to torment the very citizens they were supposed to protect and serve. The fact that their ruler and leader, Lord Dronas, himself set an example with his own reputation for epic brutality did not make it better. More than one of them secretly dreamed of joining one of the emigrant refugee groups to sneak their own families out of this vile kingdom. Those that had no families drank themselves senseless — many of them were drunk already, long before noon — and had inured themselves to the wretched cruelty of their job.

But they knew better than to show anything less than instant obedience and full allegiance. They were ready to defend their captain's honor, even though the thought of drawing weapons on a Krushan was a terrifying prospect in itself. They simply had no choice.

Prince Dhuryo did not erase the broad leering grin on his handsome face. He didn't temper his words, his attitude, or his tone. He turned to his brothers, pointing a finger at the captain.

"Brothers, he wishes to know what is so funny. Which of you will enlighten him? Dushas?"

Dushas, younger — by seconds — than his eldest brother, and the second in command of the Hundred, as the Krushan brothers were collectively known, grinned at the irate captain.

"You say that five young persons incapacitated over a hundred strong

Dronasthan men and women, all of fighting age, and many of them veterans of the militia or former military men?"

The captain frowned and nodded slowly. "That is the story the witnesses all agree on."

Dhuryo looked over the captain's head at his brothers and winked. The captain was a tall man by Eastern standards, but Westerners were taller, and the Krushan were considered giants among mortals. Dhuryo Krushan was a prime example, a hulking heap of muscle and sinew just over seven feet in height.

He continued in a mirthful tone: "And the way they incapacitated the entire hall full of fighting men is by, let me see if I remember this correctly . . . by putting them to sleep? All of them, at the exact same moment?"

The captain now looked even more resentful than when he had spoken out. He glowered beneath his bristling eyebrows. "That is what the witnesses claim."

Dhuryo nodded with a thoughtful expression. "So the fact that not even half a dozen young persons, without so much as lifting a finger or drawing a weapon, were able to somehow, magically, through unknown means, cause a hundred strong fighting men to sleep at once . . . Do you not find that amusing, Captain . . . whatever your name is?"

Now the captain was bristling all over, his temper clearly rising. "If you doubt me, question the witnesses yourself."

"I don't doubt the witnesses. There are too many of them saying the same thing for it to be doubted."

The captain's eyes narrowed, as if trying to see a double meaning in that statement. "You be doubting me, then?"

Dhuryo chuckled. "Only your manhood."

"What did you just say?" the captain asked, as if unable to believe his ears.

Dushas took a step forward. "He said you can't be much of a man if that story is true."

The captain strained against his temper. His sergeant, an older, more weathered veteran with decades of experience dealing with obnoxious royals, leaned in closer and whispered something in his superior's ear. The captain gave no sign he had heard, but he took a deep breath and released it slowly.

Dhuryo and Dushas looked at each other. Dushas laughed silently, his large head shaking.

"Seeing as I wasn't physically present at the location at the time of the incident, any attempt to ascribe blame to my command would be inaccurate," he said through gritted teeth, finishing with "*Prince* Dhuryo."

Dhuryo looked at him with an insolent smile on his face. "You mistake me for a war ministry councilor, if you even have such a thing here in this backwater pig trough of a kingdom. I don't give a hairy ass about whether you were personally present or not. I'm not impugning your masculinity personally, Captain Who-Gives-a-Fuck-What-Your-Name-Is. I'm impugning the manhood of Dronasthan's men in general."

"*What?*" the captain said, eyes widening as he leaned closer, genuinely disbelieving he had heard right.

Dhuryo sighed wearily, tiring of this charade. "Explain it in simple words of one syllable so this cretin can comprehend, Dushas."

Dushas was inserting a plug of supaku, a gummy narcotic extraction, into his mouth. His cheek bulged as he spoke around it, chewing through his words. "You Dronasthan men are all cows to let a bunch of boys take you down. Five against a hundred? No weapons used? Go on, get the hell out of here, you lot of gomunkhas!"

The last word was a vulgarism that had slight variations in almost every language across the length and breadth of Arthaloka. In every case, it had the same meaning: "cow shit eaters." In a continent where kine were regarded as wealth, and even worshipped by some faiths, it was the ultimate religio-cultural insult.

It was the last straw for the captain. With a string of curses that would have burned the ears of any priest, he drew his sword. His men were forced to do the same.

"Nobody talks about Dronasthan men like that," he shouted, "not even a damn prince!" And he slashed at Prince Dushas across a distance of barely five feet.

Dushas met the sword slash without flinching. It struck him with all the strength of the captain's muscled back and upper body. The Dronasthan guard had seen their captain strike the head clean off a man with that kind of slash. That was probably the captain's intention, since he struck at the Krushan prince's neck.

The sword blade hit skin and flesh with a sound like a hammer striking an anvil.

The sword snapped into three pieces, leaving the captain holding the hilt and a jagged shard the length of a dagger. He stared at it in confusion.

Dushas bent down, putting his face within breathing distance of the captain. He was only a few millimeters shorter than his brother, and compensated for the lack with a broader, heavier torso and a squat, overdeveloped lower body. He dwarfed the captain's six-foot height and muscular physique. "And your weapons are toothpicks."

Moving as suddenly as a striking cobra, he grasped the captain's neck between thumb and forefinger. He held it in his massive hand long enough for the captain's startled men to see it. Then he squeezed, as a normal person might when snapping a twig.

The captain's neck snapped with a very similar sound.

Dushas let the body fall to the floor of the tavern.

"If I want to put someone to sleep instead of bothering to fight them, that's how I do it," he said.

Dhuryo kicked at the captain's head lightly. It bounced on the wooden floor with a hollow sound. The captain's eyes were still open and staring upward in shock and confusion.

"Put them all to sleep," he told his brothers. "That's all Dronas men seem to be good for anyway."

2

Dhuryo emerged from the tavern with his brothers trailing behind. The rest of the Hundred, who were aware of everything that had transpired inside, looked at him expectantly. Several of them were grinning with anticipation, their hopes aroused by the killing of the soldiers inside the tavern; they were hoping Dhuryo would give them leave to have at a few hundred Dronasthan soldiers as well. It had been a while since they'd had a good slaughter.

"Would that it could be so," Dhuryo said, responding aloud to their unspoken query, "but I think our friend the Lady Goddick and our guru have something else in mind." He gestured to the road that fronted the tavern.

As if on cue, a black carriage appeared, followed by a sizeable contingent of horsed soldiers and several chariots. The carriage was a plush one, designed and built by the finest carriage maker in Hastinaga. It bore the emblem of House Goddick. The chariots were also of Hastinaga design and construction, gleaming silver-plated and with the symbol of Dronasthan embossed on their front, but unlike the carriage they accompanied, they were not designed for luxury but for war. Among them was one that stood out for its gold plating and burnished filigree inlays depicting scenes from the life of a legendary warrior.

The warrior in question tossed the reins of the four-horse team to an aide and leaped off the chariot. Even with his beard and hair whitened by age, he still posed a formidable picture of chiseled masculinity. His many scars were further evidence of his veteran status. The hooked nose and pointed, jutting jaw, the cruel hawk eyes, the air of earned arrogance were all mirrored in the many friezes embossed on the chariot, depicting only a handful of victories from a full, eventful life crammed with countless more. He strode toward Dhuryo Krushan with an attitude of commanding propriety that few mortals dared exhibit in the presence of the crown prince of the Burnt Empire.

This, then, was King Dronas in the flesh, the former guru to the one hundred sons of Emperor Adri of Hastinaga, He Who Sat Upon the Burning Throne. His was a reputation and legend equaled by few others in all Arthaloka.

"What have you learned?" he asked bluntly. Dronas was new to kingship and uncaring for the prissy formalities and elaborate rituals of the nobility. Like any good warlord, he got straight to the point — often quite literally, since he believed in ruling on his feet, and even by the point of his sword or his arrows rather than with his tongue.

Dhuryo summarized what the now-headless captain of the Dronasthan guard had told him in the tavern. He ended by mentioning that Dronas might need a new captain.

Ignoring the last, Dronas frowned at the news.

"Then my spies were right," he said, not looking pleased. "The sons of Shvate are here."

At the mention of their cousins, all the One Hundred paid careful attention.

A voice called out, "Who are the sons of Swat or whatever the uks his name is, and what do they have to do with my wedding banquet being delayed?"

Dronas ignored the speaker, but Dhuryo Krushan watched the approach of the person who had just alighted from the fine carriage with interest.

She was a storm wrapped in black velvet, her purple eyes glittering in a deep-set angular face. A single jagged streak of white stood out in her dark hair like lightning at midnight. Her body was tall and angular, but Dhuryo could tell from the way the velvet robe wrinkled and gathered that there were feminine curves beneath them. A slit in her long hip-hugging gown revealed tantalizing flashes of fine mesh stockings encasing long, ivory-pale legs — and a glimpse of a long, black-leather-sheathed dagger. Its wicked promise matched her cruel eyes. He knew from her reputation that she was a woman who loved the hunt — the kind that ended in blood and ruin, and the kind that ended in sweat-drenched sheets — almost as much as she liked to use that legendary dagger.

Shikari, whom the world knew as Lady Goddick, stopped beside her future husband and Dhuryo, her gaze fixed on the Krushan prince, thin lips curved in an insolent smile. Dhuryo knew at once that she had registered his interest and reciprocated it with a challenge: *Come and get me if you can.*

She gave Dhuryo a last flicker of her painted eyelashes before turning her attention to her betrothed. "Dronas?"

Dronas looked at her, then glanced at Dhuryo.

In that glance, Dhuryo saw acknowledgment in his former guru and new friend's eyes: Dronas knew his wife's reputation and her tastes, and offered no objection to her pursuing her target in this case.

Dhuryo reminded himself — and his brothers, who were observing the interaction vicariously — that Shikari Goddick was no ordinary cuckoldress. She was a deadly warrior in her own right, as well as an ambitious politician, and was even rumored to have killed her own late husband, Lord Goddick, when he continually failed to live up to her ambitious expectations. The word from Dronas was that she had her sights set on Hastinaga and would do whatever it took to reach that fabled metropolis. The man or woman whom she chose to align with to achieve her ends would acquire both a formidable ally and a deadly accomplice.

"My spies say they are on their way to Gwannland. Dronasthan was the most expedient route," Dronas replied to his betrothed.

"And you let them pass through?" she asked. "Is Dronasthan now a thoroughfare for any riffraff to travel?"

"Not any riffraff, my lady," Dronas replied. "These are the sons of Shvate, the former crown prince of Hastinaga. They are Krushan, and they are, all of them, quite gifted."

At the mention of the capital of the Burnt Empire, Dhuryo saw Shikari's eyes light up. "Krushan? Relatives of yours?"

The last question was directed at Dhuryo.

"Cousins. Though I've never met them. Their father went into self-exile after he abdicated the throne."

"Self-exile? Abdicated?" Shikari looked as though the words tasted sour in her mouth. She showed her teeth. "What fool abdicates the Burning Throne?"

"An honorable man," Dronas replied before Dhuryo could speak, "and a great warrior, despite his infirmity. But let us not speak of Shvate Krushan, who is dead. It is his children that concern me."

"Why does it matter," Dhuryo asked, "if they want to go to Gwannland?"

"Because of the business they have there," Dronas answered. "Queen Vensera and her consort, Gwann, are hosting a wedding contest."

Shikari laughed with delight and clapped her hands in an unexpectedly girlish way. "A wedding contest! How lovely. I love wedding contests. I had one for my own first wedding . . ." She frowned. "Or was it my third? Anyway, my contest was a simple one. All suitors had to fight each other using weapons and means of my choosing. All fights were to the death. The survivors got to face me in single combat. I was to make my selection from those who survived."

"And none did," Dronas said dryly to Dhuryo, his eyes conveying a message that his words underlined. "Shikari has never been bested in single combat."

Dhuryo raised his eyebrows, impressed. "So whom did you marry, then, if you killed off all the suitors?"

Shikari frowns. "Who was it now . . . Hmm. Oh yes, I chose the daughter of one of the suitors. She had accompanied him to the contest and acted as his aide. She was so upset with me for killing her father that she attacked me and almost managed to stab me in the side." She indicated a spot just above her waist on her left. "She was such a feisty little tigress, I was quite taken with her audacity and her beauty."

Dhuryo nodded, now intrigued. Though same-sex relationships were officially not permitted under Krushan law across the Burnt Empire, most of the aristocracy indulged their lifestyles in secret, but he knew that other kingdoms had their own mores and laws, and Dronas was more permissive in this regard. Dronasthan remained only an unofficial ally to the Burnt Empire as of now, not yet being of sufficiently strategic importance to annex; if and when that time came, they would have to pursue their lifestyles less flagrantly. It was possibly one reason why Dronas had resisted offering his loyalty officially to Hastinaga. Dhuryo's visit was in an unofficial capacity and purely owing to his friendship with his former guru.

"What happened to her?" he asked, curious. He almost expected to see the girl in question appear from the carriage. *Two for the price of one, that would be a fun game!*

"The same thing that happens to all Shikari's lovers," Dronas said matter-of-factly. "She tired of her."

Dhuryo did not ask what happened after Shikari tired of her lovers; he had heard the rumors.

Aloud he said, "This wedding contest in Gwannland, whose is it?"

Dronas raised a veined forearm as he scratched his grizzled cheek. "The daughter of Vensera and Gwann. I forget her name."

"Krushni," Shikari said promptly, her eyes glittering with that predatory expression again. "She is the one I was telling you about the other night."

Dronas frowned. "Were you, now? I don't recall. Remind me again."

"The one who they say is the real power in House Gwann. They say she was born of stonefire and stepped out of the altar a fully grown young woman. They say she has a brother who rarely speaks and is a legendary slayer reincarnated. They say she herself is the reincarnation of —"

"That will be enough," Dronas said. His face had hardened suddenly. "I know of the one you describe. So. That is Vensera and Gwann's adopted daughter, the one they prayed for through the stonefire ritual. And she is holding a wedding contest. Which the Five are attending."

"Yes," Shikari said softly, her voice almost sibilant with suppressed intensity. "And you know what that means."

"One of the Five is seeking to win that contest and wed Krushni of Gwannland. And if that comes to pass, then Gwannland will have five formidable champions in their arsenal. Together, they would make quite an army in their own right."

"Just the five of them?" Dhuryo asked, smiling. He laughed softly. "Hardly an army, Dronas."

Dronas turned his chiseled face to Dhuryo. His eyes were like icicles. "Do you remember nothing of my teachings, Dhuryo Krushan? Did I not teach you that the first rule of warfare is to never underestimate your opponent?"

Dhuryo shrugged. "Sure, but these are untested, untried, unbloodied novices. They pose no real threat. You alone could probably dispatch them. Or Lady Goddick could."

"Perhaps you think you could do the same?" Dronas asked, a hard look on his angular face as he tilted it to examine Dhuryo closely.

"Why not?" Dhuryo replied, feeling challenged and rebuked at once and not liking it. "From what your late incompetent captain told me, they didn't even lift a finger or draw weapons on the men in the tavern last night. Instead, they pulled some kind of cheap magic trick to make all the patrons fall asleep in their broths! Probably drugged the cauldron!"

He laughed again, louder than was called for. His brothers dutifully laughed in solidarity.

Dronas glanced around at the Hundred.

"Very well, then. Let us go see if a hundred titled Krushan can overcome five untitled Krushan. Let us go to Gwannland this very minute, participate in the wedding contest of Princess Krushni, and put your confidence to the test. What say, Dhuryo?"

Dhuryo's good humor faltered. He knew that by speaking the challenge aloud, his guru was questioning his manhood and his warcraft, as well as implying that neither were up to the task. He felt his temper rise and resisted the urge to lash out as he usually did — as he had done only a little while ago to the unfortunate captain of the Dronasthan guard in the tavern. Being singled out for offense by his guru's arrogance was bad enough, but he knew better than to answer back. Years of hard punishment and lessons brutally dinned into him had taught him well: the only way to answer Dronas effectively was to accept the challenge — and win it.

"Let's do it," he said, gesturing at his brothers. "Let's go to Gwannland. Any day is a good day for killing, and I've not had the pleasure of killing one of my own bloodline yet."

Dronas smiled savagely, reading Dhuryo's anger as well as his humiliation. He turned to his wife-to-be. "My lovely, this would mean —"

"Postponing our wedding," she said carelessly. "Yes, I know. In any case, the feast would hardly be ready now, and I'm intrigued too. I'd like to set eyes on this Krushni of Gwannland, and the children of Shvate as well. Especially after all this buildup about them. I am in favor of going to Gwannland."

Dronas looked pleased. "Onward, then."

He left them for a moment to issue instructions to his aides.

Steeped in his anger at Dronas's public questioning of his ability, Dhuryo did not notice Shikari approaching him. He felt her hot breath on his neck and shoulders as she breathed softly. "And I'm looking forward to watching you crush the children of Shvate, as I have no doubt you will, Dhuryo Krushan."

He regarded her. Her soft breasts pressed against his hard back as she stood closer than was required. Her eyes held an invitation, and a challenge, no less provocative than taking on the Five.

His stony face split in a shrewd smile. "With great pleasure, my lady."

He turned to face her.

"Shikari," she said softly, her hand caressing his chiseled abdomen, the movement hidden between their close-pressed bodies. "In my tongue, it means . . ."

"'Huntress,' yes, I know," he said.

Her purple-painted lips curved to match her kohl-rimmed upturned eyes. "Then let the hunt begin."

Jarsun

~

JARSUN WAS PLEASED BY the panic created by his arrival. He rode his mount through the heart of New Gwann City, deliberately taking his time.

Townsfolk turned startled faces and goggled as his procession passed. They joined heads and wagged tongues, babbling in consternation. He could guess what they were saying: *The Krushan. The Morgol. The God-Emperor. The Challenger.* It always pleased him that his reputation preceded him. Gossip and half-digested rumors built a legend more powerfully than any amount of actual knowledge possibly could. Thus were myths spun from spider-thin wisps of hearsay. Let them talk. Let them gossip. Let them share their half-heard, misheard, scraps and fragments of made-up nonsense. When the time came, the terror he would unleash would live up to all the fictions, and then some. Myths were dangerous when heroes had feet of clay. Jarsun's feet were talons, and had withstood earthquakes of some magnitude. In due course, he would confirm their darkest fears.

But first, he had a contest to attend.

And a score to settle.

"You're enjoying yourself," Ladislew said beside him.

Jarsun glanced at his companion. Somehow, even the way she rode her stallion was provocative, almost erotic. He saw many appreciative looks cast her way, even as the same faces turned darting, fearful eyes in his direction. Their confusion and mixed feelings pleased him too.

Ladislew brought a new element to his profile as a mythic ravager and conqueror. She was as yet an unknown quantity, an enigma despite her constant presence by his side over the past few years. She kept her secrets well.

Even Jarsun himself was not entirely sure of the full extent of her martial abilities, even though he had watched her spar several times. On each occasion, she displayed diverse fighting techniques and varied levels of skill. Taken as a whole, it was impossible to tell for certain if she was a truly masterful fighter who hid her true strengths well or merely a talented dabbler in multiple disciplines.

Significantly, she had always refused to spar with Jarsun himself. On the other hand, few fighters, no matter how accomplished, *wanted* to spar with Jarsun Krushan. His sparring partners had an unfortunate tendency to end up maimed for life, or dead. He was compelled to take his practice from actual combat — or when he was bored and in need of some leisure pastime. There was nothing quite like violence to keep boredom at bay.

He cast another glance over her now. She made a handsome figure, sinewy and tall, seated well on her mount, a stallion notorious for his unpredictable rages and penchant for hoofing random victims to death. The horse was blinkered at present, an essential precaution when passing through a populated area.

Ladislew met his glance with an insolent, arrogant look of her own. Her high cheekbones and almond-shaped eyes were decorated with tattooed patterns that matched the breathtakingly skillful ink swirls that covered her entire body. Only the area around her mouth was left uninked, and stood out the more sensuously for it.

As he turned his head back, out the corner of his eye he glimpsed the pattern seeming to alter slightly, the ink swirls and dots shifting ever so subtly to form new mandala-like tattoos. Yet when he stared directly at them, there was no sign of movement: they only shifted when he was not looking. Another of Ladislew's intriguing mysteries that he had yet to solve.

"It is good that they fear me. Fear breeds respect," he said.

Ladislew's eyebrows rose slightly. "I always thought admiration bred respect. But I suppose it can be earned by terrorizing as well, though I wonder if 'respect' is the right name for what these Gwannlanders are feeling right now."

Her mouth was curved in a mocking smile when he glanced back at her. She was always doing that, tossing some offhand comment or jibe that challenged his authority, yet doing so in a way that suggested playful banter. He always let it pass, as he did now. Such comments from a subordinate, or even an associate, he would not — could not — let pass unpunished. From a consort, they were borderline acceptable. Though he knew that no other consort courted reprisal the way she did. It was almost as if Ladislew *wanted* him to lose his temper or show his pique in some way—she was always goading him and pricking his pride. He would not give her the satisfaction; to lash out would only prove that he cared what she said.

Did he, in truth, care? Even an iota?

Perhaps. Perhaps not. It was hard to say. He had never known anyone quite like Ladislew. Deadly threat, conspiratorial mystery, and erotic enigma, all wrapped in one exquisitely designed package. Until he met her, he had thought nothing was beyond his ken, that his powers could grant him insight into everything, past, present, or future. Everything, it seemed, except Ladislew. She was the unknown quantity in his calculations. Perhaps that was why he kept her around, because she defied all his attempts to unravel, and because it was always better to keep one's enemies close. Someday, he would unravel her mysteries, like a priceless rug unrolled by a Red Desert merchant. And if he couldn't, well then, he would simply rip her to shreds and move on. Nobody was worth expending emotion on.

They rode on through the city together.

Ladislew

⁓

1

A FLURRY OF MOVEMENT accompanied their arrival at the pavilions. A great circle of raised platforms with tented coverings of the kind termed a shamiana by the desert peoples had been erected around a large field. The royal palace itself served as a backdrop to this venue.

An explosion of color filled the area with a rainbow-hued range of shades, from the tents, the banners outside each pavilion marking the Houses present, the gay robes, shawls, and scarves of the public, to the melee of shops and vendors that had sprung up around the pavilions to accommodate the shopping and refreshment needs of the spectators.

A wedding contest was a grand event in this part of the world, an occasion for public holidaying. Entire families were out in their finest, visitors pouring into the city from across New Gwannland and even from the neighboring kingdoms — except Dronasthan, of course, whose borders remained firmly barred to both influx and exodus. It was a circus of celebration, an occasion for feasting, imbibing, and singing the praises of their proud, rich heritage and culture. From the sheer vivacity and vitality of the crowds in attendance, and chatter overheard in passing, Ladislew gauged the adoration the people felt for their princess. To hear them speak of her, she loomed larger than life and closer than one's own kin. It was clear they doted on her in a manner that bordered on obsession.

"The sun must shine out of their precious princess's ass," Ladislew said as they dismounted before the pavilions. A half dozen courtiers clad in the ludicrously colorful Gwannlander traditional costumes bowed and greeted them with cheerful hails and wide, nervous gazes. Even their childlike smiles could not conceal their fear at the arrival of the legendary self-declared emperor of the Morgol Empire.

Jarsun did not respond for a moment, showing her his knife-edge profile. His hawkish nose and elongated features suggested he had not heard — or cared — for her comment. But she sensed something deeper in his lack of response.

"What does she do, shit gold every morning?" she added deliberately, using the languid tone she knew he hated. Like many strong, powerful persons, Jarsun considered it beneath his dignity to lose his temper over a provocative comment or implied insult, pretending to let such minor barbs go unheeded.

Ladislew knew that this false veneer eventually cracked: she had broken the resolve of strong men before, though Jarsun was not quite like any other man. Arguably, he was not a man at all; he was Krushan. Still, she hoped ultimately to provoke him into losing his temper, or to at least allowing her barbs to get beneath his skin, building up into a suppressed rage, which she would eventually exploit during a crucial, life-or-death moment. She had dispatched more than one target through this slow, patient process of attrition.

A flurry of color flashed in her peripheral vision, and she saw the approach of what was quite evidently someone of a high stature. The person's identity was revealed presently by an elaborately uniformed footwoman who announced ceremoniously, "The Queen!"

Ladislew suppressed an outburst of laughter. Ah, she had forgotten how much royals of ancient heritage loved their pomp and ceremony.

Jarsun was hypocritical enough — and shrewd enough — to pander to the same sentiment, using fantastically elaborate if more decadent and wild rituals to garnish his own stature as God-Emperor back home. Perhaps that was why he awaited the approach of the queen of New Gwannland with such patience.

"All hail Queen Vensera!" cried the footwoman, adding a string of incomprehensible titles and appellations that Ladislew ignored. She was too busy watching the very handsome figure striding toward them.

Queen Vensera was statuesque, with the athletic body of a warrior and the height of a banball player. She bore herself with a muscular fluidity that suggested middle age had not diminished her superb conditioning. This was clearly a woman who spent considerable time on the practice field and in the training yard. She carried a ceremonial sword and a set of throwing spears in a clutch bound with a gold band. Ladislew assumed the weapons served a ceremonial function as well, but there was little doubt that if the need arose, she could make excellent, bloody use of them.

Her face was long-boned and large-jawed, with curlicues of rainbow colors and starbursts painted on her features and exposed neck and deep cleavage and arms, as was the Gwannish custom. The body painting was presumably a mark of celebration, and on a more effeminate woman, it might have looked playful, even sensual; on Queen Vensera, it resembled a warrior's markings before battle.

"We are honored by your presence and look forward to showering you with our hospitality," she said crisply, in a surprisingly delicate feminine voice that belied her martial bearing, bowing formally to greet Jarsun. Ladislew noted that she had avoided use of honorifics, cleverly bypassing the thorny politics of whether to greet the notorious reaver of Eastern and Southern Arthaloka by his grandiose, self-declared title and thereby imply allegiance, or to revert to his true title of Lord Morgolia and risk his wrath. Nicely done, she thought. This was a woman she could learn to like . . . and, she noted, licking her lower lip delicately, to love.

Vensera glanced at her as if sensing her prurient interest, and while Ladislew glimpsed no trace of reciprocal interest in her grey-green irises, she felt her own desire aroused further by that direct, unabashed gaze. Ah, but how she loved matriarchal societies and their gender equality. It felt good to be in a place where genders were regarded on equal footing and women ruled in all spheres that mattered, especially after the toxic, hypermasculinized environs of Jarsun's court. It reminded her of how the world had once been, and could be again.

The sooner I finish my mission and kill this slithering snake beside me, the sooner I can be free to return to my true, natural way of life and find a lover again. Someone not unlike this fine woman.

As Jarsun and Vensera spoke briefly, formally, during their walk through the tented pavilions, Ladislew let her gaze and her mind wander farther afield.

They were strolling through the complex now, and she saw that most of the pavilions were already occupied. From the look of it, there were at least a hundred High Houses present, each with their own spacious tent appointed with luxurious amenities and sumptuous feasts. All the pavilions looked out into the enormous central field, a huge circle almost a half mile in diameter. Evidently, this was where the main contest would take place.

She wondered idly if there would be blood sport, or if this was to be just another test of skills. They finally reached their appointed pavilion and Vensera left them with a polite smile, another formal bow, and a colorful departure as she strode away, armed female attendants in tow. Ladislew saw Jarsun gazing after her briefly with a speculative look she had seen before.

"Planning to hunt for game tonight?" she asked.

Jarsun ignored the comment, as he ignored all her barbs. He regarded the contest field, then turned to stare at the pavilion two down from their own.

Ladislew looked in the same direction. She could see that it was the only empty pavilion left. Presumably, another late arrival like themselves. She wondered for whom it was reserved. Whoever they were, Jarsun had a keen interest in them. That bore watching.

Settling in hardly took much time. Jarsun's entourage was a military one accustomed to traveling long distances on war campaigns and quickly had the pavilion and its private, partitioned chambers appointed to suit his tastes and needs.

Her attention, and Jarsun's, was redirected to the pavilion beside them, also being filled now with a group of new arrivals. She saw Queen Vensera bowing to a hulking brute of a young man with a hard, handsome face, accompanied by what seemed to be several dozen young men, all armed and with aggressive body language. Vensera left, her departure closely, lasciviously observed by the entire group.

Ladislew sighed inwardly. More muscle morons. She hoped all the contestants weren't going to be the same chauvinistic testosterone-driven clichés, all bluster and grunts and chest thumping. She was so tired of all that posturing and the pointless displays of "manliness."

A glance around revealed a few female contingents. This pleased her. Hopefully, there would be some diversity of talent on display here for a change, and some skills worth watching, though she didn't get her hopes up. She found herself wondering idly if she ought to compete as well, if only for the practice and to put some of these mleccha in their place. Perhaps she would after she caught a glimpse of what this Princess Krushni actually looked like and how she carried herself. She could probably take on this bunch of hairy chest thumpers without revealing her full skills to Jarsun; she had attended contests like this one before, and the level of ability rarely went beyond champion grades.

But she knew that could not happen. She couldn't do anything that might jeopardize the very long game she was playing here. Besides, Jarsun alone could probably take on the entire lot without exerting himself, and that would be unfortunate but also interesting in its own right. If nothing else, it would make for a good week's entertainment.

Ladislew's pondering ceased as a hush fell over the crowd. The moment they had all been waiting for had finally come.

And then, something changed unexpectedly. Something she had not anticipated, even though she had known it would come in time, or that something along these lines would come.

Princess Krushni arrived.

2

Ladislew felt the change in her blood, her body, her innermost core. Like a banked fire responding to a gust of wind, her ancient instincts flared. Heat crackled at the tips of her nerves, electrifying her. It was a presence the likes of which she had never felt before.

A fanfare of trumpets preceded the proclamation.

"All hail Princess Krushni of New Gwannland!" was followed by the less boisterously though still warmly declared "Hail King Gwann, royal consort."

All the attendees were on their feet, most stepping to the front of their pavilions for a better view. The procession came from the direction of the palace, preceded and followed by a grand parade of the usual Eastern pageantry and rainbow-hued spectacles. Jugglers, clowns, acrobats, trick riders, a choir of richly voiced singers performing what she assumed was the anthem or traditional song of the New Gwann nation, all blurring past in a shifting mosaic that she barely noticed. She had eyes, ears, and senses for only one thing, one person, the figure seated on the gaily festooned throne high atop the centerpiece of the parade, a float in the form of an ancient sky ship, like a picture out of an illuminated text on the myths of the age of the stone gods. The figure on that throne might have been a stone god herself, so sublime and supreme was she.

Ladislew's breath caught in her throat. She knew she was in the presence of someone extraordinary, someone not of this realm or time or age. The appearance of an actual stone god could not have elicited a more powerful response from her instincts.

Who is this Krushni? The question danced along the edges of her ragged breath, her ignited nerves.

She began to step forward, to go toward the float that was proceeding with majestic slowness toward the largest, highest pavilion, the area marked with the flags and colors of New Gwannland and the king and queen. A spear-wielding woman in the colorful uniform of the kingdom barred her way. Ladislew's finger twitched, wanting nothing more than to tap the soldier's chest once, sharply, hard enough to penetrate through to her beating heart and drill a hole into its ventricles. She was but an obstacle in her path to the celestial figure she sought to approach on the high chair.

Better sense prevailed. Her mission was more important than satiating her curiosity. Besides, she was here, and so was this person, this Krushni. It was inevitable that an opportunity to approach her and observe her more closely would easily present itself in the coming week. It made no sense to squander decades of planning and subterfuge just to answer a question that would in any case be answered soon enough.

The eyes of the Gwannlander made contact with Ladislew's feverish, searching gaze. Ladislew registered the woman's dark pupils, her unwavering focus, and her grip on the spear that she thought she might have to use to force this foolish noble back into the pavilion and away from her princess. Ladislew released a breath slowly, letting go of the sudden, uncharacteristic impulse that had almost caused her to lose sight of her real goal, and as she returned to a semblance of her "normal" self, she sighted something in the soldier's eyes. Sympathy and empathy.

"Our princess is a special person," said the soldier, in understanding and sisterly compassion. "But we cannot allow her to be approached by all and sundry."

Ladislew remolded her face into a quick smile.

She stepped back, into the shade of the pavilion.

She watched the parade complete its journey to the royal pavilion without further ado.

Just as she thought the incident had passed without notice, from beside her Jarsun said with a faintly mocking tone, "Perhaps there is more to this Princess Krushni than you expected, after all ..." The hint of a question mark at the end mocked her earlier barbs.

He had gotten in one of his own after all. And the barb stung with unexpected bite.

Yes, perhaps there is, after all ...

Krushni

——

KRUSHNI USED THE SLOW progress of the float to view the pavilions, smiling and holding up her hand in the Gwannlander gesture that meant both "be welcome" and "be at peace." All the invitees had arrived, and every one of the pavilions was occupied to capacity.

No.

Her eyes swept back to find the gap in the crowded circle, like a lone missing tooth in a mouth bristling with sharp edges. One pavilion was empty.

She noted the position and number, recalling the allocation list prepared by herself, and was pained to see that the missing invitee was the very one she had counted on attending. How disappointing.

For a moment, she almost faltered, her smile withering, her raised arm lowering instinctively. She caught herself in time, straightened her back, kept her arm up and fingers gesturing, and continued smiling and basking in the roars of the crowds.

The people were in attendance too, tens of thousands of them, filling the general stands to capacity and beyond. She could see people standing at the backs of the public pavilions, children and even smaller adults perched on shoulders, trees, walls beyond the periphery of the great arena, surely a hundred thousand or even twice that number.

And how many more were hovering behind them, eagerly listening to the accounts related and passed on by those who had even a glimpse of the distant spectacle, latching on to every fragment and scrap of detail, how the princess looked, what she wore, how she comported herself — and those who were much too far to see, or not as well-sighted, simply made up their own idealized descriptions, embellishing, adorning, adoring their beloved icon, their legend-in-the-flesh, their one and only Princess Krushni.

She knew what she meant to the people of New Gwannland. And to the people of the neighboring kingdoms and even a few farther-flung ones. She was a symbol of hope and pride. A harbinger of a better tomorrow. The hero they wanted her to be. Whether she truly was or was not all of those things was irrelevant; that they believed she was was the only thing that mattered.

She had a responsibility to them beyond her own personal agenda. She owed them something. She owed them the fulfillment of their hopes and dreams. That was why she had taken these many years to complete her cycle of vengeance, execute her long-delayed plan for vendetta.

And the target of her plan was present here.

The pavilion reserved for Morgolia was occupied.

She could even see, with her preternatural vision, the rake-thin, tall, sticklike figure of the man, the monster, the creature that resembled a mortal human.

Her father in her last life as Krushita.

Jarsun.

He, and he alone, mattered. All others — allies, opponents, pawns, tools, sacrifices, friends, lovers — were useful but incidental in the end.

It was Jarsun she wanted.

For him she had staged this grand spectacle — this wedding contest, of all things!

Her late mother, Great Goddess Jeel bless her soul, would have laughed aloud at the very mention of such a ludicrous outdated ritual.

A wedding contest? Krushni could almost hear Queen Aqreen say with her care-lined, laughing mouth and tenor voice. Didn't that custom die out with the last of the stone gods?

Even as she continued to wave and smile and shower her attentions on the assembled guests and audience en route to her own pavilion, Krushni could hear herself respond to the memory of her dead mother.

It's the most effective way to start off the war, Mother. It allows me to confront Father in a noncombative situation, humiliate him publicly, and challenge his ego and his manhood. It will force his hand and compel him to rush into a campaign I know he is not yet ready to launch. It will stretch his resources and extend his power to its limits, beyond his capacities. It's a classic attrition strategy. And then, when the time is right, I'll make my move and go head-to-head with him myself.

Her mother laughed again, her silver-tinged hair shimmering as she tossed her head in wonder. *Listen to you, my love. You sound like one of my father's old generals! All this talk of strategy and tactics. Wherever did you learn all this warcraft? When did my little doll of a daughter grow up to be this war-mongering tactician?*

When Father murdered you in front of me, Krushni heard herself say as her float approached her pavilion, then slowed to allow a display of folk dance representing the diverse cultures and races of Gwannland — the *old* Gwannland, before Dronas had stolen away the best part of the great kingdom — in what was intended to be a hint at the coming war and reunification of the divided kingdom and merging of the old and new Gwannlands once again. She could see the flurry of outrage in Dronas's pavilion, and the amused but tight-lipped intensity of Dronas himself as he viewed what was clearly intended as a defiant rebuke to his dictatorial power grab. *When he tricked me and betrayed me and killed you as if you meant nothing to him out there in the wild sands of the Red Desert, ending all my hopes and dreams forever. Your little Krushita died that day too, of her own free will. From her ashes rose this new avatar of her soul, the Risen Avatar, Krushni. And Krushni, Mother dear, is a warrior and an empire builder. I mean to avenge you, and I knew that to do so, I would need to acquire great knowledge of warcraft and strategy in order to defeat Father in the coming clash of empires. It's taken me almost fifteen years, and that time has been hard to pass, knowing each day that he goes on living as usual, but finally the time approaches for the execution of my vengeance. I shall have it soon, Mother.*

Yes, her mother replied quietly, her laughter stilled, her smile erased and replaced with a bittersweet look of sadness, *but it will not bring me back to you.*

I know that, she said intensely in her thoughts, but even as she said it, she doubted.

Krushni, my baby, my dearest love, Queen Aqreen said, *you do realize that this long-term plan of vengeance, this campaign of war, none of this will make things as they were before. You do realize that, don't you?*

Yes. Yes! Of course I do. I know nothing can bring you back, can repair what I've lost, what we both lost. Jarsun took care of that. He destroyed everything. It's what he does. He wants to destroy all Arthaloka, to break it down, crush it, and then reshape it to please himself. He doesn't care who or how many he hurts along the way. For him the end justifies the means. But that's why he must be stopped. And this is the only way to stop him.

And do your ends justify your means?

Krushni felt the piercing gaze of her father — she still thought of him as such even in this new body and avatar — upon her, boring into her. She smiled sweetly down at him from the top of the float and waved pertly. She saw his expression change, the tips of his tongue emerge out both sides of his mouth briefly, and knew he was hissing softly without even knowing he was doing it. Beside him, the woman companion glanced at him with an interesting expression on her face and said something. With her superhuman hearing, Krushni had only to focus and could hear her every word and nuance.

"Perhaps you feel the same about her," the woman said.

From the way Jarsun ignored the woman's comment and didn't look at her, Krushni sensed something between the two. A sexual tension perhaps? No, there was more to it. The woman herself was intriguing. No mere bed companion would have dared to speak thus to the notorious Jarsun Krushan. The fact that she had and was still breathing and whole suggested something quite different indeed. That one bore looking into.

Her mother's comment bothered her almost as much as the woman's words had irritated Jarsun.

Sometimes. Perhaps. I don't know, Mother, she replied to the ghost of a memory.

What you are doing, this plan, this strategic war, will result in a terrible loss of life and great destruction as well, will it not?

Yes, probably, if he does not yield quickly or if I cannot kill him quickly enough. But all the damage will be on his conscience. I would accept his surrender and capitulation today if it were possible. Right now.

We both know that is quite impossible. Your father will never surrender. No Krushan can. They may lose a battle, even lose their life, but they never capitulate. The war goes on until a Krushan wins, even if it takes generations. That is the Krushan way.

I am Krushan too, Mother.

Yes, Aqreen said sadly. *Of course you are. But you are the best of Krushan, the* best they can be. Which is why it pains me to see you upon this path of vengeance. You know what they say about revenge, don't you?

That when one embarks on vengeance, one should dig two graves?

That too. But I meant the other wisdom. The one which says that revenge is the worst crime of all.

I cannot let it go, Mother. Please understand that. I will not let him destroy the world unchallenged.

Then let others challenge him. You are still young, beautiful, have a wonderful pair of caring foster parents and an adoring populace. You can still make a life for yourself.

Until Jarsun comes calling, his armies rampaging and reaving their way through this little kingdom, crushing it and everything good within it the way he destroys everything in his path. And by then, it will be too late to even try to stop him. No, Mother. I have thought this through very carefully and for a very long time between lives. It is the only way. I must throw down the gauntlet now at this wedding contest and provoke him into action before he is ready. It is my best chance of success.

What good success if it costs you your happiness?

Mother, please. I need your support, your love, your understanding.

You have them all. Always. In this and every life. And beyond.

Then why do you still question me about my plans and intentions?

I don't. This isn't really me, standing here in my royal regalia. It's your own mind, your memory, your conscience. You're debating the ethics and morality of your choices with yourself. It shows that you're self-aware and self-questioning, that you're not your father in the best way possible. You know this already. It's your way of thinking things through, by making me your devil's advocate and looking closely at the opposite side of the argument. That is a good thing, Krushni. A very good thing. It shows you're not deluded or harboring false hopes. You're being realistic and keeping your bearings steady.

Thank you. I can hear the "but" at the end that you forgot to say aloud.

If you know that, then you know what else I'm likely to say. After all, this is you projecting your own doubts and anxieties upon your memory of me. This argument, such as it is, will end the way you want it to end. Is there really any point in my continuing to try to make you see my point of view?

Of course there is. We all need to see through the eyes of others, to put ourselves in their shoes, to understand their points of view, their lives, their cultures and worldview; otherwise we'd all be fascist dictators like Jarsun Krushan. And you're my mother. I always want to know what you have to say.

Then, hear this: the price of war is the only prize of war.

Krushni frowned inwardly, even as she continued to smile and gesture and pose for the world. What does that mean in this context?

It means exactly what it says.

That there are no winners in war, only losers? That the death, destruction, grief, and suffering caused by war are the only real results one can hope to achieve? That there are no positive or good outcomes in any violent conflict?

That is a good reading of the words.

Thank you; I had a very good teacher, Mother, but there is no other way. There is only war.

Perhaps. Perhaps not.

What does that mean?

What do you think it means?

Mother, I am committed. I have started on this path already. I have to see it through.

It's never to late to walk away.

It is when your enemy won't lay down their arms just because you do. What I seek to do is preempt and outmaneuver Father before he comes storming into New Gwannland and destroys everything I care about. And I won't have that. I will not let him do what he did the last time. He won't deceive me again by pretending to be the repentant father. I mean to see him punished for what he did to you, and to make sure he can't do it to anyone else ever again. It is the only way.

You truly believe that? Her mother sounded sad.

Yes. I believe that is the way he is built. He cannot change. And so my path is set.

Then you have already made up your mind.

It was made up for me the day he brutally and callously murdered you before my eyes, out there in the wilderness of the Red Desert.

Then nothing I say will change that.

I honor your wisdom, I cherish your advice.

Then hear this last caution. If a time ever comes, whether today, or days from now, or years or even decades hence, when you can walk away and end the violence, break the cycle of vengeance, without further consequences or harm to yourself, then promise me you will do it.

Krushni hesitated, then said, as much to herself as to her mother's memory, I promise. If and when I can without consequence, I will walk away.

And if that does not happen, then promise me that this vendetta you have embarked on will end the day you succeed in your goal.

This time she agreed without hesitation: I promise, Mother.

Then go in peace always. Let love fill your heart, and may the rainbow brighten your sky forever. I love you, my child.

I love you, Mother.

" . . . and I miss you," she said softly, aloud. Above the roar of the crowds, nobody could possibly hear the whispered words.

But beside her Drishya turned his head, smiled in sad understanding, and put his arm around her shoulders in a brotherly hug.

She smiled back at him, even as they and the float they were on passed beneath the shadow of the great royal pavilion.

Arrow

〜

1

THE ROARS OF THE crowd were dying down when they reached what appeared to be the entrance to the pavilions. The crowds, which had been thick for a mile or two, now grew as dense as a thorn thicket and almost as prickly when asked to move.

The Five as well as their companion Vanjhani received nasty looks and unpleasant mutters in the deceptively polite Gwannlander tongue, which, fortunately for the speakers, none of them except Tshallian had any ear for. From the set expressions of the Vanjhani's faces, Arrow guessed that Brum might not have taken some of the comments too well, especially since most of them were directed at her not inconsiderable bulk pushing its way through their midst.

Being none the wiser, Brum shoved through cheerfully, offering neither warning nor apology, as was her way, although if she saw a disabled person, an expectant mother, or a child, she always slowed her pace and moved cautiously, even tenderly, around them. Not that there were any pregnant women, disabled, or children in sight. Only the hardiest, most determined gawkers had made it in this close to the city center, eager for a glimpse of the visiting royalty and nobility, no doubt.

Arrow had seen it too often to be surprised. Even in the favelas encircling Hastinaga Palace, it was said that the poor and wretched pressed in lustily to view royal events and processions, often risking life and limb just for a glimpse of the rich, the famous, the powerful. At least here in New

Gwann City, the people appeared to be better fed, clothed, and treated by their overlords than their counterparts in the Burnt Empire.

Still, Arrow had no illusions about those overlords being any better than their kind elsewhere. In a world of Haves and Have Nots, the Haves were so named not because they usually deserved what they possessed but because they were either born with it or had acquired it through dubious means, usually wrested by force from the very Have Nots and Hope to Haves who served them. A great deal had been said about this so-called legendary Princess Krushni and her famed generosity of spirit and goodness of heart. It remained to be seen if she lived up to even some of that reputation. Arrow expected not.

Finally, the Five made it into the pavilions, just as a final flourish of trumpets and conch horns blared. From the discarded flower garlands, inches-thick rose petals underfoot, and stacked platters of incense sticks, clay lamps, and assorted paraphernalia, Arrow guessed that this had been some kind of receiving area where the arriving attendees had been welcomed and escorted to their respective places. There was no one here now, so the siblings made their way through to the other side.

They stopped and looked around.

They were in one of a vast ring of similar tented pavilions, gaily decorated and marked off by partitions, surrounding a vast open field. The place was packed, judging from the bustle of sound and laughter. Every pavilion was occupied by a number of overdressed and undermannered attendees, all busy quaffing and scarfing down the wine and food provided by their generous hosts. Servers moved through the crowds bearing large offerings of food of every variety. In several pavilions, attendees were strapping on armor, wielding weapons, and otherwise preparing for the contest.

"Too late it seems we are for to be seated," Tshallian said, their heads looking in both directions.

Arrow pointed across the arena. "There's an empty pavilion over there."

Yudi and the others looked. "That must be for us. How do we get over there?"

Brum shrugged and strode out into the open. Arrow looked at the others, shrugged, and followed her. Saha and Kula came along. Yudi frowned uncertainly, but nodded at Tshallian, and they joined them.

As they made their way, Arrow saw heads turning to look at them. It was hard not to notice them, as they were the only people moving across the open space. There was a flurry of movement and gestures among some of the hosts, who could be distinguished from the attendees by their colorful attire and unusual hairdos.

"I don't think we're supposed to be going this way," Yudi said.

"Would you rather be standing around back there and waiting for hours?" Arrow asked him.

Yudi made no further comment.

They strode across the arena, Brum leading the way. A murmur of curious interest rose from the gathered crowds and attendees. More and more heads turned as everyone noticed the six figures sketching their way across the vast canvas. The murmurs grew, breaking out into a smattering of applause here and there, and a few shouts of encouragement. Apparently, some watchers presumed they were the first contestants. *Close enough,* Arrow thought. *We're the last to arrive.*

Brum responded to the mistaken encouragements in typical Brum fashion: she raised her meaty arms, turned slow circles while continuing to walk on. Then, deciding that the crowd merited some entertainment, she began turning somersaults as she went, the maneuvers growing more and more elaborate, from midair corkscrew spins followed by perfect two-point landings to half a dozen sideways cartwheels interspersed with no-contact flips. She finished with a triple somersault and a midair corkscrew, throwing out her arms and diving as if the hard-packed ground were deep water, landing with such whisper-perfect softness that Arrow heard several attendees gasp and exclaim. Brum bowed deeply to resounding applause.

"How does she such?" Tshallian asked Arrow. The Vanjhani was speaking very softly, as if anxious not to be overheard by Brum. Arrow resisted the temptation to smile; Tshallian had come a long way from his initial doubts about the Five on this trip.

"She owns the power of Wind." Arrow thought of adding more, of telling the Vanjhani that if Brum wanted, she could produce a hurricane capable of erasing this entire gathering, even the entire city. *Among other things* — but Arrow kept that part to themself.

Yudi glanced over. *Caution, Arrow. Knowledge is power. We don't speak of our abilities. We only use them when we must.*

Of course. Arrow nodded, then indicated Brum with laughing eyes. *Um, does showing off for no good reason at all count as a "must"?*

Yudi rolled his eyes. *Brum!*

Arrow laughed aloud, surprising Tshallian. *Yeah. Brum!*

Brum turned and walked backward, smiling with exaggerated sweetness as she showed them both finger gestures with tiny tornadoes spinning on her fingertips. *You're just jealous! I'd like to see you top that.*

Arrow winked at her.

2

They reached the pavilion to find it already occupied, partly at least. Several of the occupants of the neighboring pavilion seemed to have kicked down the partition and were sprawled on the cushions and rugs, enjoying their feast. They were all similar physical types: brawny, overfed, loutish males with overdeveloped muscles and egos. Arrow knew the type all too well and had encountered far too many of them to find them amusing anymore. Yudi was already stepping forward to deal with the intruders diplomatically.

Brum, on the other hand, was not interested in diplomacy. She was glaring at the hirsute men lolling about on the cushions, spilling wine and sauces as they gorged themselves with a peculiar expression that was very familiar. Brum didn't appreciate anyone taking her place or eating her food. Especially eating her food.

"You —" she began before Yudi cut her off with a gesture.

"Sirs, I believe you are in the wrong pavilion," he said.

The men continued eating, drinking, and talking without paying any heed to Yudi or the rest of the new arrivals. They appeared to be talking in the common tongue of the Northwest, the universal language spoken across most of the Burnt Empire, a simplified version of ancient Ashcrit, the official language of the Krushan. They looked, sounded, and behaved like ordinary hooligans, but Arrow had a suspicion they were anything but ordinary.

"Sirs, am I correct in assuming that that pavilion is yours?"

Yudi addressed this directly to one of the men who happened to cross his path at that moment. The man, a tall, hefty fellow with drooping mustaches and a beard that smelled like it had been washed in ale and assorted savories, sized up Yudi quickly. "What's it to you?"

"Well, if that is your pavilion, isn't that where you and your associates should be?"

The man guffawed. "Y'hear that, brothers? He called you my associates!"

"Your brothers, then," Yudi said.

The man gestured dismissively at Yudi and started to turn away. He found Brum blocking his path. She had a deep frown on her face, and her fists were loosely clenched. Saha and Kula were close by, their body language suggesting they were ready to act as well.

"That wouldn't be our food and drink you men are hogging, would it?"

The man looked Brum up and down. "What if it is . . . *Princess?*"

He said the last word like it was something lewd. Some of his brothers laughed—now that he had called them that, Arrow instantly saw the resemblance. How many of them were there, anyway? Looked like at least two dozen in this pavilion alone, and more than twice that number in their own pavilion. Suddenly, it was obvious exactly who they were.

Brum's frown disappeared, replaced by her sweetest smile. "Why, that's very nice of you, stranger. Yes, I am a princess. It's all right, though. No need to bow or scrape to me. I don't hold by those outdated formalities. Though you may, if you wish, want to kiss my pretty hand."

She held out a hand, which, Arrow had to admit, was pretty. Brum was pretty in her way, as more than one young woman—and a few older ones —had noticed in the past. It was only the male gender that usually failed to recognize her charms, but that was mostly because they were too distracted by her size and her forwardness. Arrow knew, as did all the siblings, that she could even be feminine at times. But femininity was lost on this drunken lout.

"Princess?" he repeated aloud, looking around the pavilion to attract the attention of his brothers. "Princess of what? A hog farm? No, wait, wait, maybe you're the princess of a buffalo herd! Yes, that must be it. Princess of buffaloes! Look, brothers, we have ourselves a visit from the Princess of Buffalo herself!"

A round of raucous insults and laughter rang out, attracting the attention of the occupants of both pavilions on either side. The one occupied by the remaining brothers of this lout paid closer attention. One of them was a massively built giant of a man who put down his tankard and rose slowly to his feet. Beside him was a thin, tall, white-bearded man — King Dronas, though Arrow had only known him as Guru Dronas once upon a time. And there was a woman too, a watchful dark-eyed vixen who had the physique and bearing of a warrior herself.

Of course. They would *put us here right next to Dronas and the Krushan Hundred. After all, family belongs together.*

Arrow stepped forward, coming between Brum and the lout, who was still laughing. His back teeth and his upper palate were visible. It was not a pretty sight.

Brum, let me handle this.

Arrow received no response from Brum, but could feel the stew of outrage and hunger brewing in her. Eating Brum's food or drinking ale meant for her were serious enough offenses, but to compound those offenses by insulting her to her face . . . those were capital offenses in her book of law. Arrow had known even fairly decent warriors to suffer unpleasant fates when committing similar crimes. It would probably be only a few moments before she unleashed hell on this unsuspecting bastard. They talked fast.

"Cousin," Arrow said, which got the man's attention at least. "We're your cousins. Your father, Adri, is brother to our late father, Shvate. We are the children of Shvate. And you are obviously the sons of Adri."

One of the other men sitting around drinking and chewing on a leg of mutton came forward, shoving his brothers aside. "That's *Emperor* Adri to you, peasant. We *are* the sons of Adri, and we don't hobnob with deer lice like you. This pavilion is ours by forfeit, and we don't want to be disturbed while we prepare for the contest. Now, take your fat sister and go back to your wormy hole. Begone!"

His other brothers immediately shouted in unison, "Begone, worms!"

Arrow felt even the perpetually calm Yudi starting to lose his temper at this, but pushed him — and the other siblings — back: *Give me a moment more.*

"Preparing for the contest, are you?" Arrow asked the second man.

The man made a dismissive sound. "What the hell else do you think we're doing here in this stone-god-cursed shithole of a kingdom?"

"We're here to win the contest and take the princess home," said the first lout. He glanced with a guffaw at Brum. "The *real* princess, not this hairy sow!"

All the Krushan brothers laughed at that.

"That's interesting," Arrow said, "because, you see, my brothers and sisters and I, we're here to win the contest too. And the contest can't have two winners, can it? So I think you lot had better pick up your hairy asses and move them back to your own pavilion before we crack you in half and eat you for a snack. Though I doubt even all hundred of you would be enough to make a dent in our sister Brum's appetite. She can work up quite an appetite for a fight, and just so you know, she always wins. In fact" — they gestured at their siblings — "*we* always win."

"Is that so?" said a rumbling voice from behind them.

Arrow turned to see that the giant from the next pavilion had come over. Clearly, this was not just one of the Hundred, but *the* son of Adri himself, Dhuryo Krushan, the eldest prince and heir-in-waiting to the Burning Throne. The sibling resemblance was obvious, but what was loutish and merely insolent in his brothers was wild, fierce, and frightening on this giant's craggy face. The stony eyes looked back at Arrow with the coldness of granite.

"What is this about?" Dhuryo asked his brothers, though his eyes stayed fixed on Arrow for a moment before moving on in turn to Brum, Yudi, Kula, Saha, and finally, Tshallian. Nothing in those rocky pupils suggested anything but supreme power and self-confidence.

"These peasants are trying to get us to move out," said the first Krushan that Brum had spoken to. "They say it's their pavilion."

Dhuryo Krushan looked at the Five and their companion again. He met Arrow's eyes, lingered, then moved on to Brum. He stopped there, perhaps seeing something that interested him, or just curious.

Abruptly, he turned his back on all of them and walked away, saying over his shoulder, "Let's go."

Without another word, every last one of the Krushan seated in the Five's pavilion rose to their feet, dropping whatever food or drink they had been consuming, and followed their eldest brother. Only the two who had bandied words with Brum and Arrow lingered a moment, their eyes squinting with hate. "We'll see to you lot later," said the one who had insulted Brum.

"Likewise," Kula and Saha said together.

The Krushan glared and looked like he wanted to offer a counter, but suddenly his expression changed. He walked off with his brothers.

The pavilion was empty except for the Five and Tshallian.

Tshallian looked around at the debris left behind. "Come early, we should have," they said regretfully. "Avoid misunderstandings this sort of, we would."

A Gwannlander in rainbow-hued robes indicating her high station came rushing up, accompanied by an entourage of at least a dozen attendants and twice as many armed guards.

"The sons of Shvate!" she cried. "We were expecting you hours earlier. Our profuse apologies for not receiving you at the entrance and for the misunderstanding with the Krushan."

"The *children* of Shvate," Yudi corrected her, taking charge once again. "It's entirely our fault for arriving late. We were unavoidably detained along the way. But we are here now."

Further apologies poured forth as the remains of the Krushan feasting were removed and fresh victuals and drink carried in by colorfully clad attendants. Finally, reassured that they were not offended by their brusque encounter, the Gwannlander emissary left, leaving them with enough food and drink to feast on for a week. Even Brum was content for a while.

None of the Five talked about the encounter with the Hundred. There was no need. All scores would be settled soon enough, in the arena.

Brum

⁓

BRUM WAS MAD AS hell.

The encounter with the Krushan brothers had gotten under her skin. Not because of what they had said — she was used to men strutting their machismo in her presence. They always felt threatened by her bulk and obvious strength, even before they had a chance to see what she was really capable of. Insults and putdowns were their foolish way of trying to pretend that they were superior. She had fought and laid enough men flat on their backs, many incapable of ever rising again, to know that just possessing a male appendage meant nothing. Strength and power were in the mind, the will, the heart. Brum was equal to a hundred men any day, any time, even before breakfast, and she knew it.

But this was not any hundred men.

This was the Hundred.

The Krushan brothers.

Her cousins.

They were blood kin, practically siblings.

In her mother's language, Karni had told them all when they were younger, there was no word for "cousin" as there was in the Krushan Ashcrit tongue. There was only brother or sister. Karni spoke of the Hundred as "your brothers" or as "your uncle Adri's sons."

Karni also said one thing that had stuck in Brum's mind since she was a little girl: *We don't fight our own.*

She had said it when the Five were old enough to understand that their uncle, emperor of the great Burnt Empire, had turned his back on them, forcing them to live as outcasts and outlaws in the wild jungles of Northern Arthaloka. That uncle Adri had refused to recognize them as the legitimate children of Shvate, and by doing so, he refused to acknowledge their rightful claim to the Burning Throne.

She had explained that he had done this because he was under the mistaken impression that their mother, Karni, had conspired to attack him and his mistress, Sauvali, while they were picnicking, almost succeeding in assassinating Adri himself, and abducting Sauvali. She had been pregnant with Adri's unborn child at the time and was believed to have been killed later, along with the child. Adri blamed Karni for the crime and the assassination attempt, declaring her an outlaw and placing a hefty price on her head. That alone made Karni the target of bounty hunters and outraged imperial loyalists across the land.

She told them she understood how he could issue such orders because of the misinformation he had received, presumably from Jarsun, Shvate and Adri's uncle. This was bad enough, but by turning Adri against her, Jarsun had also succeeded in achieving his true goal: to push Adri into refusing to acknowledge his own brother's children and their claim upon the Burning Throne.

When Brum had heard all this, she was incensed. She had leaped to her feet, already huffing and puffing and ready to burn a trail all the way to Hastinaga. Her siblings had been equally enraged. Even calm, quiet Yudi had said it was very wrong and something should be done to correct the lie. Their mother was innocent, and they were very much their father's children, and the world must know the truth.

Karni had calmed them down with just those five words.

We don't fight our own.

She had said the words sadly, resignedly, but also with acceptance and wisdom.

It had taken Brum years, and perhaps even now, at the still-tender age of seventeen, she couldn't say she understood completely. But she had come to accept the wisdom of that maxim. After all, she reasoned, if Brum herself gave in to every whim of temper, she would hurt everybody over time, even those closest to her. Especially those closest to her. She wouldn't want that; nobody would. So it made perfect sense. One simply did not fight one's own.

Whether that meant one's blood kin, or loved ones, or closest friends, it was all the same. There were enough enemies and threats out there in the wide, wild world, without turning against one's nearest and dearest.

Today, for the first time, she had cause to question her mother's wisdom.

Whatever she had imagined her cousins to be — her "brothers," as Karni would have put it — they were every bit as bad as she'd feared, and apparently worse. It wasn't just what they said or the way they looked or behaved. It was much more than that. Unlike her siblings, Brum couldn't always mindspeak or read other people's minds. But with the Krushan brothers, she had picked up something. It was like murmurs on the wind at night: too indistinct to make out the words but enough to guess the intent. There was something in the wind around the Krushan Hundred that was not good, for want of a better phrase. She sensed terrible urges, a history of awful deeds, and the will to do far worse in the years ahead.

Despite Karni's belief that there was "some good in every person, no matter how vile they seem," Brum's experience had shown that when it came to some people, if there was an iota of good inside them, it was buried too deeply beneath a pile of so much vileness that it was like a drop of clean water in a cesspool. It had no meaning whatsoever. Such people just had to be dealt with once and for all, because there would never be any compromising or living with them.

The Hundred were of that ilk.

She suspected they might be even worse than that, that they might even be . . . evil. Another word her mother said didn't exist in her language, but which Brum knew painfully well now was very real and more prevalent in the world than had seemed apparent at first.

That was why Brum was mad.

She could have lived with the Krushan insulting her. She would simply have insulted them back.

But she knew their insults were more than just ego-challenged male bluster and bravado.

They were clues to something far worse within those men.

Something slimy and tentacled that slithered in the dark recesses beyond morality. Something so deadly that you simply had to strike it down at the first possible opportunity, or risk it striking you when you least expected it.

So as she ate her feast and guzzled her ale, she thought about the Krushan brothers. And how she would deal with them when she got her chance. And how, when she did, she would make sure she knocked them down. And that they stayed down for good.

It was the only way.

Except … Mother had warned them about this, almost as if she had known that this encounter was inevitable. Like another one of her saws: *Some things are inevitable. Some roads turn where you turn. There's no escaping them.*

Their road to Gwannland had brought them face-to-face with their cousin brothers.

In a contest, no less.

Now all Brum had to do was to keep herself from killing her newfound kin.

It wasn't going to be easy.

She pushed away the remains of a goose carcass and looked around for something more substantial. Ah. Leg of mutton. From the smell of it, well spiced and seasoned. That would do nicely. Perhaps a dozen or so of these. And then she would be done with the appetizers and start on the main course.

She was still eating and thinking about her mother's caution and the Krushan brothers when a fanfare of trumpets sounded.

Yudi

〜

YUDI WATCHED THE GWANNLANDERS in their trademark colorful outfits walk out into the center of the arena to be greeted with loud cheers and applause. They appeared to be the hosts of the event. Yudi noted that there were exactly as many of them as there were pavilions. One of them was the same Gwannlander who had come to "receive" them after the encounter with the Krushan.

"Not good it is, pick fight with Krushan," Tshallian said beside him.

Yudi glanced at the Vanjhani. Their faces looked a little more careworn than usual, and the tendons on their arms and the backs of their necks were a little more clearly defined.

"If you're worried about us getting into a brawl, don't," he said. "My siblings may seem erratic and unpredictable to you, but believe me, our mother didn't raise any foolish or reckless children."

"True that well may be," said Tshallian, one of their hands rubbing the jaw of the face nearest to Yudi. "But say the same about the Krushan can you? Talk is their mother nurse them would not at birth and sees them rarely since. Grew up they have as spoiled princes getting their own way accustomed to. Think they own the world, they do. Mayhap, they do."

They gestured at the arena and the world beyond. "Not long will be before Arthaloka entire is Empire Burnt. Only question when will be the day."

Never, if I can help it. And since I am Krushan too, I will not and cannot let that happen. Aloud, he said, "Whatever differences we have, they will be settled out there in the arena, not in here. You have my word on that, Tshallian. And since we happen to be speaking, let me just say how much I appreci-

126

ate your accompanying us on this journey. If not for you, I don't doubt we would still be battling Dronas's guards back there."

The Vanjhani shrugged all four shoulders. "Guide you the quick and quiet way, did we. Not very much is that. You Five handle anything you can, I see. On this trip, came we to feel we are your friends. And as you perhaps know, Vanjhani make friends for life. Care for you Five, we do now. Wish you hurt to see, we do not."

Yudi nodded, smiling gratefully up at both faces. "You *are* indeed our friend, and a fine one at that. And we are honored to have your friendship and your trust. They are precious gifts in this wild and dangerous time we live in. Believe me, dear friend, we cherish your presence by our side and consider you no less than one of our own. Wherever we may end up on this journey, be it back in the jungles of the North, or in Hastinaga Palace, we would be privileged to lay a place for you at our table and provide a home for you as long as you wish to stay."

The Vanjhani turned to look directly at Yudi, something that Vanjhani rarely did. Their quadruple gaze was disconcerting. Where to look? Which face to examine for indications of emotion and nuance? Yet when they spoke, their concern and their excitement, mingled together, were evident and simple.

"True are they, then, the rumors? You Five intend to return to Hastinaga, to stake your claim for the Burning Throne?"

"Yes," Yudi said quietly. "That is our intention and our goal. Mother Goddess Jeel willing, and with the aid of friends such as you, we will achieve it."

Tshallian gestured at the arena. The Gwannlander hosts were making their way to their allotted pavilion as gay music continued to play and cheerful traditional songs were sung by choirs of singers with voices surprisingly loud enough to carry across the enormous complex. "What use this contest, then? Part of your plan to claim your throne, is it?"

"Very much so," Yudi admitted. "An essential first step. It all begins here, if it begins at all. That's why we had to come here, and your guiding us through the paths of least resistance was vital in that journey."

The Vanjhani clearly wanted to say more. Their earlier concern had given way to a flush of excitement, and they were very full of questions. Yudi found it adorable that a race of people so proud and powerful in size and strength could also be so childlike in their enthusiasms and passions. Then again, as he had learned from his childhood in the jungles, the largest, most powerful creatures were usually the gentlest. It was one of nature's many paradoxes.

Reluctantly, he raised a palm. "Friend, at an appropriate time, we shall sit together and I shall be happy to answer all your questions. But for now, let us curtail this conversation. The Gwannlander approaches, and I believe the contest is about to begin."

Tshallian nodded their heads and remained silent, though they could not conceal their change of mood or the enlivened looks on their faces.

The Gwannlander host stopped before their pavilion, just as her fellow hosts had done before the other pavilions in a perfectly coordinated formation. They now explained the rules of the contest to the attendees and assured them that a plentiful supply of food and drink would continue to be provided throughout. The contest would go on until a victor was announced, around the clock, though those not participating at any given time were welcome to rest in the accommodations provided at the rear of their pavilions until their turns were called.

"The rules are simple," said the host, smiling as she looked at each of the Five as well as Tshallian in turn. "The princess will call out a challenge, and all are invited to attempt it. Those who fail are immediately disqualified and cannot continue with the contest. They are welcome to stay until the end, but under no circumstances can they participate in further events. Those who succeed move on to the next challenge, and so on, until only one victor is left standing."

From the pavilion beside them, the sound of loud scoffing sounded in response to this announcement. Yudi cut his eyes in that direction, while keeping his face toward their own host.

"What happens if a hundred victors are left standing? Do you have another ninety-nine princesses back there?" asked the same lout who had spewed insults at Brum earlier. He jerked his head in the direction of the palace beyond the pavilions.

The hosts continued reciting their rote speeches, ignoring that and all other questions. Somehow, being Gwannlanders, they were able to do it with such polite, sweet expressions that even the Krushan brothers took no offense to having their queries ignored.

Yudi listened to the whole recitation and nodded, smiling and making a namas by way of thank you to the host. She smiled back with more warmth than before and bowed in the Gwannlander manner. "I wish you good luck. May the stone gods be with you."

"They always are," Brum said around a mouthful of roast. "I just have one question for you, beautiful."

Yudi smiled again at the host. "Please excuse my sister. She's just eager."

To his surprise, the woman smiled back and said, "It's all right, Lord Yudi. She can ask me a question now that I've finished reciting the rules."

She turned to Brum.

"What was your question, Lady Brum?" she asked.

Brum paused in her chewing long enough to say, "How hard are the challenges? I mean, the princess has had a contest like this one before, hasn't she? What was it like those times?"

"She has," the host agreed. "It is an annual event held every summer, and has been so for the past three years. But the first year, it was restricted to Gwannland united, both old and new, as we still think of it. The second year, it was expanded to include Eastern Arthaloka. This is the first year that it is open to all entrants, from anywhere in Arthaloka."

"Including the Burnt Empire," Arrow said, nodding in the direction of their neighbors. There was a trace of judgment in the gesture.

"And us as well," Yudi reminded them. "Otherwise we wouldn't be here."

"So how hard are they?" Brum asked again. "Be honest, sister. Because you have some real legends here from what we heard, and I really hope that your princess has somethin' meaty and tough enough for us to get our teeth into."

The host smiled at Brum. "The reason the princess expanded the scope of attendance is because nobody could pass the first challenge the first year. The second year, two contestants managed to achieve the first challenge, but both collapsed, and one died immediately after, while the other was stricken and lost the ability to walk and has not regained it even to this day. Truly unfortunate events, but all those attending are clearly informed of the risk and high level of ability required to participate."

Yudi exchanged a glance with his siblings, looking around at each of them. They all appeared intrigued, if not impressed.

"Bring it on!" Brum said eagerly. She finished the chop and tossed the bone back on the empty platter with a hollow clang. She slapped her hands together, producing a sound like a small thunderclap.

The host's smile faltered, and she was almost knocked off her feet. Yudi reached out and caught her in time, one hand grabbing her elbow, the other slipping around her waist.

"Are you all right?" he asked.

She blinked and regained a solid footing. "I was just . . . startled."

She gathered herself and bowed again as she backed away hastily, eyeing Brum. "I look forward to seeing you on the field, my ladies and lords," she said. "May the stone gods be with you."

She turned and walked away as quickly as she could.

"Well, this is going to be interesting," Arrow said.

Brum shrugged. "They always say stuff like that. 'It's hard, it's challenging, it's impossible.' And then they ask you to pick up a boulder and toss it, or aim an arrow into the back of another arrow, or something even a child in gurukul" — she jerked her head meaningfully in the direction of the Krushan pavilion, where Dronas was standing beside Dhuryo and the rest of the Hundred — "could probably do before they get hair on their upper lips. I'll believe it when I see it."

She stalked off in search of more food.

Tshallian was excited. "Take the prize today, the Five will most certainly. Yes? Yes!"

The Vanjhani pumped all four fists in the air.

Arrow and Yudi exchanged amused glances.

"Let's not get overconfident, shall we?" Yudi said. "We're gifted, true. But we're not unbeatable."

"You think so?" Arrow asked, with complete sincerity.

Dhuryo

⁓

DHURYO KNEW WHO THE stranger was even before he reached the Krushan pavilion. His tall, rake-thin body, hatchet face, double-tipped tongue, and nictitating eyes left no ambiguity about his identity. The murmured whispers from the neighboring pavilions, as well as the pointed fingers from those farther away, underlined the power and reputation of the God-Emperor of the Morgol Empire.

Even Dronas, who could be arrogant to a vexing degree, acknowledged the visitor with rare grace.

"Lord Jarsun Krushan," said Dronas, bowing from the waist while tilting his head at a slight angle that allowed him to keep his gaze fixed on the taller man, "you honor us with your presence."

"Dronas," said Jarsun, fixing his piercing grey-green eyes on the former guru. "I have heard of you. Your fame as a teacher of the arts of war is second to none."

Dronas bowed again, this time bending only from the neck and still keeping his eyes on Jarsun. "I am fortunate that I live in an age where few possess the skills to challenge my prowess."

Dhuryo sniggered inwardly. Typical of Dronas to praise himself to the skies while pretending to show humility.

Jarsun's eyes flicked briefly to Dhuryo, as if seeing the snigger and the accompanying thought. Something glinted deep in those serpentine pupils, something that saw the shades of darkness within Dhuryo's heart and approved of them. The thin lips did not part in a smile, not visibly at least, but Dhuryo felt that Jarsun had just acknowledged his assessment of his former guru and agreed: Dronas was an ass, but he was also the best in his field.

"And this is your famous protégé, Dhuryo Krushan."

Dhuryo bowed to Jarsun, following his guru's example and keeping his eyes on the God-Emperor. Again, he sensed rather than glimpsed a flicker of amusement in those nictitating eyes. "My lord Morgolia. Your legend precedes you."

Dhuryo felt his brothers pressing around him, eager to be introduced as well. He ignored them, as did Jarsun, whose gaze passed over them without taking notice of them, dismissing them as he might a host of serving staff. Jarsun turned to look out at the arena, where two figures were making their way to the center.

"How do you feel about today's contest, young Dhuryo?"

Dhuryo considered the question. He could easily have answered, *It's no contest at all!* But he knew that would be too obvious, too arrogant, the answer one might assume Dhuryo Krushan would give. He knew his reputation for being an arrogant, boorish oaf and had done nothing to dispel or leaven it. But this was Jarsun Krushan. Not merely one of the most powerful men in the world, but his blood kin. His great-uncle, if he had understood the family tree correctly. He knew what Jarsun was really asking, and he answered that unspoken question rather than the obvious, articulated one.

"It will give me an opportunity to see who else is out there," he said simply.

Dronas turned to look at him in surprise. The guru was frowning in curiosity.

Dhuryo looked back at him with a schooled expression. "'Twas you who taught us that in a contest, it is always best to let one's opponent display their skills first, that one might size them up and strategize how best to beat them, my guru."

If Dronas was surprised at Dhuryo using the honorific and the humble tone, he did not show it. He was arrogant enough to take Dhuryo's words at face value, since he had in fact taught him that lesson.

"Aye," he agreed, "a wise course. A true master warlord only enters the field of battle when he is in possession of all the known facts. I have taught you well, young Dhuryo."

Young Dhuryo. Had any elder in Hastinaga Palace dared to use that tone with Dhuryo, they would not have survived another breath. But Dhuryo was accustomed to Dronas's patronizing attitude and accepted it as the price for his alliance. Dronas often seemed to overlook the fact that Dhuryo was a grown man, and in line to become emperor of the world's most powerful empire, not a child in his gurukul any longer. Dronas might not realize it yet, but he served Dhuryo Krushan now and not the other way around. When the time came, he would understand this well enough. For now, Dhuryo was content to let the man have his illusions.

Dhuryo's eyes met Jarsun's, and again he saw a glint in them that reflected his own thoughts. The God-Emperor understood his diplomacy with his guru, as well as the true message Dhuryo had sent: *Let us see if my newfound cousins, these children of Shvate, have anything worth considering. They are the ones I have my eye on. Of the rest of those gathered here, I have no expectations. What chance do even the most skilled mortal champions have against demigods? Ultimately, this contest is going to be about the Hundred versus the Five.*

The thin lips pursed in what might have passed for an approving smile as Jarsun inclined his head slightly to acknowledge the responses, spoken as well as unspoken.

He heard me as clearly as my brothers hear my thoughts!

Dhuryo knew then that Jarsun truly was his blood kin.

Uncle and nephew turned their attention to the field as the two figures stopped in the middle of the arena. The contest was about to begin.

Gwann

~

1

GWANN AND VENSERA WATCHED from the royal pavilion as their daughter and son walked out to the middle of the arena, greeted by deafening cheers and applause. The king and queen looked at each other, hands firmly grasped, and smiled with pleasure at the popularity of Krushni and Drishya — and, by extension, themselves as well. Gwann reflected on how differently things could have turned out.

Ever since the day of the stonefire ritual, three years ago, he had marveled each day at the new wonders wrought by his daughter and son. He thought of them as such, as his own kith and kin, not as gifts from an unknown stone god as the result of a propriating ritual, but as his own blood. Had Vensera and he been capable of producing their own flesh-and-blood offspring, he could not have loved them more. Krushni and Drishya were to him as beloved daughter and son.

But they were more than that, he knew.

He was reminded of this fact within days of their "birth," such as it were. It felt odd to term it such. Both Krushni and Drishya had stepped out of the sacred square fully grown, as a physically mature young woman and young man of apparently fifteen or sixteen years of age. If "age" was the right term to use for an avatar! Did avatars age at all? Thus far, neither had shown any visible signs of doing so. Even his assessment of their being fifteen or sixteen at the time was purely guesswork. They could as well have been twenty, or twenty-five. All he could say at the time with any certainty was that they

134

were no younger than fifteen. He clung to that belief perhaps only because it comforted him to think of them as children yet, rather than fully grown, mature adults.

But from the very outset they had displayed talents, skills, and wisdom that suggested any attempt to relate their maturation to "normal" human stages of growth would be futile. They were clearly anything but normal.

The first incident occurred on the third day after their arrival. Now, *there* was a more apt word than "birth." "Arrival." It accurately described the moment of their emergence from the sacred square. Vensera and he, accompanied by Krushni and Drishya, were seated upon a large float, a decorated platform on wheels drawn by a team of uks, parading through the city. It was the first time they had stepped out of the palace and been shown to the people. The city streets were thronged by curious crowds, much as they were today, in fact, and the populace had come out in droves to view their newly anointed prince and princess.

Gwann knew of the rumors and gossip that had spread in the first two days after Krushni and Drishya's arrival, and the attempts by his detractors to undermine his already precarious reputation. The defeat by Dronas and the theft of the larger portion of a once-great Gwannland had severely damaged the people's belief in him. It would not have been wrong to say that the only reason they had not turned against him as yet was because they were still reeling in shock from the defeat and loss. The stonefire ritual and the arrival of Krushni and Drishya had only elevated the levels of distress and distrust. There was even talk of the king and queen resorting to Krushan sorcery. Among superstitious Gwannlanders, that was tantamount to accusing Gwann and Vensera of being demon summoners. Which made Krushni and Drishya the alleged demons.

That was why Krushni had suggested the public showing and parade.

"They think we're monsters. Let us show them we are not."

Gwann noted that she didn't say, *We're human*, possibly because, as he already suspected, they were not. Not in the sense that he and Vensera and the people of Gwannland were human at least. Human beings didn't step out of stonefire squares fully grown, clad in strange garb, and with what seemed like a demigod's knowledge and insight. Not to mention unknown powers that he had yet to see unleashed. Perhaps the rumors were not that far off; stonefire was considered evil in some cultures of Arthaloka. To the people of isolated Aranya, for instance, what he and Vensera had done was in fact demon summoning through Krushan sorcery.

But Krushni and Drishya were not demons. Anything but. That he was sure of, even if he was sure of little else.

The question was: What *were* they, then?

The question was partially answered the day of the parade.

The float was midway down the main avenue, named after Gwann's namesake, the great ancestor Gwann who had first settled the great grass-lands of Eastern Arthaloka and founded a community here. The sun was directly overhead, the day was warm and pleasant, and the crowds were ec-static. There was an air of uncertainty and even the hint of violence abroad: anything could happen. He knew at that moment that in the next few hours, his future — and that of Gwannland itself — would be decided one way or the other: either the people would turn against him and rise up, tearing him down and trampling him underfoot, or ... He could not be sure of what the alternative might be, but anything seemed better than being killed in disgrace and terror.

The first reactions had been trepidation, uneasiness, even fear on many faces. But as the new arrivals had waved and smiled and paused to greet and cross palms with the public along the way, the anxiety had gradually melted to turn into something warmer and more hopeful. Gwannland had suffered a great and tragic breaking. The people were hurting, in grief, in anger; what they needed most was hope. Somehow, in that hour after the royal procession left the palace, that hope burgeoned. Gwann could see it in the upraised faces, the tentative smiles, the nervous flutters of hands and twitching of lips. Their eyes found Krushni's breathtakingly beautiful face and graceful form, drank in the air of overwhelming goodness and splendor that she somehow bore like a fragrant cloud wherever she went, and were surprised, delighted, overjoyed. Far from the demons they had feared, they saw a goddess and god incarnate. For that was the only way to describe the effect his newfound daughter and son had on the people.

Even Drishya, despite not saying a word, somehow captured hearts and won over the most skeptical observers practically on sight. There was some-thing magnificent about the young man's physical beauty and sultry, almost feminine grace and leonine eyes. Both women and men were known to fall in love with him the moment they set eyes on him. He had only to look at a person in the crowd, to make eye contact, smile, perhaps wave lightly, and that person was besotted. What was divine and graceful and charismatic power in Krushni expressed itself as catlike fascination and magnificent lustiness in Drishya. They were like two expressions of divinity, differently phrased.

Within that first hour, he knew the parade was a great success. He exchanged smiles with Vensera and saw it reflected in her joyful eyes too. They had somehow succeeded in overturning months of rage, grief, guilt, and blame, and turned an unhappy, broken populace into a once-more joyous and proud people. How could a mere public showing achieve such a result? He didn't know or care. Just as he didn't need to know how the stonefire ritual worked; all that mattered was that Krushni and Drishya had come into their lives. And their lives had changed forever.

He watched as both his children greeted the citizens warmly, even taking a moment when possible to bend down and offer a hand for them to touch. It was a stark contrast to what he had heard of the self-declared King Dronas, who apparently traveled in a carriage with iron bars on the windows, surrounded by a phalanx of his personal guards, who were said to ride down or strike down any who dared to come in the way of the royal procession, be it an unarmed old man, woman, or child. He was proud that Krushni had insisted upon upholding the ancient Gwannland tradition of the royals being filial with their people, mingling freely with them, demonstrating that they belonged here.

That was when the assassins had struck.

2

They had chosen the perfect spot for an ambush. The largest crossroad in the city, where both the main avenue and the queen's highway intersected. The crowd was densest here, but there were also dozens of vehicles, mostly uks-drawn carts, horse carriages, some chariots, and an unusual number of uks- and dromad-drawn wagons of the kind usually seen on the great wagon trains that traversed the Red Desert.

It was from these that the assassins launched their attack.

They had placed the large, covered wagons in a rough semicircle, and as the float passed them by, they closed the circle completely, moving with expert precision, forcing the crowd back and out of the way, jostling unaware citizens aside roughly, and cutting the royal family off from the armed guards accompanying their float. Because the float had been kept clear at the sides to allow the people safe approach and time to view and greet their new princess and prince, they were exposed on both their left and right.

The guards in front and back began fighting their way through the instant they were cut off by the trundling wagons, but the enormous, heavily weighted vehicles crushed several of their number to death beneath the great wagon wheels and the hooves of the snorting uks and dromads, both of which species were already unnerved and on edge from being in the thick of such an enormous crowd of yelling, screaming humans. It would take them several minutes to reach the royals, minutes in which the assassins had probably expected to be able to dispatch all four without much resistance.

The assassins poured out of the sides of the uks wagons being used for the blockade, a shocking number of them, all dressed in black from head to foot, their heads covered with cloths that hid their faces except for eyeholes. The common uniform, their numbers, and the practiced efficiency of their movements suggested a highly organized and well-funded assassination plot.

All wielded large curved weapons with a razor-sharp sword edge on one side and a jagged sawtooth on the other, ending in a wicked, sharp hook. Even accidental contact was enough to maim or dismember, as Gwann saw with horror: several innocent citizens, caught within the trap intended for the royals, were struck in passing by the blurring samtarns. Blood spray, severed limbs, and screams of agony filled the air even before the first assassins reached the royal float. They arrived not merely climbing onto the raised moving platform, but by somersaulting and flipping multiple times in midair, like veteran acrobats.

Krushni and Drishya were poised to welcome them.

Unarmed and dressed in richly brocaded flowing robes, the new prince and princess met the flying assassins with hands that were empty one moment — and then armed the next. Gwann had not so much as blinked, but there they were, weapons of a kind he had never seen nor heard tell of before, in his new daughter's and son's hands, already moving through the air to strike.

Drishya had a golden disc the width of his hand, balanced on the tip of his forefinger, which he held at shoulder height. The disc was spinning even as it appeared on his finger, its resplendent surface glowing as it blurred at impossible speed. As the first assassin came somersaulting at him, launched from the vantage of the higher wagon before the float, Drishya curved his hand in a tight arc ending at the assassin's body.

The golden disc cut through the assassin's bent forearm, biceps, then his neck and chest, and down the length of his torso as he threw himself through the air; it finally emerged from the side of his waist without so much as a spatter of blood. The assassin's wickedly bladed and hooked weapon, poised to puncture Drishya's throat, passed within millimeters of the prince's neck before dropping to the wooden floor of the float, where it clanged uselessly, still gripped by the severed fist and forearm of the dead assassin. The rest of the body fell in two separate parts into the dust of the avenue.

At the same instant, Krushni met her first attackers.

A black-clad assassin somersaulted over the hump of a dromad, samtarn flashing downward in a curving arc. The tip was aimed at Krushni's throat, the jagged back-blade poised to rip through her torso as the assassin passed over her. It was a fatal strike. Gwann, watching with horror from the carriage yards behind Krushni and Drishya's, knew that no weapon, neither sword nor axe nor both combined, could counter such a strike entirely. Even if Krushni had been armed with both weapons, she would have sustained a gory wound at the very least, almost certainly a ruined shoulder and damaged arm. That itself would have ensured her demise when the second and third assassins, already flying at her from different angles, struck.

Weaponless, faced with an impossible-to-counter attack, Krushni made no attempt to avoid the weapon, or even to strike it away with her hand, as any unarmed warrior would have done instinctively.

Instead, she let the samtarn pierce her throat and penetrate her neck and upper torso. Gwann heard himself shriek in terror as he saw the ugly thing cut into his daughter's earth-complected skin. Beside him, Vensera was on her feet, raising her ceremonial scepter as if about to hurl it, for all the good it would do. Even she, a veteran at arms, knew there was no way anyone could reach Krushni in time to save her now.

The assassin's spinning curve reached its end and they yanked at the samtarn's hilt, expecting it to follow in accordance with the laws of gravity, spilling blood and gore in satisfying quantities.

Instead, they found themselves holding only the hilt of the weapon.

The assassin stared uncomprehendingly at the stump that marked what remained of the samtarn's cruel double blade, turning their masked and hooded head to look back at their intended victim. Gwann's eyes followed, expecting to see what the assassin probably expected as well: that the samtarn had snapped off to leave most of its length still imbedded in Krushni's body.

Instead, all the assassin, and Gwann, saw was Krushni, still seated on the carriage, unharmed, unhurt, and without a hint of injury.

Gwann blinked several times, staring but not understanding what he was seeing.

How was it possible?

There was no time to wonder, for the second and third assassins were already upon her. They had launched themselves only instants after the first and were already committed before their comrade's failure. They descended from both sides, samtarns flashing in a scissoring arc that was perfectly coordinated for a double decapitation. Overkill perhaps, but deadly efficient.

Krushni met both attackers without flinching. The lethal crisscrossing blades hit her exposed neck on ether side — and were severed as neatly as if they had been struck with Inadran's hammer, the fabled stone god's mythic weapon that could shatter any metal forged by human hands.

The two assassins completed their leap, landing lithely on the road on Krushni's side of the carriage, and stared at their truncated weapons. Their confusion was obvious in their stances and darting eyes, all that Gwann could see of their faces.

A fourth, a fifth, a sixth, seventh, and eighth assassin followed suit in blurringly quick succession, all burying their weapons in Krushni's body. Beside her, Drishya dealt out death with his golden disc, slaughtering as many assassins as came at him.

Krushni remained standing still, unarmed and unharmed.

The eight assassins who had attacked her and failed all stood beside the carriage, staring up at her in mute wonder. What had happened to their weapons? How could they have failed? Why did her smooth, soft skin not show so much as a single nick or cut? Where was the blood, the gore, the body parts that should have been severed and strewn?

Gwann had never seen the likes of it, and neither, he assumed, had the assassins.

The answer came a moment later, when Krushni began to move.

Her hands rose in a dramatic gesture, as she spoke words that Gwann could not hear — nor could the assassins, he suspected, to judge from their reactions — and then, with startling violence, she plunged both hands into herself. Into her flesh. Into her body.

Blood spurted, bright red spatters glistening in the sunlight, as Krushni bent over double, clearly in agony, clawing *inside* herself, like a crazed being tearing its innards out.

Gwann cried out, raising his own hands, unable to understand or bear the sight of his daughter suffering so. Even though it had been only three days since she rose from the stonefire, already she had seared a brand onto his heart. Decades of longing for a child, an heir, and the painful memory of the stillborn children that Vensera and he had birthed in the first years of their marriage, as well as his intense spiritual commitment, had all coalesced into a powerful, burning attachment to his new wards. In that moment, he was every father watching his daughter suffer terribly, and could not bear the sight.

The assassins reacted too, though not in quite the same way. They exchanged masked glances, their eyes dancing with smiles. They thought their attempts had finally borne fruit. That whatever power had been shielding Krushni from their concerted assaults had finally failed, and that she was now suffering the results of their efforts. That she appeared to be doing this to herself made no difference: they had struck her, and she was now clearly dying. That was all that mattered.

But their celebration was premature.

With a howl that was audible even above the chaos and cacophony of the square, the roar of the crowds, the shouts of the guards battling to reach their king, queen, prince, and princess, the lowing of panicked uks, shrieking of injured dromads, and other assorted screams and cries, Krushni reached deep into herself and pulled out something impossible.

She drew it out slowly, by degrees, howling and gnashing her teeth, fling-ing her hair and head about in agony, spitting foam and blood and obsceni-ties, as if every inch caused her unspeakable pain.

Gwann watched. Vensera watched. The assassins watched. The people watched.

Krushni drew from her body a samtarn, dripping blood and gore. *Her* blood and gore.

It was no ordinary samtarn.

Several times the size of the weapons wielded by the assassins, it was as long and broad as Krushni herself. Impossibly large and, Gwann assumed, impossibly heavy. Yet she held it above her head in one hand like it was any broadsword, her body settling into the practiced stance of a veteran swords-mistress. She held it aloft, high enough for all to see, and the tip of its wick-edly curved hook dripped blood. A bead caught the sunlight and glinted like a ruby. Krushni threw back her head and howled one more time, the sound as bone-chilling and terrifying as the mythic shriek of urrkh, the storied demonic race of yore.

Krushni turned from the waist, swinging the giant samtarn in an arc so swift, so powerful that Gwann's eyes saw it moving before his mind com-prehended it was in motion. Before the assassins on the road could react or move, the bloody weapon cut through them, accomplishing in a single strike what all eight of them had been unable to achieve with their combined as-saults. It hacked through bone and muscle, gristle and sinew, blood vessels and organs, eyes and limbs, like they were nothing but empty air. It reaped an eightfold harvest in a single blow.

Eight butchered corpses fell, thrashing, writhing, spewing gore, in an assortment of body parts. But more assassins were already coming at her, flying at her with weapons swinging and eyes glittering hate.

Krushni swung the great weapon in a beautifully executed arc, as grace-ful as any classical dancer in Gwann's court, and slew them as easily as she had the rest. She continued reaping more victims as the remaining attackers struck at her and Drishya. But the assassins were now on a suicide mission, and the end was inevitable.

At last, a deathlike silence fell over the great boulevard.

Tens of thousands stared in wonder and horror.

Then, with a resounding roar that deafened Gwann and could probably have been heard miles away, they let loose their joy and exultation.

They had accepted their new princess and prince.

3

Now Gwann watched with rising anticipation as Krushni and Drishya demonstrated the first challenge.

Krushni spoke in her quiet way, not raising her voice or shouting — although across that vast arena, even the loudest shout would have been little more than a whisper — and yet each word was audible to every person gathered in the pavilions, as well as the crowds beyond. Gwann had witnessed this phenomenon before, and the people of New Gwannland were also familiar with it by now, as they were with many of Krushni's and Drishya's extraordinary deliveries. But to the contestants in the pavilions, it was one of several mysteries that would remain unanswered that day. Even though she was over a hundred yards from the pavilions, her voice was as clear as if she stood before each person.

"The first challenge," she said simply.

She took a bow and a single arrow offered by an attendant in colorful garb.

She held up the arrow, turning around slowly, so all the contestants could view it in turn. Even at a hundred yards, the feathery fletching on the tail of the arrow was visible. As was the eye painted on the fletching.

Krushni placed the arrow on the bow, raised the bow high, pointing it directly up above her head.

She drew on the bowstring until the stretched bow seen from Gwann's view resembled a large circle. It took considerable strength to do that, for the longbow was an oversized one constructed of ironwood and weighed an unusual three hundred pounds. Not even the strongest archers in New Gwannland could lift the bow, let alone draw it that far. Krushni made it look as easy as working a child's sugarcane bow.

The bowstring twanged with a vibration that made Gwann's back teeth sing. He felt a sharp pain deep in his gums, reminding him that that particular tooth was loose and needed pulling. He ignored it, as he had for the past several weeks, willing it away — ever since he had been a boy, he hated having a tooth pulled and always waited until it was impossible to sleep with the discomfort. A crystal flute in the personal collection of one of the more finicky contestants shattered with a sharp sound, startling the person holding the drink. Dogs began howling, their sensitive ears picking up the sound inaudible to human ears, and were promptly stilled by their owners.

All eyes followed the arrow as it shot up straight into the blue sky.

Its trajectory could not have been straighter if a weighted line had been dropped from a cloud down to the earth.

Gwann's neck creaked and crackled as he looked up to the limit of his ability.

Just as the arrow slowed to a halt, it was followed by a second, quicker one.

Gwann's — and everyone else's — eyes flicked down to see Drishya holding his own bow, a slimmer, lighter one than Krushni's, the bowstring still twanging in the wake of the loosed arrow.

Drishya's arrow shot up toward Krushni's arrow, somehow managing to meet its sister at the exact point where the first arrow reached the apex of its flight and hung motionless for an instant before starting its inevitable fall back to earth.

Krushni's arrow turned, presenting its side for a fraction of a moment, before it began its descent. In that instant, the eye painted on its tail was visible, but only to those with the keenest vision.

Drishya's arrow shot up and met its sister, striking the painted eye and piercing the fletching of the arrow. Both arrows hung in midair for another fraction, then began their united descent, now coupled together.

Drishya caught both arrows before they could reach the ground. The fact that they had descended as precisely as they had risen was only one of the many impossible marvels that were accomplished by that display of bowcraft.

Drishya held up the conjoined arrows to show the contestants.

A ripple of murmurs traveled through the tented areas. Several were accompanied by curses and cries of "Impossible!" and "Cannot be done!" which were quickly silenced.

Gwann smiled and looked at Vensera.

She smiled back.

"Attempting to match that will eliminate most of them," she said, "if not all of them, as it did the first year."

"That it will," Gwann said, "but I have a feeling this year we may actually proceed to the second round, if not the third."

Vensera looked thoughtful, then inclined her head. "Perhaps. We do have some interesting guests this year."

Gwann felt his own face grimace. "That's not the word I would choose to describe them."

Vensera looked at him sympathetically. "You know Krushni has a plan. She always has a plan."

"I know, I know. But this time, the stakes are higher. We have let the wolf into our henhouse. You can hardly expect him to leave without his supper."

Vensera smiled that superior, enigmatic smile that both infuriated and aroused Gwann, depending on when it was deployed. "I think this wolf may find the hens in this house aren't mere chickens."

Gwann grinned despite his anxiety. "I like that. Yes, I'm hoping that will be the case."

She reached out and caressed his face, brushing an errant lock off his eyes and stroking his cheek. She let her hand slip down to his shoulder and then his biceps. "You know that watching these contests always arouses me."

Gwann pretended to make a face, catching her wrist and lowering her hand to her side. "Name one thing that doesn't arouse you, Vensera. And do keep your hands to yourself. I'm trying to watch this contest."

She winked at him. "You do that, my love. And to answer your question, the answer is probably nothing. But some things do arouse me more than others. And watching the bastard tyrant who stole our kingdom, who is terrorizing our people, get his ass kicked and handed to him on a royal platter does rank quite highly on the list of stimulants. Maybe later we can slip away and take advantage of that."

Gwann pretended to sigh and ignore Vensera. But when her hand found its way back to his waist, he didn't object. Truth be told, the prospect of watching his worst enemy get trounced today did arouse him too.

Arrow

~

"NOW, *THAT IS WORTH* the trip here," Brum said. She had paused in chewing a mouthful of some local sweetmeat. The bowl containing the rest of the black, gooey dish was in one hand, her other hand resting on the rim, fingers dripping treacly juice.

"Aye, worth our lives risking across Dronas, it is. However did they that trick?" said Tshallian. Both the Vanjhani's faces gazed upward in wonder. Their hands rubbed and scratched at their beards and chins, reminding Arrow that none of them had bathed in days.

Yudi, Kula, and Saha made similar sounds of appreciation, with Saha also marveling at the bowcraft.

"What do you think, Arrow?" Kula asked. "How did they do it? I mean, I'm sure you could do it, but I'd never have believed there was a bowman who could pull off such a feat in all Arthaloka!"

"Bow*woman*," they said distractedly. Arrow had been watching the challenge but with eyes turned not up at the sky, where the arrows had met, but on the ground. They were still staring at the same spot, the center of the arena a hundred yards away, where the princess and prince of New Gwann-land stood basking in the cheers of a hundred thousand throats.

"What was that?" Kula asked, frowning.

Arrow pointed at the princess, standing now with her bow lowered, her head bowed as well, acknowledging the applause. "It was no trick. The mastery was in her shot, not his. To loose an arrow straight up into the air, that high, from a bow of that size, in just such a manner that it did not falter an inch from its path despite a wind of some twenty miles an hour over seventy yards up, and so that the arrow at the peak of its rise would hang still for a moment before starting its descent, that was a shot worthy of Parshu himself. If there is a better bow master in all Arthaloka, I have not met them. And to answer your remark, no, I don't believe I could pull off such a feat myself."

The four other siblings turned to stare. After a moment, the Vanjhani turned their heads as well, looking at Arrow curiously.

Arrow shrugged without returning their looks, still pointing at the princess. "It was remarkable. *She* is remarkable."

As if sensing the attention and praise, she raised her eyes just then and gazed directly at them. Not merely at their pavilion, or in their general direction, but at Arrow. Personally. Her eyes met theirs and held them. Her lips parted in a soft smile.

She winked.

Arrow's hand shivered slightly. They lowered it to their side.

A heat and a chill both thrilled through Arrow's body simultaneously, lighting a fire and dousing it at once. Spice and sugar. Lust and inertia. Doom and glory.

They took a step back, blinking rapidly.

"Arrow?" Yudi asked. "Are you well?"

Arrow shook their head, eyes shut tightly. When they opened them again, the princess had turned away and was awaiting the first contestant, who was already striding across the arena.

Arrow looked at their siblings, each in turn, and saw an unusual range of reactions reflected on their faces: curiosity, surprise, wonderment, disbelief. The Vanjhani's two expressions were not as easy to read but could be summarized as puzzlement too.

Looks like Arrow's been struck!

Smitten!

Shot through the heart.

Brum's meaty hand slapped Arrow on the back. "Looks like you're human after all."

"Only partly," they said, "but I guess that's true of all of us."

Arrow grinned to show that all was all well but sensed from their thoughts that this came off looking more like an invalid trying to pretend to be perfectly healthy.

Brum's powerful arm pulled her sibling closer, close enough for their foreheads to press together. "I'm talking about your lack of interest in matters below the waist," she said. "We were all starting to think that you might not be interested in such matters at all. Not that there's anything wrong with that. It's perfectly fine if you don't choose to indulge your nether urges. But it would be a shame for this beautiful body and gentle, loving nature to go unenjoyed."

"A very beautiful body," Kula said in agreement. Kula was something of an expert in beautiful male bodies, after all, just as Brum was one when it came to female bodies.

Arrow said to Brum's nose, "Sister, your dessert is in my hair. And my ears."

Brum's eyes flicked to her hand, still mealy and dripping sticky black juice, and rubbed her fingers across Arrow's mouth. Arrow saw the gleam in her eyes an instant before she did it, and read the intent in her mind before she was aware of it herself, but didn't try to break away and instead endured the drubbing, and the subsequent backslap by Brum, before she relaxed her iron grip, laughing broadly.

"Welcome to the land of love and honey!" she said.

Arrow grinned at her. "I was just admiring her bowcraft, that's all. I didn't say anything about love."

All of them laughed at that, including both of Tshallian's heads.

Arrow shrugged. It was impossible for any of them to hide their true feelings from the others.

Besides, it turned out to be quite enjoyable to be teased about this sudden, almost instantaneous fascination with the princess of Gwannland.

Dhuryo

~

"WAIT," DHURYO SAID, STOPPING his brother with a heavy hand. "Let all the fools try first and fail. Once they're all back in their pavilions, red-faced with shame, we'll go out there and show them how it's done." He turned to the packed pavilion full of mustached and bearded faces. "Won't we, brothers?"

"Aye!" they boomed in unison.

Dhuryo turned back and crossed his arms across his chest, watching as the first contestant attempted to pierce the fresh arrow that Krushni shot up into the air.

On either side of him, Dronas and Jarsun watched the arena, but it was clear their interest no longer lay in what was actually happening out there. Like Dhuryo and his brothers, they were probably mulling over that extraordinary shot and wondering how it had been achieved. Dhuryo thought he had an insight into how that might be accomplished. In order to best it, or match it at least, it was first necessary to understand how it was done. Dronas had taught them that in their later years at gurukul, when they were ready to advance to the higher levels.

"That is a wise choice," Dronas said now, affirming Dhuryo's decision.

Jarsun said nothing. He seemed focused on the princess. Dhuryo didn't like that. He intended to win the princess's hand today. Jarsun had best not get in the way of that. He had heard the stories of Jarsun's powers and was not impressed. However powerful he might be, Jarsun was still just one Krushan. Dhuryo and his brothers were a hundred strong. What could one Krushan do against a hundred?

As if sensing his thoughts, Jarsun's eyes flicked to Dhuryo. His eyelids closed and opened. Dhuryo looked away. The nictitating eyelids irritated him. So did the reed-thin, ridiculously tall body, hairless head, and hatchet-sharp profile. Everything about Jarsun irritated him. His long-lost uncle was a freak. No matter how formidable his reputation and powerful his growing empire, Dhuryo felt no fear. He was crown prince of the Burnt Empire. Once he succeeded his father and ascended to the Burning Throne, he planned to launch a campaign of conquest that would bring all Arthaloka under his rule. Let Jarsun build his puny sand-blown empire in the East. Someday, all that was his would be Dhuryo's too.

Jarsun chuckled softly.

The sound puzzled Dronas. The former guru looked up at Jarsun. "What prompts your mirth?"

Jarsun glanced over Dronas's head, his piercing eyes meeting Dhuryo's. "We all have our plans and our ambitions, but when it comes time to be tested, none of that matters. The only thing that counts in this world is power and the knowledge of how to wield it."

He flicked his twin-tipped tongue out at the arena. "Those fools will all fail today. Only a handful will pass the first challenge. Even fewer the second. And in the end, when it comes time for the princess to choose from the winners, none will be left standing."

"What are you saying?" Dronas asked. "That the contest is rigged?"

"The contest is a facade. A display of their strengths. A demonstration to put on notice all who dismiss this tiny kingdom as inconsequential."

"It *is* inconsequential," Dronas said in a tone that allowed no room for debate. "It is a flea on the rump of my kingdom. If it irritates me overly much, I shall squash it into the dirt and take what I desire from it."

Jarsun looked at Dronas with a sly smile that bordered on challenge. "Why not do it now, then?"

Dronas stared up at Jarsun with a frown. Dhuryo was amused. Dronas was not a man accustomed to being questioned or challenged. The fact that he did not strike out at Jarsun suggested he harbored some fear of the Krushan. In any other man, Dhuryo might have called it respect, but Dronas respected only power and his own opinion: everything else was expendable. For him to tolerate Jarsun's challenge was a sign of the awe he felt.

A look matching Jarsun's sly smile creased the guru's lined face. "What makes you think I have not already begun my takeover?"

Jarsun laughed, a strange hacking-hissing sound that made all the Hundred look up from their imbibing. In the neighboring pavilion, the son of Shvate named Yudi looked as well, an inscrutable expression on his face.

Jarsun hissed approvingly. "Perhaps we may be allied in our purposes after all, Dronas," he said.

Takeover? Of New Gwannland? Dhuryo was not surprised to hear of it. Dronas was always a man of opportunity. Here, he had all the resources he could possibly desire to accomplish what he had long craved. The Hundred, his former pupils, owed him a lifelong debt for having taught them their skills and mastery of warcraft.

Unlike other gurus, Dronas had chosen not to demand that debt be repaid by their father, Emperor Adri, when they graduated a year ago. It was an opportunity few others, if any, would spurn. Had he desired wealth, titles, land, it had all been available for his asking. By ancient Krushan custom, a guru could demand anything, including the life of his pupil, and a pupil was obligated to honor his request.

By keeping his debt in abeyance, Dronas had retained an influence over the Hundred that he could draw upon at any time he chose. Dhuryo suspected that the invitation to visit Gwannland, and New Gwannland, was no accident of timing. Dronas had intended this all along, to this very purpose.

Dhuryo shrugged mentally, sharing these thoughts with his brothers, who approved heartily. Any excuse for a fight was a good excuse for the Hundred. So be it. If Dronas wanted them to use their powers to take over New Gwannland and complete his vengeance against his childhood friend Gwann and his wife, Vensera, Dhuryo had no problem fulfilling the debt to his guru.

It would give him an excuse to acquire a much-desired prize for himself as well: the princess Krushni. The more he saw of the woman, even from across the span of the arena, the more he desired her.

You will have her, brother, he heard his brothers say silently. *We will win this contest!*

Of course they would, he thought to himself.

But whether they did or didn't wasn't really of consequence. One way or another, Dhuryo Krushan intended to take possession of the object of his desire.

Yudi

⁓

YET ANOTHER CONTESTANT TRIED and failed to meet the challenge. Miserably. Good as they were with bowcraft, none of them were of sufficient skill. What Princess Krushni and Prince Drishya had demonstrated was a level beyond the reach of any of these overconfident, hyperaggressive suitors.

Even Yudi, who knew he was only marginally better than the best of those oafs strutting out there, knew that much. But the men and women making fools of themselves out in the arena were either too pig-headed or too vain to accept the fact. Even more laughably, not a single one of those in attendance had the good sense to step away and concede. They had to go out there and attempt something that they could not possibly accomplish.

The thing was, Krushni and Drishya had made it look easy. That they had been able to do it was testament to their prowess, but of course, these idiots couldn't see that. They thought, well, if a young woman and boy who've never been tested in battle yet can do it, of course I can.

And so they paraded out into the arena in their well-oiled leather skirts and jerkins, displayed their pompously pumped-up bodies, and made utter disgraces of themselves. Some returned with their tails between their legs to their pavilions, others ranted and raved and demanded another, and another, and yet another try, until they had to be escorted off the field firmly by New Gwannland's very competent hosts.

None of this actually interested him very much. He had never been to a wedding contest before, but he had enjoyed brushes with royalty and nobility before and knew their kind. Born privileged and with the self-assurance that came of never wanting for anything, they assumed they could do anything they set their minds to.

After all, there had been a time when all royalty had been presumed gods by virtue of their high birth alone. That was a legacy of the days of the stone gods, when the only royalty on Arthaloka had indeed been gods; it persisted long after the stone gods passed from the earth, and imbued even mere mortals with the false belief that they were owed the same adoration and awe the stone gods had received in their time.

And so, he had to admit, it was actually fun to watch these contestants discover that there were severe limits to the privilege of birth. Brum and the others shared in his enjoyment. They didn't have many opportunities to attend fancy events like these, and to watch this parade of princes doing the human imitation of a rock trying to fly like a bird was immensely entertaining.

Brum probably enjoyed it the most. Her laughter grew louder and more uninhibited with every new hopeful who aimed his or her bow skyward and shot themselves in the foot (metaphorically speaking). Yudi knew the ale had something to do with that lowering of inhibitions, but he also knew better than to try to curb Brum. She was having a roaring good time, and if she had to let loose, surely this was as good a venue as any.

She was not the only one either: Yudi could see most of the occupants of the pavilions consuming impressive amounts of food and drink, judging from the scurrying to and fro of Gwannlander attendants. There were probably more roast pigs and barrels of ale being carted around than arrows shot in the air.

Brum's laughter was infectious. Other pavilions, many of them occupied by contestants who had failed only a moment earlier, began echoing her laughter at each new attempt. Soon, the entire arena was ringing out with laughter punctuated by vulgar catcalls and comments. Some of the heckling was quite entertaining too. The only silent pavilions were those occupied by contestants yet to make their own attempts.

In time, there were very few of these left. Perhaps two handfuls or less. One of them, Yudi noted, was the Krushan pavilion. He could see the stick-thin figure of Jarsun Krushan standing alongside the usurper Dronas and his ward Dhuryo Krushan, seated now with their backs to the arena, engaged in conversation. They were the only ones pointedly ignoring the contest. That suggested either supreme arrogance or indifference: Yudi suspected it was the former.

He linked minds with Arrow for a moment. The flood of emotions that had overwhelmed his sibling had abated for now, but Yudi could feel Arrow's attraction still present, a banked fire needing only a fresh spark. He felt the others noting and wondering at the infatuation. It was the first time any of them had known Arrow to feel such powerful attraction to someone.

Usually, it was the other way around: people were attracted to Arrow. So much so that it had led to some embarrassing, awkward, and in many cases, quite hair-raising escapades. But this was the first time that Arrow had exhibited strong feelings for anyone. It was a notable moment, Yudi knew. Arrow's first infatuation.

Is that all you think it is? he felt Arrow demanding of him with a trace of indignation, but also curiosity.

What do you think? Or rather, what do you feel? Yudi asked.

You know how I feel, Arrow replied, looking at him reproachfully.

Yes, but . . . Yudi hesitated. While they could all read each other's hearts and minds as easily as a Krushan priest an Ashcrit scroll, with maturing adolescence, they had begun to acquire the ability to cloak their thoughts and feelings too. They were not always successful: Brum after an all-day/night binge of ale and roast spewed far more of her innermost thoughts and feelings than Yudi ever wanted to be privy to. She was about as capable of concealing her true feelings from her siblings as she was of stopping at only one pork chop. Brum apart, they could all shield parts of themselves they didn't want to share with their siblings, if they chose to.

The last part was the crucial one: *if they chose to.* The truth was, until now, there were few things they wanted to conceal from one another. As intimately linked by heart, mind, and blood bond as identical twins, the Five were as a single heart and mind shared by five bodies. But the needs of the body are not always those of the mind, and Yudi knew that they all held some secret, however small or large, that they did not wish their siblings to know.

During the years they had been separated, each of them had undergone their own tests of fire, in a manner of speaking, and it had left its marks on each one. Their bond, unassailable though it was, still held cracks and crevices within which each one held their most secret shames, desires, unspoken urges, and who knew what else. Such was the way of all flesh.

When it came to this emotion, though, Yudi sensed Arrow spoke the truth. They were concealing none of their feelings about Krushni from the others. This attraction toward her was an open scroll.

Then you intend to take the shot? Yudi asked instead.

On this his sibling was not as decisive.

Should I? Arrow asked him, turning to look Yudi in the eye.

Yudi frowned. *Why not? We came here to meet her and her brother, and that would be the simplest way.*

We can still do that without my participating.

What do you mean . . . Yudi started to ask, then broke off. Arrow was still looking at him with that familiar, penetrating gaze, the look that seemed to see into the innermost corners of Yudi's mind. Just as their mastery with the bow enabled them to place an arrow where it seemed impossible to do so, Arrow could see into people more deeply and surely than they themselves could at times. Yudi had never been able to determine if that was one of Arrow's powers, inherited at birth from their stone god father, or an acquired survival skill.

You should take the shot, brother, Arrow said. And their gaze and tone revealed something to Yudi that even Yudi had not known he felt until that instant. *You are powerfully attracted to her as well.*

Ladislew

~

LADISLEW LOOKED OVER AT the Krushan pavilion. Jarsun was still there, now engaged in deep conversation with the old bearded one named Dronas. The Krushan Hundred, on the other hand, were deeply engaged in feasting and drinking. From the way the eldest one glanced over at Ladislew from time to time, she guessed his interests were more inclined toward ravaging flesh than eating it.

"We could share him," said her companion.

Ladislew turned to Lady Goddick.

The woman winked slyly at Ladislew. "He is young and virile enough to keep us both entertained."

Ladislew reached out and caressed the woman's bare shoulder. "I'm sure we can find ways to keep one another entertained that don't involve a man."

Lady Goddick arched her shaped brows. "A woman after my own inclinations. If that's your preference, I second it. Although I do like both kinds of entertainment, or even more than two kinds."

Ladislew shrugged. "I'm game for anything."

"And any*one*?" Goddick asked shrewdly, eyeing her from beneath her painted lashes. "Because I sense a certain . . . lack of attraction for the eldest Krushan. I saw the way you were looking at him just now. He might as well have been a dung beetle."

"Isn't he?" Ladislew asked sweetly. "After all, that's all the Krushan do, isn't it? Continue to pile up their mountain of dung and feed off it?"

Lady Goddick threw back her head and laughed throatily. She wagged a long, tapered nail. "How refreshing! Finally, someone of stature who isn't afraid to criticize the Krushan. In most realms, that comment alone would earn you instant ostracism, or worse. But I like it! I like it! You're not afraid to speak your mind. But then, I suppose being the consort of the one person who has openly declared war against the Burnt Empire means showing a certain loyalty."

"I'm not afraid to speak the truth," Ladislew said. "What Jarsun does or doesn't do is of no interest to me. He is Krushan himself, in case you've forgotten."

Lady Goddick sipped her drink, an exotic oily black concoction Ladislew had never heard of until her companion ordered it. "Then you do not support your man's imperial interests?"

Now it was Ladislew's turn to laugh. Except when she did it, it came off sounding like an exhalation during combat. "He is not my man, nor I his woman. Our association is one of convenience."

Lady Goddick examined Ladislew for a moment. "More and more interesting by the minute. So it is no significance to you that he might well succeed in his goal to take over the Burnt Empire? Many say it is inevitable now that he has conquered the East and South."

"The Southeast, you mean," Ladislew corrected her. "The peninsula of Aranya remains unchallenged, as do the Island Kingdoms and the Archipelagoes."

Lady Goddick waved a ring-laden hand. "Wild jungles and barbarian backwaters. The parts of Arthaloka that matter are within his reach now. Word is that he only awaits the right moment to launch his final campaign against Hastinaga, and once he does, victory will be his."

Ladislew shrugged. "Men and their war games don't interest me. What one takes today, another will take from him tomorrow. Their one-upmanship goes on through the ages, and achieves nothing in the end."

"Of course. But that is what men do. When they're not fornicating, feasting, or drinking themselves stupid. The business of men is war. Wealth, land, and resources keep exchanging hands, and every time they do, someone profits from the exchange. If a woman is smart enough, she can build a nice fortune of her own. Provided you aren't too stuck up about morality."

Ladislew smiled thinly. "I'm no merchant. Whatever I need, I can hunt, or acquire through my wits. Wealth and property slow a woman down, tie her to a place. I value my mobility. Freedom is the richest possession."

"You don't care about power, wealth, property, or men. Whatever interests you then, Lady Ladislew?"

"Just Ladislew is fine. I'm no lady."

A soft chuckle greeted this casual self-disparagement. "Neither am I, if I'm being honest. It suits my interest to carry the title, and prevents men from acting too familiar. You can call me Shikari."

"Shikari, there are more important things than material possessions."

"Don't tell me you're one of those stone god revivalists! Or some other brand of religious fundamentalist? Is that why you don't imbibe? I've hardly seen you touch a morsel or a drop yet."

"I eat to survive, not live to eat as some others here." Ladislew cut her eyes to indicate the Krushan brothers' pavilion. "And I'm no fanatic either. I just believe in very old-fashioned values."

"What could be more old-fashioned than wealth, power, sex, property, possessions?"

"Honor," Ladislew replied quietly. "Oath fealty. The love and respect of your sisters. The perpetuation of the Maatri."

Shikari's eyebrows rose again. "The Maatri? You mean the ancient network of matriarchs at the dawn of time?"

Ladislew looked at her carefully, her dark eyes hooded and intent. "What do you know about it?"

"Only what I have read in old texts, or heard from an old woman. It was some kind of sisterhood of goddesses and demigods, wasn't it? They were all daughters of the River Goddess Jeel, whom they regarded as the creator and supreme deity. Their faith was based on the power of the feminine. Their symbol was the female sex organ; what was it called in ancient Ashcrit? Oni?"

"The yoni." Ladislew was quiet for a while, continuing to regard her companion. "This old lady you speak of, is she still alive?"

"Passed away two sowing seasons ago. She was my great-grandmother. Or my great-great-grandmother, nobody would say for certain. She was very old, though. Nobody knew exactly how old."

Ladislew turned her attention to the arena. "The daughters of Jeel live a very long time. Less, if they choose to become mothers. To each daughter they birth, they give a part of their immortality. It is part of their sacred pact with mortalkind. They rarely cohabit with humans, but when they do, the offspring are always beings of significance."

She looked back at Shikari. "What is your age, Shikari?"

Shikari smiled and told her.

Ladislew nodded. "You look younger than your age. It is the Mother's gift. Enjoy it. If you choose to bear a girl child, you will pass on part of your power and longevity. I hear some choose that path willingly, others do so for a purpose. Whatever your choice, choose wisely."

Shikari was silent as she considered this. Finally, she said, aloud, "Thank you, I will."

They sat companionably for a while, watching the fiasco as contestant after contestant attempted — and failed at — the challenge. Shikari sipped her drink.

Shikari said quietly, "Well, I am glad I accompanied that boor Dronas to one of these events for once. Usually, all I meet are the typical arm dressing and cheap concubines clothed in expensive trash. But today, I met you."

Ladislew gave her a knowing look and a sly smile. "I think perhaps we could be of great use to one another, Shikari. I'm glad to have met you too."

Krushni

〜

1

THE LAST CONTESTANT HAD been eliminated. That they would all fail had been a foregone conclusion. Even the best among them were barely capable of shooting an arrow high enough to reach the first one. Some fell several dozen yards short, or lost their line in trying too hard. The one or two who managed to strain their overdeveloped muscles to come close to the mark were a good yard or more short, close enough to have hit the center of a coin-sized target at three hundred yards on a still day, but wildly off in this challenge.

"It is impossible!" ranted the last loser, throwing his bow to the ground. It bounced and twanged in the dust, dislodging one of the precious stones embedded in its woodwork. His aides scurried to retrieve the weapon and the gem. "No one can hit that shot!"

"And yet, as you witnessed, my brother did so," Krushni said calmly.

The ranting and denials were to be expected. Men rarely accepted that something was beyond their capabilities. Their inborn sense of privilege had bred into them the conviction that they had only to try hard enough to accomplish anything they imagined. Only the rarest and wisest understood that there was no trying, there was only accomplishment. Either one did it or did not. One gave one's best every single time, or else there was no point in participating. Yet the vast majority of men persisted in their masculine fantasy of being able to exceed their own abilities.

The irate prince looked as if he wanted to say a great deal more, but mercifully restrained himself and stormed off the field in a flurry of dust and curses.

Krushni gestured at her staff. Her hosts would ensure that he received a case of her best vintage, as did all the other losers. She did not need to soothe their injured male pride, but she did need to retain good relations with their counties and territories. New Gwannland would need their numbers and swords when the time came. At least now when that happened, they would not question her ability to lead them into war.

"Is there no one else who will accept this challenge?" she called.

For the first time this morning, the pavilions were silent. The crowds watching were silent too, waiting to see if any new challengers came forward.

Then, a movement in the shade of one of the tents.

A figure stepped out onto the field. The person walked across the arena toward Krushni and Drishya. As they approached, their silhouette resolved into that of an aging bearded man.

Dronas. Former childhood friend and gurukul mate of her father. Former guru of the Krushan Hundred. Invader, conqueror, and usurper of Gwannland.

The crowd remained silent as the contestant's title and name were announced by the hosts and the proclaimers. Slowly, like an angry wind gathering force in the wadis of the Broken Lands, their response built from a murmur of indignation to a full-blown outburst of hatred. They booed, yelled, cursed, and vented their rage at the man who had slaughtered their kinsmen, stolen their land and houses, enslaved their brethren, and turned one of the richest nations in Eastern Arthaloka into a country of refugees.

Buffeted by the storm of outrage, Dronas walked in stately pride to the center of the arena.

His deeply lined and weathered face looked on Krushni, studying her closely. When he was done examining her, he shifted his gaze to her brother, Drishya. What he saw or felt was not revealed in his face.

His eyes, granite-grey and as sharp and alert as those of a man fifty years younger, turned back to Krushni.

"Princess Krushni, I take this opportunity to thank you for your kind invitation. I must say I was surprised to receive it."

Krushni acknowledged his artifice with a formal reply. Unlike his, hers was sincere. "It was the least I could do after all you had done for my father."

His eyes narrowed slightly at that. He considered her meaning. She didn't give him time to dwell on it. "Although I heard that you did not intend to accept the invitation. Not until you heard that the offspring of Shvate were bound here as well."

At that, he blinked. He did not speak at once, but she knew she had struck her target.

"It seems even small kingdoms have excellent spies," he replied.

She smiled. "What need for spies when our enemies are so transparent?"

He did not respond to that, but she knew he was stung. His mind was working to try to figure out how she could have acquired her insights, but he would be thinking of all the usual ways: spies, informers, treacherous allies, a straying lover . . . She could have shocked him further by assuring him it was none of these usual methods that had secured her the information, but where would have been the fun in that?

"You wish to accept my challenge?" she asked.

He gathered himself at once: the advantages of maturity and a lifetime of self-discipline. Yet little did he know that those were the very things that would cost him this contest — and his pride today. But then, those were the very least of the things he was about to lose. Krushni had been looking forward to this.

"I do," he said stiffly, reverting to his usual pompous, arrogant persona.

She raised the bow, keeping her eyes fixed on him with a casual, relaxed smile. He stared back at her, keeping his face inscrutable. Yet even the effort it took him to do this communicated volumes: he was off guard and suspicious. He had expected to stride out here and overwhelm her with his masterful display. Things weren't going quite the way he'd expected. *Get used to it,* she thought.

Perhaps something of her thoughts conveyed itself through her expression. Just before she loosed the arrow, she saw his eyes blink once, registering now his realization that this was intended to be something more than just a wedding contest, that this challenge was meant to be a personal one for him. He was wise enough to know that there must be some other agenda for his enemy's daughter to invite him to her event, but whatever he might have expected, this was not it. That was because Krushni was not following the playbook of war that he took for granted; she was writing her own. When she loosed the arrow with a mocking smile and kept her eyes on him, his pupils widened in surprise.

Dronas looked up, following the path of the arrow. His eyes flicked back to her once, then up again, then a second time, as if unable to believe that she, the one firing the arrow, had not looked up even once, not even to aim. To his mind, trained to shoot what the eye saw, that was inconceivable. Yet, as he watched the arrow shooting skyward and her smiling mockingly at him, both at once, he saw that she had indeed done so — and done so flawlessly.

Even as his eyes flicked back and forth between her and the arrow, his body and hands worked their practiced magic. Long decades of muscle memory took over in his moment of confusion, functioning with expert efficiency. If age had caused any dimming of his faculties, it was not evident. With a muscular ease that dozens of other contestants far more developed and youthful than he had lacked, he lifted the bow and loosed the arrow in a single motion, his eye and mind and body judging and determining the exact instant and trajectory.

She knew without having to look up that his arrow would find its mark.

In its own way, Krushni thought, it was almost as impossible as her own feat. But while she had kept her eyes on him to deliberately communicate a message, his divided gaze conveyed an unintended one: he had underestimated her.

The pavilions and crowds exploded with raucous applause and roars of outrage both at once.

The first were jubilant that finally someone had broken the losing streak and successfully matched the princess's challenge. The latter were enraged that their greatest enemy had done so.

2

Dronas lowered his bow and looked at Krushni with his chin raised, a stance that he probably used to convey his sense of superiority and disdain for others. It failed on Krushni, who was slightly taller than him and began speaking before he could pronounce some sage guru aphorism.

"We move on now to the second challenge," she said. Around the field, her hosts echoed her words to each pavilion individually. A reluctant silence had fallen across the field and its environs, with an undercurrent of murmuring anger.

Dronas frowned and seemed about to say something. Krushni didn't wait for him. She shot Drishya a glance, and he turned to gesture at an attendant standing some distance away. The attendant turned toward the palace and raised a rainbow-hued flag bearing the sigil of the House of Gwann, waving it to and fro to catch the attention of his counterpart waiting on the roof of the High House.

The attendants on the roof of the palace released a small object into the air that rose higher and higher, moving toward the field and over it. As it came closer, it was recognizable as a dove, its milky white feathers blending in with the cottony clouds. Those with the sharpest eyesight might glimpse that it held in its beak a long, feathery object that echoed the rainbow hues of the nation's flag.

When the dove was directly overhead, Drishya abruptly raised his bow and shot an arrow straight up. The watching thousands held their collective breath as they gazed into the cerulean sky.

The dove dipped in its flight for an instant but recovered at once and continued on its way without visible distress. It faded into the distance, a tiny white dot.

Krushni raised her hand and lowered it almost at once. She now held the arrow Drishya had released, with a peacock's feather impaled on its shaft. She separated the feather from the arrow and held it out for Dronas to inspect. Drishya's arrow had pierced it in such a manner as to bring it down virtually undamaged.

Krushni tucked it into her luxuriant hair, just above her right ear, and smiled sweetly at the man who had stolen her adopted family's lands, massacred and tyrannized their people, and sought to extinguish their entire civilization.

She held a hand out to indicate the attendant standing on the high ramparts of Gwann Palace with a second dove.

"Whenever you are ready, contestant," she said.

3

Several moments passed.

When Dronas still did not respond, Krushni said sweetly, "If you wish, I can demonstrate the challenge again for your benefit."

Dronas's face had hardened even further, the age lines deepening and new furrows plowing between his bushy eyebrows. His eyes burned into Krushni's, and she felt the heat of his resentment.

She was used to it.

Men who had tied their sense of self to their prowess at warcraft always felt threatened by women who challenged them to prove themselves in public. Dronas's resentment went even deeper: he had come here expecting the usual series of one-on-one combat exercises, perhaps a melee, a few assorted displays of skill with various weapons, and maybe one archery event. Adversarial challenges, pitting men against other men. Shows of strength, raw power, willingness to unleash one's most brutal urges.

That was what most wedding contests were about.

By restricting her challenges to bowcraft alone, Krushni had forced the contestants to rely on pure mastery. This was Dronas's area. As the preeminent teacher of warcraft in Eastern Arthaloka, his entire reputation was built on his unmatched skill with weapons, strategy, and tactics. Had she simply stated the tasks and challenged him and the other contestants to attempt them, Dronas would have been well served. The others would still have failed, and Dronas would have taken center stage to show his superiority over them all, reaffirming his legendary stature and giving those who failed the opportunity to say, "An impossible shot! Only the great Dronas could have pulled off such a feat!" thereby saving face themselves and retiring with their male egos secure and masculinity intact.

Instead, Krushni and Drishya had emasculated Dronas, and every other male contestant present here today.

That they had done so not once, but twice in a row with such flawless perfection conveyed a powerful, unignorable message: *We can do it easily. Can you?*

To fail after the bride-to-be herself had pulled off the impossible shot with such easy elegance would be the death of Dronas's reputation. To fail in front of the watching eyes of all these other young upstarts and old royals, almost every one of whom had studied with him or sent their sons to study with him, would be utter humiliation. And to fail before tens of thousands of spectators whom he had been responsible for displacing from their homeland, the slaughter of their kith and kin, the continuing atrocities against their people and great nation, would be to ruin him forever. Not just his reputation; Dronas himself would never recover from such a blow. He had never experienced such a loss, and at this age, with so much power and wealth and resources at his disposal, he had no stomach left to digest it.

Succeed or fail, it was all the same. Either way, the contestant lost something. And at best, he would win the very woman who had cost him so dearly.

Krushni saw something move inside Dronas's mind. The legendary wizard of warcraft was churning through stratagems and tactics. He had understood what she had left unsaid: that this was not just a contest between the participating attendees, it was a contest between them and their host herself.

To beat the challenge and truly win, Dronas must find a way to defeat Krushni publicly. He had to show the world that not only was he every bit the legendary master of bowcraft, he was also master of womancraft. To Dronas, this was now a test of his masculinity and his reputation. It was personal. He had to find a way to win and to upstage Krushni.

She saw the glint in his eye and knew that he had found it. He had hit upon a way to kill both birds with the same arrow: to win the contest as well as show that he was superior to her. Good. Very good indeed.

She had been counting on him finding a way.

"I am ready," he said in a smugly arrogant tone. "Release the dove."

She inclined her head slightly, matching the action with the hint of a smile. "Remember, not a feather on the dove can be harmed."

Dronas blinked.

He stared at her blankly for the duration of another eyeblink or three.

He wanted to lash out, she knew, to tell her that she had no idea how wedding contests were supposed to be. That she was just a so and so, such and such, and so on. She had heard it all before; every woman had. Even in Eastern Arthaloka, where cultures were far more progressive than the antiquated, male-dominated Burnt Empire, there were still men like Dronas, drunk on their own power and masculinity, who felt threatened by strong, powerful women.

Ultimately, she knew, that was what this contest would come down to in the end. For most of the attendees, the wedding contest was about winning her, not proving their own prowess. The original meaning of these events had been to demonstrate the multifarious skills of the suitors, the better to judge them by. In the Gwannlander way, there would have been dances, carpentry, masonry, sewing, animal husbandry, and a slew of other events for contestants to prove themselves. Today, it was nothing more than an unabashed display of male pride.

And Dronas's pride was injured. He felt challenged, threatened, called out. But he was committed now. He could hardly back out without losing face. He pursed his lips, pressing them tightly together, and put an arrow to the bow. "Release the dove."

Krushni gave the signal.

Moments later, the dove took flight from the palace ramparts, swooping low before rising and climbing higher as it passed over the arena.

Dronas loosed his arrow.

He lowered his bow slowly with a controlled, measured motion.

He looked directly at Drishya, as if mocking him, then at Krushni as if to threaten her.

His messages were clear: *Who are you to challenge me? I am Dronas, guru of warcraft.*

Krushni smiled sweetly, answering his threat with her own: *I am Krushni. Let's see if you're as good as you believe you are.*

She held out her hand.

The arrow fell into her palm with a soft impact.

She looked at the peacock feather impaled on the shaft. It was as perfect as it had been when it had been shed by the bird.

She held up the feather to show the stadium.

A roar of admiration burst from the throats of the contestants.

A growl of disgruntled rage rumbled through the citizenry. They were not as belligerent as the first time. For all their hatred of Dronas, they respected their princess's decision and had faith in her.

Krushni intended to repay their faith, and reward it richly.

"We shall move on to the third and final challenge now," she said. "Unless you wish to take a recess to refresh yourself, Dronas."

She saw his eyes narrow at the casual use of his first name. Among his people, she knew, elders were always addressed by their title, gurus especially. To strip him of his title and call him just Dronas was insulting. But he knew too that she was not of his people.

"I am ready when you are, girl," he said, showing his teeth.

She turned away to offer Drishya a wink. *Our ploy is working, brother. Dronas is irate.*

I never doubted it, sister. He will be more than irate in a few moments, I wager.

I will not take that bet because you would win it!

She gave the signal to her attendants, who passed it on to those waiting on the palace ramparts.

4

This time, a whole flock of doves were released, several hundred taking flight at the same time. Their white wings blended with the cottony clouds above, making it hard to distinguish each individual bird. The peacock feather clutched in one dove's beak was a tiny speck in that crowd. Yet when Drishya raised his bow and loosed, the arrow that returned brought with it the rainbow-hued feather as before, falling into Krushni's outstretched hand.

She held it up for Dronas to see. He kept his angry eyes on her, brows furrowed.

"As before, not a feather on a single bird must be harmed."

Dronas stared at her with proud arrogance. "Release."

She smiled and gave the signal.

The second flurry of doves took flight to sudden silence in the arena. All eyes were raised to the skies, watching to spot the target dove amidst the melee.

Yet Krushni sensed one pair of eyes watching her. From the pavilion.

She glanced in the direction of the Dronas pavilion, expecting to find Jarsun watching her.

He was not. Jarsun had his back to the arena, in fact, and appeared uninterested in the contest. Krushni smiled at that show of indifference because it only proved the opposite.

Her gaze flicked to the neighboring pavilion, that of the children of Shvate.

She saw a handsome young person watching her with a relaxed stance but a watchful gaze. There was something in their body and posture that suggested great intensity, not the kind of hypermasculine muscularity of the male contestants, but the pantherlike power of the finest warriors.

Beside the person, a sister and brother appeared to be watching Dronas as he pulled his bowstring for the shot, but it was obvious their interest lay in her as well. The other two siblings were looking up at the sky like two persons engaged in conversation, though their lips were not moving. The only one who appeared less interested in the contest than in the occupants of the neighboring pavilion was the Vanjhani accompanying the Shvate children. Their two heads alternated between watching Jarsun and the Krushan Hundred.

Krushni felt a frisson of sensation, like when her soul-brother, Drishya, communicated with her without speaking. Except it felt unfamiliar, strange . . . interesting. She could make out that it was one of the three Shvate siblings looking at her — and pretending not to — but could not tell for certain which of them it was. Their three consciousnesses reached out with a filial similarity that made it difficult to distinguish between them.

She sharpened her attention, trying to go deeper, to separate one from the other. She was intrigued by what she found. She sensed each one's personality, so unique and distinct from the others, and their mutual attraction toward her.

Except that one, the born warrior, was more than attracted. They were *besotted*. She felt it as surely as she felt the pull of their personality and soul. There was heat in their gaze; her body felt it and reciprocated.

Yes, she was powerfully attracted as well.

She smiled across the distance that separated them.

Abruptly, the pavilions exploded with a deafening roar that was counterpointed by the sullen silence of the city.

She snapped out of her reverie to see the felled arrow clutched in her outstretched hand.

She looked at it closely.

The peacock feather was intact.

Dronas smiled for the first time, a predatory grin that matched his avaricious eyes. Almost instantaneously, his hatred and resentment had transformed into lust. He had conquered her challenge, and now he regarded her as a hunter would look at felled prey. He was ready to claim his prize.

Krushni met his gaze with a cool smile that conveyed her complete lack of acknowledgment. She showed him neither defiance nor acquiescence, the two typical reactions he would have expected. Instead, she showed him smug superiority. She saw his smile falter, the anger returning to his eyes as he tried to interpret her unexpected reaction.

She held up the arrow, turning it over to show him the other side of the peacock feather.

A single red stain marked the feather, barely a drop of blood from the dove. Yet it was there, and it was proof.

"You have failed," she said.

Dronas stared at the smidgen of blood on the peacock feather as if he could not believe its existence.

His eyes swept the skies. The doves were flying westward, arranged now in a more organized pattern.

"The dove is unharmed. It flies on."

She shook her head. "You caused it to shed blood. That violates the conditions of the challenge. You have failed. Kindly return to your pavilion and allow the next contestant to attempt the challenge."

Dronas stared at her, then at Drishya, who had moved closer to Krushni, his smooth face turned toward Dronas without any visible expression, yet somehow managing to convey extreme menace. Dronas stared at him, the hatred back in his gaze, directing his rage now at Drishya, and then, as he swept across the attendants and hosts, all standing ready to come to Krushni's aid should she need it, at every other Gwannlander. For his failure meant not only the loss of the prize, but also a supreme loss of pride. To fail in this particular contest, in this particular place, was to show the world that he, the One and Only Dronas, was not the matchless master he was famed to be. It would mean the ruin of his reputation.

"My shot cannot be bettered," he said, looking not at Krushni, but at the doves now, mere specks against the bright horizon.

Krushni smiled. She had been hoping he would say just that.

She gestured to her attendants. They hesitated, but obeyed.

From the ramparts of the palace, another flock of doves was released.

Dronas looked at them, a frown appearing on his lined brow, then at Krushni. His eyes showed bafflement, disbelief, and something else ... shock.

He could see that Krushni meant to challenge him back now.

Krushni looked at him until the last instant, neither watching the flight of the flock, nor stretching her bowstring until the flock was directly overhead.

In a single flawless action, she pulled, raised, and loosed.

The twang of the bow echoed in the deathly silence that had fallen across New Gwann City.

Dronas stared at her with open disbelief now. The beginnings of a smile gathered at the corners of his drooping lips.

Krushni reached out and caught the felled arrow without looking at it. She had not so much as glanced up even once, not even to distinguish the target dove from the flock. She had loosed entirely by instinct and unerring judgment.

She showed Dronas the peacock feather, immaculate and pristine.

She turned it over to show him the other side of the feather.

"It can," she said simply, responding to his boast.

Then, she turned away as if losing interest in Dronas. "You have failed. Return to your pavilion."

She felt the rage of the man behind her, the fist gripping his bow tightly, the other hand moving the arrow toward the bow, the inexorable instinct to respond to her humiliation and emasculation with violence. She sensed Drishya stepping forward, showing Dronas his face, and felt Dronas reevaluate his position.

A long moment passed, in which the calling of the doves above was the only sound. That, and the fluttering of flags in an easterly wind.

With a final look of murderous rage, Dronas threw down his bow and strode back angrily to his pavilion.

The other pavilions fell into a shocked silence for a moment before the citizens erupted in an exultant roar of jubilation that filled the city for miles around.

Seated in the royal pavilion, Krushni could see her father and mother staring in stupefied joy. Both Vensera and Gwann broke into broad grins.

Arrow

~

1

ARROW WALKED OUT OF the pavilion with his siblings and Tshallian. The Vanjhani did not intend to compete, but he had no wish to stay in the pavilion alone, hemmed in by the Krushan brothers on one side and Jarsun's pavilion on the other.

They strode out to a mixture of angry muttering and sullen silence; the other contestants were having some trouble digesting the shock of Dronas's loss. As they began to notice the Shvate siblings walking out into the arena, the chatter subsided briefly.

Arrow could feel their puzzled, suspicious eyes. Nobody here recognized any of them. Their ignorance was soon dispelled by the Gwann hosts announcing the next contestants.

"The children and heirs of the late Prince Shvate of Hastinaga, eldest prince of the Burnt Empire, by his wife Princess Karni of Stonecastle, Yudi and Arrow and Brum; by his late wife Princess Mayla of Dirda, Kula and Saha."

At once, interest perked up. Those who had been sitting or distracted by arguments over the loss of Dronas turned to look at the new contestants. Several of them swore in surprise and stared at the first Krushan they had seen in their lifetime.

Arrow knew that the Krushan were more feared than admired in this part of the world, and any of the nobles here would give their right arm to meet a Krushan, any Krushan. The tale of Prince Shvate's sudden abdication, self-exile, and subsequent assassination was the stuff of legend, liberally embellished over time, and even though a shadow lay over his widow Karni's and his children's official status in Hastinaga, they were still Krushan, and that was a powerful name.

The citizen audience grew quiet for a moment, then cheered loudly. Arrow was pleased to hear their enthusiasm. Mother had always said their late father was dearly loved for his campaign against Jarsun's tyrannical allies in Reygistan and central Arthaloka, but it was quite another thing to hear a strange crowd of hundreds of thousands cheering for him even after all these years. Arrow hoped to achieve something one day that would make so many people remember them fondly after their death. It was not easy walking in the footsteps of a legend.

It also raised the stakes today.

What the Five sought to achieve was not merely to win a contest and a bride, but to start the arduous process of repairing their family's damaged reputation. And, if all went as Mother planned, to see them ride through the gates of Hastinaga Palace as heirs to the Burnt Empire.

2

The surge of emotion that had overtaken Arrow upon first setting eyes on Krushni returned as they came closer. She was standing facing the siblings, prepared to welcome the new contestants. She was exceptionally attractive, yet it was not her physical appearance that drew Arrow's eyes and mind to her, but rather a powerful sense of connection. She was a blazing orb emitting light in a dark forest, and Arrow was walking through the densely packed trees toward the brilliance. The closer the light, the more illuminated their world, their life, their mind felt. The doubts and uncertainties that had plagued them — plagued all five of them — since leaving their humble forest hut and their mother weeks ago, seemed to evaporate in the heat of Krushni's presence. She shone out and filled Arrow with the warmth of surety. Anything — *anything* — could be accomplished in the presence of this woman.

And so you can, Arronesh, for you are the greatest warrior of this age.

Arrow startled at her presence in their mind and at her knowledge of their full birth name, the intimacy of her soft voice as unexpected as it would have been had she suddenly strode up to actually whisper in their ear. Even though Arrow had been hearing the Five's voices internally since they were born, it was unnerving to have this inner space so casually breached by someone who was, after all, a complete stranger.

A stranger? Is that really how you view me, Arrow?

"No," Arrow said aloud, unaccustomed to conversing with another person this way; another person who was not a sibling, that is.

Kula looked at Arrow curiously. The others were all intent on staring at Krushni. Arrow saw that their sibling evidently didn't hear Krushni's voice in his head. That was new too. When the five of them communicated, they spoke to all their siblings at once. It was impossible for any one of them to speak or think a thought directed at just one sibling, not without all the others hearing it as well. Although, over time, they had all grown adept at making out which communiqué was meant for which one. But whatever this connection with Krushni was, it was direct. One-to-one. From Krushni's lips to Arrow's ears alone.

Arrow responded silently this time. *Who are you? Have we . . . have we perhaps met before now? You seem . . . so familiar.*

We know each other well, you and I. We have known one another for eons, and will always know one another in eons to come. Our link is eternal. It endures like the stars and the force that unites all things.

The Five had come within a few yards of the Gwannlander prince and princess now. Drishya stood silent and statuesque, a magnificent specimen of a man. Even at a glance, Arrow could see that he was not unlike Arrow themself, a being born for physical excellence. Their eyes met, and Arrow acknowledged him with a polite but not unfriendly face. Drishya did the same. Then Arrow turned to Krushni.

She is beautiful! This came from Brum, who, as always, could never contain her exuberance and poured out her feelings at first sight. *I don't just mean her body and face, which are gorgeous, but there's just something about her that pulls me like a rope drawn by a horse team. I could marry this woman without knowing another thing about her!*

Yudi's calm, cool voice intervened: *Remain tranquil, Brum. We are here for a bigger purpose. Don't forget what is at stake.*

What's bigger than meeting the love of your life?

Arrow couldn't resist smiling at her outpouring of joy. Her passion and vivacity were contagious, recalling Arrow from the more ethereal state of a moment ago when Krushni had said those extraordinary things about the two of them. A moment later, it struck Arrow that none of the others, not just Kula, appeared to have heard or commented upon Krushni's silent conversation. How strange. Did that mean that only Arrow could speak with her? How was that possible? They had not shielded themself — how could they have known Krushni would speak into their mind? — and the Shvate siblings had shared every thought, every emotion, since birth.

We have a link that is greater than time and physicality, Arronesh. Do not question it or wonder why. My connection with your siblings is very special too, but you and I are beyond everything and everyone. Our relationship exists in a space outside of time and matter. It is as old as creation and as young as the emerging future. Look within your heart and soul, and you will know it to be true.

Arrow hardly knew what to say or think of that. And yet, somewhere in their heart they felt instinctively the truth of Krushni's words. The two of them *were* connected. Arrow had felt that the instant they first glimpsed her, and even before, when Mother first said that they must go to New Gwann City. Now, meeting Krushni in person, it felt like they were old, intimate friends reunited after too long a separation.

Before there was time to think further on these matters, a disruption broke out in the pavilions. Arrow saw the Gwannlander hosts shift their gazes to look at someone or something behind the Shvate siblings. They turned to see a large group leaving the shade of the pavilions to walk toward them. Several hosts, serving in their capacity as security, were engaged in tussles with the group. They seemed to be insisting that the intruders return to their pavilion. As Arrow watched, the intruders retaliated with far more force than necessary, striking down, shoving aside, and in some cases, even cracking skulls and stomping Gwannlanders who tried to stop them.

"The Krushan Hundred," Yudi said, not sounding surprised.

Dhuryo Krushan strode at the head of the group, bearing down on the arena with his bow in hand. Every one of his brothers carried a bow as well. They were clearly the worse for all the wine and ale consumed, and some of them staggered unsteadily; Arrow saw at least one bend over and expunge the contents of his stomach. One of his brothers slapped him on the back, making him fall over into his own vomit, and the others laughed raucously.

As they approached, Arrow glimpsed several more Gwannlanders rushing to surround their prince and princess. He glanced back just in time to see Krushni gesture to them to stand down and step aside. Reluctantly, they withdrew, but they remained within easy reach, just in case. He looked at Krushni. She had fallen silent after their last exchange, but her smile evoked familiarity and intimacy. The rest of the Five noticed this as well, and all of them turned to look at Arrow curiously.

Looks like Arrow has found the mark yet again. Saha thought this in a mildly amused tone.

Arrow looked at her disapprovingly. She shrugged. *Just saying what's true. This isn't the first time. The most attractive ones are always attracted to you.*

Like bees to nectar, Kula agreed.

Or bears to honey, Brum said, pretending to grumble, but then giving Arrow a wink that showed she bore no malice. Jealousy was one thing that never reared its ugly head among the Shvate children. They were all secure in their bond, and their deep connection meant that few things came as a surprise to any of them.

They don't know that Krushni and I can communicate without any of them hearing, Arrow thought. *I should tell them.*

But there was no time. Dhuryo Krushan had covered the ground between them with impressive speed. The prince and heir to the Burning Throne bore down on them with the look and manner of a rhinoceros intent on bulling his way over them.

"Here we go," Yudi said.

3

"We shall take our turn now," Dhuryo Krushan said in a tone that allowed for no argument. He took up his bow and held out his hand. One of his brothers put an arrow into it. Dhuryo Krushan jerked his chin at Princess Krushni.

"Release the targets."

All eyes turned on Krushni. She stood, imperious and elegant, impervious to Dhuryo Krushan's rude manner.

"The children of Shvate stepped forth first," she said. "They will take their turn now. All others may await their calls. If you wish, you may return to your pavilion and continue partaking of our hospitality. I shall summon you when your time arrives."

Dhuryo and his brothers all bristled visibly at this. Arrow suppressed a smile at their indignant expressions.

Bet no one ever told Dhuryo Krushan that he *would be summoned,* Kula said, in his laughing tone.

Bet no one ever refused that buffalo and lived long enough to regret it, Brum said. She didn't sound amused.

It's about time, then, Arrow said.

The buffalo hadn't taken Krushni's orders well. He glowered at her. But Dronas, who had followed the Krushan brothers, had arrived in time to overhear the exchange. Dhuryo's former guru said something to him that did nothing to diminish Dhuryo's outrage but caused him to hold his tongue.

Arrow saw that the rest of Dronas's party had arrived as well, joining the Krushan Hundred. It consisted of only one man, if he could even be called that. This, of course, was Jarsun Krushan.

Arrow's eyes met Jarsun's briefly, taking the measure of the man. So this was the most feared and hated man in Arthaloka.

Jarsun was intent on Krushni, his thin face sharpened to bladed points as he stared at the princess of Gwannland. Arrow couldn't tell if his expression was one of loathing or something else. Whatever it was, it was not pleasant. Nothing about Jarsun Krushan could be remotely termed likeable.

So this is Father's murderer, Brum thought. She was outwardly calm to look at, but Arrow could sense her breathing deepening and quickening, and could feel the telltale signs.

Tranquil, sister, Yudi said quietly into their minds. *The time will come.*

What better time than now? Brum asked.

Arrow knew she was wrong, but also shared her anger. Jarsun was right there, mere yards from them. The bastard who had killed their father in cold blood, taking the form of Grandfather Vessa for the purpose, then disappearing through supernatural means before either of their mothers could react. Arrow had been a mere babe at the time, but the memory was as painful and jagged-edged as if it were a shard of glass imbedded in their brain only moments ago. Arrow was ready to confront Jarsun right then and now; all five of them were. They had been ready for fifteen years.

But Yudi was right. This was not the time. Not yet. Their time would come soon. Then they would know if all their training, their inborn talents, their learned skills, were good enough. Whenever it happened, it would not be easy. That, and not the wedding contest, was the real challenge.

A voice broke into the siblings' mindtalk.

"Children of Shvate, Karni, and Mayla, heirs to the Burnt Empire, who among you wishes to take the challenge?"

Arrow glanced around at them. There was a flicker in Yudi's eyes as he responded to the warmth of Krushni's tone and noted her choice of words.

Heirs to the Burnt Empire. She shows us great respect by acknowledging our claim.

That's not how Dhuryo Krushan and his brothers are taking it, Kula said wryly, grinning as he mindspoke.

Who gives a fart what Dhuryo Krushan thinks? Brum said. *I think I just fell in love with the princess.*

She also acknowledged Mother Karni and Mother Mayla, Saha and Kula sent in unison. *Most people only call us by our father's name; it's so infuriating.*

Especially since Father didn't actually participate in our procreation, Arrow added. *But coming to her question . . .*

"All of us," Yudi said aloud.

The hosts, as well as Tshallian, who had stood silently by all this while, looked surprised at that. Only Krushni smiled.

"So shall it be," she said, clapping her hands. "Release five."

The attendants passed on the message to their colleagues on the palace ramparts.

The siblings removed an arrow each and fixed it to their bows, keeping them pointed down at the ground as they had been taught. It was impolite — and dangerous — to point weapons at anyone unless one intended to use them. Arrow could still hear Grandfather Vessa's voice drilling this into their ears over and over again. That was a long time ago, but the lesson stuck.

Arrow sensed a commotion from the back just as the palace attendants released a flock of birds. The Krushan brothers were restless. It wasn't too much of an effort to ignore them.

Arrow allowed themself to fall into the state of intense focus that took over every time they used their skills. All sights and sounds faded, leaving only the sound of the birds beating their wings, the wind pushing them sideways as they flew southward, the smell of dirt and dust and Arrow's own body odors, the perfume of Princess Krushni, and also her own scent. She was sweating a little in the searing noonday sun, and Arrow found the aroma powerfully arousing.

They used the arousal, taking the emotional power and channeling it into kinetic energy. The energy gathered in the muscles of their neck, back, shoulders, and arms as Arrow gazed nowhere in particular, using peripheral vision to track the birds without actually seeing them. The sun was directly overhead now, and when the bow was raised to fire, it would be blinding for a moment. That was all right. Arrow had no intention of looking up. They were going to aim based on sound and intuition.

As the flutter of wings grew closer, it sounded deafening, filling the senses. Arrow smelled the pungent avian odors of bird droppings and urine, felt the ticks crawling on their torsos and head, knew each bird intimately. Arrow was one of them, was the flock. They soared above the arena, the city, the world laid out below like a rolling carpet. They sensed themself standing, a puny figure when seen from this height, merely one of countless insignificant creatures on the face of Arthaloka, no more important than a single tick on the dove's head. They felt the weight of the arrow, felt its longing to leave its dust-bound existence, if only for a moment, felt the grain of the wood, the tiny speck of rust in the pointed metal tip, the force of the bowstring launching it, and now Arrow was the peacock feather itself, not just the flutings or the wispy ends but the eye of the feather. Only this eye existed, rainbow-hued and exquisite, curling at its base to form a paisley pattern, the eye and that arrow, and nothing else in this whole wide world. The eye welcomed the arrow. In midair they met and joined with furious vigor, the dove trembling momentarily as it felt the brute force of the arrow's upward thrust, then released the feather which was now conjoined with its spouse, the arrow.

Falling now, falling through wind and air and sky and emptiness . . .

Falling into . . .

An open hand, a single palm.

Krushni

~

KRUSHNI HELD UP HER closed fist. It clutched five arrows, each sporting a peacock's feather on its tip. She separated arrows from feathers and examined them closely. There was not a speck of blood on any one of them.

But even as she did this, the sky was filled with the sound of violence.

Around her, there were not five bows raised as ought to have been the case, but a hundred and five.

The Krushan brothers had fired as well, even though they had been forbidden to take their turn. Dhuryo Krushan wore a look of supreme pride on his handsome face. His brothers all looked as if they shared a mutual jest and had just heard the punch line.

With a rattling repetition, a hundred doves fell to the arena, landing in sickening thuds around the group of people gathered in the center, but none fell on them. The arrows that struck the doves had been carefully aimed to drop the birds away from their killers. Every dove had a single arrow through its eye, oozing black blood.

Silence fell over the city and the arena.

Krushni saw her father and mother in their pavilion, risen to their feet.

She looked in their direction, willing them with that single look to stay in their places, and allow her to handle this matter. She saw their concern but could not address it just now. For better or worse, her plans were coming to fruition, and there would be violence, great and terrible violence. That had always been a given. The only thing that mattered to her was that she had not been the one to draw first blood. Not even the blood of a dove.

She raised the five arrows in one hand, the five peacock feathers in the other.

"The children of Shvate have won the contest. All five of their arrows struck true."

The watching spectators, visitors as well as citizens, remained silent. Everyone knew that she was not done speaking. The Krushan Hundred still grinned arrogantly at her, clearly defying her. Their guru Dronas now came forward to stand beside Dhuryo Krushan, bow in hand, staring with intent eyes at her, making it clear that he stood with his pupils in this matter. Krushni had never doubted that. He and his cohorts, the Krushan brothers, had come here to New Gwann City with the express intention of initiating aggression.

They had issued their challenge. Now it was time for Krushni to rise to it. "The sons of Krushan have violated the terms of the contest, disobeyed the rules, and insulted the hospitality of Gwannland," she said. "They are hereby banished from the realm and forbidden to ever enter its borders again. They will leave immediately and never return, under penalty of death."

She deliberately used the traditional name for her father and mother's kingdom. Not "New Gwannland." So, too, was her pronouncement deliberate; as royals, especially royals of a much more powerful and greater kingdom — the Burnt Empire, no less — protocol would have been satisfied with her admonishing them gently and requesting them to kindly withdraw from the contest, giving them the chance to save face and dismiss their act as a jest. Thus did royals and the privileged classes get away with the worst atrocities, by terming their own misdeeds as "horseplay" while punishing those of lower status, class, caste with the severest penalties for the smallest missteps. She didn't give a damn about protocol, or the status quo. Krushni had set out to start a war, and the Hundred had just delivered the opportunity she desired. She was going to show them that when it came to pain and death, all were equal under Jeel's judging eye.

"Sons of Krushan, I hereby declare you ... *mleccha!*" she said, ending the pronouncement and issuing her first countermove. The word "mleccha" meant "uncivilized barbarian," a derogatory term used by the Krushan themselves to denigrate the nomadic groups that roved the great continent or occupied its most remote, unexplored corners. Quite distinct from the aboriginal peoples such as the Aran who dwelled in the dense jungles of Aranya, mleccha were the lowest of low, cannibals, head-hunters, animalistic in their lifestyles and savage in their interactions, fiercely resistant to peaceful dialogue, hygiene, or any trace of civilized behavior. To call a Krushan — let alone heirs of the empire itself — mleccha was the most unforgivable insult. No Krushan could tolerate such abuse, and Krushan law demanded that the speaker apologize, prostrate themselves, and accept whatever punishment was deemed fit or be put to death.

Krushni had just issued a death challenge to Dhuryo Krushan.

The smiles on the faces of the Krushan Hundred disappeared. The lowered bows rose at once, and a hundred arrows were nocked in an instant — no, a hundred and one, for Dronas had raised his own bow as well. Now, a hundred and one arrows were aimed directly at Krushni.

The moment of reckoning had arrived.

Ladislew

~

"NOW THIS GETS INTERESTING," Shikari said, leaning forward in her seat. They had elected to return to the pavilion to partake of more wine. "You would think the princess would know better. She seems like a bright young..."

She stopped speaking and crinkled her eyes, thinking. Ladislew noted that when she did, her snub nose crinkled as well. Despite her aggressive, brash personality, the Lady Goddick was very cute. A very enticing combination of cute and sexual, with the promise of aggression. Ladislew wondered idly how she might be as a lover.

"You think she intended things to go this way?" Shikari wondered aloud.

"Clearly," Ladislew said.

Shikari glanced at her with a raised brow. "You mean, she planned this very outcome?"

"She probably set up this contest with this very goal in mind."

Shikari crinkled her eyes again. It really was quite attractive, and wholly unlike the insolent, challenging expression she wore when speaking to men. Yes, she was promising as a lover. "But the wedding contest has been held three years in a row, the host said. So..."

Again, she stopped and thought about what she had just said.

She inhaled.

"You mean," she said softly, thinking aloud, "that the princess set up the contest with the express intent of attracting the attention of the Krushan brothers and setting up a confrontation with them?"

Ladislew shrugged. "Something along those lines."

Shikari frowned at her. "Something ... so not exactly that. What, then?"

"She knew the contest would attract Dronas's attention. And the Krushan brothers visit him at least once a year, paying off their guru debt by doing the things he tells them to. Dronas can't be pleased that King Gwann and Queen Vensera have prospered since he ousted them from their homeland and stole the bulk of their kingdom. It injures his pride to see his enemies still thriving. Only his preoccupation with the internal strife in his own newly formed kingdom kept him busy until now. He's always looking for an opportune moment to pounce on this tiny nation and swallow it whole, putting an end to his once-friend and sworn enemy and his entire lineage once and for all. The invitation to this contest provided him with that opportunity. And now Princess Krushni's insult to his pupils provides him with the perfect excuse."

Shikari's shapely eyebrows had risen while Ladislew talked. They were almost even with her hairline now. Her snub nose also rose quite a ways, Ladislew noted. She felt a familiar stirring in her nether regions.

"You know a great deal about Eastern politics," Shikari said.

"It's part of my job," Ladislew said.

Shikari looked skeptical. "You have a job?"

Ladislew smiled. "Political advisor to the God-Emperor of the Reygistan Empire."

Shikari laughed. "Nicely done!"

She looked into Ladislew's eyes and saw her arousal. She inclined her head, acknowledging it with a sly upturn of her lips. Shikari put her hand on Ladislew's thigh. "I've never slept with a political advisor to the God-Emperor of Reygistan Empire before."

"*The* political advisor," Ladislew corrected her, smiling. "He's quite particular about emphasizing that. Announcers who misspeak titles are corrected quite harshly in his court."

"I'm sure they are," Shikari said. She looked at Ladislew. "And yet I don't take you for someone who gives a damn about the *God-Emperor's* rules — or his punishments. In fact, it makes me wonder, why is someone like you with Jarsun Krushan at all?"

Ladislew allowed her face to relax into a sly smile. "Isn't it impressive, the things we sometimes do to let a man to believe he is in charge? The enduring patience we display when we want something and know it can't be had in a day?"

Shikari smiled back. "We have much to talk about, don't we?"

The sound of raised voices from the arena turned both their heads again.

Shikari

~

DHURYO KRUSHAN WAS SPEAKING.

"*Mleccha?*" he repeated, fist tightening on his bow till his biceps bulged and the veins on his face stood out like white worms. "*You* are the uncivilized one here. You dare insult our guru, the great Dronas himself, by accusing him of failing? And then you deny us our legitimate turn? We, the sons of Krushan? But most of all, you insult us by acknowledging *these* mleccha, bastard spawn of a disgraced exile! How dare you let them take their turn before us?"

Krushni bore this tirade calmly. "It is you who have insulted Gwannland. By killing our national mascot, these sacred doves, symbols of peace and prosperity, you insult all our people, our culture, our tradition, our heritage. In addition, you have violated the rules of the contest and are hereby barred from ever taking part again. Only mleccha would behave thus. As punishment, I exile you from Gwannland for life. Leave now with your lives intact, or face the consequences."

Dhuryo Krushan stared at her, then turned and looked at his brothers. As one person, they all burst out laughing.

Krushni saw her father and mother standing still, looking intensely anxious now. They were speaking among themselves. She was aware of the Shvate siblings standing around her, and Drishya beside her, all in stances poised for action, their bows held by their sides and ready for use. As were all her security team, the several dozen hosts, who had come up during this last exchange to surround the Krushan Hundred. There were many more held in abeyance, but she had no intention of summoning them. She knew how this was likely to play out, and shedding either Krushan blood or Gwannlander blood on the dust of the arena was not part of the scenario.

When the Krushan brothers finally stopped laughing, Dhuryo turned back to look at her in amusement.

"This one has spirit, brothers, has she not?" he said.

"Aye!" they replied, like a well-trained military company.

Dhuryo Krushan eyed Krushni from top to bottom, his gaze lingering in all the expected places. "And something more as well," he said thoughtfully. "Yes, yes. I think you would make a fine companion for my nights. At least for a week or two. After that, I shall decide whether to keep you in my palace of concubines for my brothers to enjoy or dispose of you by other means. The brothels of Hastinaga always have a place for Eastern beauties like yourself. For some reason, your kind don't last long there. Too soft to survive the rigors of Western men? It matters not. There's plenty more where you came from. But for a week or two, you will be a fine addition to my night's entertainment."

Krushni walked closer to Dhuryo, swaying her hips and moving in the most explicitly feminine manner. She stopped within inches of his taller, broader, overbearing frame, and leaned closer, close enough to kiss his grizzled jawline. She said in a soft, breathy voice, turning her face sideways as if she meant to kiss him on his temple, "If you stand here and continue talking any longer, I shall unman you so thoroughly that the only entertainment you'll enjoy at night is singing baul laments in praise of lost love."

As if to underline her meaning, she jabbed the point of the shortsword that had suddenly appeared in her hand into Dhuryo's groin.

Reacting instinctively, he yelped and jumped back, bending over to clutch at his pricked ego with the hand not holding the bow.

Laughter burst from the lips of one of the Shvate siblings.

The short, fat one, Shikari noted, the one they called Brum. She was the one who had been putting away ale and food in the pavilion like she hadn't eaten in weeks, and impressed Shikari as being quite a character. She proved this right by laughing so hard at Dhuryo's discomfiture that she had to bend over, leaning her bow on the ground to support herself and slapping her meaty thighs as she shook with laughter.

"The way he yelped," Brum said through tears of laughter. "Like a dog slapped on the nose by a cat!"

Around her, all her siblings grinned as well, except for the serious-looking one named Yudi, who appeared to be their leader.

Dhuryo Krushan straightened up, his face murderous. He had not exploded at the use of the epithet "mleccha" as Shikari had expected, which meant he was much smarter and more self-controlled than his unruly brothers, but he was furious now.

"Nothing like an insult to his manhood to make a man lose his temper," Ladislew said.

Shikari chuckled. "Men. So *predictable.*"

Ladislew

~

DHURYO KRUSHAN SMILED AT Krushni as a jaguar might seem to smile at its prey. Except, the jaguar's smile was no smile at all: it was a promise of deadly intimacy. Whatever spark of lust had appeared in Dhuryo's eyes at the prospect of possessing the princess of Gwannland had just been doused. In its place was hot fury.

"I have changed my mind. I would not want you in my bed for even one night. You are not deserving of the privilege. Instead, I shall put you in my House of Truth."

Ladislew caught her breath. The legendary House of Truth was a feature of Krushan "civilization." There was one in every Krushan-governed city across the expanse of the Burnt Empire.

Most legendary of them all was the progenitor, the original House of Truth in the capital city of Hastinaga. Rumored to be a vast underground labyrinth of perpetually dark chambers, where unknown terrors roamed and did what they pleased to the incarcerated occupants. Whatever they did left no permanent mark on the unfortunates condemned down there, but damaged them deeply enough to scar their souls and minds forever. When they emerged, if they ever did, it was as things bereft of any trace of human empathy or other emotions. They spoke only the truth, naked and raw, and obeyed the will of their Krushan overlords unquestioningly, even to the point of death. In short, they became mentally enslaved for the rest of their miserable mortal lives.

As if to mock the truth of this house of horrors, the structure that rested atop this nightmare warren was a hideously beautiful monstrosity, an insanely fascinating architectural marvel that both attracted the eye and repelled the senses. The rumors also claimed that the structure itself was constructed out of the bodies and bones of those who had once been incarcerated below. When their masters no longer had use for their services, they ordered the brainwashed mindservants to return home to the House of Truth: a command that had only one meaning.

Those thus instructed returned to the building that had stolen their souls and humanity, and ended their lives upon it. Some impaled themselves on its jagged points, others crushed their limbs and skulls into crevices and crannies, many chose to simply lie on the vaulting roof until they died of exposure and starvation. None actually entered the building itself again, or ventured belowground to the catacombs that had been the cause of their loss.

It was said tens of thousands had been thus condemned, most of them vanquished enemies of the Burnt Empire — kings, queens, princes, princesses, nobles, generals, champions — but many were people who had once served the Krushan loyally as maids, servants, personal guards, lovers, spies, or merely the bastard offspring produced by the more flagrantly lustful members of the dynasty. If there was a literal definition of a fate worse than death, the House of Truth was it.

When Dhuryo Krushan said the words, it was evident he meant them. That promise would have made any foe's blood turn to ice. It made Shikari's own rising desire for her companion curdle momentarily. She had seen — and administered — enough torture and punishment to her enemies and betrayers not to take such a threat lightly. It was not the same as merely threatening to kill someone: every warrior expected death by combat. But to be sent to the House of Truth was not death, it was the ultimate terror that could not be fought by any means.

Yet Krushni shocked Ladislew, and the Krushan Hundred, by laughing loudly. Her laughter rang out, strong and vibrant, the mirth of a strong woman confident in herself and her place in the world. She threw her head back to reveal a lovely black throat, muscular and well shaped. Ladislew had a personal soft spot for throats. There was something erotic about placing one's lips, one's teeth, on another person's throat while making love. One could kiss, bite, nibble — or bite deep and rip out. That dual death-love combination made it particularly arousing to her. Krushni of Gwannland had a throat she would love to make love to.

Dhuryo Krushan was eyeing it with somewhat less than amorous intent.

Krushni ceased laughing and looked at him with an expression of amusement. "You are such a cliché," she said. "Are you sure you're not a traveling troupe of performers here to put on one of those old plays about the age of the stone gods and how the world was governed by Truth and Honor, and men . . . always *men* . . . walked the earth as gods and masters of all they surveyed? What next, are you going to threaten war? To crush my little kingdom with your vast and powerful armies?"

Dhuryo Krushan stared at her with a look so hateful, Ladislew could feel the heat of his fury even in the cool shade of the pavilion. "You are a child playing with forces far greater than you can understand, princess of Gwannland. You do not understand yet what you have unleashed. You think we Krushan came here to participate in some worthless contest? To win the hand in marriage of an insignificant royal from some Eastern Kingdom that isn't even important enough to appear on the maps of Arthaloka in the royal map room of Hastinaga? You are a fool among wise giants if you think you or your kingdom matters!"

Krushni shook her head, a mocking smile on her face. "And yet here you are, a long way from home, in the eastern corner of the continent, hundreds of miles from even your former guru's kingdom. Which is called Gwannland, not Dronasthan, as he has pompously renamed it, and which I now intend to take back control of, by force if necessary. So if you didn't come here to win a bride or to show off your mastery of bowcraft and arms, then why are you here, Dhuryo Krushan? Because you are wasting my time and the time of these worthy contestants on the field by standing here bantering and badgering to no end."

Dhuryo grinned, turning to show his brothers his teeth. They laughed and bared their teeth as well. He turned back to Krushni. "We came here for a purpose. And I suppose this is as good a time as any to reveal that purpose. I think this conversation has gone as far as it can. So let us show you the real reason for our visit to your little speck-of-shit kingdom in the corner of nowhere."

Dhuryo turned and gestured at someone in the pavilions.

For a heart-stopping second, Ladislew thought he was beckoning to her. Then she saw that he was gesturing in her direction — or rather, the direction of the pavilion beside the one she and Shikari were seated in.

The pavilion of Jarsun Krushan.

Dhuryo

~

1

DHURYO HAD WATCHED AS Jarsun rose to his feet and began walking. The tall, thin figure cast a shadow as thin as a spear stuck in the ground with a skull on its point. In a way, Dhuryo thought, his uncle was just that. A spear upon which a human-like head had been impaled. There was little sign of humanity about him. He could as well have been a shaft of hardwood; his mind was as rigid as iron, fury as deadly as a honed blade. Truth be told, Dhuryo was a little frightened of him. His brothers were far more than that: they were scared shitless. They parted to make way for the God-Emperor as he strode through their ranks, none daring to look directly at him. Jarsun was the only living being before whom the sons of Adri lowered their gazes.

Even Dhuryo felt the powerful urge to do the same. He compelled himself through force of will to keep his chin straight, and his eyes to stay on Jarsun's face. From a distance of several yards, the feverish intensity of Jarsun's eyes was white-hot, the hooded gaze of a red rattlesnake in the Reygistan desert, patient enough to wait weeks for prey to move close enough to attack before launching a strike. Once a red rattlesnake struck, it did not retreat, and almost never failed to secure its prey. Jarsun was far deadlier than that: he could strike at his enemies without their even knowing he was there, and then it was too late.

Again, not for the first time since their association, Dhuryo dreaded that venomous gaze being turned on him. Had it been up to Dhuryo, he would have handled this his way. The Hundred were more than capable of overrunning this tiny backwater republic themselves. They didn't even need Dronas and his army, although that was there to handle the dirty work of ravaging and pillage, burning cities and towns, slaughtering civilians. Dhuryo had no special enmity against these Easterners, at least he hadn't until today. He had come here only because his guru had summoned him. The Hundred had done this kind of work for Dronas before, most notably when the guru had announced his retirement from active teaching and desired a kingdom of his own to rule for the rest of his days.

When Dronas had made his wish known to Dhuryo's father, Emperor Adri in Hastinaga, Dhuryo had been present. Adri insisted on him being present in court more and more often these days. Dhuryo found politics and the day-to-day governance of an empire too boring, but sooner or later he would be sitting up on that same stonefire throne, and he might as well get used to enduring these tiresome chores. He had been present when Dronas had approached Adri and taken a knee to show respect to the Burning Throne.

Stonefire burned deep blue before changing hues to indigo, then orange, then red and yellow. Adri had tilted his head, as if listening to someone speak into his ear, even though the packed court was deathly silent. Dhuryo *felt* rather than heard the susurrating voice of the Burning Throne as it spoke to the mind of its occupant. It was like being near a perpetual bolt of lightning, a jagged line of light and power linking the earth to the heavens; it crackled in one's blood, singed the senses, and cycled through colors unseeable by human eyes. To ordinary mortal humans, it was said to sound like the screaming of countless demons, and if they were exposed to the presence of the throne for too long, it drove them insane. The court of Hastinaga had a very high turnover of servants and guards.

"Guru Dronas," Emperor Adri had said in his sonorous voice, blind eyes raised to gaze sightlessly across the vast chamber. "I believe you have a wish."

Dronas inclined his head in acknowledgment. "One can say nothing that is not already known to He Who Sits Upon the Burning Throne," he said. "Indeed, you speak verily. I wish to ask for my guru debt to be paid."

Adri was silent a brief moment. Dhuryo sensed the susurrations of the supernatural flames speaking in its alien tongues and wondered, as he always did, what it was saying.

"It shall be so," the emperor replied. "I see that you do not wish it to be paid in coin, treasure, or titles. State your wish, then."

"I desire to possess my own kingdom, the kingdom of Dronasthan."

"And where in Arthaloka would you wish to reign?"

Even though the Burnt Empire did not comprise all of the great continent, those in Hastinaga never acknowledged this fact. To their minds, all the world that mattered was under Krushan rule. The rest was mere barbarian wilderness, areas fit only for mleccha.

"In the East," Dronas replied. "In the region presently known as Gwannland."

Adri raised his head, the blackness in his eye sockets staring at the vaulting, carved ceiling of the great theatrical space. A forest of jagged, sharp-edged rocklike formations descended from the distant height, an upside-down forest of deadly design. The entire chamber had been burned out of a mountainous rock by stonefire eons earlier at the formation of the empire.

The legends said that in ancient times, anyone who lied, betrayed, or otherwise thought, spoke, or acted against the interests of the current occupant of the throne was impaled or crushed by the spontaneous dropping of one of those jagged spurs hanging from the ceiling. Dhuryo did not want to put himself in the place of the countless mortals who had appeared before the emperor, constantly aware that the slightest false move — even an errant thought or emotional response — could bring a life-ending shard of stone from above, without word or warning.

Adri contemplated this mouthful of jagged black teeth patiently awaiting their next morsel. Without lowering his gaze, he said, "You were born and grew up in that region, Dronas."

A sudden intake of breath was the only indication that Dronas was taken aback by the statement. Dhuryo smiled to himself. No matter how many times outsiders heard about the legendary powers of stonefire, they still found it awe-inspiring when they actually encountered it. Like all gurus, Dronas had shrouded himself in a cloak of secrets, allowing no indication that he might have had something resembling a childhood, or even that he had been born at all. Part of a guru's ability to command depended upon an almost supernatural awe of his knowledge and skills. But there were no secrets from the Burning Throne. Stonefire had ferreted out the secret details of Dronas's childhood in an instant.

Dhuryo's father continued speaking.

"Your family was slain by marauders when you were an infant. Queen Gwannsin happened to be passing and slew the miscreants. She adopted you and raised you alongside her own son, Gwann. You grew up as friends and brothers until your later youth when you had a falling-out. You had sworn oaths as children that when the time came, you would rule jointly. Eager to hasten your ascent, you slew your own adoptive mother, Gwannsin. Prince Gwann ascended the throne and banished you from Gwannland. You dedicated your life to vengeance, acquiring the knowledge and skills that you planned to use to take back what you believed was your rightful inheritance. Now you believe the time has come."

Dronas was silent for a long moment, clearly rendered speechless by the emperor's depth of knowledge. Finally, he said, "Your Imperial Highness knows all. I ask then that you grant my wish and command the armies of your mighty empire to accompany me on my conquest of Gwannland."

Adri said, "Your request is denied."

Dhuryo blinked, startled by his father's reply.

Dronas raised his eyes and stared in surprise at the blind emperor seated atop his high throne. The jagged, misshapen form of the dark, vicious being that was stonefire loomed above him, flickering with flames of more hues than human eyes could absorb. "Your Highness?" he cried, shocked. Then, with a flash of the notorious temper that had earned him his reputation as a merciless tutor, he said, "You deny me my guru debt? This is a violation of Krushan law!"

"Watch your tongue, teacher," Emperor Adri said sharply. "I only deny your request for my armies, not your guru debt. Your debt shall be repaid in full and then some. The armies of Hastinaga are not required for a task this minor. It would take such a large mass years to travel to the far eastern end of the continent and return. The capital cannot be left unprotected for such a length of time. Nay, I say you do not need the armies of the Krushan to accomplish this conquest. My sons alone shall be quite sufficient."

"Your sons," Dronas repeated. "The Krushan Hundred." His eyes sought out and found Dhuryo, who stood a little straighter and taller, acknowledging his guru with the customary namas. "I see. Yes, of course. You are quite right. I have taught your sons much of warcraft. And their natural talents make them equivalent to an army in themselves. Once again, your wisdom is faultless, your words impeccable. I shall accept the service of the Krushan Hundred as my guru debt."

"In that case, you may take them and leave at your earliest convenience. Make sure they return by the start of the Festival of Vish. They are required for the annual parade and assorted other duties."

Dronas bowed and took his leave, taking Dhuryo and his brothers with him. They had done as instructed, overrun Gwannland and made it the new kingdom of Dronas. When King Gwann, his queen, and a small but fiercely loyal number of his followers had fled farther east, Dronas had wanted to give pursuit and run them down, slaughtering every last one. But Dhuryo had his orders from his father. "Guru, my father instructed me to return with my brothers before the Festival of Vish. We must take our leave now. We have accomplished your task, you now have your kingdom. The handful of survivors and the sliver of land left are insignificant and can be dealt with in due course."

"Very well," Dronas had said with obvious ill humor, "but I shall summon you once more to finish the job. I shall not consider the guru debt fully re-paid until all Gwannland is mine."

And now here were Dhuryo and the Hundred once again, and they were in New Gwannland, on the verge of fulfilling their plan and completing Dronas's conquest.

But there was a condition to their service, one that Dronas had not been made aware of when he was granted his wish by Dhuryo's father.

He was about to learn what it meant to be touched by stonefire.

2

Jarsun stopped within yards of Dhuryo and Krushni. His hatchet face was inscrutable as ever, but Dhuryo thought he glimpsed a flash of something when he looked at the princess.

"Princess Krushni of Gwannland," Jarsun said in his susurrant voice. The tips of his twin-edged tongue snaked out the corners of his mouth.

"Jarsun the Exiled," Krushni said, the smile on her mouth counterpointed by the icy glint in her eyes.

If Jarsun took offense to the lack of use of his formal title, he did not show it. Instead, he gestured with both hands outspread and palms held up.

"So this is where you wish to be," he said. "Among these . . . people?"

"This is my home," she replied. "This is my family."

"You could have had an empire. The world. Everything and everyone at your feet. Instead, you chose this." He sounded incredulous, skeptical, disgusted.

"Everyone does not crave power as you do," she said, "or abuse it as you do."

He shook his head. "You take after your mother. Foolish woman."

At that, Dhuryo saw a change come over Krushni for the first time since he had first laid eyes on her at the start of the contest. She seemed to visibly bristle, her skin flushing, her entire body drawing tight. Something moved within her, like a mole burrowing its way just under the surface of the earth, rippling over her lean, lithe form. He frowned.

"You have lost the right to speak of my mother," she said harshly. "Do not speak of her again."

Jarsun laughed softly. "Ah, my dear. You are still the same. The body changes, but the spirit burns eternal. Still the little headstrong, hotheaded little girl I last saw in the Red Desert."

Dhuryo blinked. Jarsun had met Krushni before today? It was the first he was hearing of it. There was something very strange about this conversation. He glanced at his guru and saw that Dronas was frowning, his brow furrowed. So he too was unaware of what Krushni and Jarsun were talking about.

Krushni said, "Did you come here intending to take part in the contest?"

Jarsun smiled. "Contest? Of course not. No matter how lowly I am in your view, there are lines even I will not cross. Your little contest is of no interest to me."

"Then why are you here? To cheer for your nephews, the sons of Adri? Or for your new friend, Dronas?"

"They are my nephews, yes, and he is my friend now, although 'ally' would be a better description. We have mutual interests in this region. But to answer your question, no, I am not here for either of them. You might even say that they are here because I am. We had arranged to meet here."

Krushni's gaze sharpened, her eyes drew tighter. "To what purpose?"

Jarsun smiled again. "The same as yours, young Krushni. War."

"Who said anything about war?"

Jarsun shrugged. "What else is there worth doing? We are kings and queens and warriors. We exist because of war. War exists because of us. It is an eternal cycle."

"Perhaps it's time for the cycle to end. For a new one to begin. An era of peace."

"Peace is a noble dream. An impossible dream. As long as mortalkind exists, war will thrive. It is in our nature, it is in our blood."

"Only a power-mad despot like you thinks that way. The people of the world want peace and prosperity, not violence and mayhem."

Jarsun chuckled. "The *people* of the world. Is it for them that you do all this now? Is that what you are in this life? A servant of the people?"

"I am one of the people. Their interests are my interests. I work for their upliftment and betterment. When we rise, we rise together."

"And when you fall . . . ?" He waved off the last remark. "Never mind this pointless bantering. It will lead us nowhere. Let us come to the main matter at hand. You seem to have invited the wolf into the sheep's fold, so to speak."

Krushni smiled. "Yes, I have."

Jarsun nodded. "I am sure you did so with a plan in mind. You knew that Dronas and the Krushan Hundred would come, intending to use the opportunity to size up your strengths and weaknesses and launch their offensive against this tiny realm, completing the conquest of Gwannland begun some years ago. You intended in turn to lure them in with this hope, and turn the tables on them by inviting the sons of Shvate here as a surprise. I take it that the sons of Shvate will now fight on your side in the coming conflict, lending their considerable gifts to the clash?"

Krushni shrugged. "The best plan is always a simple one. The difficulty in war is not coming up with a plan, it's executing it effectively."

"I have no doubt you will execute this one very effectively," Jarsun agreed. "Except for one small thing."

"Let me guess," Krushni said, with emboldened confidence. "The fact that you decided to come along and join their side in this fight? I was counting on it."

"Of course you were," Jarsun said. "Now you can settle multiple scores with a single battle. Gwann and Vensera and the people of this little republic will have the chance to avenge themselves on Dronas for invading their kingdom and committing his atrocities. While you will face me and seek to avenge your mother's death."

"Murder," she said, her eyes flashing like fireworks were exploding behind them. "Death would be of natural causes. She did not die naturally. She was murdered and betrayed by one closest to her."

"Yes, of course," Jarsun said conversationally. "And I have no doubt that the sons of Shvate —"

"Children of Shvate," Krushni said sharply. "That's the third time you called them 'sons.' They are of more than one gender, the five of them."

Jarsun inclined his head in acknowledgment of his oversight. "The children of Shvate. I have no doubt they will be quite the match for the Krushan Hundred, pitting one set of cousins against another, and setting out to redress the wrong done to their father Shvate, and declaring their arrival upon the theater of the world."

"Your assumptions are accurate for the most part," Krushni said. "Now can we stop bantering, as you said, and get on with this?"

Jarsun raised his wire-thin brows. "Of course, Princess. As I said, war is the primary purpose of human existence. That is why we are all gathered here today. I am always ready for a good battle. There is no better exercise of the mind and body."

He raised one blade-thin hand. "But first, we must introduce the last and most important participant in this conflict."

Dhuryo saw Krushni frown. Even the Shvate siblings exchanged glances, looking as nonplussed as the princess.

Jarsun rubbed his palms together briskly, muttered something in ancient Ashcrit that Dhuryo thought sounded vaguely similar to the ritual chantings of the priests in Hastinaga at stonefire ceremonies, then spread his palms.

Hovering beneath his palms was a glowing black-tinged ball of light.

3

The ball of black light pulsed and glowed.

Jarsun spoke more Ashcrit, spreading his hands wide, then suddenly made a shoving gesture.

The ball broke free of his palms and spun out into empty air. Dhuryo's brothers scattered quickly, distancing themselves from the sorcerous orb. Even though they were all Krushan, they knew that stonefire was no servant to their bloodline. It was its own power, using mortal instruments to accomplish its unimaginable goals in ways that sometimes served the interests of the instruments themselves. Like any sane person, they respected and feared its power. There was soon a space large enough to contain a herd of uks in the center of the arena.

In this space, the black ball of light spun, gaining speed and size. An intense, high-pitched scream rose from it, making the hairs on Dhuryo's body and face prickle with discomfort. The black ball expanded till it was the size of an elephant, then stabilized, slowing.

It irised open to reveal another place, far from the dusty arena and eastern grasslands of Gwannland.

Visible through the portal now was the Burning Throne itself, and seated upon it, the emperor of the Burnt Empire, Adri Krushan.

Yudi

~

IT LOOKS LIKE THE fox has just been outfoxed, brother, Arrow sent to him.

Yudi didn't reply at once. He was still staring at the unseeing dark pits of his uncle's eyes. Emperor Adri was turning his head slowly from side to side, as if examining each of them in turn. He lingered for a moment on Yudi, and Yudi felt the burning sensation in his brain that signaled another Krushan, a close blood relative. He strengthened the walls guarding his thoughts and feelings against the intruding heat. It felt like a white-hot spear was being pushed into his head. Gritting his teeth, he resisted.

Suddenly, the spear disappeared, and he saw the emperor's face continue its circuit, passing over Yudi's siblings, pausing finally on Princess Krushni.

"Princess Krushni of Gwannland," said the emperor of the Burnt Empire.

"King Adri of Hastinaga," said Krushni as politely as if she were greeting another contestant.

"King?" Adri's tone was surprised. "I suppose I am still king of Hastinaga, am I not? Though it's customary to address me by my greater title."

Krushni said nothing in response to that, merely smiled politely.

This is not something we had expected, Arrow sent.

Most definitely not, Yudi admitted. *But as we learned in kul, no battle plan survives actual engagement. We knew our enemies would have tricks up their sleeves.*

Tricks, sure, but this is no trick. This is stonefire sorcery of the highest level. If Emperor Adri is involved in this conflict, that means . . .

Arrow, I know what that means.

Yudi turned to look at Arrow, who nodded, acknowledging, then shrugged. *Okay then, let us see where this goes.*

Yudi turned his attention back to the scene unfolding before them.

"Princess Krushni," Emperor Adri continued, "I hear you have insulted my sons and violated Krushan law."

Krushni's smile broadened. "Have I, now? And here I thought they were the ones who insulted my people and me, and it was they who violated Gwannland law."

Adri made a dismissive noise. "Gwannland is not a recognized entity. No such nation exists."

Krushni raised a brow. "Gwannland has existed in one form or other for seven millennia. Almost as long as there's been a Burnt Empire."

"Hastinaga does not recognize such a nation. Krushan law is the only law that matters."

"In your Burnt Empire, that may be true, King Adri," Krushni said, "but here in Eastern Arthaloka, we have our own laws and customs. You are merely a visitor here — an uninvited guest, as it were — and have no say in what is or is not law."

Emperor Adri spread his arms wide on the arms of the Burning Throne. Behind him, flames of deep blue and greenish hues undulated slowly, curling up and changing shade as they unfurled like war banners on a battlefield.

"I will not banter with you, young woman. Let me state this simply for your benefit. This entire region is now granted to King Dronas by my decree. You and your people may stay on as servants of Dronas or emigrate at once. I address you thus to give you one opportunity to depart peaceably and leave the borders of the kingdom of Dronas. You have until sunrise on the morrow. After that, anyone claiming to be a Gwannlander will be dealt with by Dronas as he sees fit."

Princess Krushni smiled, shaking her head slowly.

Emperor Adri raised his head, his face gripped by an unpleasant frown. "Do you find this amusing, Princess? I am giving you and your people less than a day to leave this land or face death!"

"Oh no," Krushni replied, "I don't this amusing. I find it typical."

"Typical," Adri repeated.

"Yes. Typical of Krushan arrogance. Your high-handed assumption that you are superior to all other peoples and cultures of this vast continent. You think that you have the right to whatever you wish to possess and that you can just take it. As you have done for thousands of years."

Yudi saw Arrow looking at him. Arrow's eyebrows were raised. Yudi didn't respond, but he felt Arrow's admiration of the princess. She had some guts to stand up to the most powerful being in the world, even if she was just telling him the truth.

The emperor sat back in his seat. Behind him, the hues of fire cycled through warmer shades of green and purple, the flames flickering faster.

"The world was a dark and desolate wasteland before the Krushan," Adri said. "My ancestors brought light, culture, organization, civilization to this barbaric continent. We built the world you now live in. What have you Gwannlanders done in all that time?"

"We created all the things you claim to have brought to Arthaloka. You simply stole them from us. When I say us, I don't mean us Gwannlanders, I mean all the ancient aboriginal peoples of Arthaloka. You Krushan came as alien settlers, empowered by the privilege of your otherworldly power, a power drawn from a sentient thing whose motives and goals remain unknown even today. You serve its needs, its drives, selling your souls for the power it gives you and your kin, and use that power to torture, massacre, steal, appropriate, and dispossess countless millions of their lands, their lives, their cultures, their heritage, their history. You are a scourge upon this world, and you come as settlers bent on destroying everything good that you find in our native nations, to replace them with a form of political structure that serves only your base needs and ambitions. It is we who own this land, this world, and you who are the intruders. I task you and all the Krushan to leave Arthaloka, and return whence you came, or face the consequences."

Emperor Adri smiled. The flames around him were dancing deep orange and vermilion now.

"A champion of the people, are you? Seek to give every person a say in the governance of their nation? I have met your kind before, Princess Krushni. You are full of talk and passion, but in the end, you are corrupted as easily as anyone else. If you had come to me to petition for acceptance into the empire, I might have considered acknowledging your puny kingdom and admitting it into the Burnt —"

Dronas spoke out in outrage. "That is not what we agreed, Your Highness. You promised me all of Gwannland as my own kingdom."

"*Silence!*" Adri said.

A small shard of flame shot out from the portal, darting with the speed of a flung dagger at Dronas, who sidestepped it just in time. It struck someone several yards behind him, and the man burst into flames and was incinerated even before he could open his mouth to scream. The ashes fell onto the dust of the arena, dusting the bloodied corpses of the fallen doves. Dronas's temper subsided. He lowered his gaze and stepped back several feet.

"As I was saying," Emperor Adri continued, "I might have considered such a petition had you approached me before Guru Dronas brought his request to me. But now it is too late. I was willing to grant you leave to depart peacefully when this conversation began, but now it is too late for that as well. Krushan law dictates that all those who speak out against the empire must be dealt with severely, without exception. I withdraw my offer to let you and your people leave. It will now be up to King Dronas to deal with you as he sees fit."

If Princess Krushni was alarmed or dismayed at this, she showed no sign of it, Yudi thought. She stood just as tall, proud, and erect, and spoke without a trace of nervousness. *I hope she knows what she's doing,* he thought.

I think she's incredible, Arrow sent. *I wager no one has ever spoken to Uncle Adri this way in his entire life.*

She's a leader of her people, Yudi sent back, *and she just condemned them all to a genocide. I hardly think expressing her sentiments was worth the risk!*

Krushni smiled at Adri. "Your Krushan law means nothing here, neither do your pronouncements. You have no authority here. This is sovereign Gwannland property, and you are trespassing. I think this discussion has outlived its usefulness. Now, it's time for you and your sycophantic sons to leave my people's kingdom."

She raised her hands and chanted. Yudi felt a shock as he recognized the syllables as ancient Ashcrit mantras, similar to the ones Jarsun had invoked when he summoned the portal.

With a sudden deflating sound, the giant orb of the portal collapsed in upon itself, taking with it the Blind Emperor and his Burning Throne.

Krushni

—

1

ENOUGH WAS ENOUGH. SHE had tolerated Adri's presence only in the interests of exploring every possibility. She knew that what was about to happen next would cause the deaths of many of her people, and many more deaths on the enemy's side. The killing was regrettable, but unavoidable. There was no bargaining or negotiating with the Krushan. Their idea of diplomacy was to issue decrees and for their allies to follow the letter of the decrees without question; anything else was a punishable offense. Diplomats who sought fair dealings ended up in the House of Truth.

She looked at Jarsun now. He was chanting furiously, hands held apart. Smoke and light swirled and sparkled between his spread palms, but each time they began to coalesce into something resembling an orb, the structure collapsed. He tried once more, scaly skin glistening with effort, and this time he managed to build an orb and expand it to about the size of a yard's width.

Through the opening portal, she could see the flames of stonefire. They now raged a bright orange, angry red, and glaring yellow, reflecting the wrath of their current occupant. A hand, and then a knee of the emperor became visible, then his robes and the crest of the House of Krushan.

Jarsun breathed in deeply, his anxiety declining as he spread his hands, seeking to expand the orb into a full portal once more.

The orb collapsed again, this time blowing inward into a pinpoint of darkness so suddenly, the resultant force was felt by everyone in the arena, and those in the pavilions, with the impact of an explosion. Even Krushni

felt the air sucked out of her ears, nostrils, and mouth, leaving a ringing tinnitus for a few seconds.

Several of the Krushan Hundred were knocked off their feet, except for
Dhuryo Krushan and some of his brothers. They sprawled on the dust of the
arena, crying out with surprise. Dust swirled, clouding the air for a moment.
She heard Dronas coughing.

When the dust cleared, a new figure stood on the ground of the arena. A
tall, long-bearded male clad in dusty red ochre robes, with intense eyes and
a hooked nose.

"Greetings, Guru Vessa," Krushni said, joining her palms together in a
namas.

2

"Vessa!"

Jarsun spoke the name like a whipcrack.

Vessa met Krushni's eyes, then he turned and looked at Jarsun. He said
nothing.

"I should have known it was your doing! No one else is powerful enough
to countermand my mantras."

Vessa said, "You always did underestimate your enemy, Jarsun Krushan.
It is the failing that will be your downfall."

Jarsun laughed. It was not a pleasant sound. His nictitating eyelids shut-
tered and reopened, tongue tips flickering in the air, dripping viscous white
fluid. Only a few drops fell to the dust of the arena, but the ground sizzled
and burned from the ones that did. A black hole marked where each droplet
landed. "Princess Krushni, as she calls herself in this life, overestimates herself. She has played her hand too soon. She precipitates her own downfall."

Jarsun pointed at Krushni. "You thought you were being very clever,
hosting these games, inviting the sons of Adri and the children of Shvate
to participate. What was your original plan? To set up a confrontation between the cousins, launch a dispute over the right to sit upon the Burning
Throne? Use Dronas as a scapegoat to start a war in this region? To what
end? A war with the Burnt Empire? Do you really think these five bastards

and you and your brother can take on the might of the Krushan? Your naive scheme was doomed to failure. The Krushan Hundred and Dronas alone are sufficient to destroy you seven as well as conquer this puny kingdom. All this will be nothing but ash and corpses within days. You have sealed your own fate."

Krushni said nothing, merely held the polite smile on her face as if enduring a particularly obnoxious petitioner in her mother's court. She knew Jarsun wanted her to respond, so he could engage her in a war of words. She would not give him the satisfaction.

Jarsun pointed at the Five. "You whelps should stayed in the wilderness where you have remained in hiding all these fifteen years with your mother. You could have eked out an existence for a few years more. Neither I nor your uncle Adri were particularly in a hurry to extinguish your lives. You were not worth the effort, especially after this sage used concealing mantras to cloak you from my divination mantras. But instead you chose to show yourselves in the most public way, and to pit yourselves against the very forces that seek to destroy you. By joining this foolish young woman's cause, you have doomed yourselves. None of you will leave this arena alive. You will die as easily as your foolish father."

Krushni saw Brum start forward, a roar of fury bursting from her throat. Arrow and Yudi turned and caught her shoulders, restraining her. Neither of them spoke aloud, but she knew they were addressing her silently through the mindspeak that the five siblings used to communicate mentally with one another. Brum snorted, her barrel chest heaving, but she remained standing where she was. She glared at Jarsun with eyes that sparked hatred.

I feel your pain, cousin. That man deserves to die. Not only for killing your father and my mother but for his many, countless crimes against humanity, and to prevent the further countless crimes he will continue to commit should he not be extinguished. His end will come, I promise you that, but it will be in its time and when the forces all align. Believe me as a sister to another sister.

Brum's eyes flickered and swiveled to look at Krushni. She blinked.

I think she heard me that time, Krushni thought, *or felt the essence of my communication. I believe that in time I will be able to bridge the divide and communicate with all five as easily as they do with each other.*

But that would have to wait. Now she had to pay full attention to the next stage of the plan about to unfold.

3

Vessa said, "Jarsun Krushan, you appear to forget that you and your allies are in our territory now. This is Gwannland soil you tread upon and Gwannland air you breathe, and you are no longer welcome here. You have been asked to leave at once, and I reiterate the order. Depart swiftly and do not return."

Jarsun chuckled. "Sage, it has been so long since we last exchanged words and blows that I forgot how you love to issue commands. Where have you been the past fifteen years? Concealed by the same cloaking mantra that shielded these five whelps from my sight? I expected better of you. We have unfinished business. It will give me great pleasure to settle my scores with you as well here today. All my enemies together in one place! Truly, the princess's naive plan has provided me with a golden opportunity. I can now kill a bush full of birds with a single stone."

Vessa sighed softly. "You always were too proud of your own powers, Jarsun. It was a fault as a boy and one that is so deeply ingrained in you that you have forgotten what it is like to confront one more powerful than yourself. Do you remember your first encounters with me when you were a child? I should say 'brat', because you were a spoiled little brat drunk on your own power and abusing it at every opportunity. You were the equivalent of the boy who tortures pets and little animals only to revel in their suffering. Except that your malice was directed at other children. You used your stonefire-given abilities to bully your own playmates and cousins, feeling no remorse when you caused their deaths or maimed them or worse. The more they suffered, the more you enjoyed it. Because of your status as a prince of the Krushan, there were no consequences of your actions. Your father, Melinger, brother to Sha'ant, was too preoccupied with his own campaign of conquest in the North and West to notice you. You grew up ungoverned and unchecked. And before he could return to correct you, he was slain in battle, making you his heir and putting you in direct line for the Burning Throne, which only increased your power and your boldness. And so you assumed that you were all-powerful and could do anything you pleased to anyone you wished. But that day in the forest, when you were slaughtering every animal in sight, you experienced your first rebuke. Do you remember that day?"

Jarsun's face lost its humor. He hissed softly but said nothing. His eyes bored into Vessa.

"What will you say now? You would rather I never mention that day again. But I must. The world must know that even the greatest evil in existence has a vulnerable side and can be defeated. For that day, Jarsun Krushan was defeated and made to remember that he was not omnipotent and supreme."

Vessa turned to address everyone else in the arena, as well as everyone watching the contest. "That day, I came across a boy in the forest, a boy who was slaughtering every animal of that habitat not for sport or for the royal kitchens, but simply for the joy of murder. I rebuked him as one rebukes any errant child who has gone far beyond the bounds of human decency. I used no power nor mantras to do it, but my own two hands."

Vessa raised his calloused, age-wrinkled hands and turned them to show his palms. He had very large hands, and each palm was the size of a small boy's entire face.

"I slapped him. He was so shocked, he fell back in a pile of dung and burst into tears."

Silence met this revelation. Krushni saw the Krushan Hundred and Dronas trying very hard not to look at either Jarsun or Vessa. They probably would have liked nothing more than to be thirty thousand miles from here, back in Hastinaga Palace.

"I went to see his father, Melinger Krushan, and told him of his son's misdeeds. He was furious. He vowed to punish Jarsun when he returned to Hastinaga. Unfortunately, that day never came. Melinger was killed in battle."

Vessa pointed at Jarsun. "Eventually, your poisonous blood showed itself and cost you the throne, Jarsun. You were exiled by the elders and forbidden from ever ascending the throne. And ever since then, you have dedicated your life to battling the Krushan, your own family, and regaining the very seat of power that you were disinherited from."

Jarsun had remained silent. He now shook his head, face slitted with a grim smile. "You are wrong, old man. I have no quarrel with the current generation of Krushan. They are my blood kin. As you can see for yourself, I am here in alliance with Emperor Adri and his sons. They have accepted me and acknowledged the unfair treatment I received at the hands of their ancestors. I wish them no ill will. All I seek is my rightful inheritance restored."

"And how will you achieve that with Adri still upon the throne?"

Jarsun smiled but did not answer.

Vessa turned to look at Dhuryo Krushan, addressing him directly. "The only way Jarsun can sit upon the Burning Throne is if he eliminates your father, you, and all your brothers as well as your one sister."

Dhuryo Krushan crossed his arms and raised his chin to look down at Vessa, but said nothing.

Vessa turned back to Jarsun. "You insinuated yourself into Adri's confidence somehow. But he does not know that it was you who orchestrated the attack on him and his beloved Sauvali years ago."

Jarsun kept smiling. "Wrong again, old man. That was the work of the mother of these whelps in cohorts with a traitor in the emperor's own palace."

Vessa shook his head. "You can lie, you can change your appearance with sorcery, you can assassinate and murder, but you will never achieve your goal, Jarsun Krushan. The Burning Throne will never be yours to possess. It is beyond your reach."

"Why are you so concerned with what I do or do not achieve, sage? Concern yourself with the crisis you and your wards now face. You successfully shielded these five whelps and their mother from me. Now they are out in the open, and I will gut them all like rabbits for a cookfire. As for this ingrate who calls herself princess of Gwannland, she and her brother in this life will both share the same fate. That is all you need concern yourself with."

Vessa spread his palms. "Do you plan to fight us here and now? In this arena today? If so, then let us have at it. I tire of exchanging words with you, Jarsun Krushan. The more you speak, the more lies and deception spill out of your vile lips."

Jarsun laughed. "You would like that, wouldn't you? For the principals in this conflict to all confront each other in a single clash, pitting us directly against one another. Simple. Direct. Conclusive. But that is not how empires are won and built. There are many more players in this game than you are aware of. What is at stake here is not the ill-conceived plan of an immature young princess and five children of the jungle. It's the fate of Arthaloka itself."

Vessa raised his bushy eyebrows. "You think too highly of yourself. This is a simple family disagreement. Let it be settled by family. The rest of the world has nothing to do with it."

"That is where you are wrong. For this family is the Krushan family. And our home is the whole world. We are destined to rule the entire continent. The Burnt Empire as its borders stand today covers more than half of the world. I intend to bring the rest of the world under our aegis."

Jarsun turned and addressed the spectators at large. "I, Jarsun Krushan, God-Emperor of the Reygistan and Morgol Empires, join forces today with Emperor Adri Krushan, ruler of the Burnt Empire, and willingly subsume my territories to Hastinaga. Henceforth, all my realms will be included in the Burnt Empire!"

4

Krushni gritted her teeth. With those two empires added to the Burnt Empire, most of Eastern and Southeastern Arthaloka would come under the control of the Burning Throne. Only the wild jungle peninsula of Aranya and a few remote corners of the continent would remain unsecured. With that single pronouncement, Jarsun had doubled the size of the world's largest empire. Over two thirds of the known world now bowed to the blind king of Hastinaga, Emperor Adri.

Jarsun turned to look at her. She straightened her face, determined not to let him see her irritation. But Jarsun saw it anyway. She saw the look of satisfaction in his serpentine eyes.

"That leaves only this tiny but rebellious region upon whose ground we stand," Jarsun said, speaking to the crowd but looking at her. "In anticipation of your resistance, and on my advice, Emperor Adri authorized the armies of the Burnt Empire to secure the authority of Hastinaga and eliminate any opposition. Even as I speak these words, the greatest armed force in the world approaches your little kingdom of New Gwannland. Any attempts at resistance are in vain. Suffice it to say that every rebel of Gwannland who dares challenge the authority of the Burnt Empire is now outnumbered by a factor of several thousand to one."

He raised his arms and turned slowly to execute a full circle. "Surrender now and submit your lives to the authority of Hastinaga, or face extinction. That is your only choice. I was authorized to give your people until tomorrow morn to flee into permanent exile, but your beloved Princess Krushni cost you that reprieve. Her hasty words and ill-planned actions have denied you your only opportunity to buy yourselves more time. Now you are all doomed."

Krushni knew this was a lie. Even if she had taken the "reprieve" and fled with the entire population of New Gwannland, the armies of Hastinaga would have hunted them down and slaughtered them, every last man, woman, and child. But Jarsun was the consummate liar, which made him the perfect politician. He made dying tomorrow seem like freedom.

"And now," Jarsun said, "my kin and I will take our leave. We depart this so-called 'contest' and go to prepare ourselves for battle. I suggest you do the same, Princess Krushni."

Jarsun's eyes settled on the Shvate siblings. "And you, offspring of Shvate, are welcome to join their fate as well, if you seek early deaths. It will be quicker and simpler than living your lives in hiding, never knowing when or where or how I will find you and finish what I started when I killed your father."

Brum roared again, and this time even her brothers made no attempt to stop her.

She rushed at Jarsun again, but before she could reach him, he laughed and gestured.

An invisible wall blocked Brum's way, stopping her dead in her tracks. She battered at it with her fists, hammering furiously.

Jarsun gestured and built another orb from sorcery, expanding it quickly until it was large enough for an entire company to pass through. Krushni could see green grassland on the far side of the portal. Jarsun beckoned to the Krushan Hundred, and they went through the portal quickly. Dronas followed. Jarsun was the last to go. He paused, looking back at Krushni directly. She sent him a message of pure hatred through her eyes.

Jarsun laughed one last time and passed through the portal. It irised until it was reduced to a pinpoint, then disappeared.

Adri

~

THE BITTERSWEET SCENT OF jameen preceded Jarsun's arrival. Adri was expecting him. Stonefire had whispered it into his ears. The Burning Throne had had much to tell him after the abruptly aborted dialogue through the portal.

When he had been cut off in midsentence, Adri had felt rage flare within him like wildfire. He had wanted to demand that he be transported directly to Gwannland, to use the power of stonefire to burn down that impudent upstart Krushni and everyone who stood with her.

The throne had talked him down.

It had whispered into his ears, telling him — no, more than that, *showing* him — everything that transpired after he had been cut off from Jarsun and the rest. It had flashed into his mind's eye the complete scenario of what had been said, by whom and to whom.

When it ended with Jarsun reopening the portal and sending Adri's sons and Dronas through, then stepping through it himself, Adri had been filled with another flash of anger. How was it that Jarsun had been able to open a portal now, when he could not keep it open the first time? Stonefire had posed the question. It had caused Adri to stop and consider the implications.

How indeed?

What if, the throne had whispered into his mind, what if Jarsun himself had caused the portal to close, deliberately cutting Adri off in midsentence?

"Why?" Adri asked aloud. The courtiers in the throne room heard him speak but did not react. They were habituated to the emperor's one-sided dialogues. None of them ever spoke of it to anyone else, not even to each other. The price for that would be instant death, not from being overheard by spies or being ratted out by one of their own, but by the throne itself.

Even though the turnover of staff in the throne room was high and almost none lasted more than a few weeks, there were a rare few who had survived service in this cursed chamber for several years. It was even rumored that one courtier had lived long enough to retire comfortably on the handsome income he earned merely from being known as the emperor's personal staff. No one had actually met him, but the rumor persisted. Each hoped to live that long, even though they had seen enough of their number incinerated on the spot for far lesser transgressions than speaking of the emperor behind his back.

But when they were on duty and these one-sided dialogues occurred, they could also sense the screeching, hair-raising sound just beyond the limits of human hearing that they knew was the throne itself speaking. In what language, by what means — how could a rock speak at all? — they knew not. It put the fear of the stone gods into their hearts, and they shivered in their boots as they stood at their posts, praying to Mother Jeel that she would let them live long enough to go home to their children and their spouses when their duty was done for the day.

This time, the dialogue was particularly intense. The voice of stonefire, if it could be called be that, was especially grating, like a pair of ice-cold needles inserted into the brain from either side, seeking out and puncturing nerve endings and blood vessels. They endured the almost soundless shrieking as a homeless person might endure a storm, praying only that it would pass and they would still be alive when it had gone.

To undermine your authority, stonefire said to Adri, in answer to his question.

Adri mulled on that. These dialogues with the throne were not straightforward ones. Most of the time, stonefire said things that made very little sense to him, often it spoke what sounded like gibberish. But of late, it had become more coherent, seemingly adapting to his mind and vocabulary to articulate clearer messages.

"Why would he do that?" Adri asked aloud. The question echoed in the vast chamber, faint reverberations sounding in the distant eaves of the high ceiling.

His goals are not your goals.

Adri thought about that. On the face of it, it was self-evident. Jarsun had his own agenda, and that agenda was transparent. He wanted the throne. But so long as Adri sat upon the Burning Throne, no one could unseat him by ordinary means. Stonefire did not pit one Krushan against another; it chose one or the other. The only exception in history had been when it accepted both Adri and his brother Shvate, making them the first Krushan to rule jointly. With Shvate's death, only Adri remained. Jarsun could not simply assassinate him to gain the Burning Throne; stonefire would not tolerate it. The Burning Throne was called so for a reason: anyone who sat upon it had to pass the Test of Fire. If the throne found them unworthy, it incinerated them on the spot. Jarsun would not risk such a fate. The only way he could seek the throne was by aligning himself with one accepted by stonefire. As of now, that was Adri and Adri alone. So what would Jarsun gain by plotting against him?

Adri was still mulling over this question when the bittersweet scent of poisonous nightflower filled his nostrils. He raised his head, sensing the presence that had arrived through the sorcerous portal.

"Waywalker," he said.

"I have not been called that name for a very long time," Jarsun said, sounding amused. "Where did you hear it?"

Adri tilted his head to indicate a shrug. "One of the elder wet nurses, some old woman reminiscing about bygone days of yore. She said you were nicknamed so after your mother found you missing from your bedchamber night after night. They finally discovered that you had learned to pry open portals to other worlds, other ages, and were exploring them nightly. Waywalking, as it was called in past ages."

Jarsun's voice moved as he walked around the throne. His footfalls were soft, barely audible, but the acoustics of the throne chamber were designed to direct every sound, every whisper to the one seated upon stonefire. Adri could follow his every move without having to turn his head. "It is as you say. I discovered waywalking accidentally. It was the discovery that changed my life."

"They say every Krushan possesses the ability from birth."

"Yet few use it. The elders discourage it, and everyone in Hastinaga is forbidden to speak of it to the young. Entire generations grow up without ever hearing or knowing about it. Without constant practice and expert guidance, the ability to waywalk is quickly forgotten. This suits the purpose of the elders."

"How so?" Adri had not desired a discussion on the intricacies of waywalking; he was only using the conversation to try to work through what he had been thinking about when Jarsun arrived. Sometimes a person allowed more information to escape while talking about unrelated matters than when questioned pointedly. Maybe by understanding Jarsun a little better, he could understand his real motives. Know your friends; know your enemies even better. He had no illusion that Jarsun was truly his well-wisher. It was merely expedient for the two of them to be aligned. For now. What would happen after that?

"Waywalking is one of the most powerful gifts of the Krushan. There are paths that can lead one to unimaginable riches and wonders, and also darker ways, paths that lead to places from which there is no return."

"Did you go down such paths?"

Jarsun paused. "I did not know what I was doing at first. I believed I was dreaming. But there was one night when I wandered into a realm that . . ." He broke off. "Suffice it to say that there are places in the universe that are not meant to be explored. By anyone."

"Was that what changed you, Uncle?" Adri asked with the perfect tone of innocent curiosity.

"Changed." Jarsun mulled the word. "Shifted my consciousness, yes. It moved me from assuming that this physical plane is all that exists to a state of being where one accepts that there are more dimensions and hues to what we call reality than can be experienced by the senses alone."

Adri was not sure what that meant. To avoid a philosophical diversion, he asked, "Is that what made you turn to dark sorcery?"

Jarsun sounded amused when he spoke again: "Urrkh sorcery. The forbidden arts. Yes. I found that Krushan law has its limits. The only way to transcend it is to go beyond them."

"So you broke the laws of our people, then?"

"We are Krushan. We make the law."

Adri did not comment on that. "That is how you gained your powers, then? By the use of urrkh sorcery?"

"Even the most potent sorcery cannot imbue someone with powers they do not possess to begin with. All I did was enhance my abilities. It is no different from using a tool, or a weapon, instead of one's bare hands."

"Tools do not infest one's mind. Weapons don't corrupt the soul."

"Infest. Corrupt. You speak of it as if it were a disease."

"Isn't it? The scrolls speak of urrkh sorcery as being the downfall of many ancients, even some of our own ancestors. None who used it ever prospered or thrived. It leaches one's rational mind of all reason, driving one insane over time."

Jarsun said, amused, "Do I seem insane to you, nephew?"

"You pursue your own path."

"Doesn't everyone? Don't you?"

"Are our paths the same?"

"Why must they be? All that matters is that they are headed in the same direction."

"One can reach the same destination by different roads, different means."

"The end is the same, is it not? Total domination of the world by the Burnt Empire. You become the first Krushan to unite all Arthaloka under the aegis of the Burning Throne, bringing the light of civilization and Krushan law to the dark barbaric outposts of the continent. Your name will be engraved upon the scrolls of history forever."

"Is that your goal as well?"

"It is for now."

"And once it is achieved, then what will you seek?"

"A fair share."

"What will that be? You have never spelled out what you seek to gain from our alliance, Uncle."

"We are family. Blood kin. Your gain is my gain. I am content being the orchestrator of your rise, nephew."

"What of you personally? What is your ambition?"

"I have told you already."

"Yes, but will you be content with merely seeing me reign over all Arthaloka?"

"I will."

"How can I believe that? You must want something more."

"What more is there?"

"Power. Glory. Your name above all others. The usual things that mortals desire."

"I will have all that and more merely by being there by your side, accomplishing the conquest of the untamed regions."

"So you will be my general? My regent? My mentor? My guardian?"

"I will be what I am now: your uncle. Jarsun Krushan."

Adri was silent for a long moment. Then he said, "Why did you allow the portal to Gwannland to close before I was finished speaking?"

"I was unable to keep it open. Vessa arrived."

"Vessa?" Adri had not expected this. He inhaled. "I thought you were the most powerful Krushan alive."

"Vessa is a waywalker, perhaps the most accomplished. He also ages differently, living on a different timeline from the rest of us. He has been waywalking far longer, and learned many more things than I have. Sometimes knowledge and insight outweigh power."

"I see. He bested you, then?"

Jarsun made a scoffing sound. "He knows a few tricks more than I, in some matters. In others, I know things that he cannot or will not attempt." Jarsun paused. "It was unfortunate, showed disrespect to you. That was as he intended."

"Vessa is my forebear, he fathered me."

"Yet he showed disrespect for you. In case you have not noticed, he follows his own agenda as well. Do not forget that he was the one who assassinated your brother Shvate in his forest hut."

He lies, stonefire said to Adri's mind. Adri heard Jarsun's footfalls halt abruptly and sensed the older man raising his head and looking around, his robes whispering. Adri knew that as a Krushan elder, Jarsun heard more and understood better what the throne said, but he could not decipher the exact words, as they were addressed solely to Adri.

Adri did not press Jarsun on the matter of Shvate's death. It was history, and he was more concerned with the here and now. "What transpired in Gwannland after I was cut off?"

"It went as we expected. I have declared your intentions against Gwannland and the East. Our armies move into position as we speak."

Adri nodded slowly, using the gesture to think. "It is impressive, the way you transported millions of our troops, animals, and equipment across tens of thousands of miles in an instant. My people say that it would normally have taken several years, perhaps even a decade to move them that far across the continent."

"I merely opened a portal large enough for them to pass through. It was like opening a door."

"As I said, it was impressive. The sheer logistics of transporting our forces across that great distance was the main hurdle keeping us from completing our conquest of the continent all these many centuries. You accomplished it within days."

"As I said, nephew, our interests are aligned. I want nothing more than to see the Burnt Empire cover the entire known world."

"Even if it replaces your own Reygistan Empire and Morgol Empire?"

"Those were placeholders, intended to secure the territories until the time came for Hastinaga to recognize me and accept my claims."

"Your claim to the throne, you mean? You know that the elders have still not acknowledged it as yet. I have no power over their decision."

"Their decision is irrelevant. Possession is all that matters under Krushan law. Dowager Empress Jilana and Prince Regent Vrath can spend the rest of their lives in council debating the legalities of my claim, they cannot deny the real contribution I have made today to the empire."

"Still, even once we have conquered all Arthaloka, it does not mean they will accept you — or embrace you."

Jarsun laughed, a hollow sound. "I care not for their acceptance or their embrace. They are obsolete specimens who follow a bygone moral code. Their views are worthless. You, Adri, are the emperor. Only your word matters."

Adri could not argue that. He had the power to bypass the elders and make his own rulings if he so chose; the authority of the emperor was absolute. The will of the elders was just that, their will. He could not be compelled to obey it nor constrained by its strictures.

"So now we go to war?" he said.

"We go to war," Jarsun agreed.

"And the children of Shvate are engaged in the conflict?"

"They stand by Princess Krushni, as does Vessa."

Adri frowned. The presence of Vessa on the side of the enemy was a new,

unexpected wrinkle. He would have to consult the throne on that question after Jarsun departed. There were nuances and subtleties here that he
needed to explore further. Most of all, the nagging question of Jarsun's true
intentions, which he had not deciphered yet.

"Was she present?"

Jarsun knew whom he meant. "Your sister-in-law Princess Karni was not
present at the time, but I have no doubt that wherever her children are, she
cannot be far. She will show herself before long."

"And you remember my instructions for dealing with her?"

"To be brought in chains before you, to be questioned by you personally."

And by stonefire, said stonefire. The words sent a chill into Adri's heart.
He had witnessed stonefire "questioning" suspected traitors before. Those
were times he was glad he was sightless.

"Then go with the stone gods and crush our enemies into the dust," Adri
said.

"So shall it be," Jarsun replied. "Allow me to take your leave, my emperor."

Adri gestured dismissively.

A moment later, Jarsun was gone, leaving behind only the remnants of
energy from the portal he had stepped through, and the scent of jameen.

And so it begins, Adri thought.

And so it ends, stonefire sang.

Part Two

The Beginning of the End

Brum

~

1

FROM THE RAMPART OF New Gwann Palace, Brum watched the armies of the Krushan approaching.

She could see almost thirty miles out. New Gwannland was a small country, barely a hundred miles in length by eighty miles wide. On the east, it ended at the ocean. To the north and south, it was bounded by hostile nations allied to the Reygistan and Morgol Empires, both of which were controlled by Jarsun. To the west, Dronasthan. The population of New Gwannland was barely a hundred thousand souls, the fraction that survived when its homeland was overrun by Dronas and the Krushan Hundred three years ago.

Our cousins were barely twelve at the time, when they aided their guru in the pillaging and ravaging of Gwannland. That might have seemed ludicrous to ordinary folk, those fortunate few who lived most of their lives without seeing war: she wondered at times if such people even existed. Perhaps to them, twelve might seem too young.

In fact, at twelve, most Krushan were veterans of violent combat. The Krushan brothers had been champions, possessed of the unfair advantage of their extraordinary talents as well as their privileged education, training, and command of any resources they desired. They had run through a nation of five million in days, slaughtering almost a tenth of that population — a task in which Dronas and his notorious Dronasthan guards had performed the bulk of the massacre — and terrorizing the rest into surrendering, forced to choose their lives over an illusory freedom.

Only this small minority, the remnants of the armed forces and their families and relatives, had had the courage to accompany Gwann and Vensera and a few high-born loyal to them into this far corner of the continent. They lived on this sliver of land, poised between the prospect of another invasion from the West and the looming threat of Jarsun's imperial ambitions in the North and South. Every day for the past three years, they had known that someday Dronas would invade again, finishing the task he had begun. That day had finally arrived.

Except that this time, the odds were not merely insurmountable, but absolutely absurd.

As Brum watched the seething horizon churn dust clouds the size of mountain ranges, she cursed Dronas, her cousin Dhuryo, her uncle Emperor Adri, and her evil great-uncle Jarsun. They were so power dazed that they had to send a giant to crush a beetle. How many strong was that Krushan army gathering out there? A million? Five million? Ten? It was beyond comprehension. Jarsun had said they would be outnumbered a thousand to one; at the time, Brum had thought he was exaggerating as warlords always did in the old legends Guru Vessa had taught her and her siblings. But now she saw that he had meant it literally. For every warrior that New Gwannland fielded, including children of fighting age, the old, the disabled, and the infirm, the Burnt Empire had sent a thousand fighting-fit warriors fully equipped, with armored horse cavalry, elephants, chariots, regiments of archers, and Mother Jeel knew what else.

"Stone Father!" Brum said, spitting liberally over the top of the rampart.

Beside her, Saha cleared her throat. "There are other levels below this one. With soldiers manning the lookout."

"Oh," Brum said, blinking. She peered over the edge, trying to see through the crenellated arrow slits. "Sorry!" she called out sheepishly.

"This really is overkill," Saha said, meaning the Krushan army.

"You think?" Brum said bitterly.

"This isn't what we expected when Mother told us to come east."

Brum sighed. "To be fair, Guru Vessa did say to be prepared for anything."

"Sure, but this, Brum? This is beyond impossible. No matter what we do, a lot of people are going to die."

Saha indicated the city below them. "City" was too strong a word for what was essentially a very large town, with only the palace and a few dozen permanent buildings clustered together. The farther houses and structures were little more than temporary cottages, sheds, and even tented housing. Three years was not a great deal of time to rebuild a city, let alone a nation. "They don't stand a chance. This will be a massacre."

"Genocide, more like it," Brum said. "That bastard Dronas means to finish the job he started. He won't stop until every last Gwannlander is dead or driven into the ocean." She paused. "Which is the same thing, isn't it? I mean, Coldheart Sea isn't exactly a warm pond one can take a dip in. Even the bluebellies swim south for the winter so their young don't freeze at birth."

"Coldheart Sea is to the north of Arthaloka, Brum. To the south is Mother of Seas. Here on the east coast, I think it's called just 'ocean.'"

"Well, I suppose I wasn't paying attention to Guru Vessa during our geography lessons, but my point is there's no way to run from here. Whatever happens in New Gwannland, stays in New Gwannland. And I mean that in the sense of a death trap."

"I hear you, sis. But that's why we're here, isn't it? To do our best to save as many as possible."

"'As possible' being the key words, Saha. What are we supposed to do?"

"I guess we fight."

Brum snorted. "You know I like a fight as much as anybody. Well, probably *more* than anybody. I really like fighting. But this isn't a fight. This is a mountain being used to crush a pebble."

Saha took a deep breath and released it slowly. "I hear you. But I have faith in Guru Vessa." After a moment, she added, "And Princess Krushni."

At the mention of Krushni, Brum grew thoughtful. "She's quite something, isn't she?"

Saha turned to look at her sister, a sly smile lighting up her face. "My, my. Is our little Brum infatuated? You are, aren't you? You're totally smitten by her!"

"Shut up," Brum said furiously, her rounded cheeks turning pink.

Saha laughed, put her arms around Brum's neck — which took some doing, since Brum's neck was the size of some people's waists — and squeezed affectionately. "My little sister is in love!"

"Shut up before I punch you so hard it sends you flying out to land on your butt in the middle of that Krushan army out there," Brum said, still blushing.

Someone cleared their throat behind them.

The pair turned to see Arrow trying very hard to keep a straight face.

"War council," they said.

2

Brum was the last to enter. The chamber served as throne room, court, and council hall for the nascent kingdom of New Gwannland and was modest by any standard. Every seat but one was taken. Apart from herself and her four siblings, there were Tshallian, Guru Vessa, Princess Krushni, Prince Drishya, Queen Vensera, King Gwann, and several others she didn't recognize at all but who were clad in the colorful garb of Gwannlanders. Yudi frowned at her as she slipped into the empty seat between Arrow and Saha.

Queen Vensera was speaking. "That Dronas would attack us someday, we knew already. What we did not expect, could not expect, was that the Krushan would support his cause so openly."

Vessa said, "The Krushan have always supported him. He is guru to the royal princes. Their involvement is not entirely unforeseen."

"By you, perhaps, great one," Vensera said. "You are a master of *Auma* and a legendary walker between worlds and times. Our resources and knowledge are limited. All we knew was that Dronas had asked Emperor Adri for the use of his sons for a military campaign, as payment of their guru debt. That is not the same thing as officially sending the entire Krushan army to destroy us."

Vessa inclined his fierce face to acknowledge Vensera's words. "What you say is true, Queen Vensera. Yet it is no secret that the Burnt Empire has sought to complete its conquest of the continent for many generations without success. Until now, no Krushan was powerful enough to open and sustain a portal that could bear the transport of such a great army. Without a waywalker's help, the physical journey and supply chains would have cost the Burnt Empire decades and risked exposing Hastinaga itself to attack.

With constant unrest in the Western and Northern regions, no Krushan emperor could undertake such a campaign and risk losing the seat of the empire and, most of all, the throne itself."

"And now, with Jarsun's help, the impossible has become possible," Vensera said sadly, "but what I do not understand is why he would join his cause to theirs. It was my understanding that he was a sworn enemy of the Burnt Empire until now. After all, it was the refusal of the elders to acknowledge that his daughter Krushita passed the Test of Fire and was worthy of the Burning Throne that caused his declaration of war against the Burnt Empire. It was to build an army of his own capable of taking on the Krushan that he undertook his own campaign of conquest of the Desert and Eastern regions. He is an emperor in his own right now."

"A *God*-Emperor," King Gwann pointed out.

"Indeed," Vensera continued. "He has built a formidable empire of his own. He even fought and lost to your own late father, Prince Shvate, who took back Reygar and part of Reygistan by force almost two decades ago, which territory Shvate regained after the Krushan army withdrew. Subsequent to Shvate's passing, no Krushan has dared to come east or south to challenge Jarsun's dominance. He is the undisputed lord and master of this entire part of Arthaloka. In time, he could have mounted his own invasion of Hastinaga, and he might well have succeeded."

"Indeed, he could have," Vessa agreed. "For Emperor Adri, who was once a strong prince and a leader of armies equivalent to his brother Shvate, has long since fallen into a dark pool of depression since a personal tragedy befell him some fifteen years ago." Vessa looked at the five siblings. "For which he believes — falsely, I add — your own mother was responsible."

Brum frowned. This was news to her.

Don't fret about it, Brum, Arrow sent. *It is probably Jarsun's own doing. We knew he's been seeding lies and fake truths for years.*

Vessa looked at Arrow and nodded once.

Indeed, it is so, young Arrow. It was Jarsun who seeded the lie that your mother, Karni, was behind the attack on Emperor Adri and his lover Sauvali. In fact, the perpetrator was Jarsun himself.

Brum blinked rapidly. *Guru Vessa can mindspeak to us? All of us? Can he mindspeak with anyone he pleases?*

Brum, Arrow, would you two keep it down, please? We're trying to hear what they're saying. Aloud, I mean, Yudi sent. *We can ask Guru all the questions we like after the council.*

Vensera, who was not privy to these silent mind exchanges, was saying, "... then why would Jarsun retreat from his aggressive stand and join forces with Hastinaga suddenly? It makes no sense to me. After all, it is the same Hastinaga which he declared war against, the same elders who denied him his inheritance. That they were right to do so is not in dispute, as Jarsun was exiled and cast out of the Krushan forever. But from what I know, Jarsun believed he still had a claim to the throne and was willing to fight for it, no matter how long it took or how much damage he caused. What changed?"

Vessa nodded slowly. "A good question, Queen Vensera. In truth, nothing changed. Jarsun remains as determined as ever to assert his claim and sit upon the Burning Throne. He still vows vengeance against the elders, and they still stand by their rejection of his claim. Neither party has changed their stance."

"Then what prompted Jarsun to join his enemies now?" King Gwann asked.

"Perhaps it would best to hear from someone with a vested interest in that question," Vessa said. "With your permission, Queen Vensera, I would like to open a portal to allow these parties to join us briefly for this part of the council."

Vensera looked surprised. So did Gwann and the other Gwannlanders, whom Brum supposed must be ministers or generals or both.

"You wish to summon strangers here from another kingdom?" Gwann asked, half rising to his feet. "Is that not dangerous?"

"Are they hostile to us in any way?" Queen Vensera added.

Vessa shook his head once. "If anything, they are sympathetic to our cause. I cannot say they are on our side, due to the complex nature of their political predicament, as you will surely understand yourself, but they are not hostile. Of that, I give you my personal assurance."

Vensera and Gwann exchanged a glance. Vensera looked at Krushni as well. Brum felt a flush of heat in her chest as Krushni nodded, smiling reassuringly.

She is beautiful, Brum thought. *And not just in face and body. There is something about her that is so completely captivating, I can't take my eyes off her.*

"We are in your hands, Guru Vessa," Queen Vensera said. "We trust your wisdom. If you feel these visitors are necessary for our war council, then we give you leave to summon them."

"Their presence is essential," Vessa replied. "Thank you for your leave."

Without further ado, the guru gestured, drawing obscure Ashcrit symbols in the air. Their outlines sparkled, leaving a trail of glittering motes, as he chanted softly.

Brum felt her hairs and nerve endings prickle as some unseen energy sparked in the chamber.

With a rush of air and an unfamiliar scent, a portal irised open in midair. It expanded to an oblong shape, from the floor to about nine or ten feet in height. Through it, she glimpsed an opulent chamber with a level of luxury she had never seen before or heard of except in scrolls. Two figures, both dressed in rich, luxuriant robes and wearing ornate gold and platinum jewelry, stepped through the portal and into the throne chamber of Gwann Palace.

3

Guru Vessa closed his open hand and the portal irised shut. Only the perfumed scents of the distant location lingered. And the two tall figures.

Brum looked up at them curiously.

One was a woman much older than Brum's mother. She was darkskinned, almost ebony, and her wild head of hair had been tamed by gold needles crowned by a jeweled tiara. Her face was exquisitely boned, with angular features and eyes almost diagonally raised at the ends. Her manner and bearing were equally sharp and angular; she moved with an imperious air, a woman long accustomed to being the unchallenged ruler of all she surveyed.

The other was a man with long, flowing tresses of ivory-white hair, and a beard that accentuated the heavy, handsome ridges and bumps of his face. His head was large even in proportion to his body, and he was one of the tallest men Brum had seen, almost as tall as Tshallian the Vanjhani. He loomed over the chamber, dominating it with his physical presence and that indefinable sense of banked power.

This is a demigod, Brum sent to her siblings, not even aware she was mind-speaking. *Isn't he?*

Kula said, *I think that's our great-uncle Vrath. His father was Krushan, but his mother was Mother Goddess Jeel herself. He's said to be the most powerful Krushan alive.*

And the lady is most definitely our great-grandmother Jilana, Vessa's mother, Saha added. *Um, she's mortal, isn't she?*

Yes to both, sent Yudi. *Now could you keep it down while we focus on the council?*

Saha sent to Brum privately, *What's the point of being able to communicate without other people knowing if you can't do it with other people around?*

Brum grinned at Saha. *Even when he was a little tyke, Yudi always spent more time listening to the gurus at council than playing with us. I think he should have been born with a beard!*

Saha buried her laughter with her hand, turning it into a cough. One of Tshallian's heads looked at her curiously, then shook itself and turned its attention back to the discussion.

"I give you Dowager Empress Jilana and Prince Regent Vrath of Hastinaga," Vessa said to the chamber at large.

There was a moment of awestruck silence.

Yudi broke the silence when he rose to his feet and approached the two imposing figures.

"Grandmother, Uncle," he said, performing a namas with his head bowed low, "I am Yudi, son of Shvate and Karni. These are my siblings, Arrow, Brum, Kula, Saha."

Brum and her siblings rose and bowed low as well, greeting their elders with a namas.

Both Vrath and Jilana looked at the five with frank curiosity and a certain warmth that Brum found encouraging. While she lacked Yudi's deep insight into the inner workings of people's minds and motives, and Kula's acuity for reading a person's intentions through their body language, she didn't need either talent to tell that here were two people with genuine affection for herself and her siblings.

"The children of Shvate, Karni, and Mayla," Jilana said, going to each one of them in turn and looking them over closely. Brum smiled shyly upward when Jilana stopped before her. Jilana was an imposing, impressive woman.

As a young child, when Brum had first learned the words "emperor" and "empress," and the power they wielded, she had formed a certain idea in her mind of what they might look like. Jilana fulfilled and even exceeded her expectation of what an empress ought to be. She marveled at the much older woman's prominent cheekbones and angular, striking features.

"You are beautiful, Great-Grandmother," she said instinctively.

Yudi sighed mentally. He didn't approve of Brum, or any of them, speaking their minds to people without knowing where their loyalties lay. Brum didn't care: this wasn't just any new person. Jilana and Vrath were family. And Brum was Brum.

Jilana's stern face softened in a smile. "And you are lovely, young Brum. I have heard great things about you from your grandfather Vessa. About all of you," she said, sweeping her gaze across Brum's siblings.

Vrath remained standing where he was, looking down from his vaulting height at each of them in turn with what Brum assumed was his natural resting expression. Despite his imposing size and formidable aura of power and authority, he seemed not unkind to her. When he looked at her directly for a moment, she saw that his eyes were a bluish grey, almost the color of clear water.

The demimortal son of Mother Jeel herself, Brum thought, awestruck. Their mother had talked about Great-Uncle Vrath and his adventures with a tone of voice that she used only when reciting legends and myths from the age of the stone gods. She could feel the power rolling off him in waves, like heat off a desert floor. When she looked into his eyes, it felt like looking into the river Jeel itself: on the surface it seemed calm and blue, but the longer you peered, the more you sensed the darker undercurrents and the movement of unidentifiable creatures. She swallowed nervously. She was glad he was on their side. At least, well, she thought he was. Wasn't he?

As if sensing Brum's anxiety, his eyes turned a warmer blue, glinting with a light like a sunset refracting off the river on a warm summer's day.

He lowered his great shaggy head an inch, still holding her gaze.

It felt like a smile and an assent.

4

"You are wondering if we are here as allies or enemies," Dowager Empress Jilana said.

Her words were clipped and precise, like everything else about her: her hair, her garb, her accessories, her manner. There was nothing loose or relaxed about this woman, Brum thought. She was completely in control. Although Brum had learned that could often be a disguise people wore to conceal their inner messes, in Great-Grandmother Jilana's case, it seemed to be true.

"I will start by setting your minds at rest. We are not hostile to you." Her gaze swept the chamber, pausing on the five siblings briefly, then moving on to Queen Vensera, King Gwann, Drishya, and Krushni. "We have no enmity with you. If anything, we would gladly extend the flower offering of friendship."

She means the traditional Krushan offering of a metal platter piled with flowers, Yudi sent to his siblings. Neither Brum nor her siblings commented. They were accustomed to Yudi interjecting stray trivial observations of etiquette, tradition, history, lore, and any other relevant, or even irrelevant detail, that he felt would broaden their perspective. To his credit, Yudi did spend an awful lot of time poring over scrolls or, as was more often the case in their largely forest-bound childhood, listening to the oral recitations of the forest hermits who carried the vast library of collective knowledge in their heads, passing it on to anyone who asked, expecting nothing more than something to eat and perhaps a place to rest their heads overnight.

"But our hands are tied by the actions and intentions of young Emperor Adri, and his sons."

Young Adri? Brum sent to Saha. *She makes Uncle Adri sound like he's our age!*

She's old, Saha said, always empathetic to others, even more when it came to those unlike herself. *To her, we're probably newborns.*

"For reasons we find difficult to understand, Adri has chosen to ally himself with his distant cousin, whom he terms 'Uncle' Jarsun. Despite being aware of our strictures against Jarsun, and his banishment from the family and Hastinaga, Adri has begun communicating with him privately. To what end, we are as yet unaware, although we have some theories."

Jilana glanced at Vrath as she said the last part.

He inclined his leonine head. "We believe, based on Jarsun's claims and challenges, that young Adri believes that by joining forces with the Exiled One, he can become the first emperor of the Krushan to take control of the entire continent. This is a delusion, for an empire is not gained by conquest alone. Any king can lead a great army to subjugate distant nations. The real task begins after the conquest, in the work of building trade and cultural relationships with those remote territories, encouraging and facilitating commerce and the transport of people freely between the capital and the satellite nations, building a symbiotic bond that will endure over centuries and millennia.

"Empires can be hastily erected overnight, and torn down just as speed-ily. It is administration, trade, and mutually profitable exchanges of ideas, technology, knowledge, art, culture, literacy, food, goods, services, that make each one depend upon the other, integrating and assimilating those territo-ries into the body of the empire. The great Kr'ush, forebear of our race, did not merely set out to rule the whole world; he sought to unite, uplift, and educate the peoples of the world into a single cohesive, integrated structure that would stand over time, just as a great edifice endures over generations, resisting all the vagaries of nature and climate.

"What Jarsun is offering Adri is nothing more than hasty conquests achieved through brute force and aggression. Such means lead only to un-imaginable bloodshed and loss of life and property. When an entity as large and powerful as the Burnt Empire invades and massacres a distant king-dom a hundredth or even a thousandth its size, all it does is alienate and radicalize its victims, turning them into rebels and resistance fighters who dedicate their lives to destroying the empire. We saw this happen with the first ill-advised attempt by my ancestor Sala'shar Krushan to conquer the northern and western reaches of the continent, both areas which remain obdurately resistant to the rule of law even today, almost seven hundred years later. Adri may indeed achieve a temporary victory over the East and South through his alliance with Jarsun. But he has not stopped to weigh the cost of that alliance, nor the consequences of those victories."

Vrath paused, as if aware that he was speechifying, and added, "Yet, so long as he remains linked with Jarsun, we elders of the House of Krushan have little choice but to support his efforts, if not actively, then passively. I have already made clear that I will not be fighting on the side of the Krushan in this eastern offensive, but I will not be able to fight against our armies either. It is forbidden under Krushan law for any Krushan to violently confront his own emperor. And as you may be aware, our ancestral bond with the being we call stonefire enforces this ban by whatever means it deems appropriate."

Is he saying what I think he's saying, Yudi? Brum sent. Her siblings all echoed the same question.

Yes, Yudi replied. *If a Krushan uses violence against the seated emperor, the Burning Throne will reach out and punish that Krushan severely.*

Meaning what, exactly? Kula asked.

That stonefire will deal with them as it deems fit, Yudi said distractedly. *Now, can we focus on what Great-Uncle Vrath is saying? This is important.*

"So you are sympathetic to our cause, but cannot offer us actual help?" Queen Vensera asked, looking vexed. "Is that all you bring us? Words and well wishes? These are of little use to us in this moment of crisis. We need an army, enough fighting forces to equal the odds against the Krushan army knocking at our door. Failing that, the assistance of one such as yourself in actual combat would help even the odds. All Arthaloka knows that the great warrior Vrath is an army unto himself. Fight with us on the field of battle. Your presence alone will demoralize the Krushan army and aid us in turning the odds."

Vrath nodded, looking sympathetic. "I hear your words and feel your need, Queen Vensera. Were it possible for me to do such a thing, you would not need to ask. I would offer my sword gladly in your service. But as I have explained, both Krushan law and its prime enforcer, the throne, prohibit it."

Jilana spoke up: "There is another reason why our direct participation would be disastrous. What Adri is doing is foolish, what Jarsun is doing is reprehensible, but as long as they are acting in the empire's interests, we are obligated to support their actions, no matter how misguided. For us to openly defy the emperor's actions and battle our own army would destroy the Burnt Empire itself. You might win the coming battle with the mighty warrior Vrath fighting on your side, but you would damage the Burnt Empire itself permanently. The resulting fractures would destabilize the entire continent, leading to an era of lawlessness and anarchy that would bring many other enemies to your doorstep. You would only be trading today's army for tomorrow's, and the day after's, until the end of time."

"Even if that be so," Vensera said, "if we don't survive today, we will not live to see tomorrow or any other day. What can you offer us that will enable us to face this crisis, apart from words and speeches?"

The queen is angry, Brum sent to Saha.

Can you blame her? But look at your beloved princess. She isn't getting upset like her mother. She's as calm as a forest pond on a windless day.

She's not "my" beloved princess, Brum sent fiercely. *Stop calling her that.*

But she did look at Krushni. The princess looked as calm — and just as beautiful — as if they were in a perfectly routine session, discussing matters of taxation and administration.

"The queen speaks truly," Vessa said, "yet I fear that noble Vrath and honorable Jilana are indeed constrained by law and their commitment to the House of Krushan."

"In that case, what purpose does their being here serve?" Vensera asked sharply. "If they are not with us, they may as well be against us!"

Vessa looked at Vrath and Jilana. "Queen Vensera's anger is justified. Will you not tell her what purpose your presence here serves?"

Vrath and Jilana exchanged a look. Even though no gestures or words passed between them, Brum understood that Vrath was deferring to his stepmother.

Jilana said, "The same Krushan law that constrains us from openly supporting your cause also demands that we oppose Jarsun Krushan."

The temperature in the room changed immediately. Quiet murmurs were exchanged in the rear of the chamber, and Queen Vensera, who had been sitting back in her chair and frowning, straightened and sat up, her face clearing.

"As elders of the House of Krushan, it is our responsibility and our duty to ensure that the edicts and dictates of previous emperors and empresses are followed, no matter how opposed the current occupant of the throne may be to them. Jarsun Krushan was exiled for actions and crimes against the empire and his own family. He was judged by the throne itself, and for reasons unknowable by mortal minds, stonefire chose not to punish him physically, but demanded his exile and excommunication. From that moment, he was no longer considered a legitimate member of the House of Krushan, and as such, was not entitled to any of its powers and privileges, or its protections. He is, in all senses of the term, an outlaw, and we are in no way constrained from acting against him and those who support him."

Vensera had risen to her feet, accompanied a moment later by Gwann. "What does that mean exactly?" she asked. "Is that a legal loophole that allows you to join us in this coming battle?"

"Regretfully, not quite," Jilana said. "We still cannot join your cause openly nor fight on your behalf. But we are required by law to act against Jarsun and are free to do so at any time of our choosing."

Jilana indicated Vrath. "A long time ago, when Adri and Shvate were but boys with hairless chins, they led the Krushan army against an uprising of disgruntled nations. This uprising was instigated and, in some cases, forced, by Jarsun himself, under the guise of a rebellion against the Burnt Empire. He personally took the field, seeking, we believe, to extinguish the lives of both Adri and Shvate. Their premature deaths would have created a void at the seat of the empire, leaving the Burning Throne vacant. He hoped to fill that void by sending his daughter Krushita to Hastinaga to demand her right to undergo the Test of Fire again. Under those circumstances, she would have become the empress of the Burnt Empire. She could then have passed an edict forgiving her father for his past crimes and sins, and Jarsun would have achieved his aim.

"However, Vrath took the field as I have said, and engaged Jarsun directly. Jarsun was diverted from his goal of slaying Adri and Shvate in combat, and compelled to fight Vrath himself. In an epic confrontation, Vrath got the better of Jarsun that day. Jarsun fled the field, fearing for his life, abandoning the foolish alliance who had supported him. The rest, of course, you already know. Adri and Shvate survived, grew to young manhood, and Shvate ascended the throne. He later abdicated and tasked his brother Adri with the seat, choosing to go into exile over an inadvertent crime he had committed, the accidental slaying of a sage and his spouse, which had drawn upon Shvate a terrible curse prohibiting him from ever bearing offspring. Considering himself no longer suitable for emperorship, Shvate went into the forest with his wives, Karni and Mayla, never to return to Hastinaga. In time, they found a way to bear children through the use of a powerful mantra that Karni had gained as a young girl, and summoned the stone gods to father children upon herself and her sister wife, Mayla. The results are the five impressive young people who are in attendance here today."

Jilana smiled kindly at Brum and her siblings as all heads turned to look at them.

"But I digressed in my narration. The main thrust of my explanation was to say that Vrath battled Jarsun once and defeated him. He nigh killed him. There is little doubt that he would do so again, and this time almost certainly finish the task. And as it so happens, an opportunity has now presented itself to justify his taking the field again."

Jilana turned to Vrath. "Son?"

Vrath bowed his head to his stepmother. "My mother speaks truth. In the decades since the Battle of the Rebels, we have wanted only for an opportune time to resume my duel with Jarsun. Due to my responsibilities in Hastinaga, I could not roam the world in search of him. It would have been pointless to do so in any case, since he is a waywalker and could simply escape to other worlds or dimensions at any time. My stepbrother Vessa here has attempted to chase Jarsun through the ways, and battled him on other dimensional levels numerous times, never being able to pin him down physically long enough. So the only practical way was to wait until I knew for certain where and when Jarsun would be, so I could confront him once and for all."

To kill him, he means, Brum sent to her siblings.

We're not the only ones he's wronged, Arrow sent back. *I would love to have the chance to face him myself.*

We all would, Brum sent.

"And today," Vrath continued, "that day has finally come. Jarsun has committed himself to taking the field and fighting alongside the Krushan Hundred in the invasion of Gwannland. I intend to be on the field at that battle, to confront Jarsun personally, and finish what we began decades ago."

King Gwann frowned. "It was my understanding that under Krushan law, you are forbidden from acting against the empire's interests in this conflict. Forgive me if I misheard or misinterpreted your words."

Vrath nodded. "You heard correctly, and the law forbids me from battling Hastinaga's forces. However, Hastinaga has offered military support to Dronas. Jarsun happens to be an ally to Dronas only at the present moment.

He remains a free agent and an exile and outlaw to the empire. The law does not protect him personally. I still cannot engage him openly in battle if it would involve the deaths of Krushan soldiers. However, there is nothing to forbid me from responding to a challenge by Jarsun and defending my honor and my life, as well as the empire, by engaging him personally. Jarsun and I have unfinished business from our last encounter. For him to leave the field without challenging me would be to admit his own cowardice before his allies, his followers, and his enemies. It is likely that at some point during the conflict, Jarsun's pride will get the better of him and he will issue a formal challenge to me to fight him in a duel."

"And if he does not?" Queen Vensera asked.

Vrath shrugged. "Then I will challenge him. He will have no choice but to accept."

He added calmly, "When he does so, I will slay him."

5

"This is encouraging news," Queen Vensera said. "For we understand that behind all this is Jarsun's hand. He, it was, who told Dronas to bring the Krushan brothers to Gwannland to precipitate this conflict. He has been relentless in his pursuit of expanding his empire across this part of the world for decades. Until a few years ago, Gwannland had escaped his avaricious gaze. That changed when he encouraged Dronas to use his old feud with my husband, Gwann, to justify his invasion of our homeland. These past three years, we have lived under the shadow of Jarsun's ambition, knowing that it was only a matter of time before he turned his piercing scrutiny in our direction once more. Now that day has finally come, and the wolf is at our door.

"But it is a far greater enemy than any we could ever have imagined. To have you, the legendary Prince Vrath Krushan, join us in this fight against Krushan would be a great aid. But I fear it will not be enough. You will engage Jarsun and no doubt slay him as you intend. But what of the Krushan army? What of the Krushan Hundred? What of Dronas and the other champions he has assembled? In the invasion of Gwannland, the Krushan Hundred, Dronas, and his relatively smaller army were enough to rout our forces and drive us out of our ancestral lands, giving him control of the greater part of the nation and the populace. We have only a tiny splinter remaining with which to battle that great host. Add to that the vast army of the Burnt Empire, whose numbers beggar the imagination, and we are doomed.

"Can you not do something more to aid us, great Prince Vrath and my noble sister liege Jilana? You have come so far and brought us so much hope with your presence and support. Now surely you must find it in your hearts to offer us more tangible aid?"

Jilana looked at Vrath, then at Vessa, the latter of whom nodded once.

"May I approach you, Queen Vensera?"

Vensera looked surprised. "Of course, sister."

Jilana went forward, her robes rustling, and took Vensera's hands in her own. Clasping them, she said, "You call me sister liege. In this brutal war-riddled world, we are indeed sisters, and sisters must stand by one another in their time of need. Jarsun's evil has infected much of the civilized world, filling vile men with mad ambition, facilitating a campaign of terror unprecedented in the history of Arthaloka. Not even in the age of the stone gods has such atrocity and cruelty been witnessed in our world.

"Yet the rise of this breed of rapacious brute has also engendered an opposing resistance. The forces of good have toiled and battled in secret, offering fierce resistance to his imperial ambitions across the continent. Tiny pockets have struggled on despite all odds, suffering greatly but enduring over time and learning much from their struggles. With the aid of my son Vessa, whose ability to waywalk and cross the barriers of time and distance grants him unique privileges, we have worked in secret, privately and discreetly seeding, encouraging, and building a growing network of resistance forces against Jarsun and his brutal allies.

"Some you have been aware of this through public knowledge, such as the queendom of Reygar, which has been successfully reinstalled after three attempts by Jarsun over fifteen years. That is the most publicly known success of the resistance. Another notable one that you are well aware of is the slaying of Tyrak by the prophesied Slayer."

Vensera nodded. "We heard of the slaying of Tyrak in the kingdom of Mraashk. It is one of the great ancient kingdoms of Eastern Arthaloka, and only a thousand miles north of Gwannland. A very long time ago, it is said, all the grasslands were united and lived in peace and harmony. We have ancient ties with Mraashk, and it pleased us greatly to hear of the overthrow of the tyrant Tyrak. Since his slaying, we have also heard tell that Jarsun's hold on the region has been weakened and challenged by the repeated uprisings and rebellions against his forces. There have been many assassinations and strikes against his minions and figurehead governors, each of which brought encouragement and hope that someday, Mraashk and Arrgodi may also free themselves of the cruel yoke of Jarsun's power. But what do they or the Red Desert kingdom of Reygar have to do with us here in Eastern Arthaloka?"

"More than you know," Jilana said.

She turned and looked at Prince Drishya, seated to the side of Vensera. "The Slayer of Tyrak was none other than your own son, Drishya, in his previous avatar."

Vensera caught her breath. "Drishya . . ."

Both Gwann and Vensera looked at Drishya. So did everyone else.

Drishya rose slowly to his feet. His handsome face and sculpted body glowed with youthful vigor and good health. He performed a namas and bowed his head low before his mother and Jilana.

"Mother Vensera. What Dowager Empress Jilana says is truth indeed. I have lived many lives before this one. The life I occupied immediately before coming to your house was in Mraashk. It was in that life that I slew Tyrak, the tyrant."

Vensera and Gwann looked at each other, their faces revealing their amazement. Gwann rose to his feet and came toward his son.

"Son, I have always known there was something extraordinary about you. Today, my belief is confirmed. I have no trouble believing that you are the legendary Slayer of Tyrak reborn. Additionally, I am certain that in your previous avatars, you have performed equally legendary feats. Your mother and I are privileged to be your parents in this lifetime. We thank the stone gods for bringing you to us."

Gwann embraced Drishya with tears of joy in his eyes. After him, Vensera embraced her son as well, looking at him with a mother's adoring gaze.

"We are proud to serve as your family, Drishya. You honor us with your presence in our lives."

Drishya bowed his head, accepting the praises of his parents.

Jilana continued, "Both Drishya and his sister, Krushni, came to you through the stonefire ritual wholly formed as grown young adults, much as they are today, did they not?"

The queen and king of Gwannland exchanged surprised glances. "Yes, that is so," said Gwann. Vensera nodded.

"In fact, the idea of conducting the ritual and the tiny piece of stonefire required to perform it came to you, Gwann, I believe," Jilana said.

Gwann nodded, still looking surprised. "While fleeing the Krushan Hundred and Dronas, I went into the woods to lose them. Stopping to rest, I encountered a hermit living off the land. He gave me water and shared with me his meager store of wild roots and berries, which I accepted gratefully to sustain myself. He also tended to my injuries with herbs and watched out for my pursuers while I slept. When I woke the next morning, I offered him the most precious thing I carried at that time, my signet ring. He accepted it, and in exchange gave me a fragment of stonefire wrapped in protective red ornash leaves and bound with the vines of the arrowroot tree, cautioning me not to open it and handle it out of curiosity. He told me a myth from the age of the stone gods about how great beings who had unfinished business on Arthaloka could regenerate themselves spontaneously in new avatars in order to fulfill their purpose. He put into my mind the idea that if I would conduct a stonefire ritual to summon such a personage, my desire for revenge and reparation would be successful. When I finally made it back here, I told Vensera the tale, and she agreed that we should perform the ritual."

"And out of that ritual fire stepped Drishya and Krushni," Jilana said.

"Yes," Gwann said, reaching out to take Krushni's hand, rubbing it fondly as he smiled at her. She smiled back, clutching his arm in daughterly fashion. "It was one of the happiest days of my life — our life," he added, including Vensera, who smiled as well, "and the turning point of our days. Against all odds, we raised a city and a kingdom out of the ashes, achieving levels of prosperity in three short years that we had never seen in thirty years before. It has given me hope that good can triumph and defeat evil, that the vile and wicked will be punished for their crimes, and the righteous will prevail."

"Indeed," Jilana said, "and now it is time for you to meet that forest hermit once again, and if you wish, thank him personally."

Jilana gestured to her son, who stepped forward. With his wild hair, bushy eyebrows, mustache and beard, and fierce eyes, Vessa looked the part in every sense right down to his dirt-encrusted toenails and gnarled feet. He nodded at Gwann, who stared at him with open-mouthed surprise.

"Guru Vessa? But your appearance..."

"Was somewhat altered at the time," Vessa agreed. "It was a necessary subterfuge. I am pleased that you took my advice to heart. That is how Krushni, Drishya, and I were able to complete our plan to defeat Jarsun. It would not have been possible without your patronage."

Gwann stared at his daughter and son. "Krushni?"

Krushni patted her father's arm gently. "In my last life, I was Krushita Krushan, daughter of Jarsun Krushan."

Arrow

~

1

ARROW SENT TO THE siblings, *Guess we're not the only family with a tangled history.*

Definitely, Brum sent back. *This lot has even us beat. Although being children of stone gods sort of beats being only Krushan, doesn't it?*

Saha sent Brum an image of herself rolling her eyes. *Always the competitive one, Brum!*

So this means . . . that we're cousins to Krushni and Drishya? Kula asked.

Cousins, Yudi said, *but only to Krushni. Drishya is . . . something else.*

Vensera was saying to Krushni, "We knew there was something special about Krushni from the start. But *daughter of Jarsun? Mother Jeel!*"

Krushni reached out and touched her mother's shoulder reassuringly. "That was another life, as I said. A life that I ended by my own choice."

She paused, looking down. "It was not a happy ending."

When Krushni said nothing further, Vessa spoke up.

"Jarsun killed Krushita's grandfather when he refused to go to war against the Burnt Empire. Her mother, Queen Aqreen of Aquila, feared for her own life and her daughter's future. To Jarsun, the little girl was nothing but a pawn to his ambitions, a means for him to claim the throne of which he had been deprived. Aqreen took Krushita and fled across the Red Desert on a caravan bound for Reygar. The journey was long and arduous with many attacks by Jarsun himself and the foul beings he summoned through the use of his urrkh sorcery. Despite it all, Aqreen persevered, and with the help of a valiant Vanjhani train leader named Bulan, was within sight of Reygar when Jarsun struck at them with the vilest deceit, tricking them into believing he had repented and wished to make peace with his wife and daughter. Jarsun was able to get close enough to murder Aqreen in front of Krushita, who was only a young girl at the time. The shock of her mother's murder by her father's hands changed Krushita forever. She vowed that she would avenge her mother and destroy Jarsun, no matter how long it took."

Everyone looked at Princess Krushni. Arrow's heart filled with a deep sadness.

She saw her mother killed by Jarsun, we saw our father suffer the same fate, Arrow sent to the siblings. *We are more than cousins. We are joined at the heart, bound by grief and pain.*

"Drishya and Krushita were already joined through a common ancestor, the stone god Vish," Vessa said. "Both have been, in other lifetimes, avatars or amsas of Vish, sent down upon Arthaloka to rid the world of a terrible evil. I took them both under my wing, taught them to walk the ways, and indeed, everything else I know of warcraft and the use of weapons, both physical and intangible. Each is a formidable warrior in their own right; together, they are indomitable. In their current avatars, both are tasked with the same mission, to end Jarsun Krushan's reign of evil. They are our greatest weapons in the coming battle. Each is the equivalent of an army. With them on your side, Queen Vensera and King Gwann, you have no need of great numbers. They are sufficient to deal with the Krushan army. As my stepbrother Vrath has undertaken the mission to face Jarsun personally in combat, Krushni and Drishya will direct their attention to the forces of Dronas and Krushan."

"This is excellent," said Vensera with a look of wonderment. "I am overwhelmed to know that two personages of such illustrious heritage are under my roof, my own daughter and son! It gives me new hope and heart for Gwannland's odds of surviving this conflict. But even two of the greatest warriors cannot be everywhere at once, and the sheer numbers being thrown against us are so vast, and our own numbers so minuscule in comparison, that I fear our losses will be too immense. Our brave warriors — I refer now to those of us who are merely mortal, including myself — will fight as valiantly as these great champions, but unlike them, we have no powers or talents. The first wave of attack may well wipe us out. What good is it if our champions go on to defeat Jarsun and his allies, if we too are slaughtered?

Krushni, Drishya, Vrath, all will achieve their goals, but we will not be alive to celebrate their victories. Gwannland is more than just soil and grass and air; it is people. How will we, the outnumbered, survive in the face of the infinite numbers marching against us?"

2

"Guru Vessa," Krushni said. "Great Mother Jilana. May I speak?"

"Of course, Krushni," Jilana said. "My son and I were merely setting the stage. Ultimately, this is your show. You are the protagonist of this great undertaking."

Krushni bowed her head to thank her elder. Then she turned to her mother and father.

"Mother, Father," Krushni said. "None of us are here merely for vendettas or personal glory. We are aware, every one of us, that many precious lives are at stake. What good is it for us to win this war if we lose Gwannland and all its people? I cannot guarantee that none of you will die in battle. That is the nature of war itself. Even a victory comes at a price. As a legendary hero of Aranya once said, in another age, 'The price of war is the prize of war.'"

"Aptly quoted," Vensera replied. "I am a warrior born and bred; I know that casualties are inevitable. My concern is that this could be a massacre, or even a genocide."

"You have my word," Krushni said, "that it will not be so. While Vrath engages Jarsun, keeping him at bay, Drishya and I will deal with Dronas and the Krushan Hundred. They are the ones who have sworn to slay both of you and as many Gwannlanders as possible. They are the greater threat, and my brother and I will dedicate ourselves to keeping them at bay, and if possible, ridding the world of them forever."

Vensera and Gwann nodded, looking a little less anxious. "That is encouraging," Vensera said. "But what of the armies of Dronas and the Krushan? How will just two of you fight a hundred and one powerful enemies as well as engage the millions of invading warriors?"

Krushni smiled. "Drishya and I will not be alone in defending Gwannland. We also have among us several other allies, each of whom brings their own considerable talents and powers."

She raised her hand and indicated the children of Shvate. As their eyes met, the warmth and power of her gaze thrilled Arrow's senses.

"The children of Shvate, who were my distant cousins in my past life, are all demigods, sired by the stone gods themselves."

Krushni turned to address the Five directly now.

"Will you rise and present yourselves as I call upon you?" she asked.

3

Yudi rose to his feet. "We are here for you, Princess."

Krushni acknowledged him with a nod. "Yudi, the eldest by a short span, is the legitimate son of Karni and Shvate under Krushan law, sired by the grace of Shima, the stone god of death and duty."

Yudi bowed formally.

"Brum, second-born child of Karni and Shvate, is an avatar of Grrud, stone god of wind and power."

Brum stood, shuffling her feet awkwardly, and raised her hand in casual greeting. Arrow knew she was never comfortable being noticed, especially under such intense scrutiny, and sent her an invisible hug. *Thank you,* she sent back.

"Arrow, child of Karni and Shvate, fathered by none other than Stone God Inadran, Lord of Storms and War."

A ripple of murmurs passed through the chamber. Of all the stone gods, none was considered more fearsome in battle than Inadran. The legends claimed that it was Inadran who created war itself, as a means of settling the eternal dispute between the stone gods and the urrkh once and for all, and laid down the rules that governed the waging of it even today. Arrow stood, remaining as impassive as possible, despite feeling a burning heat. They avoided meeting Krushni's gaze directly, not wanting her to see the intensity of their attraction for her. Arrow also shielded these feelings from the rest of the Five, even though the shielding would convey some meaning to them.

Thankfully, Krushni passed on to his siblings without lingering on Arrow.

Both Saha and Kula had stood together.

"Lastly, the twins, who are both avatars of the twin equid gods known as the Asvas. Saha, fourth-born child of Mayla and Shvate, is the avatar of

Stone God Shravas, Lord of Animals and Kindness. Kula is twin to Saha, and the avatar of Uchchaih, Lord of Animals, Speed, and Good Health. Though born gendered, both twins chose to use their powers to transition to their present genderfluid identities."

Krushni joined her hands together in a namas. "It was Guru Vessa who advised the mother of the Shvate Five to send her children east to Gwannland. Their guide was the Vanjhani seated beside them, Tshallian."

Tshallian rose and bowed both their upper halves. They belatedly remembered to namas as well, and the gesture was responded to in kind by Queen Vensera and King Gwann.

Tshallian addressed their words to the king and queen. "On behalf of Vanjhani tribes, thank Gwannland I wish to for harboring our people when forced they were to migrate lands overrun Jarsun and his warlords by. Granted you them refuge at a crisis time. Many Vanjhani slain or enslaved were by that evil Krushan and minions his. Not for your generosity and grace were it, many more suffered the same fate would have."

"We only did what was humane," Vensera said graciously. "The Vanjhani are an honorable race and ever a friend and ally to our people over generations. My ancestors and I have fought alongside your tribes more times than I can recall. My own great-grandmother had a captain of her guard who was Vanjhani. Their name was Morajuan."

Tshallian bowed their heads again. "Our uncle on our mother's side was Morajuan. Many tales told they us of adventures together. To train you as a young girl, they lived long enough. Recall we them saying one of the finest you were of long line warrior queens Gwannland."

"Indeed," Vensera said, pleased by the compliment, "that is high praise. And Morajuan was never one to praise their pupils to their face. In fact, I don't recall them ever complimenting me, except maybe for the one time when they grudgingly admitted I was 'starting to learn.' This was after I had routed an entire swarm of Ferrigneus from the grasslands."

Tshallian raised their eyebrows. Ferrigneus were hybrid beings that rarely ventured into human-occupied territories, but on the rare occasions they did, they could be lethal. "Sounds much Morajuan like, it does. Praise they even the stone gods were they descend today, I doubt!"

There were smiles all around.

Arrow could feel the tension in the room easing a little, now that people realized that the odds against them were not as impossible as they had seemed before this council began. They smiled inwardly, looking forward to the next announcement.

Yudi spoke next, at Tshallian's urging. "Tshallian wishes me to inform you that they are very pleased to say that as a show of gratitude for Gwannland's long friendship with their people, the Vanjhani will also take the field and aid you in the coming battle."

Vensera and Gwann looked very happy. Even happier, Arrow noted, than when they had learned that the Shvate Five were to fight for their side.

That's because they know what the Vanjhani can do in battle, Yudi said, *while they've yet to see us in action. And we are quite young to their eyes, after all.*

I guess we'll just have to show them, then, Brum said. *Won't we?*

Yes!

Oh yes!

We will, Arrow sent.

Arrow wasn't sure which thought was more thrilling, the prospect of going into their first real pitched battle against a truly formidable enemy, or fighting alongside Princess Krushni. They kept this thought to themself.

4

"We are reassured," Queen Vensera said, addressing Vrath, Jilana, and Vessa, since they were the elders and had begun the discussions. "Before this council began, I feared the battle would be over within an hour at most, the outcome a foregone conclusion. Now I glimpse sunrise on the horizon. With the Vanjhani fighting alongside us, and this extraordinary group of champions, our odds have improved considerably."

"Mother," Krushni said gently, "the odds are better than you think even now. You have yet to meet a few remaining allies who have joined our cause. I think you will take great satisfaction once you do."

Krushni clapped her hands, gesturing to the guards at the doors to allow entrance to someone waiting outside.

The doors opened, and a small group of people walked in. Two were women, both of whom Arrow had seen before. The third was a young man, perhaps a few years older than the Five. This latter had a certain look about him and a bearing that was oddly familiar.

That one is Krushan, Yudi sent.

Are you sure? Brum asked.

Of course. If I wasn't certain, I wouldn't offer an opinion. See for yourself. Probe him.

Arrow did as Yudi suggested. While Yudi lacked the physical talents of his four siblings, in the realm of the mind and intellect, he was head and shoulders above them. Perhaps because of this, his ability to probe minds — his siblings' as well as others', even non-Krushan — was exceptional. Arrow couldn't probe a stranger's mind as deeply and easily as Yudi, but tried.

Surprisingly, Arrow made contact with the young man's mind almost instantly, only slightly less easily than with the siblings. Minds were not dissimilar to handprints and facial features; each had its own distinguishing qualities and unique features. Arrow could sense at once that there was a familial relationship with this young man.

Yudi is right, Saha sent. After their eldest brother, she was the next most sensitive of them. *He is a Krushan, perhaps even a relative.*

All Krushan are related, Kula sent.

Well, I mean closely related, then, Saha shot back at her twin.

"I present to you," Krushni was saying, "Shikari and Ladislew."

The two women bowed from their necks to greet Vensera and Gwann, both of whom frowned.

These two were in Jarsun's pavilion, Arrow sent to the Five.

"You are allied with Jarsun Krushan," Vensera said to Ladislew.

"And you with Dronas," Gwann said to Shikari.

"I am," Shikari admitted, looking unabashed. "I am betrothed to him. We were to have been married but chose to make this journey to your brave young city instead."

"And I share the God-Emperor's bedchamber and his privy," said Ladislew, looking perfectly composed.

Vensera and Gwann looked at each other, then at Krushni, frowning at her.

Krushni smiled. "Who better to know of our enemies' weaknesses than those closest to them? Shikari and Ladislew are indeed intimate with Dronas and Jarsun respectively, but they pursue independent agendas. Their goals happen to coincide with ours today, and so they have come to us of their own volition, seeking to ally with us in secret against their lovers."

"Is that so?" Vensera asked skeptically.

She looked both women up and down. "How do we know you are not merely here to spy on us on behalf of our enemies?"

Ladislew replied, "Because Jarsun already knows, and has known for several years, that I lie with him only so that I may be present at the time of his defeat and demise."

"And Dronas and I have been mortal enemies for far longer than we have been lovers," Shikari said. "In fact, you may even say that we are only lovers because we are enemies."

Both Vensera and Gwann looked taken aback. As did everyone else in the chamber.

Now, this is getting interesting, Arrow thought. The other siblings all shared the same thought, except for Yudi, who, as always, had a ready answer.

They're telling the truth, Yudi sent. *Ladislew is actually —*

Shut up, big brother, Brum sent affectionately, *I want to hear her tell it.*

By *her,* Brum meant the princess of Gwannland, of course.

Yudi shut up, none too pleased about it.

You do tend to lecture us at times, Arrow sent to Yudi privately, *though I know you mean well.*

Yudi didn't respond, but Arrow knew he wouldn't stay miffed for long. For all their youthful adventures, none of them had experienced anything quite like this war council before. And there was something else, Arrow noted: Yudi too wanted to hear the princess speak. In fact, all five of them did, quite eagerly. Though perhaps Arrow and Brum were a little more eager than the others.

"To save time," Krushni said, "I will explain briefly. Ladislew is from an ancient order of female assassins who live very long lives. Her issue with Jarsun stems from her ancestral relationship to his ancestors; theirs is a long and ancient enmity. Jarsun knew this at their first encounter but realized that if he slew her, she would simply be replaced by another of her order. The feud dates back eons and is endless. Instead, he chose to accept her as his lover in order to keep her closer."

Vensera looked at Ladislew with fresh, curious eyes. "I have heard of such generational feuds. Your goal, then, is to slay Jarsun? What keeps you from striking at him at any time? Why not this very day?"

Ladislew smiled. "Yes, that would remove a considerable blight from Gwannland's doorway, would it not? But it is not as simple as that. Jarsun is not an easy being to slay. The day I choose to make my move will end with at least one of us dead. Until now, the odds did not favor my being the survivor. Do you play the game of chaupat, Queen Vensera?"

Vensera raised her eyebrows. Arrow knew of chaupat, a Krushan war game played on painted boards with carved figures representing the various cadres and players. "I have some knowledge of it," the queen said.

"I expected you would. You come from a long line of warrior queens. I am from a similar order. I have learned to play chaupat during my time with Jarsun. The game has infinite combinations of strategies and tactics and can conceivably go on indefinitely, if both players are evenly matched. The only way to declare a victory, then, is for one player to admit defeat. But so long as a player believes they have a chance, however slender, of success, they would not wish to be the first to declare."

"Naturally," Vensera agreed. "A warrior never surrenders unless there is no other option."

"Precisely. The game I play with Jarsun is just as intricate but far deadlier. We attack one another through other players, those more disposable than ourselves, ending their lives when we can, while circling each other in anticipation of the endgame."

"I think I understand," Vensera said. "Do you see your endgame in sight anytime soon, then?"

"I believe that by joining forces with you, I have begun my endgame," Ladislew said.

Vensera and Gwann both nodded at that.

"We are privileged to have you on our side," Vensera said.

"Shikari's story is quite different, though the result is the same for us," Krushni said. "She is from a tribe that resisted Dronas's attempts to recruit an army of his own several years ago. Dronas attacked her people and used his formidable skills to slaughter a number of them. Fearing total annihilation, their chief approached him under cover of a peace banner and made a request."

Shikari took over the narration. "The chief was my father. It was I who told him to propose a truce. In exchange, we would provide a limited number of our warriors to support Dronas's forces, because to send all would render our own tribal lands defenseless and in danger of starving since our warriors were also our hunters. To sweeten the deal, I offered myself as Dronas's wife. He accepted but kept me instead as his mistress. He is not a man given to trusting easily, and it is only recently, after I slew one of the rich merchants who was refusing to support him and took over his estates, that Dronas finally decided I could be trusted enough to marry."

Gwann said, "I am sure that Krushni has chosen to trust you for good reason. You will be an asset to our efforts."

5

"There is one final ally whom I must introduce," Princess Krushni said.

She put her arm around the young man Arrow had noticed earlier and gestured to Jilana and Vrath first. "Dowager Empress Jilana, Prince Regent Vrath, allow me to introduce a fellow Krushan. This is Ekluv."

Jilana looked curious. Vrath retained his inscrutable impassivity.

"I thought I knew every Krushan alive," Jilana said. "I have never met or heard of Ekluv."

"He is your grandson," Krushni said to Jilana. "And your great-nephew," she said to Vrath.

Both stared at the young man, who bowed gracefully.

Another cousin? How many more are there? Brum sent. *And why did Mother and Guru Vessa never tell us of this fellow?*

Good question, Yudi sent back, caught without an answer for once.

"Grandson? Nephew?" Jilana replied for herself as well as Vrath. "I don't understand. How is this fine young man related to us?"

Krushni smiled. "He is the son of your own grandson, Adri," she said to Jilana. "Fathered upon his maid and lover Sauvali."

Jilana's eyes opened wide in understanding. "The one who perished in the assassination attempt?"

"There was no assassination attempt. The attack on Emperor Adri and his secret lover was planned and orchestrated with the sole intention of abducting her. She was eight and a half months pregnant with his child at the time. The plan was to keep her alive just long enough to deliver a male child, then slay her. But another party intervened, and she was liberated from her captors and taken to a safe refuge, where she stayed until recently. The child she gave birth to shortly thereafter is this young man, my cousin in my former life, Ekluv, son of Sauvali and Emperor Adri."

"Great-Grandmother. Uncle." Ekluv's voice was as quiet and understated as his manner. "My mother sends her deepest regards and prays that you will forgive her for violating the sanctity of your household by having relations with your grandson. She asks for nothing for herself but that you accept me as your own and grant me the honor of your recognition."

Both Vrath and Jilana looked closely at the young man with renewed interest. So did everyone else.

"Ekluv," Jilana said in wonderment, "son of Adri. Another heir to the Burning Throne. I am very pleased to meet you, my great-grandson. Tell your mother she did nothing wrong. I know everything that occurs in my household. I was aware of her every tryst with my grandson Adri, as I am aware that it was he who initiated the relationship which she entered into only hesitantly at first. Adri was lonely, and his wife had no interest in sharing either his bed or his life. He was in need of companionship, and your mother was a good friend to him in that time of need. Whatever transpired between them was no liaison, it was genuine love. You are the child of that union and, by Krushan law, a legitimate part of our line. I welcome you to our family, young Ekluv. May you live long and be ever victorious."

"I shall not repeat the Queen Mother's words," Vrath added, "except to say that I can sense the Krushan blood flowing within you as a river senses the proximity of a tributary. I find no fault with you or your mother. Would that you could have been part of our lives and your father's life all the years since your birth. He has been twice as lonely since he lost your mother and you."

Ekluv bowed low to acknowledge and show respect to both his elders. He performed a perfect namas.

That was when they all noticed it for the first time.

His hands, Saha sent, *look at his hands!*

He has no thumbs, Kula sent.

They have been severed with a single blow apiece from a very sharp blade, wielded by an expert swordsman, Arrow replied as he examined the nubs of the missing digits.

Jilana's and Vrath's eyes lingered on Ekluv's hands too, but neither said anything to call attention to the amputations.

Jilana's eyes swept across the Shvate Five. "My, my. Dhuryo and his brothers are going to be quite irate when they meet all of you. Six more rivals to their precious throne!"

"Wait till they meet us on the battlefield!" Brum replied with her usual outspoken manner. "They'll be crying 'Mama!' all the way home."

Krushni flashed a spontaneous grin at Brum. Brum blushed and then recovered enough to wink back at Krushni.

Really, Brum, Yudi sent disapprovingly, *this is a war council, in case you'd forgotten.*

So? Brum shrugged. *Haven't you heard? All's fair in love and war.*

"I'm sure they will, young lady," Jilana replied, smiling at Brum and including all the Five in her warmth. I do wish the six of you had been part of our lives all these years. Still, we are very pleased to meet you at long last."

Queen Vensera looked at her daughter. "Krushni, my dear, do you have any more surprises for us? A few more Krushan hidden under your skirts perhaps? A lost uncle or two? A rainbow-colored elephant?"

Krushni giggled, covering her mouth with her hand. "A rainbow-colored elephant would be lovely to ride into battle, wouldn't it? The perfect mount to represent Gwannland! But sadly, no. No more surprise guests to be introduced. That's it from me."

"Very well, then," Vensera said. "Now that all the players have been introduced, let us proceed to the main business of this war council. Planning a strategy for the battle against Jarsun, Dronas, and the army of the Krushan. I need not remind everyone that our very lives, as well as the fate of all Arthaloka, rest upon this battle. Despite all these new allies joining our cause, our enemies are still immensely powerful, and their resources far, far greater than our own. The odds against us remain just as impossible, and yet we must fight."

"We *will* fight!" Gwann said passionately.

And so will we, Brum sent.

Jarsun

~

1

JARSUN SURVEYED THE FIELD of Beha'al. He was pleased by what he saw.

All day today, the day before, and the day before that, the armies of the Burnt Empire had continued emerging through the portal. The aperture itself was vast, a mile in width and several yards high, to allow clearance for the massive war elephants that would pass through. It was a phenomenon unto itself, certainly the largest he had ever engineered, and even the Krushan troops and war animals passing through it looked up at its flickering, strobing edges fearfully, taking care to avoid coming within a hundred yards.

It had taken a considerable expenditure of power on his part and used up a great deal of his precious store of urrkh *Auma*, the hard-won energy earned solely through sustained meditation on the Forbidden, the urrkh deities who had once been numbered among the stone gods before being cast out of the tribe and relegated to permanent excommunication. It taken him centuries to accumulate that store of urrkh *Auma*, centuries spent floating in the hellish dimension that urrkh worshippers termed Nrruk, a void where nightmarish apparitions tormented constantly, their sole goal being to distract the supplicants from their meditation. He had thought long and hard before deciding to utilize that much of his painfully gained store.

Viewing the results now, he had to admit it was worth all that effort and expense.

The army that assembled on the enormous grassland field was vast beyond even his expectations. He had estimated that about a thousand soldiers were able to pass abreast through the portal every minute or so. Three days since the influx had begun, and they were still coming through. Even Dronas, seated on a mount beside Jarsun, had spent the better part of the past hour simply watching the endless rows and columns pass through the portal. It resembled the longest victory parade ever imagined.

"I knew the army of the Burnt Empire was vast," Dronas said, "but even so."

"I impressed upon Emperor Adri the importance of a show of strength. Eastern Arthaloka is tens of thousands of miles from Hastinaga. There are some in this distant corner of the continent who think of the Burnt Empire as a myth, a nighttime fable for grandmothers to tell errant children to put them to bed. Not a real, living, flesh-and-blood thing. I told him that this was the moment his ancestors had dreamed of, and he had a chance to achieve those dreams. If we struck with only a portion of our full strength and achieved anything less than total victory, it would diminish the stature of the empire. He must show these barbarians in this stonegodforsaken part of the world that the Burnt Empire was everything they had heard of and feared for centuries: it was even greater and more fearsome than they could have imagined. His response was to issue an empire-wide draft, summoning not just Hastinaga's considerable standing army, but also the individual armies of every one of its satrapies and allies, far and wide. What you see here is not just the Krushan army, but five hundred armies combined to fight under the Krushan banner."

He indicated the battalions that had just begun coming through the portal. At their head, their bannermen held flags of their individual tribes behind a larger, preceding flag marking the Vanga nation. The Vanga flag, a barbed mace wielded by a roaring bear, hung below the larger flag of the Burnt Empire, a blood-red flag with the outline of the black throne of Hastinaga and seated upon this throne, a grinning skeleton wearing a crown, bathed in roaring orange flames.

"I hear your words and understand them," Dronas said, "but my eyes and mind are still having some difficulty processing the reality they are witnessing."

Jarsun hissed, allowing himself a thin smile. "It is quite a sight, I will admit."

After a moment, Dronas said, "I will not forget what you have done for me here, my friend."

Friend? Jarsun almost laughed aloud at that, then reflected that the reaction might confuse Dronas. Mortals could be quite dense-headed when it came to appreciating the irony of their own words, though they were quick enough to point out the irony in other people's words.

Dronas turned to look at him directly. "I expected you to use your own powers, perhaps bring your own armies here to aid me, but you have exceeded my expectations. Whatever I might have expected, *this*" — he gestured at the lines upon lines of war chariots now rumbling through the portal — "this is far beyond anything I imagined. This is an army capable of conquering the entire world, not just Gwannland."

Jarsun frowned. Could Dronas really be this dense? He had expected the legendary guru and master of warcraft to have a better understanding of strategy.

"You do know that this army is not just here to help you to get your revenge on your childhood friend Gwann," he said. "Don't you?"

"Of course," Dronas said. "Even payment of my guru debt does not require Emperor Adri to send all the armies at his command to serve me. He has larger plans after he aids me in my conquest of Gwannland. Which" — he chuckled as he gestured at the bellowing elephant brigades that were passing through the portal — "will now be accomplished within an hour at most!"

He turned to Jarsun. "I am not a guru of warcraft for nothing, my friend. I know that the Burnt Empire has long aspired to extend its borders to the far corners of the world. With your help" — he gestured at the portal — "that can now be accomplished. And with a strong king such as myself dominating Eastern Arthaloka, Hastinaga will have an ally they can trust and depend on."

Dominating Eastern Arthaloka? Jarsun wondered how Dronas had extrapolated his conquest of a key but still relatively minor kingdom in the East to control of this entire part of the continent. Despite his claim to the contrary, Dronas *did* fail to see the larger implications. His sense of self-importance deluded him into believing that this entire mobilization centered upon him and his petty vendetta against his childhood friend.

So be it, Jarsun mused, let the guru nurse his delusions. The icy cold air of harsh reality would soon slap him in the face.

"Jarsun," said a voice from behind.

He turned to see Ladislew. "The wanderer returns."

She ignored the comment. "We need to talk."

She jerked her head at Dronas. "Your fiancée would like to have words with you as well. She is waiting back in the war tent for us."

Without waiting for a reply, she turned and walked back toward the camp.

Dronas watched her go with no attempt to conceal his lust. "That one must give you some wild nights."

Jarsun's already low estimation of the man sank another inch. "She gives me nothing. She takes."

2

Both women were standing in the comfortably appointed tent. Dhuryo Krushan was with them, glowering. Jarsun glanced at the eldest son of Adri with some amusement. Which of the two women had dealt him an acid putdown when she rejected his advances? Both perhaps. Despite their physical differences and apparent dissimilarity, Ladislew and Shikari were cut from the same cloth.

Dronas made a show of seating himself on the thronelike chair that had been brought all the way from Dronasthan for his comfort before asking everyone to be seated. Ladislew and Shikari looked at him with identical expressions of disdain. Dronas noticed neither.

"Well, then," said the guru who now thought himself a king and soon-to-be emperor of Eastern Arthaloka. "The armies are marching, and I plan to finish off Gwann before I break my fast on the morrow. What have our pretty spies found out for us that could be of use at this late stage? Speak up, now, do not be intimidated by my reputation. I am a fair king and will reward you well for any information of value."

Both women ignored him. Ladislew addressed her words to Jarsun directly.

"The Shvate Five are with Gwannland, as you suspected. But there are many more allied with them than you believed."

Jarsun shrugged. "Let me guess. The rebels yipping at my heels back in Mraashk and Arrgodi? Some other malcontents and anarchists, anti-imperialists and other sellswords? They can have them, for all I care. It will give me the opportunity to rid myself of them once and for all. When the dog leaps in the river, the fleas will all drown."

Dronas frowned, probably wondering who was the dog in this analogy.

"Them too, but they're not the ones I meant," Ladislew said. "I speak of Dowager Empress Jilana and Prince Regent Vrath."

"The Krushan elders?" Dronas said incredulously. "Impossible! They would never involve themselves with insignificants like Gwann and Vensera."

Shikari looked at her fiancé coldly. "They were present at the war council, and openly expressed their support. In fact, Vrath said he himself would fight in the battle."

Dronas rose from his seat. "I cannot believe this. Vrath is the most honorable man that ever lived. He swore the terrible oath of lifelong celibacy and abstinence in order to ensure that his progeny would never challenge his father's heirs for control of the Burnt Empire. He would never dishonor his family in this manner!"

"I do not believe it either," Dhuryo Krushan said angrily. "He is my great-uncle. He would not take the field against me and my brothers! Your information is wrong."

"He will be upholding Krushan law," Ladislew said, speaking carefully and slowly as if addressing a child. "He will not be taking the field to fight you or your brothers, Dhuryo, nor you and your forces, Dronas. He will be fighting only one opponent."

She turned to look at Jarsun.

Jarsun had already reached this conclusion while Dronas and Dhuryo were ranting denials.

"Yes," Jarsun said, "that would be in keeping with the law. Jilana and Vrath cannot subvert Adri's orders or interfere with the invasion of Gwannland, but they can move against me. I am a declared outlaw and an enemy of the empire."

"Ah," Dronas said, settling back in his seat with a grunt of relief. "That does seem logical. So long as it does not affect my campaign, it is of no consequence. Jarsun, you will probably welcome the opportunity to confront Vrath on the field and finish what you almost accomplished in the Battle of the Rebels decades ago."

Dhuryo stared at Dronas. "You are speaking of killing my great-uncle."

Dronas shrugged. "Jarsun is your great-uncle too. Or is it great-great-uncle? I can never get that straight. In either case, you will lose one of the two tomorrow. You have the rest of the evening and all night to prepare your eulogy."

Dhuryo glared at Dronas but subsided.

"So I will face Vrath on the field tomorrow," Jarsun said, not letting those present see how that made him feel. "What else have you learned?"

Shikari spoke. "Vrath and Jilana both favor Gwannland in this conflict. And their newfound nephews and nieces in particular."

"Shvate's brats?" Dronas snorted. "Dhuryo alone will be sufficient to deal with the lot of them. It will probably take him barely one morning. Is that not so, Dhuryo?"

Dhuryo nodded but said nothing.

Jarsun thought that perhaps the pupil was smarter than the guru. Their eyes met briefly, and Jarsun saw and assessed the young man — only a boy, really — more carefully. Their mutual link to stonefire smoldered within their veins, connecting them in a way that was indescribable and incomprehensible to non-Krushan.

Yes, perhaps the lad has the makings of a good warrior, he thought. But he would still wait till the morrow to see how Dhuryo fared in actual combat against his cousins. He had a feeling that those five might give not just Dhuryo but all the hundred Krushan brothers a strong challenge. It would be interesting to see how they fared.

The two women recounted briefly all that they had seen and heard at the council in Gwannland.

When they finished, Dronas waved dismissively.

"So far you have brought us no great insights or revelations," Dronas said, forgetting that only moments earlier he had been shocked at the news that Vrath and Jilana were supporting his enemy. "If you have nothing of value to impart . . ."

Shikari smiled, stepping forward to raise one manicured hand and stroke Dronas's sinewy arm. "There will be one more Krushan taking the field tomorrow than you expected." She glanced at Jarsun coyly. "Perhaps one more than anyone knew existed."

Dronas frowned. "Stop talking in riddles, woman! If you have any intelligence worth sharing, spit it out. We have a battle to plan and the sun nears its nadir."

"There was a young man, about the same age as Dhuryo and his brothers, as well as the Shvate Five. He was handsome, in a dark, intense way, the kind of man who would probably be as effective an archer in bed as on the battlefield."

Dronas grabbed a handful of her hair. "Enough nonsense. This is no time to speak of bedrooms and innuendos."

He looked at Jarsun and Dhuryo with a leer. "This is why women should know well enough to remain in the bedroom themselves. It is the only thing their minds run to."

Jarsun ignored Dronas's boorish comment and actions, but was not surprised to see Dhuryo Krushan snigger in response: the Krushan boys did have a reputation for debauchery. He spoke to Shikari directly.

"Whom do you speak of?"

Shikari looked at him through her long, painted lashes. "He calls himself Ekluv. He claims to be the bastard child of Emperor Adri and his former maid Sauvali."

Jarsun felt heat flare within himself. "You are certain of this?"

He realized only belatedly that he had crossed the breadth of the tent and was gripping Shikari tightly by both shoulders.

She looked up at him without any sign of fear at his reaction or the iron vise in which he held her. "Your own mistress was there. Ask her if you doubt my word."

Ladislew said, "It is true. He is the eldest born of his generation and next in line of succession after his father, Adri. He is heir to the Burning Throne."

"Impossible!" Dhuryo Krushan shouted. "You lie! Both of you!"

He lunged at Ladislew and Shikari with a raised fist.

Jarsun slapped him backhand, the impact hard enough to fling him across the tent. Dhuryo skittered across the carpeted floor, tumbling over to land in a jumble of cushions.

Before he could leap to his feet and attack again, Jarsun held out a finger in warning. "Think very carefully about what you do or say next, boy. You may be accustomed to having your way with women and those younger, smaller, or weaker than you, especially back home in Hastinaga, where you are no less than a god, but here, tonight, in this tent, you are only the third strongest person here. If you wish to stay alive and keep the use of all your limbs and wits, I suggest you keep your mouth shut. Open it only if you wish to apologize to my aide here for daring to raise your hand to her."

"That's all right," Ladislew said, glancing over her shoulder at Dhuryo. "He would never have landed the blow, but you did save him from losing an arm at least."

Dhuryo Krushan glowered at her, then at Jarsun, rising to his feet with a sound that was more snarl than speech.

"Stand down, acolyte," Dronas snapped in a tone that left no room for disobedience. "My friend Jarsun is right. You are outmatched, and I would rather not lose my star pupil to a pointless brawl the night before the most important battle of our lives."

Dhuryo stopped short at his guru's words. He continued to glare daggers at Jarsun and Ladislew, but made no further move. He picked up a goblet of wine and quaffed it like water, sprawling on a seat with the goblet in one hand and a flagon of wine in the other. He sat and drank through the rest of the discussion and the battle strategy council that followed.

"If Ladislew says it, it is true," Jarsun said to Dronas. "Adri Krushan did indeed father a child upon his maid. She was abducted in a surprise attack on Adri while he was on a leisure trip away from Hastinaga. She was pregnant at the time and only a few days short of birthing the child. I personally attempted to track down the woman, without success. It now appears that she survived long enough to bear the child and that child survived into manhood."

"It's more than that," Ladislew said, looking at Jarsun. "Jarsun, they know that you were the one who sent the assassins to attack Adri on that trip, and that you were responsible for the abduction of his lover and unborn child. Your intention was to cut the child out of the mother and raise it as your own, to use as your means of claiming the Burning Throne. Everyone knows the truth now, including the mother herself and her son, Ekluv. They both survived and were kept safe by Guru Vessa in a secret place until now. They have emerged from hiding to avenge themselves upon you and are sworn to end your life."

Jarsun stared at Ladislew. She stared back, undaunted. The others were staring at him as well, Dronas with suspicion, Shikari with derision, Dhuryo with eyes narrowed and brow furrowed.

Jarsun broke the silence with laughter. He spread his hands in that "so what" gesture that mortals always used when they were overwhelmed by news. "What of it? It is a fact that I was deprived of my legitimate inheritance. I should be upon the Burning Throne, not Adri, and definitely not that self-righteous Shvate, whom I did the world a service by killing. I will do whatever it takes to regain my rightful seat, no matter whom I have to kill or how many. So what if I kidnapped the maid Sauvali? How she escaped my assassins is still a mystery to me! I knew it had to be Vessa who stole her away from them. I tried tracking them down, chasing them through the ways, but never found them. Now you say they are alive? That they want revenge? To see me dead? Welcome to them, I say! How many others want me dead? A million? Ten million? A hundred million? Even the clerks of Hastinaga would go mad trying to tally the count! What does one or ten or a thousand more enemies matter? I am Jarsun. I am the rightful ruler of this world. Arthaloka is my domain, to rule and to shape to my wishes. No one, mortal, Krushan, or stone god, can deny me my right."

They were all staring at him. Except for Dronas, who was staring into the distance, face frozen in contemplation.

"Take it as you will," Ladislew said, a slight smile on her face. "I just thought you might like to know. Oh, and you already know about the Shvate Five. They and their mother and their guru Vessa have all sworn an oath as well, to avenge the murder of their father and kill you on the field tomorrow."

Jarsun chuckled, even though what he was feeling right now was rage and frustration more than humor. "Anyone else? Everyone in Gwannland, perhaps? And Arrgodi? And Mraashk? And Reygistan? And Aquila? All of Arthaloka? A wolf rules the sheep. He does not expect the sheep to love him. They are sheep, nothing more. Their love or hate does not matter. When the time comes, he tears out every one of their throats, and they can do nothing to stop him."

He turned to Dronas. "Enough of this. Now, let us lay our plans for the morrow. Dronas, I will outline my strategy for the battle. Here is what I propose."

Dronas turned to him, the lack of expression on his lined, aging face speaking more eloquently than words. "I will plan my battles myself, Jarsun. Though I thank you for offering your suggestions."

Jarsun stared at him. He had never found ordinary mortal expressions and moods easy to interpret. Often, their words, tone, body language, manner, all contradicted one another in subtle yet somehow meaningful ways. He had never cared to learn their subtleties and intricacies: What did it matter? Mortals who cooperated with him, he rewarded. Those who did not, he killed. It was a system that had worked well enough for him for all these years.

"Dronas," he said with as much patience as he could muster, "I have built an empire across Eastern and Southern Arthaloka and have experience in these matters."

He did not need to add that he had a personal stake in this battle, far more than Dronas, even. After all that Shikari and Ladislew had said, and he himself had spewed, it was obvious. Perhaps a little too obvious, he now reflected.

"Yes, and I value your experience and your support, Jarsun," Dronas said with careful precision, the more casual tone and the repeated uses of the word "friend" now suddenly vanished. "But I am the expert in warcraft and strategy. I have, as they say, written the book on the subject, and that book contains every strategy and tactic you may have used in your conquests, and many more you might not have. I am capable of planning and executing this battle in the most effective way possible."

Dronas indicated Shikari and Ladislew. "I believe you have been made aware of several powerful enemies who aim to see you dead on the field of Beha'al on the morrow. It might behoove you best to spend your time preparing and planning your own defense strategy. Vrath alone is no simple opponent, and from what I saw on that battlefield over two decades ago, he came very close to ending you."

Dronas paused and squinted into the distance. "In fact, if I remember correctly, you left the field quite abruptly at a crucial point, just when it appeared that he might be gaining the advantage. So the contest was never really completed, was it? Tomorrow it will not be as easy for you to flee the field. It will be instructive to see how you play out a full challenge. It can end only one way, as you well know, with one opponent dead. And Vrath, need I remind you, is a demigod and nigh invulnerable."

Jarsun stared at Dronas. He took in the awkward silence and averted gazes of Dhuryo, Shikari, and Ladislew, all of whom had found other corners of the tent more interesting to observe than his conversation with Dronas.

He looked back at Dronas again. The aging guru was showing Jarsun his profile, and it was not a pleasing one. Jarsun could have smashed that face in with a single blow, killed the rest of them with another, aided by urrkh sorcery, with only Ladislew giving him resistance. Although, in his present mood, he would have been willing to take her on as well, if only for that smug expression she wore, even as she kept her face averted.

"I am Jarsun Krushan," he said to Dronas, to all of them, to the world at large. "I cannot be defeated."

He turned and left the tent.

Adri

⁓

BORN BLIND, ADRI HAD never possessed the gift of sight. Even now, he knew that what he was experiencing was not true sight. It was . . . something else.

Yet, to his mind, if felt as if he were *seeing*. How else to describe it?

He had viewed every face, every expression, every action and word at the war council in Gwannland Palace. He had seen and heard every nuance in the tent on the field of Beha'al. It was as good as being there.

No.

It was *better* than being there.

Not being physically present, and with no one there aware of his presence, he could see, evaluate, and judge every detail, every pause, intake of breath, flicker of expression, with perfect clarity.

The power of stonefire did even more than that.

It enabled him to sense the innermost thoughts and feelings of those who were Krushan.

Of which there were a considerable number of key players. His five nieces and nephews. Uncle Vrath. Birth father Vessa. His own long-lost son, Ekluv. *Sauvali's son!* Even Princess Krushni, who, although she was in a different identity and body in this lifetime, remained resolutely Krushan in her spirit and strengths, drawing on the same infinite reservoir that empowered Adri to view these distant scenes.

And Jarsun.

Jarsun Krushan, his great-uncle. Or was it distant cousin? Regardless which branch of the family tree connected them by blood, Jarsun *was* his blood, his family.

And yet Jarsun was the one who had acted against him.

Jarsun had killed Shvate.

Adri had had a complicated relationship with Shvate when they were children. There had been a time when he had felt for his brother nothing but eternal love, gratitude, and reverence. That had changed the day of the Battle of the Rebels, when Adri had felt betrayed and abandoned by Shvate, whose albinism had forced him to flee the noonday sun, leaving Adri alone and bereft in a great press of enemy chariots; it was only thanks to Uncle Vrath that Adri had survived that terrible day. Perhaps it had begun to change even earlier, when they had been taken to the remote jungle by Vrath and left there to study under the gurus. Things had never been the same between Adri and Shvate after that.

But however complicated, even conflicted, his feelings for Shvate had been, one thing was indisputable: Adri had loved Shvate.

When he had received the news of Shvate's death from the person he had then believed to be Vida, his second brother, Adri had been devastated. Before he could begin to process the shock and to grieve, he had been enraged. The person he had thought was Vida had told him that Shvate had been murdered by their birth father, Vessa. At the same time, Vida had also said that Karni was behind the attack on Adri and Sauvali and the abduction and supposed death of Sauvali and her unborn child, Adri's unborn child.

At first, he had believed it completely. Had been out of his mind with fury at both Vessa, for doing such a terrible deed, and Karni, for stealing away the only person who had brought a lamp of joy into his dark, lonely life.

But after that Vida had left, Adri had learned the truth.

From stonefire.

The Burning Throne itself had spoken to him directly.

It had told him several things even more shocking than what that Vida had revealed.

Vida was not Vida at all; he was Jarsun in the form of Vida, seeking to deceive and manipulate Adri.

Jarsun had lied about everything.

Vessa had not killed Shvate. Jarsun had killed Shvate.

Jarsun had also orchestrated the attack on Adri and Sauvali, had Adri's beloved abducted by ruthless mercenaries, and had planned to rip Adri's unborn child from her womb and raise it as his own.

All this, and far more, Jarsun had done in order to carve a way, no matter how illegitimate, bloody, and violent, to the Burning Throne.

Jarsun was the one who had forced Hastinaga's own allies to fight against it in the Battle of the Rebels, the battle where Adri's bond with his brother had been tested and frayed.

Behind all these terrible things that had befallen Adri, Jarsun was the one responsible.

And yet he had repurposed the same events through his clever design and machinations to appear to be the fault of others, seeking to estrange Adri from his birth father, his sister-in-law, even his own wife, since Jarsun, disguised as Vida, had also implicated Geldry in the abduction and alleged murder of Sauvali and the boy he now knew as Ekluv.

Once Adri knew the truth, he had been chilled to the bone.

What monster would go to such lengths, commit such terrible crimes — against his own family — merely to serve his illicit ambitions?

Jarsun.

How to counteract such moves, such contrived and elaborately planned and deftly executed maneuvers on the vast chaupat board of life? How was Adri, blind king and reluctant emperor, supposed to defend himself against the future aggressions of Jarsun?

Stonefire could tell him.

Stonefire could tell him everything.

Stonefire spoke to Adri, and Adri listened.

Stonefire was honest to him; it spoke only truth. A terrible, unendurable truth, but truth nevertheless. It would never lie to him, deceive him, abandon him, turn on him; it had no ambitions other than his own: to rule the world justly and fairly, even if that meant inflicting violence on those that opposed its power.

Stonefire was his friend, his true life companion, his family.

The only family that mattered.

So long as he listened to stonefire, he would be safe. He would be strong. He would be powerful.

He could even see, in a manner of speaking, by surrendering himself completely to the supernatural flames that blazed around him as he sat upon the dark, living rock. Its heat blazed into the membranes of his eyes and took control of his mind and body, showing him those distant scenes where his enemies plotted and schemed against him, even as they depended upon his power, his mercy, his armies.

Adri knew all.

Saw all.

Heard all.

And soon he would have his vengeance.

They would burn.

Every last one of them.

Burn, sang the throne.

Burn, agreed Adri.

Burn.

Part Three

The Battle of Beha'al

Krushni

~

A SUDDEN GUST OF wind billowed Krushni's rainbow-hued Gwann-lander robe, painting the grey world with dancing colors. The grey was the endless ocean of Krushan troops nearly encircling the Gwannland army in a semicircle that seemed to fill the edges of the visible world.

The field of Beha'al was uniquely shaped, a mile-sided squarish patch of flat land surrounded on all sides by rising slopes that undulated in waves for a score of miles in every direction. The result was a bowl-shaped space where the luxuriant grass that thrived in this part of the continent grew only sparsely. Perhaps even the land knew that there was little point in growing green shoots only to have them trampled by a million feet, she thought, turning slowly to scan the horizon.

"They mean to crush and erase us where we stand," Vensera said grimly, her jaw tight as she fastened the strap of her war helmet.

"Or push us into the sea," Gwann added, indicating the city behind them, beyond which lay the body of water in question.

"You have to admit, though," Krushni said, turning back again to review the enemy. "It is quite a sight."

"The Krushan believe in spectacles," Vessa said, squinting up at the sky. "The display of power and its trappings is the bedrock of their culture."

"You are Krushan too, great guru," Arrow said, "as are we. None of us find this sight spectacular. It seems to me a sign of weakness in an otherwise strong enemy."

"Speak for yourself," Yudi countered. "I agree with Krushni. It's an impressive display of imperial power."

"Oh, so that's what it is," Brum said, her tone heavy with irony. "And here I thought it just another convention of fart lovers."

Vessa chuckled, surprising Krushni. "Young Brum does well to keep a sense of humor at a time like this. When faced with such odds, there is little point in worrying overmuch."

"Tell Yudi that, Grandfather," Saha said. "He does nothing but worry."

"The only jokes he knows are probably about worrying or thinking too much about something," Kula agreed.

Vessa smiled again, his yellowed teeth contrasting sharply with his pristine white beard and facial hair. "I am pleased to see that the five of you made the journey safely. As I suggested at the time, I would have been glad to have transported you through a portal, as I have done for your mother."

He indicated the woman who stood nearby, engaged in conversation with Tshallian and two other foreigners. They had arrived shortly before.

Krushni regarded Karni, her distant cousin in her previous lifetime, widow of Prince Shvate, sister-in-law to Emperor Adri.

She was a woman of middle age with attractive features that had seen some hard living and a fair bit of combat as well. Her lean, lithe body and toned arms and legs testified to almost two decades of living in the wilderness, far from the imperial comforts of Hastinaga Palace. There were scars on her arms, back, one thigh, and even one on her neck, just below her chin. For a warrior of middle age, those were not too many; it was hard to say if she had not seen very many battles or if she was just that good. From the looks of her, and the fact that she had survived the transition from princess to exile, and exile to outlaw, and was still alive and in robust health and physical condition, it would seem she *was* that good. There was an air about her of self-control and quiet watchfulness, as if she had spent the decade and a half since her husband's assassination ever on the alert for another attempt.

Krushni knew how that felt; she had watched her own mother die on the red sands of Reygistan, within sight of their destination after long, hard years of travel and struggle, betrayed and murdered by the very man who was oathsworn to protect and love her to the end of her days. Even in this lifetime, as Krushni, princess of Gwannland, who had no ostensible connection to Jarsun, Aqreen, or their bitter marital dispute, she still carried the pain and weight of that shocking death. Her senses were ever alert and would remain so, she knew, until she herself breathed her last.

As if sensing her eyes and her thoughts, Karni turned and glanced at Krushni. She finished speaking to Tshallian and the other two strangers and came over to her.

"Princess Krushni," she said in a voice that was oddly quiet, despite the inevitable background roar of the vast numbers gathered all around. "Our fates and lives are joined now."

"They are," Krushni agreed. "United by a common bond and purpose."

"To kill Jarsun Krushan and end his long reign of evil," Karni said.

Krushni smiled. "And, if possible, launch a new era of justice, equality, and inclusivity. A new age for Arthaloka."

Karni raised her eyebrows. "Then it is true. You intend to use this battle as the first step in your aim to take Hastinaga and control of the Burning Throne."

"To take *back* Hastinaga," Krushni said. "But it is not I who will sit upon the throne. I gave that up when I ended my life as a Krushan and took this new mantle of flesh. It's your children that I hope to see installed as lieges of the empire."

Karni gazed out at the field, watching the rippling waves in the distance that indicated troop movements.

Krushni followed her line of sight and saw what appeared to be war elephants being positioned behind foot infantry, several tens of thousands of the former behind several hundred thousand of the latter. She could feel the vibrations of all those ton-heavy beasts in the soles of her feet, even from all these miles away.

"I only want for the family to give my children what they rightfully deserve."

"And Grandmother Jilana and Uncle Vrath both said that they deserve the throne. Shvate abdicated for only one reason, because he had been cursed by the sage to never bear offspring. That was negated the instant you and your sister wife, Princess Mayla, birthed the Five. Under Krushan law, they are legitimate heirs to Shvate and as such to the throne. Adri must step down and yield the throne to them. As their mother and guardian, that means you ought to be empress regent until they come of age. Both Jilana and Vrath have said so."

"Grandmother Jilana and Uncle Vrath mean well. They have only the interests of the empire and the family at heart. They are keepers of the law and tradition, and if they say so, it must be so under Krushan law. I am neither a lawkeeper nor do I care about tradition. I have only the welfare of my children at heart. I want them to be happy and fulfilled. If they wish to take the Test of Fire and claim their right to the throne, I will support that decision."

"*If?*" Krushni asked, puzzled. "Where is the *if* in this decision? They *must* take the Test of Fire and claim their rightful inheritance."

Karni looked at Krushni. "Why does it matter so to you? You hardly know them. Why do you care if they want to be rulers or if they simply choose to wander the earth doing as they will?"

Krushni nodded. "A fair question. I suppose it's because I would rather live the life of a princess than survive in the jungle."

When Karni frowned, Krushni said, "I know this is neither the time nor place to bring this up, but I only met your children because they came to my contest." She paused and added slowly, "My *wedding* contest. Which they won."

Karni stared at her.

"I promised only that I would choose my possible suitor from among the victors," Krushni went on, eager to finish now that she had started. There was something in Karni's face, in her eyes, that made her wish she hadn't started at all. "And I have made my decision."

Karni raised her eyebrows expectantly. "You wish to marry one of my sons?"

"I wish to marry all five of your children."

"All of them?"

"Yes. Gender is unimportant to me."

Karni was silent for a long moment. The background noise of the battle-field grew steadily. Someone brought word to Vensera and Gwann that the rebel forces had arrived from Mraashk, Arrgodi, Reygar, Aquila, and other places, and the united armies of Arthaloka, as they had mutually decided to term their side, were now ready for battle.

Krushni waited, knowing for that long, seemingly endless moment how petitioners must feel when they approached her mother Vensera in her court for justice. At this moment, she was not a princess or a woman of power; she was just a young woman praying with all her might that she would get the partner she desired. *Five partners, in this case.*

"We shall speak of this after the battle," Karni said. "Assuming we survive."

Krushni nodded. She knew better than to counter that caveat with something glib, if only because she knew painfully well that one could never be sure of victory. If anything, the odds were heavily stacked against them. Even their brave alliance barely made a difference. To go into battle against not just the powerful Jarsun Krushan and the Krushan Hundred, as well as the formidable Dronas and all the other legendary champions from the Burnt Empire, but all the armies of the empire as well, was not something to take for granted.

We will be lucky to survive — and not all of us will. Which was why I hoped to get your blessing before the battle at least, Karni.

Aloud she said, "I shall look forward to that talk."

Karni started to turn away, then paused. She looked at Krushni once more, this time sizing her up not as a fellow combatant but as a woman. Perhaps even as a mother might view her prospective daughter-in-law.

No, you're just overthinking it again, Krushni. Sometimes a look is just a look.

"I wish you success in all you desire, Krushni," Karni said, laying a gentle hand on her shoulder. "May you find it upon this field today, and in all your endeavors."

Krushni smiled as Karni walked away. Now, *that*, that was a blessing.

Yudi

⌒

YUDI STARED OUT AT the sea of humanity, hypnotized.

A hand thumped him on the back. Brum. Of course.

"Brother," she said cheerfully, "you look like a man condemned to the gallows staring at the scaffolding as he crosses the prison yard."

Yudi sighed. "Admit it, Brum. Even you have never seen a sight like this before."

"Of course not," she shot back. "Nobody has. I heard Vrath and Jilana telling Vessa how this is the largest mobilization that either of them has witnessed in their lifetimes."

"That's *Great-Uncle* Vrath and *Great-Grandmother* Jilana."

"Sure, sure, but it's still the biggest damned army footslogging it, isn't it?"

He nodded. "So you agree that it's impressive? Awe-inspiring? Magnificent?"

She reached up and grabbed his chin forcefully, twisting his face to examine it closely. Their noses touched briefly. He bore it patiently. She was his little sister, after all. "Magnificent, did you say? You do realize that monster of an army is here to kill you, big brother? Kill all of us, and our new friends, and everyone who stands with us. And then, after they're done stomping our bones into the dust, they plan to roll on like the stone god Inadran, laying waste to all Arthaloka — the parts that aren't already under the Burnt Empire, I mean. You do remember that minor detail, don't you?"

"Of course," he said. "An army of that size wasn't transported thirty-seven thousand miles across the continent just for nothing. This is our uncle Adri's chance to complete the Krushan conquest of the rest of Arthaloka. If he succeeds, he will be the first Krushan in history to unite the entire continent."

"To run through it like a stampeding bull elephant, you mean," Arrow said, coming up beside Yudi. "The Eastern and Southern Kingdoms don't need imperial rule. They have their own cultures, their own languages, their own laws and customs and traditions. They don't need the Burnt Empire to shove Krushan laws down their throats."

"Especially after these armies are done pillaging and rampaging through those independent kingdoms," Saha added.

"Or if those kingdoms will even survive these armies passing through," Kula said. "I can say with confidence that Gwannland won't survive, if that army wins this battle."

"Yes, yes," Yudi said. "I see your points, all of them. But the fact still remains that we are Krushan, and those are our armies too. Someday we will control all those forces, and when we do, we will face the same political situation and complications and problems that Uncle Adri faces now. I'm just saying that we need to learn to see things from his point of view as well."

Brum squinted at him, then peered around at their other siblings. "Do you, any of you?"

They all shook their heads. Kula grinned.

Brum turned back to Yudi, taking him by both arms. "I don't think so, brother Yudi. We don't like the idea of seeing through the eyes of someone, anyone, who is willing to kill their own nephews and nieces, and a whole bunch of other very nice people, just because he has a big fat army and all the power and wealth in the world at his command. In fact, at this moment, looking at that army out there, what I feel for Uncle Adri, I can best express with a single word. And that word is . . . wait for it . . ."

Brum bent over, made a face, wriggled her backside a little, then let go of a mighty fart.

Arrow, Saha, and Kula burst out laughing. Even Yudi smiled reluctantly.

Brum looked at him with a satisfied expression. "That translates into every language. No interpreter required."

She sniffed and wrinkled her nose. "Ah. Beans. They were good, though!"

Yudi shook his head, grinning. "Brum, you're too much."

She shook her head. "No such thing. Now, if you've stopped admiring the view from the Barfing Throne, could we get ready to go to battle? Pretty please? I haven't had a good battle in a while, and this one looks like it's going to be such fun."

Yudi shook his head. "Brum, sometimes I worry about you."

"That's okay, brother," she said contentedly, picking up her mace and hefting it. "It saves me the trouble of worrying about myself — or anything else, for that matter. I mean, let's face it, who has the time, when there's so much fun to be had, right? All right, let's do this."

Dhuryo

~

DRONAS WAS LAYING OUT the last details of his briefing.

"Remember, watch for my signal at all times. I will be observing the enemy and indicating to you which tactic to use when. Otherwise, you boys have a tendency to expend needless energy just bashing and smashing."

"Bashing and smashing work really well for us," said Nubanyer, one of Dhuryo's youngest brothers, although this only meant that he had been born a few seconds later than most of them.

Dronas turned to look at Nubanyer. "I'm sure it does. But sometimes one needs to move on to other tactics to keep the enemy on the defensive. Constantly changing tactics confuses their army and creates chaos."

"With our numbers today," said Jogan, one of the middle brothers, "we could probably just run over them and pound them into dust."

The rest of the Hundred shouted out their agreement.

Dronas looked at Jogan, then at the Hundred in general.

"We are not the army. We are not mere foot soldiers. Or chariots. Or horse cavalry. Or elephants. We are *champions*. We are master warriors. We pick and choose our fights; we make use of our intelligence and our warcraft, not just our weapons and brute strength. We strategize and are tactical as required. We outmaneuver and outwit the enemy. Our battle is not merely the battle of the body and blade, it is the battle of the mind and the heart. Do you understand me, Krushan?"

A sullen chorus of ayes acknowledged him.

"Good. Remember, you are Krushan. You fight not for personal glory. You fight for the bloodline. You fight for the Burnt Empire. You fight for the ancestors who spent their lives waging war that you might have the privi-

285

leges you were born with. You fight for the people of the empire, who give their livelihoods and hard-won earnings to pay you the imperial tax that makes all your armies and palaces and luxuries possible. You fight to bring Krushan law to the unschooled barbarians and savages of the far corners of the continent. You fight for the honor of your elders, who guide you and administer the empire on your behalf. And above all else, you fight for stone-fire itself, the rock that gives you the power that you will wield on this field today. You fight for the Burning Throne."

This speech got a more than enthusiastic response. Every last one of the Hundred was on his feet and roaring with approval by the end.

Dronas nodded to Dhuryo and stepped aside.

Dhuryo stepped forward, facing his brothers.

"You know me well in battle. You have seen me fight."

"Aye!" shouted Manafor, one of the eldest. "And every time you fight, you win!"

Dhuryo raised his hand. "I win because I respect the law, I honor my elders, I repay my debt to the people who serve me, I commemorate our ancestors, I represent the dynasty. Guru Dronas has already reminded us what we fight for, so I won't repeat it. I'll just say one thing more, and then we shall go to battle. I know you are as impatient as I am to bash in skulls and separate heads from bodies."

"And smash bones!" yelled Firono, one of the youngest and most boisterous. "I love smashing bones the best!"

Everyone laughed at that, even Dhuryo.

"You shall have plenty of bones to smash, brother. There are enough to go around today. But remember, we are not facing any ordinary enemy on the field of Beha'al. We face Krushan as well."

The noise and laughter subsided a little, but several voices still rang out defiantly.

"We are the best and mightiest of all Krushan. Even Guru Dronas says so. We will crush their bones and skulls as easily as the other poor bastards!"

This came from Venmak, who had already drunk more ale this morning than most men drank in a week.

"Perhaps," Dhuryo said mildly, knowing better than to dampen their spirits. He could feel their eagerness and shared it himself. But he still needed to make his point.

"But let us not make the mistake of underestimating our enemies. Let us use the strategy and tactics that Guru Dronas has designed for us so artfully. Without them, we might well win anyway, but it could take us longer and perhaps pose some difficulties. Remember, the entire Krushan army is on that field today. We are not in some taproom bashing skulls in a brawl. The whole world will be watching us. We must not simply win by *any* means; we must win *decisively* and *shrewdly*. We must show the world that Krushan are indomitable and that to stand against us is a futile and foolish choice. We must drive terror into the hearts of our enemies and into the hearts of our own warriors. For they must look upon our exploits on the field and say to themselves, 'Fight the stone gods. Fight an army of urrkh demons. Fight all the champions of the world. But never pick a fight with a Krushan!'"

"Krushan!" roared the Hundred.

"And when we face a fellow Krushan out there," Dhuryo said, building now to the crux of his speech, "remember that we have something they do not. We have the power and weight of stonefire itself behind us. Our father sits upon the living rock from which our ancestors sprang. That rock empowers us all and gives us superhuman strength, power, and speed. Even another Krushan foolish enough to stand against us cannot overcome that advantage. Because when anything threatens stonefire, what does it do?"

"Burn!" cried his brothers with one voice.

"And that is what we will do on the field of Beha'al today, my brothers. We will fight, we will smash, we will crush, and we will burn. Burn every last one of our enemies."

"Burn! Burn! Burn!" They repeated the word over and over again, thumping their feet on the ground till the hillside itself shook and troops turned their heads from a mile away to gaze fearfully in their direction; elephants trumpeted, and horses whickered.

Jarsun

~

JARSUN HEARD THE ROARING of the Hundred. He ignored it.

He no longer cared about Dhuryo and his brothers.

He didn't give a damn about Dronas and his vendetta against Gwann.

He knew how this game was played.

Dhuryo believed he was heir and crown prince, in direct line to the throne. Dronas thought the same and was fixated on the possibility of Dhuryo, his star pupil, making him commander in chief of the armies of the empire. He thought that the title and all the glory and riches that came with it were within his grasp now. He aimed to get his revenge on Gwann, expand his personal fiefdom, and act as the satrap of the empire in the East.

Dhuryo believed that once he completed this expansion, he would be credited as the first Krushan to conquer the entire continent. Even though the credit would go to his father first for daring to make such a bold move, Dhuryo was the one on the ground risking his princely neck, and he would have glory and recognition like he'd never known before. He thought he would succeed his father soon, perhaps even in the next few years. And then he would be master of the world.

They were both forgetting one crucial thing.

Jarsun.

Jarsun had not played the game and worked so hard for so long just to see an arrogant self-serving *teacher* and overprivileged *brat* reap the spoils of what he had sown. Did these fools think that because Dhuryo was crown prince and the armies of Hastinaga were at his command that they could shunt Jarsun aside like this and still succeed? Without Jarsun, this vast army would not even be here. If Hastinaga had been capable of reaching as far as the East and South and taking over those remote territories, it would have done so centuries ago. Only Jarsun's portal made it possible for the greatest armed force in the history of the continent to be transported more than thirty thousand miles in a matter of days. And how did they think they would return home?

All he had to do was shut the portal and refuse to reopen it, and they would be stranded here for years. Desertion, attrition, hostile climes, and treacherous geography would whittle away their vast numbers until, by the time the remainder staggered into Hastinaga, they would be a pale shadow of their present imperial might.

Meanwhile, Hastinaga would be left unprotected except for a couple hundred thousand city troops, barely sufficient to withstand the usual uprisings and rebellions of the civil populace, vulnerable to any tin-hat despot who saw a way to quick glory and riches.

It would destroy the empire.

He could destroy the empire.

Jarsun breathed deeply, exhaling with a dual hiss, his split tongue flickering out the corners of his mouth, tasting the air heavy with humidity and the salty sweat of millions of unwashed bodies strapped into leather harnesses and metal armor.

He could destroy it, but he would not. That would negate all that he had worked for.

Instead, he would show them all who they were truly dealing with.

He would win this battle first. Decisively, conclusively.

He would crush these enemies, all conveniently gathered together in a single place — how nice of them — and grind their bones into the dust of this field.

The Shvate Five, because so long as they lived, they threatened his claim to the throne.

The bastard son of the maid, Ekluv, for the same reason.

Gwann, Vensera, and the rest of Gwannland's rainbow-clad flower gatherers and their rebel sympathizers from Arrgodi, Mraashk, Reygistan, Aquila, and whichever other holes they had crawled out from, would all be easy pickings — they would not survive the first hour of battle facing these odds.

That would leave the four main opponents, the heavy hitters.

Vrath. Vessa. Krushni. Drishya.

First, he would have to deal with Vrath, of course. He had a strategy in place for that. Did the fools really think Vrath's participation came as a surprise to Jarsun? He had planned for every eventuality, anticipated their every move, and prepared for it accordingly.

That left Krushni and Drishya and the waywalker.

Krushni, he had a personal score to settle with. Drishya would have to die because he was with her and because he had slain Tyrak, Jarsun's son-in-law and the surrogate son he had mentored and groomed for kingship. He had hoped at the time to give Tyrak charge of the Reygistan Empire, so Jarsun could concentrate his attention on the heart of the Burnt Empire itself, on the far side of the continent. By slaying Tyrak, Drishya had knocked that wagon train off its wheels, setting back Jarsun's plans. Tyrak had been hard to replace; a dozen, or even a hundred minor sadists hardly compared with a single genocidal dictator.

Lastly, Vessa.

He knew he could not hope to defeat Vessa in open combat. The guru would simply escape through the ways, avoiding direct confrontation. That was the infuriating thing about his kind; they were not warriors, so they cared nothing for the codes and rules of battle. They did not consider running away a form of retreat; they considered it simply a tactic.

But he knew that the surprise he had in store for all of them, the revelation he would make when the time was right, would compel Vessa and Vrath to back down. After Jarsun revealed the truth, they could not possibly fight him openly. They would not dare to. It would violate Krushan law, and if there was one thing that even their combined powers could not make them overcome, it was that.

Krushan law.

Which brought him back to Krushni. He did not doubt he could kill her. At most, she could cause him some small inconvenience, perhaps even difficulty. But he would destroy her; he had no doubt of that. And when it was all said and done, Dronas, Dhuryo, and everyone else on this field would bow down before him and acknowledge him, Jarsun, as God-Emperor of all Arthaloka.

This battle was his for the winning.

The empire was his for the taking. Within his reach at last.

He grinned, unfurling his mouth, peeling it back to reveal his fanged jaws, dripping venom, and let his eyes flash with lightning. He could see the troops and their mounts whicker and mutter in fear at the sight, shifting uneasily in their massed ranks. It was strange indeed to them to be on the same side as the very being whom they warned their children of at nights as a cautionary tale. Jarsun, the monster who prowls Hastinaga at night in search of children to steal or murder; Jarsun, the demonlord who ravages entire cities, entire nations, just by walking through the streets and laying hands on the water or food, or breathing the same air. Jarsun, the terrifying. Jarsun, the unspeakable. His name itself was a legend, a myth come to life, that struck terror into the hearts of even the staunchest of champions.

And here he was now, in the flesh, as monstrous as they had heard and been told.

He rode through the ranks, the lines parting hurriedly to let him pass, giving him a wide berth, fearful of even his glance, holding their breaths till he went by for fear of breathing in the air he had exhaled.

He rode toward the front of the lines, to where the enemy awaited the start of battle.

The sun was just beyond the distant hills, threatening to shine its gaudy glory onto this abattoir's slab. The air was cool, redolent of grass, animal shit, and the stench of millions of living beings gathered in a few square miles.

He reached the frontlines and then broke free into the open space between the opposing armies. Only a few hundred yards away stood the pathetically smaller forces of Gwannland and its allies. Colorfully clad even in battle, their banners whipping in the steady morning breeze, their troops arranged in circular, horseshoe-shaped, floral, and other ludicrously impractical formations. Were they here to entertain children at a spring festival or fight a battle?

Jarsun asked the question aloud to the nearest Krushan commander. The man smiled nervously but chuckled and passed the joke along to his subordinates. By the miraculous speed of battlefield camaraderie, it rippled down the seemingly endless lines until Jarsun imagined that the chuckles were echoed miles away by the soldiers fortunate enough to be at the tail end of this gargantuan beast of an army.

A little way to his left, Dronas and Dhuryo heard the joke repeated and the name of its originator, and glanced coldly in his direction.

Jarsun raised one bony hand and offered a mocking gesture of greeting.

He smiled to himself. Yes, this was his army now, whether Dronas and Dhuryo liked it or not. Neither they, nor Jilana, Vrath, or even Adri himself could deny Jarsun now. When this battle was done and won, he would unveil his biggest revelation and make his final move. This was the endgame, and none of them could stand in his way.

He would be emperor of the Burnt Empire soon. And within his grasp, the Burnt Empire would encompass the world.

The first ray of sunlight stole over the horizon, gleaming darkly in his peripheral vision. He felt it glancing off his cold cheeks, the needles of warmth prickling his scaled skin. He smiled. Yes, he tasted victory already. It had the flavor of blood and terror, and it was both pungent and sweet. He savored it.

"Sound the start of battle," he said.

Yudi

～

CONCH HORNS SANG OUT in the cool sunrise, overriding the susurration of the armies. The two armies, unequal in numbers but interlinked by the common brotherhood of battle fever, heard the sound and thrilled to it. Like whale song over the soughing of the ocean, the breathy notes carried across the field of Beha'al. A million hearts tightened in a mixture of fear and relief. Fear for the inevitable possibility of one's own death. Relief that it would now begin and that meant it was closer to ending.

Yudi read the temperature of the battlefield through a thousand signs and sounds, processing every detail through his knowledge of the history of war.

The Krushan armies were cheerful, boisterous, and confident. They knew they outnumbered the enemy. They had legendary champions on their side. They had the fearsome demonlord himself, the dreaded Jarsun. They had Guru Dronas, the greatest master of warcraft that ever lived. They had Dhuryo Krushan and the Krushan Hundred, whose brutality and mercilessness in battle were already notorious. Opposing them were unknown strangers, foreigners in absurdly colorful garb and with neither reputation nor numbers nor lineage.

Some wondered why they were even here, so far from home, in a foreign land under strange skies, brought this vast distance to crush this puny force. Were they even required here? Did it take an elephant to smash this ant? None voiced these questions aloud: under Krushan law, any questioning of orders was regarded as treason and punishable by death. But they thought it. They *had* to be thinking it.

There were other things that passed through Yudi's busy mind. Things not as obvious, yet equally self-evident to him.

The enemy believed they would ride over and trample the united armies of Arthaloka in minutes, ending this not-quite-a-battle within the first hour.

That was obvious even to their own side. Unrestrained by the strictures of Krushan law, the rank and file of Gwannland spoke their fears and doubts openly.

The fact that they were still here on this field, ready to fight and give their lives for the cause of freedom from tyranny, said all that needed to be said.

They believe we will die here today, this very morning, he thought.

They might well be right.

There had been a wave of laughter on the enemy side, just before the battle conches sounded. Yudi thought it might have been in response to something Jarsun had said, thought it spoke to the same state of mind: the utter certainty that the Krushan side would demolish the enemy in a flash.

It might also have been provoked by amusement at the colorful pageantry of Gwannland's forces. Yudi had to admit the irregular, exotic formations of troops and positioning of the united armies was cause for merriment. It looked funny, even absurd, to anyone familiar with tried and tested battle tactics and formations. He could only imagine how hard Dronas, Dhuryo, and the Krushan Hundred must be laughing at the sight of all these gaily decorated legions and the dancing bannermen and bannerwomen who pranced at their heads.

They must think we are children come to play a deadly game without understanding of the dire consequences.

But nothing could be further from the truth.

Arrow

~

1

EVEN BEFORE THE BATTLE conches ceased their wailing, the enemy began their charge.

They're eager to get this over with and reap the spoils of war, Arrow thought, then glanced around.

The rest of the Five stood to either side. Also there was Ekluv, bow in hand. He looked calm and expectant, as if he were ready to face death. Arrow would have liked to have had time to get to know this cousin better. He was interesting, if somewhat enigmatic. Ekluv changed his grip on the bow.

Arrow looked further down the line. There were Krushni and Drishya, side by side. Again, at the sight of Krushni, Arrow felt something leap inside their chest. She evoked such powerful feelings; they could not begin to be described. Yet it had only been a few days since they had met, eventful days with so much to do, so much to talk about and think about, that it had hardly been possible to begin to get to know her.

Arrow sensed something in her profile and knew she was about to turn a fraction of an instant before she did. Their eyes met. There was a shock of connection. It was like and yet unlike the psychic connection the five siblings shared. In the case of the Five, Arrow felt a warm familiarity when exchanging a glance or a thought with one of them. But at Krushni's look, the ground shuddered underfoot.

Without moving her lips or changing her expression, she conveyed a smile of regard and good wishes. This was clear even though Arrow did not feel the mind-to-mind connection that meant she was communicating.

Somehow, she was speaking even without words. They tried to do the same, to wish her a good battle, but were unable to tell for certain if they had succeeded. She was again looking down at the charging enemy lines, her attention never wavering, yet they felt that they had communicated.

You need to get your head back in the fight, Arrow told themself. *Not indulge in childish fantasies.*

Arrow felt the other siblings' minds, aware of their presence despite being shielded from them. They were all watching the enemy advance, waiting for the time to act. Brum was already breathing deeper and quicker, preparing for one of her leaps. Yudi's mind was burning at feverish speed, processing everything he saw and heard through his vast library of knowledge, even while remaining outwardly calm and composed. Saha was fretting about the animals being used in the conflict who would be injured or maimed, and who would mostly die awful, cruel deaths. Kula was watching the Krushan Hundred carefully, waiting to see where and how they would strike first.

Arrow looked down at the field. Because of the unique geography of Beha'al, they were standing on one of several terraced levels above the lowermost point. Far behind them was the highest point. The Krushan elders Vrath and Jilana were there, along with Guru Vessa. The lowermost point was ahead of Arrow, the midpoint between the two armies. That was where the advancing Krushan army would expect to meet the Gwannland army in the first clash.

But Queen Vensera had not yet given the order to charge. The queen herself, and her consort, King Gwann, stood astride their chariots on the level behind and slightly above the one on which the frontline stood. She too was watching the advancing Krushan army. Arrow admired her calm and poise.

Arrow could feel the thrumming of the enemy advance through the soles of their feet, shuddering in every bone and joint of their body. It was a scary feeling, to know a force that enormous and powerful was coming toward you with no intention except to kill you and crush you into the dirt. If they, Arrow Krushan, the birth child of Stone God Inadran, Lord of Storms and War, could be chilled at the prospect, how did it make these *mortals* feel? To the best of Arrow's knowledge, only the Shvate Five, Ekluv, Krushni, Drishya, Vrath, and Vessa were empowered. Apart from the ten of them, every other body on this side of the field was painfully, vulnerably, mortal.

How did they endure the knowledge that in a few moments, many of them would lie bleeding, broken, dying, dead, or incapacitated?

It was pointless thinking such thoughts. Besides, it was not as if Arrow, or the other empowered, were immortal or invulnerable either. They each had their weaknesses. If their opponents, even a perfectly ordinary Krushan soldier, knew just how and where to strike, each could be killed. Unlikely, nigh impossible in some cases — Vrath and Vessa, in particular — but doable. Who could say that some fateful arrow, spear, or sword might not happen to catch them at their weakest point, if not by knowledge, then by accident? In the madness of war, stranger things had happened. Arrow had not lived long nor read a fraction of the histories Yudi had scrolled through, but they knew that much. Nothing was certain until it had happened. Only then could one say, yes, it happened that way.

I could die here today. Or I could lose any of my siblings. Or one of the other members of the family whom I met only yesterday for the first time.

The enemy reached the midpoint and continued their advance up the first slope on the Gwannland side.

Still, Queen Vensera did not give the order to advance.

The enemy was now less than five hundred yards from the frontlines of Gwannland. Though the incline they were negotiating was a gradual one, Arrow knew that a gentle slope could be deceptive. In a few moments, tens of thousands of Krushan infantry had crossed the midpoint and were working their way up the terraced hillside. The Gwannland army remained exactly where they were, standing at ease, observing the enemy's approach but making no move.

Arrow saw horses galloping to and fro on the enemy side. Messengers seeking advice from their commanders on whether to continue advancing uphill. Several riders reached the little knot of the Krushan Hundred where Dhuryo Krushan and Dronas were mounted on their chariots. Almost immediately, the riders turned and started back with their orders. The Krushan kept advancing.

Four hundred yards now.

The enemy advance was a little slower, thanks to the rising incline. But the day was young, the troops were fresh and eager, with the scent of easy victory and spoils in their nostrils, and they kept coming.

When they were three hundred yards short of the Gwannland front-lines, Arrow saw Queen Vensera lift her hand to issue a signal.

2

Everyone along the line raised their bows, arrows already notched, draw-strings pulled.

Arrow had tested the wind a moment earlier with a wetted fingertip and had judged it to be blowing easterly at a diagonal angle across the field at about fifteen miles an hour. They corrected for the wind and distance, and held their aim. The arrow was pointed upward at the clear grey-blue sky, angled forward toward the first hill on the enemy side, slightly to the right to allow for the wind.

"Loose!" Arrow called.

The thrum of the bowstring vibrated down their arms and shoulders to their spine. They felt the familiar thrill in the gut that came with the first use of weapons in battle. The shower of arrows rose up into the early morning sky, the metal tips catching the rising sun and gleaming darkly as they traveled in long, slow arcs across the field. Arrow glimpsed the Krushan troops pausing to glance upward, raising their shields defensively, then lowering them as they saw that the arrows were aimed far behind them.

Our strategy puzzles them and confuses their leaders, Arrow thought, and imagined the enemy believing that Gwannland had just wasted a perfectly good volley. Dronas would probably assume in his arrogance that Vensera had given the signal too late, misjudging the pace of the enemy advance, and missed the chance to slow the Krushan advance.

The Krushan advance resumed, the troops roaring with derisive laughter, mocking the foolish Gwannlanders who couldn't even aim a bow properly.

As in all Krushan battles, there was a certain order to the formations in which the four branches of the army assembled and advanced. Up front were the infantry, who were now committed and well on the enemy side, barely two hundred yards from the Gwannland frontlines. Next came the chariots. Then the horse cavalry. And finally, the elephants.

Strike, wound, scatter, crush, as the scrolls and gurus taught. It was a classic Krushan war formation.

The chariots had staged at the top of the first hill, the better to give them momentum when they advanced. They were spread across the horizon, perhaps a thousand chariots abreast and a hundred deep. A hundred thousand Krushan chariots, enough to crush an army five times that number.

The storm of arrows reached its zenith, seemed to hang in the air, then started its earthward journey.

The volley was aimed, not at the oncoming foot soldiers, but at the chariots.

3

The volley struck the Krushan chariot regiments with a sound like hail on a tin roof. Arrow could hear it even from a mile away. That was the sound of the arrowheads striking the metal wells of the chariots: those were the ones that missed their target. Perhaps only about two or three in ten arrows actually struck flesh and bone: those were the ones that struck home.

He saw the charioteers cry out in surprise and shock as they lowered the shields they had hurriedly raised to stare at their horses. Each war chariot housed two men — a driver and an archer — and was drawn by two horses. While the men were interchangeable, and a good charioteer could drive and fight at the same time, a chariot was not much use without its steeds.

Gwannland's archers had aimed only at the horses.

Arrow heard Kula cry out as the volley struck a few thousand horses. The painful sound of equestrian screams rang out. The charioteers cried out just as loudly, as pained by the suffering of their beloved mounts as they were outraged by the unexpected assault.

They didn't have much time to grieve.

Arrow and the others along the Gwannland frontline had already loosed a second and a third volley before the first had landed. They were about to loose the fourth when the first one struck and the screaming and shouting began.

The advancing Krushan infantry faltered in its advance, half a million heads turning to look back up the hill on their side. They saw their chariot ranks being targeted and heard the screams and cries. Then their captains ordered them to look ahead and continue their advance. They roared uneasily and resumed their uphill charge.

By now, they were only a hundred yards short of the Gwannland frontlines. Arrow could see the faces of the first Krushan soldiers, light eyes glaring hotly beneath the trademark helmets marked with the icon of the Burning Throne. The soldiers charging up at him and his siblings were spear wielders, as were most of the frontlines of Krushan infantry all along the battlefield. Once they expended their spears, they would switch to swords. Standard Krushan tactics again.

By the time Gwannland had released its twentieth volley, they were almost within throwing range. Arrow glanced down between arrows to see the lieutenants bickering with their captains. The rules called for them to start throwing when within fifty yards, as they would be in a few moments. But the tactic was not intended to be applied to the throwing of spears fifty yards uphill. They had expected to meet the enemy at the midpoint of Beha'al, where the ground was level, not on a rising slope. There was no time to send back word to their commanders for a change of tactic, so they would have to decide what to do.

Gwannland continued firing volleys without pause. Twenty-one, twenty-two, twenty-three . . . then the sound of orders being yelled in Krushan commonspeak. The lieutenants and captains had decided to follow standard procedure. That was as expected: it took a direct order from a royal or a very high-ranking officer to countermand Krushan procedure. Drilled into the soldiers from their earliest years of training, in an empire that mandated military training and service as compulsory for every youth over the age of twelve and the enlistment of at least one young member of every family, the protocols and procedures were standardized and followed strictly to ensure uniformity across the empire. That could be a powerful tool when facing a like enemy.

But in this battle it was about to prove lethal.

The Krushan frontlines paused to raise their spears over their shoulders, take aim, and throw. The first volley of throws mostly fell far short of their mark. The deceptively gentle incline curved sharply before peaking at the top of the hill, creating a soft lip where the grass grew tall, obscuring the Gwannlander frontlines when viewed from the slope below. Most of the

Krushan spears fell into the grassy lip, embedding themselves into the dirt. Only a few reached the top, injuring a small number of archers.

As their plan required, the Gwannlander archers continued their volleys without pause, ignoring the spears and the approaching enemy. Thousands of Gwannlander arrows rose and flew through the air, arcing across the field to cull the chariot horse teams of the Krushan by the thousands.

But the Krushan were not entirely unsuccessful in their advance. By the third and fourth spear volleys, the throwers had begun to find their marks. More and more archers cried out, screamed, and fell, many toppling over the edge to roll downhill into the path of the enemy. These unfortunates were quickly dispatched by spears jabbed into their writhing bodies. The luckier ones were able to stagger back or sit down on the lip of the hill. With resolute effort, they continued loosing arrows, determined to take as many enemies down as possible before they met their end.

The Krushan advance continued. The slope's curve at the top made it impossible to throw upward without losing one's balance. After several throwers began falling backward, crashing into their comrades behind them, the leaders gave the order to switch to swords. The gleam and flash of tens of thousands of swords shone in the rising sun's light as the Krushan infantry prepared to make direct contact with their enemy.

It was then that Queen Vensera gave the order to the archers to switch targets.

With a rippling motion, the frontline of the Gwannlander forces lowered their bows to aim directly at the approaching infantry. Arrow saw the eyes of the soldiers directly below widen as they saw what they were now climbing toward.

In a battle fought on flat land, archers were useless on the frontline. The enemy could rush at them too quickly to allow them to retreat, cutting them down even as they tried to notch arrows to their bows. But this was not flat land, and Gwannland had seized the high ground. Had the Krushan leaders not been so arrogant and eager to crush the enemy, they would have realized this basic error and switched to a different tactic for the first assault. But they were Krushan, drilled to mindless obedience by the dictates of protocol, and they were so supremely confident in their superiority of numbers that they had pressed on regardless.

Guru Dronas's famed teachings emphasized that "the weapon fits the target." The maxim referred to the use of suitable weapons and tactics for each set of circumstances. The Krushan seemed to have forgotten their own leader's teachings.

They were about to pay the price.

4

It was like shooting wooden peacocks in a country fair game. Arrow could see the startled eyes of the climbing Krushan soldiers below him as they realized, too late, that the enemy archers they were so used to cutting down in droves had the advantage on them in this battle.

The thrum of the drawstring vibrated in their fist, sang through their body, as they loosed.

The arrow punched into the throat of a soldier, producing a small explosion of blood, gristle, and cartilage before passing through and into the neck of the soldier behind, and then the one behind him. The power of the longbow, pulled to its fullest extent, was enough to carry the metal-tipped arrow several hundred yards with enough force to punch through armor, leather, and bodies. When aimed at point-blank range, downhill, it was like a sledgehammer striking at a clapboard wall. That first arrow took down a dozen or more Krushan soldiers before splintering and breaking apart as it struck bone, the metal head wounding the last one, into whose shoulder it embedded itself with enough force to make the man cry out and drop his sword as he clutched at the wound. The Krushan who were killed or wounded fell back onto their climbing comrades, starting a human landslide that disrupted the entire Krushan advance and caused further casualties and chaos.

That first volley stopped the Krushan advance dead in its tracks, like a hammer blow to the groin.

Not all the Gwannlander archers were endowed with superhuman strength like the Five, but they fared well enough, each taking down at least two or three enemy soldiers with each volley.

It only took four or five volleys to completely break the Krushan advance.

Barely moments after they had begun aiming downhill, Arrow paused to take stock.

The Krushan infantry army was in complete disarray.

Perhaps a hundred thousand, possibly twice that number, now lay wounded, dead, or dying on the grassy slopes of Beha'al. Those below and behind them were struggling to rise to their feet, injured or bruised by their falls or cut by friendly blades and spears that had pierced them as they fell.

Not a single one was interested in advancing or attacking anymore.

A wave of cheers rose from the Gwannland frontlines as Queen Vensera praised the archers for their staunch stand and excellent bowcraft. From west to east across the battlefield, colorfully clad archers raised their long-bows and belted out the Gwannland national song in their language. It was a gay, cheerful tune tempered by notes of sweet sadness, and it was a fitting rebuke to the harsh, guttural Krushan shouts and curses echoing below.

But the battle was still young and the enemy still formidable.

We will pay for this early advantage, Arrow sent to the Five.

Yes, we will, Yudi replied grimly.

Dronas

~

"FOOLS!" DRONAS ROARED. "IMBECILES. Cretins. Feeble-witted . . ."

He continued in this vein as he drove his chariot through the massed ranks. The shouting served to warn the Krushan troops ahead of his approach, forcing them to scatter to either side. A few were not quick enough and were trampled under the hooves of his horse and wheels of his chariot. Their screams were cut off abruptly as the knife-edged spokes of his wheels finished what the hooves and wheels had begun.

He reached the top of the foremost rise, overlooking the midpoint of the field of Beha'al, and drew his team to a halt. The horses squealed as he yanked the reins roughly, stamping their feet and tossing their heads. Dronas pointed at a startled infantry captain standing nearby, struggling to bring order to the chaos that had descended upon the frontlines.

"You! Sterile son of a dromad! Heed my words!" The captain listened as Dronas rattled off orders. "Well, what are you waiting for?" Dronas shouted when he was done. "For your mother to remember who fathered you? *Move!*"

The captain saluted him in the Krushan style and began passing on the instructions to his lieutenants.

Dronas sent several of his aides, all of whom had followed him on horseback, to pass the same instructions along the frontline. "And if any officer balks at following those orders, put an arrow through his face and promote the first soldier you see."

The aides galloped away, calling out to the troops to make way, and began passing on his instructions.

Dronas fumed and watched as the word spread across the Krushan frontline. "That's what you get when you give a boy a man's job," he muttered to himself.

He turned to the remaining aides. "You lot," he said, indicating another dozen or so, "take these orders to the chariot regiments."

He rattled off a series of instructions specific in detail and phrasing. They involved the charioteers using the surviving horses to form new chariot teams, with the drivers and archers doubling up.

"Tell them to execute those orders then assemble behind the infantry frontline preparatory to an assault."

His aides saluted and rode away.

"Guru!" called a voice from behind him.

Dronas turned to see Dhuryo Krushan approaching in his own chariot, followed by a hundred more chariots carrying his brothers.

"Dhuryo," Dronas said, "I was just thinking of you."

"Guru," Dhuryo said. "Our frontlines are ravaged. Those fornicating Gwannlander archers!"

"Archers are archers, boy," Dronas said. "It's up to the commander of the army to know how to counter them. Who taught you to send spearmen uphill, charging at the enemy's best archers?"

Dhuryo frowned. "It's standard protocol for the first wave advance."

Dronas cursed under his breath. "I know *that*. I wrote the damned protocols for the Krushan army decades ago. But the protocol also has exceptions."

Dhuryo shrugged. "I didn't know that. I just told the officers to follow standard procedure. How was I supposed to know the enemy would take a stand on the hilltop instead of down at the midpoint? Isn't that a violation of the rules of war?"

"Boy, that's the point of being a commander! You expect the enemy to use unexpected tactics. It's up to you to use a countertactic. Have I taught you nothing?"

Dhuryo looked put out. "I'm not an officer. I'm the prince, Great Guru. It's not my fault if my father's officers don't know how to use tactics."

Dronas resisted the urge to snatch up a javelin from the well of the chariot and ram it into Dhuryo's mouth. "Your *father's* officers, as you call them, are *your* officers. You may be prince now, but one day you will be emperor, and the emperor is supreme commander of the armies of the Burnt Empire. And right now, since you're here on this battlefield and your father isn't, that makes you equivalent to a supreme commander. It's your job to tell your officers what to do and when to do it. Think of this entire battlefield as a vast theater populated by actors playing the parts that you script. It's up to you to tell them what to do, when, how, and where. You are the master of this stage, a god of the theater of war."

Dhuryo Krushan looked around the field of Beha'al, thronged by the vast armies of the Krushan and their enemy. "I don't care about all this strategy and tactical stuff, Great Guru. You know that. I like to fight. So do my brothers. It's easier to just go in and break skulls myself instead of sitting up here and telling other warriors what to do."

Dronas shook his head despairingly. "Sometimes I wonder why the stone gods even made you prince."

Dhuryo said nothing to that.

They both looked out at the field below. The chaos in the Krushan frontlines had reduced considerably. The reason for this was obvious: the infantry soldiers who were still able-bodied were going over the field and dispatching their badly wounded or maimed comrades with quick thrusts of their swords and spears. Leaving the fallen where they lay, the rest regrouped in squads and platoons, forming up as larger regiments and taking up attack positions at the midpoint line once again. Those had been Dronas's orders.

Just as they finished, his aides began returning, reporting that the chariot teams had carried out his instructions and were moving forward to form up as ordered.

"There's one thing to be said in praise of Krushan troops," Dronas said, "they take orders well. Now, boy, you said you like to fight, didn't you?"

Dhuryo perked up at once. "Aye, Guru."

"Then let's go fight."

Dhuryo grinned, showing his teeth.

Dronas grinned in response, slapping his pupil on his broad back.

They urged their horse teams forward, and the chariots began rolling downhill. The rest of the Krushan Hundred followed.

The newly re-formed ranks of the Krushan infantry parted to let the hundred and one chariots through, then hurriedly scattered as the main chariot regiments also followed them.

Dronas glanced to his left and then to his right to see what appeared to be tens of thousands of chariots moving forward along the Krushan front, replacing the traditional order with a formation in which the chariots were now the frontline, with infantry behind them. From what he could tell at a glance, the better part of fifty or sixty thousand chariots remained in action. That was a heavy loss, considering that the enemy had suffered almost no casualties yet, but it was still a formidable number.

The thunder of sixty thousand chariots rolling over the field of Beha'al could be felt even through the floor of his chariot well, thrumming under the soles of his feet.

He looked at the chariot riding alongside his own.

Dhuryo Krushan looked like a wolf about to descend upon a lamb, his long angular jaw parted in a lupine grin. His aide crouched in the well of his chariot, prepared to hand him weapons from the cache stashed there as he called for them.

Dronas found the presence of the aide to be an unnecessary indulgence: it was one thing to use aides to pass on orders or carry messages, but to use one to pass you weapons in battle was just plain laziness, and inefficient as well. Often Dronas did not consciously know which weapon he would use next. His hand simply reached down and picked up the right one. As he liked to tell his pupils, "I let my hands decide for me." In the heat of battle, the body and limbs knew what to do faster and more efficiently than the mind could anticipate.

That caveat apart, he knew that Dhuryo was a born warrior. That had been obvious since he had received the Krushan brothers into his kul at a very young age. Even as a little lad, Dhuryo Krushan had loved violence and bloodshed; Dronas had taught him to hunt and kill small animals — rabbits, fowl, dogs, cats, squirrels, at first — all of which seemed easier to track and kill in Guru Dronas's training camp than they were in the jungle.

By the time he moved Dhuryo up to the larger predators, the boy had a killing urge that reminded Dronas of his own idyllic blood-spattered childhood. They bonded over the gutting of a pregnant deer from whose womb they had dragged out a still-breathing-and-kicking unborn fawn. Dhuryo had begged Dronas for the privilege of killing the infant, and Dronas had watched as the boy had ended the small, bleating life with an expression of pure ecstasy on his little face.

Since that day, Dhuryo had killed many more times. Dronas considered that the first true mark of a future emperor: one had to be willing to kill any number of people, regardless of their race, age, gender, or physical condition, in order to rule over millions. Power came at a cost; absolute power came at the highest expense.

Dhuryo Krushan had many failings: his carelessness as a leader was one, his limited capacity for thinking strategically was another. There were a few other minor deficits. But on one count he satisfied Dronas's expectations completely: he was a born and gifted killer.

Dronas saw the frontlines approaching rapidly. A few last buffoons, nursing bruised or broken limbs and slow to move out of the way, screamed as the thundering chariots ran them over. Dronas hardly felt the bump as the soldiers disappeared beneath his left wheel. By the time the chariot regiments had passed over them, there would be nothing left of their bones but powder. War was not a game for the slow, or the slow-witted. What the Krushan Hundred lacked in wits, at least they made up for in power and skills. Those who lacked any of these were mere lambs for the slaughter. They deserved to die — quickly, if they were lucky. The world was meant for the strong and the powerful; nobody else mattered.

His chariot flew over the midpoint and raced toward the rising incline that led up to the first hill on the Gwannland side. At the top, the frontlines of the enemy awaited, bows raised and arrows notched. Dronas recognized the colorful, billowing robes of Princess Krushni among them, near her brother, Drishya, and their parents, King Gwann and Queen Vensera. That was his target, personally. Dhuryo and the Krushan Hundred would focus on the Shvate Five and their companions. The chariot regiments would deal with the rest of the Gwannlander frontlines.

Dronas whipped the reins of his team around the hooked horn at the head of the chariot well, keeping them at just the right amount of tautness. The horses were specially trained to maintain a steady course, even when racing uphill, and would hold the line.

He raised his longbow, fitting a specially crafted arrow to the string, and aimed it high.

The sky above was laden with large, cushiony clouds, hanging low in the early morning sunshine, catching the golden and orange hues of the risen sun. Beyond the clouds, the sky was a proud, rich blue.

Dronas loosed the arrow, confident in the knowledge that it would hit its mark.

Then he took hold of the reins again and changed direction just as the chariot reached the foot of the hill.

Dhuryo

~

DHURYO CROWED WITH LAUGHTER as he saw his guru's arrow shoot upward at the large grey cloud hanging directly over the enemy frontline.

"He's doing it!" he called out to his brothers, who surrounded him on both sides, their chariots keeping pace with his. "I told you he would do it."

Dhuryo and the Krushan Hundred watched as the arrow rose up to meet the belly of the cloud, piercing it and disappearing into the dense grey mass.

For a long moment, nothing happened. The arrow did not fall back to earth as it might have been expected to ordinarily — but there was nothing ordinary about the arrow. Like all gurus, Dronas had spent decades in harsh penance, meditating on the stone gods with intense fervor, performing arcane rituals and sacrificial offerings to the deity of his choice, in the hope he would be rewarded eventually with a boon. He had succeeded. His boon had been the gift of astras, celestial weapons of the stone gods. The astras themselves came in the form of mantras, locked and embedded into the consciousness of the person thus rewarded. When uttered with the proper respect, they turned ordinary mortal weapons into the weapons of the gods.

Dhuryo and his brothers knew the weapon Dronas had just unleashed. It was one of the mythical weapons used by the stone god of storms and war, Inadran himself, Dronas's patron deity. When the mantra was uttered in conjunction with the use of a weapon, it called upon the elements to obey the will of Inadran. It could not be refused or countered by any mortal or godly weapon.

The grey cloud suddenly turned dark, blackening as if the light of the world had gone out. In the blue sky, the sun continued to shine brightly down, bathing the field of Beha'al in slanted spears of brilliant yellow and

310

gold. Other clouds, some white, some grey, drifted indulgently in the morn-ing sky, unaffected. Only that one grey cloud, poised above the Gwannland frontlines, just over the heads of Queen Vensera, King Gwann, and their son and daughter, blackened and turned dark and stormy in an instant.

Out of the stormcloud, a blinding flash exploded, racing down to earth. The jagged white streak shone so brightly, it left multicolored spots on the backs of Dhuryo's eyes. He blinked them away, roaring with laughter. His brothers echoed his merriment. They had seen this before, on a small scale, in an earlier conflict against another warlord whose daughter Dronas had coveted. But this time, it was far bigger in scale and intensity. The lightning bolt that struck the royal family of Gwannland on top of the hill was ten times the size of most lightning bolts and struck ground with the force of a dozen storms at once.

The thunderclap that followed instantly was deafening, the impact of the grounding fierce enough that even Dhuryo and his brothers were buffeted hard by the blast. Infantry troops on the frontline were knocked off their feet. On the hill above, dozens of Gwannlander archers were blown off the top, tumbling through the air like broken dolls, their rainbow robes ablaze. Even at a half mile away, the sound clapped Dhuryo's ears like his guru box-ing his ears to punish him for making a minor mistake in training. At the point of impact, it would cause ears to bleed and deafen many permanently.

Guru Dronas had summoned the lightning.

Dronas

~

THE SMOKE FROM THE lightning blast cleared to reveal a jagged hole in the hilltop almost an acre in size. Gwannlander bodies lay strewn along the slope and atop the hill, their clothes scorched and still smoking. Wisps of smoke rose from the hole.

From close behind him rose the sound of laughter and loud cheers. He looked back to see Dhuryo and the Krushan Hundred raising their fists. Their cheers were echoed by a resounding shout across the battlefield as the Krushan celebrated the first assault on the enemy.

Dronas laughed with them. "That will show you, Gwann, old friend," he said.

He peered up at the hilltop but could no longer see Gwann and Vensera. They might have fallen into the hole carved by the lightning, or been vaporized by the lightning itself, or flung away by the impact.

But there were others still standing, even next to the point of impact.

Seven figures lit golden by the morning sunshine.

Dronas's smile disappeared.

The Shvate Five, Vrath, and Vessa.

They remained upright, seemingly unaffected by the giant bolt of lightning that had struck the ground only a few dozen yards from where they were standing.

As he gazed up at them, muttering an oath, two more figures appeared, climbing up from the smoldering crater created by the strike.

Drishya and Krushni.

A moment later, he saw Gwann and Vensera also appear, climbing up on the far side of the crater, their backs to the frontlines as they helped each other out.

So.

All the main villains had survived.

Oh well, Dronas mused, he hadn't expected to fell the most powerful among the enemy with his very first arrow. It would take a lot more to kill a Krushan, let alone one as powerful as Vrath or Vessa.

They weren't his targets anyway.

He had been aiming for Gwann and Vensera, Krushni and Drishya.

They might still be standing, but from the way that the king and queen of Gwannland supported one another, he knew they had taken a beating.

Good.

That was only a taste of what lies in store for you and your family, Gwann. Before the sun sets on the field of Beha'al, all four of you will lie broken and bleeding on this grassland. I, Dronas, swear that by my deity, Inadran himself.

He raised his arm, turning to address the leaders of the chariot regiments now forming on either side of him and the Krushan Hundred.

"On my order, prepare to attack!" he shouted, confident his words would be passed along through the ranks.

As tens of thousands of chariots assembled on the Krushan frontline, forming into a neat, seemingly endless line that stretched as far as the eye could see in both directions, Dronas raised his bow and selected another arrow, picking out a sinuous one that curved and bent all along its length, culminating in a snake-mouthed tip. He whispered the mantra that went with the arrow, calling upon his stone god, and loosed.

The arrow whipped through the air, undulating as if alive as it flew.

Aimed directly at the tall, stately woman standing at the top of the hill, it ought to have reached its target within a few seconds. But as it flew upward, it shivered, seemed to shed parts of itself, and before the naked eye, split into two arrows. These two split into four, which split into eight, which became sixteen, and so forth. The dividing happened in a blink of an eye, each new arrow the same length and thickness as the first one, with each spreading outward in a wide parallel line that stretched hundreds of yards in the time it took the arrow to reach its destination.

By the time it struck, the single arrow had divided into thousands, perhaps even tens of thousands of others. Dronas knew not exactly how many, nor did he care. All that mattered was achieving its purpose.

To kill Queen Vensera, and if possible, Princess Krushni and Prince Drishya, while King Gwann, whom he had deliberately aimed to miss, watched in horror and grief.

Krushni

~

1

A CRY OF DISMAY had hardly begun to rise from the Gwannland ranks when it was abruptly choked off and turned into a cacophony of screams of terror and pain.

The screams came not from the victims whom the arrows had struck, but from those behind, above, and around them.

The ones who were felled had simply dropped dead. Their bodies hammered out a death rhythm as they went through their last throes, their hearts already stilled the instant the arrowheads had entered their flesh.

Krushni had been struck by one of the arrows too. She had known even as Dronas fired the arrow that it could not be avoided. Those around her who tried to dodge found the missiles turning with them, striking them regardless of how they moved.

The arrow that had struck her had entered her chest, beneath her right shoulder and just above her right breast. The impact was not as hard as one might expect an arrow shot from a longbow at this range. In fact, it had barely tapped her in the soft fleshy gap between her first and second ribs. The head held on after it connected, biting into the flesh to draw blood, and clung on. It hung loosely, dangling limply at first as if momentarily dazed from the impact. Then, as she looked down at it, it began writhing and undulating again, coming alive. She could see the mouth of the serpent arrow clasped to her chest, the curved black fangs embedded in her flesh, the body and tail writhing from side to side as it hung on greedily. She felt the venom pumping into her veins, blackening her blood, killing her flesh instantly.

315

Guru Dronas had loosed a serpent arrow. A celestial one that split in midair and multiplied ten thousandfold before it struck.

Every one of the ten thousand serpents was deadly venomous. For most of their ten thousand targets, the moment of contact was also the moment of death. Their hearts were stopped instantly; their bodies and brains took a few moments longer to die, thrashing and suffering agonies before succumbing to the lethal venom.

All across the Gwannland frontline, Krushni could see and hear the cries of the Gwannlander forces as they watched their fellow warriors fall dead, slain by a single arrow.

And then, after the first ten thousand were dead, the real horror began.

2

The instant its first victim was dead, each serpent arrow detached its fangs from the flesh and raced away in pursuit of the next victim.

All the wailing Gwannlanders who were trying, unsuccessfully, to revive their stricken comrades, or simply close by when the volley struck, suddenly found themselves facing a reed-thin black serpent with razor-sharp ivory fangs. The serpents moved like a flash, slithering several yards in seconds. Those Gwannlanders foolish enough to turn and run — these were few — were struck in the back by the relentless serpents. Those who stood and stared in shock, or merely attempted to deflect or strike away the lunging fangs, were similarly bitten and killed. Only a few hundred who were quick-witted and fast-acting enough to strike at the serpents with their daggers or swords succeeded in severing the heads from the bodies. In these latter cases, the moment the serpents' heads were parted from their bodies, the bodies stiffened into perfectly ordinary blackwood arrows. The heads hissed and spat for a few seconds before collapsing and expiring, oozing milky white venom and garish black blood. As they died, the serpents' heads turned into black ironheads with pointed-tongue tips, as inanimate as any arrow in the Gwannlander archers' own quivers.

The serpents that were successful in killing second victims then went on to seek out third, fourth, fifth, and even more victims, until someone cut them down. Impossible as it should have been, their supply of venom was limitless. Krushni knew from the writhing serpent head pouring its venom into her flesh with relentless vigor that it could produce venom enough to kill an infinite number of victims.

She saw her brother take hold of the writhing tail of the serpent that had struck his abdomen and slice off the head with a single quick stroke. The body straightened at once into a black arrow shaft. The head continued thrashing for a few more seconds before succumbing, then released its hold on Drishya's flesh and fell to the ground. Drishya rubbed at his belly, erasing the wound as if it had never existed.

Krushni allowed the serpent to continue pumping its venom into her flesh, curious to see how much it could release. She was also draining it for another reason. Drishya turned to watch her, nodding as he gleaned her intent.

The Shvate Five and their elders, Vrath and Vessa, had similarly survived their own serpent strikes without any difficulty. It took a great deal more to kill a Krushan than a few snakebites, even from a celestial arrow. Jilana, Karni, and the more vulnerable members of their group had retreated at the start of battle to a holding position several hundred yards behind.

Krushni had wanted her mother and father to do the same, but they had refused. Vensera for one had insisted that she would be in the fore, leading from the front as per Gwannland tradition. Even when Krushni had warned her that this would not be a traditional battle in any sense of the term, and that their enemy would use any means at their disposal to win, Vensera would not hear of it.

She turned now to see Gwann kneeling on the ground, holding a body in his hands.

Her heart leaping in her chest, Krushni crossed the yards to them in a trice. Drishya was beside her.

"Mother," Krushni said, feeling tears prickle her eyes.

Gwann looked up, and below his upraised face, Krushni saw the pale, limp features of her mother, her eyes closed. On the ground beside her was the black shaft of a severed arrow and the oozing head of the serpent arrowhead. In her hand was the dagger she had used to sever it.

"She moved like lightning, as always," Gwann said, his face drawn and sickly in grief, "but it managed to get one fang partly into her, breaking the skin."

Krushni crouched down and examined the skin of Vensera's right shoulder. Gwann had already ripped off the armor that had protected that area. Somehow, Vensera must have managed to turn just enough to take the arrow on the pauldron, then hacked off the head at once. Her warrior's instinct had told her what to do on reflex. She had acted with incredible speed for a mortal. Yet it had not been quick enough.

Vensera's eyes flickered open, startling Krushni.

"Mother, you're alive!" she said, astonished.

Vensera looked up at her through bloodshot eyes rimmed with black discoloration. "I had heard about the serpent arrows of Stone God Inadran from my great-aunt Fiaravol. She . . ."

She hacked involuntarily, coughing up blood and a blackish pus-like phlegm that was wholly unnatural.

Gwann reached up and grasped Krushni's forearm. "Save her," he said. "I know you can."

Krushni stared down at him, then covered his hand with her own warm palm. "I cannot give life to the dead."

"She's not dead," Gwann said. "I know you can prolong her life."

Krushni looked at Vensera, who had shut her eyes again and was wheezing now, close to the end. "Perhaps. Perhaps not. Even if I do succeed, it will not be for long."

"She just wants a chance to die fighting," Gwann said.

Krushni started to shake her head, ignoring the hot tears spilling down her cheeks. One found its way to Vensera's bloodless forehead. A second hand snaked up to grasp Krushni's other wrist with surprising strength.

Vensera's eyes were open. She stared up at Krushni, pleading. "Please, daughter. Do it."

Krushni was silenced. She blinked away her tears, glancing up at Drishya, seeking his advice. He nodded once, grimly.

She lowered her gaze to Vensera and Gwann, acknowledging them.

Gwann nodded and moved aside, giving her room.

Krushni released Vensera's hand from her wrist, gently, and placed both her palms on her mother's chest, pressing down hard until she felt the ribs of Vensera's chest under her palms.

She uttered a mantra subvocally, opening a doorway in her mind, reaching out beyond dimensions to beings and powers that were unfathomable by human minds.

A flash of blinding light filled her for a brief, shocking instant.

When her vision cleared, she was sprawled on her back, next to Vensera, and there were spots before her eyes and tinnitus in her ears.

Slowly, almost hesitantly, Vensera sat up, looking down at herself. She touched her own chest, then her legs, then her face. The color had not come back into her face entirely, but she had stopped coughing and her eyes had returned to some semblance of normality.

"I am not as I was," she said softly, as if realizing it from her own assessment of her inner body.

"You never will be again," Krushni said, crying freely now. "I'm sorry."

"Thank you," Vensera said, embracing her. Vensera's fingers felt cold against her hot neck and back. "Thank you for giving me a little more time. I will not waste it."

Krushni allowed herself another moment, then detached herself reluctantly from her mother's embrace. Gwann's face was wreathed with a confusion of relief and guilt.

Krushni kissed Vensera, then Gwann, then rose to her feet.

She walked back to the frontline, her eyes flickering darkly.

3

Krushni felt rage boil up within her.

She saw the crater formed by the lightning blast and the bodies strewn across the hilltop and slopes below.

She saw, heard, and felt the agony of thousands of Gwannlanders who had died of the vicious serpent arrow bites. Thanks to the quick reactions of their comrades, almost all the serpents had now been decapitated. In the intervening minutes since Dronas had fired the lightning and serpent arrows, the Krushan chariot army had made considerable progress, pushing forward into Gwannland territory. They were now within arrowshot of the Gwannland frontline.

Even as she watched, the wave of chariots sweeping up the hillsides toward her defending warriors bristled with raised arrows as the charioteers prepared to loose their first volley. Her frontline was in complete disarray with most of her archers downed; her mother the queen, the symbolic and literal commander of Gwannland's forces as well as the united armies of Arthaloka, was incapacitated and in no condition to continue to lead. Krushni had prolonged her life — and her pain — for a time, but even she could not be sure how long this might last. Vensera could drop dead within moments, or hours at most.

Dronas. Dronas had killed her mother and shot at Krushni and Drishya, while deliberately sparing Gwann.

His intention had been to kill all three of them, leaving Gwann alive to witness his family's horrific demise, sparing his life so that Dronas might take it himself. No doubt Dronas intended to do so in some especially gruesome and agonizing manner.

The rage built within her as the first volley of Krushan arrows began flying. Suddenly, the air was stained with deadly shafts hurtling past like horizontal black rain. She felt the wind of their passing and the sting of the ones that nicked her skin.

One struck her in the hip, striking bone.

She absorbed it, the arrow dissolving and disappearing into her body, leaving the skin with nary a blemish. She would need its constituent elements for what she was about to do next.

"Give the order to advance," she said to Drishya.

Drishya turned and signaled their expectant warriors. The officers who had been slain by the arrows had been replaced, and the lines were starting to form up as he gestured silently to them. They put away their bows and drew their cutters in quick, efficient response. Gwannland had drawn first blood but had suffered grievous losses. They were ready and eager to join blades with their enemy.

Yudi acknowledged the command on behalf of the Shvate Five. Behind them, Vrath and Vessa stood on the second hilltop, observing the progress of the battle and awaiting the right time to enter. Drishya's command did not apply to them. Nobody gave orders to the Krushan elders. They would join the battle when they deemed fit.

Drishya turned back and looked at Krushni inquiringly.

She took a deep breath. "Dronas is mine," she said as she felt the storm building within her body. "Everyone else can pick their targets freely."

Drishya nodded once and raised his forefinger. The air around it began to shimmer and spin, whirling like a tiny tornado balanced upon his fingertip. Motes of gold sparkled in the early morning sunlight, flashing brightly and casting spinning dots of golden reflection in every direction. In a moment, the celestial disc materialized, a golden blade-thin shape with serrated edges that hummed and sang hungrily. She could hear the song of Sarshan, the celestial disc, in her mind, its notes and lyrics too high to be heard or understood by anyone upon this mortal plane except the two of them and perhaps Vessa, possibly even Jarsun.

Drishya was ready.

Krushni shrieked her rage and grief as she plunged her clawing fingers into her own torso, ripping skin and cracking bone, digging deep into her hot, steaming flesh.

Inside her chest, her heart crackled and flared, its dark crimson flames pulsing. Despite her rebirth, Krushni was still a Krushan at heart — quite literally. As with every Krushan, stonefire was an integral part of her biology, the powerful element concentrated most heavily in, around, and of her heart. But not every Krushan could do what she could. That burning heart within her gave her the ability to absorb everything that entered her body, the way that any mortal body absorbed nutrients from food. The venom and the other elements of the serpent arrows that had struck her were contained inside her. As were the ordinary arrows shot by the charioteers now almost at the top of the hill. She had also drawn upon other things she had consumed and absorbed before the battle, further elements as required from other dimensions and worlds, using her ability as a waywalker to open pinhole portals *within* her body.

Now she put all that work to good use, constructing and shaping out of all that she had absorbed a weapon she would use to battle the enemy of Gwannland, the tyrant who had tormented a nation, her mother's assassin.

She drew the weapon, steaming and dripping her precious blood, out of her body, and held it up in the morning light. A final scream of rage and exultation escaped her lips as she raised both arms. Her body healed itself, the mortal wounds repairing themselves and closing in the blink of an eye. By the time she stood holding up the weapon for the world to see, she was whole and unmarked, ready for battle.

"*Dronas!*" she cried as she flung herself down the hillside.

Jarsun

~

"*DRONAS!*" SHRIEKED KRUSHNI, THROWING herself down the hill-side. Her rainbow robes billowed as she flew, her feet never touching ground or grass. The chariots about to crest the top of the hill faltered, their horses rearing back in fright as Krushni came at them like a crazed stone god out of ancient myth.

Jarsun admired her rage and intensity. He could still see the little girl in her, the Krushita who had challenged him in the Red Desert when he had confronted her mother. That little girl had attacked him with a burst of power far beyond anything even a Krushan her age ought to have been capable of; she had surprised him then.

Now he watched with paternal pride as he saw how she had learned to harness and tame her fury. She still used too much energy, expending the valuable resource of *Auma* that flowed from within her as freely as water in the River Jeel. He could have shown her ways to trim that usage, pare it back and hone it until she was able to let it loose only at the very moment of assault. But there was something glorious, magnificent about her untamed rage, the way she *flowed* down the hillside like a waterfall of multihued rage.

Dronas had driven his chariot most of the way up the incline. In another few moments, he would have breached the crest, close enough to his lifelong adversary Gwann to toss a sword through the man's heart. He was taken by surprise by Krushni's mode of attack.

Arrogant fool, Jarsun thought with delicious amusement, relishing Dronas's shock and surprise. *Did you expect her to simply use arrows and spears? She is no Gwannlander. She is a Krushan, regardless of who she poses as in this lifetime. The blood that runs through her beautiful veins is alive with stonefire, the same blood as mine. She is one of the most powerful and gifted of my race. You should have known better than to come at her directly.*

He watched as Krushni struck the front well of Dronas's chariot with her weapon. The enormous swordlike object was entirely bladed, with only a hand grip in the center. On either side of the handgrip and hilt was a double-sided, wickedly curved blade a foot and a half in width. From one end to the other, it was some nine feet in length, he estimated, taller by far than Krushni's own five and a half feet. Yet the ease with which she wielded it, turning and weaving it through the air like a simple shortsword, made her seem twice as tall and ten times as formidable.

The weapon sliced through the well of the chariot like it was made of scroll paper. The team of horses, already terrified and rearing high, fell back onto the split chariot. The entire contraption collapsed and tumbled downhill in a mass of writhing horseflesh, flailing feet, and equestrian screams. Krushni remained suspended in midair, floating a yard off the grassy slope, her face wreathed in a ghastly grin.

Jarsun glimpsed Dronas's shocked face as Krushni's blade bit into the chariot well. The guru's shock had not prevented him from reacting with his razor-sharp reflexes. He threw himself sideways and out of the destructing vehicle, turning a full somersault before landing on the grass. He rolled several times before righting himself.

He rose to his full length now and faced Krushni.

His lips were parting, Jarsun saw, uttering another God Mantra.

One had to admire how Dronas's advanced age had not dimmed his senses or his skills. If anything, the guru was at the peak of his powers, his natural athletic abilities and vast store of knowledge further enhanced by the celestial weapons and countless little tactical surprises he possessed. Krushni and Dronas might seem as far removed from one another as an adolescent granddaughter and a very senior grandfather, but in truth, Jarsun would say they were almost evenly matched. What Dronas lacked in demigod powers and Krushan blood, he more than made up for with his warcraft, experience, and specially endowed gifts from the stone gods.

A new weapon appeared in Dronas's hands, a crackling rope of chainlike links. It was silvery bluish in hue, surrounded by a glowing effusion that increased steadily in intensity. The rope itself was several dozen yards in length and several inches thick, gnarled and embedded with spikes, spokes,

blades, and every manner of lethal cutting object. At the very end of the
rope was an ugly bludgeoning tool shaped like an irregular spherical block
of solid iron, and from the far end of this deadly mace protruded a whirling
point.

Dronas wielded and worked the rope the way the farmers of Mraashk
might use a hemp rope to lasso an errant steer or horse. He spun it overhead,
whipped it out into the air, struck a rock about fifteen yards away. The rock
shattered into neatly sliced splinters, and with another twitch of the rope,
Dronas smashed them with the bludgeon head, turning them into lethal
missiles flung straight at Krushni.

*Inadran's Lasso, the very one the god of storms and war used to capture the sa-
cred bull of the First Vessa.* The bull in question had been a demigod incapable
of being captured by any ordinary rope or means, so Inadran had commis-
sioned the smith of the stone gods, FireShaper, to craft a special rope that
could do the job. *How many celestial weapons does Dronas have?* Jarsun had
a feeling that would soon be known. It would take everything Dronas had,
and then some, to do what he intended on this field today.

The deadly splinters of rock flew at Krushni. She made no attempt to
avoid them or deflect them. Instead, she spread her arms wide, embracing
them.

A dozen irregularly shaped splinters embedded themselves in her head,
face, throat, torso, arms, and thighs. The rest flew past her to strike the next
unfortunates in their path: the Krushan chariot teams driving up the hill.
The men and horses struck by the shower of shards tumbled, some dying,
some dead, their chariots turning over to fall and strike other chariots below in a cascade.

Krushni closed her arms, crossing them over her chest. Even from where
he stood, Jarsun's Krushan vision could see that she had absorbed the splinters of rock.

*It seems the young whelp has learned new tricks — or been well schooled by
someone wise in the ways.*

His gaze flicked to Vessa, standing motionless, staff in hand, white beard
and unruly hair striking against the colorful garb of the Gwannlander lines.
Beside him stood Vrath, equally impassive, observing the battle.

Vrath's face tilted upward slightly, his eyes finding Jarsun across the mile
of distance separating them.

The two men stared at each other intently for a moment.

Soon, cousin, I will face you on this field. For the second and last time, Jarsun thought, his tongue tips flicking out in anticipation of the taste of Vrath's blood.

He sensed Vessa looking at him as well, but ignored the old sage. He was not concerned with Vessa; once Jarsun won this battle and killed Vrath, Vessa would fall into line. For all his eccentricities, Vessa would do as his mother, Jilana, ordered, and Jilana in turn would always do what was right for the family and the empire. Jarsun was confident that by the time this battle was over, she would see that Jarsun was indispensable to the House of Krushan and would accept him into Hastinaga. She would simply have no choice once she knew the secret that Jarsun would reveal to them at the opportune time.

The secret that Jarsun had kept for fifteen years.

Krushni

~

KRUSHNI REACHED INTO HERSELF and began to extract the weapon she had forged inside her body from the shards of rock mingled with enough metal to make it cohesive and sharp edged. She screamed uninhibitedly at the pain. The process of transmuting everything she absorbed into new weapons did not kill her: as a Krushan, very few things could kill her, and ordinary weapon wounds were not among them. But the pain of being wounded was real, and the pain of drawing the remade weapons from her body, ripping flesh and organs, shattering bones, was horrendous beyond belief. She drew it out as quickly as she could, mere eyeblinks in real time, but in the realm of physical sensation, it was infinite agony. This particular weapon was worse than others because of its shape and form.

Then it was over, and she held the weapon, still dripping with her own blood.

The weapon she now raised was something she could not name because no such weapon had ever existed. It was a sphere about three feet wide. Not a smooth, perfect orb, but radiating outward from a central base with a grip intended to be held by a human hand, dozens of branches zigged and zagged to end in a multitude of cutting edges and shapes. It weighed over a ton. If flung at anything, human, animal, or object, it would simultaneously ruin and crush the target. What possible defense could deflect or shield against such a thing? The only challenge was lifting and throwing it, and doing so with accuracy enough to strike one's intended target from a distance, without killing oneself in the process.

There was no name or history for it, not even in myth or legend. Krushni had created it on the spur of the moment, knowing she needed a weapon against which even the world's greatest champion would have no defense.

She was pleased by the result.

Krushni decided to call it the Gobramauth — "ball of death" in common parlance — and raised it like it weighed nothing, her hand holding the iron grip at the center of the tangled web of jagged branches. The points, edges, and blades cut her flesh in a dozen places, drawing streams of blood. She ignored them, ignored the pain, the weight, the sheer impossibility of using such a weapon.

Across the hillside, some dozens of yards away, she saw Dronas stare at the deathball. She knew his brilliant mind was racing to find a weapon that would counter it.

She drew her arm back, feeling the pressure on her shoulder, her back, her entire body, as the ton-heavy Gobramauth strained even her Krushan powers to their limit.

Dronas's lips began to move, uttering the arcane syllables of ancient Ashcrit. He was using one of the God Mantras. She had no way of knowing which one or what it would do once completed.

She braced herself for the attack, ran forward, drew her arm back, and released.

It ripped free of her grip, tearing chunks of flesh and cracking bones as it left her, and hung in midair for an instant, the air thick with particles of her blood like rain flying away and upward. Then it began its loping flight toward its target.

Dronas finished the God Mantra just as the deathball arced out over the chariots racing up the hill between himself and Krushni. The charioteers as well as their straining horses gaped up as the black and grey orb passed over them, seeming to float rather than fly. The first chariots were already cresting the hillside as the Gobramauth cast its shadow over Dronas, who watched it approach with the stillness of a rabbit that looks up to see an elephant leg descending.

Krushni released one more scream, cutting across the cries and animal sounds and metal noises of battle. It was a terrifying, banshee scream, shrill and piercing, filled with her pain, her anguish, her rage, her grief.

Dronas

~

DRONAS WATCHED AS THE Gobramauth left Krushni's hand, tearing swaths of skin and flesh, watched it rise through the air, arcing toward him. He watched its inevitable descent as its sheer weight caused it to drop sharply. With impeccable judgment, he knew it would land a little short of him, perhaps just on the edge of his chariot. It mattered little. It would still crush him, the chariot, the horses, and tamp them several feet into the ground on impact. Instant death.

The God Mantra he had uttered was answered a fraction of a second before the deathball hit.

A cloak of crimson light fell upon him instantly, covering his body as closely as a second skin. He felt unchanged, and as he saw the Gobramauth fill his field of vision, he was unable to stop his jaw opening involuntarily. Whether to curse or to scream, he did not know, because in the next instant, the orb struck the edge of the chariot as well as his left shoulder and arm with an impact that ought to have crushed his bones to pulp.

The chariot collapsed with a soughing sound like a wine bladder giving up its last dregs. The horses, flung backward by the force of the impact, toppled heels over head, falling onto the deathball. The deadly points and blades impaled all four horses but did not grant them the mercy of quick deaths. They thrashed and screamed, shattering fetlocks and causing even more ruinous wounds.

Dronas was flung like a wood chip snapped free from a block when the axe bit. He fell several yards away, onto his side, and ought to have felt the impact on his neck and back, surely breaking both.

He regained his feet slowly, examining himself. He was completely unharmed. The Cloak of Vish had protected him from the Gobramauth as well as the fall. Inside its protective skin, he felt completely normal. It had successfully deflected the monstrous orb, and only the impact of the weapon had thrown him free of the chariot.

He stood and turned to look back at Krushni, now even farther away. Around them, the Krushan chariot legions thundered up the hillside, smashing into the Gwannland frontline. The Gwannlanders were fighting back fiercely, and every dozen chariots or so, one had its charioteer or its horses cut down, and tumbled back down the slope, but for the most part, the Krushan army was overrunning the enemy front.

Dronas made a show of dusting himself off, not because he had been sullied by the fall, but in order to demonstrate that he was unharmed and whole.

"Is that the best you can do, Princess?" he called out, knowing that Krushni, like all Krushan, would be able to hear him over the furor of the battle. "Not quite good enough, was it? Now, let me show you how I take down my enemies!"

With a shrug of his shoulders, he released the Cloak of Vish. He only hesitated a moment before doing so, aware that, like all the God Mantras he had acquired, that particular one would not work for him again. That was the price of acquisition of the weapons of the stone gods. They worked but once. Perhaps, as the sages believed, the stone gods feared that any mortal who was able to use them repeatedly might use them to challenge the stone gods themselves. It did not matter. Dronas did not have many more mantras left. In fact, he had only one powerful enough to guarantee victory. He paused a moment to weigh the consequences of unleashing that weapon. The decision was inevitable. He *would* win this battle. He *must* win this battle. Once he had taken Gwannland, he would be able to take all Eastern Arthaloka, and after that, he would be one of the most powerful men in Arthaloka. His legend alone would make everyone fear to challenge him. He would not need any more God Mantras. He was Dronas. His name alone was a mantra that cast terror in men's hearts.

The Krushan Hundred, already at the top of the hill and watching from their chariots, paused to cheer their guru's thwarting of the Gobra-mauth.

Dronas acknowledged them with a raised hand.

He would give them something to remember.

He would show them how to kill a Krushan.

He uttered the Ashcrit syllables of another God Mantra.

Krushni

~

SISTER, SHALL I SLAY the guru?

Krushni replied silently without turning to look back at Drishya. *No, brother. I will deal with him. You must stay close to Father and Mother and make sure they are not harmed again.*

She turned her attention back to Dronas.

He was summoning another gift of the stone gods. The air around him shimmered and heaved. He raised both arms, spreading them wide with palms apart. A bluish-reddish haze grew brighter between his palms, roughly shaped like a semicircle. It coalesced into a three-dimensional object that resembled the front of a chariot. It continued to expand as she realized it didn't just resemble a chariot, it *was* one. Dronas's hands moved faster, and he stepped back as he released the light, which had now taken the form of a chariot designed in the ancient style. Until now, Krushni had only seen it portrayed in ancient art, but even at first glance, she knew at once what it was. As did every other charioteer on the battlefield.

Inadran's chariot! By the stone gods, however did Dronas receive use of that as a boon? He must have done something extraordinary to persuade the Lord of Storms and War to grant him use of his own chariot.

As far as she knew, it had never been done before. In all the legends and tales of yore, none told of Inadran's fabled chariot being used by any mortal. There were countless tales of stone god weapons being gifted to mortals, Krushan, and even urrkh, but not one of this particular weapon.

There was a reason for that. She had no doubt Dronas knew the reason well, but either the old guru did not care or he was too eager to eliminate her so that he could have at Gwann and Vensera and achieve his vengeance.

Still. That's Inadran's chariot. It's not just a weapon, it's . . .

She hardly had words to describe the devastation the chariot was said to bring.

It even had a name, given for good reason.

Warbreaker.

Inadran's chariot was not merely used to attack an opponent, unless of course they were a stone god. It was a device of mass destruction. An instrument of annihilation. It could neither be aimed nor controlled. Once unleashed, it simply rampaged until everything in its path was destroyed, be it friend or foe.

"Dronas!" she cried out over the noise and clamor of battle. "You would destroy everyone for your own selfish victory? Do not do this, I implore you. Face me one-on-one, as two warriors, as the rules of war dictate."

Dronas laughed.

The chariot had now turned fully solid. It was twice the size of Dronas's own four-horse chariot, and glowed like burnished gold set with countless dark jewels that glittered and gleamed like the eyes of unseen monsters. It hovered a foot above the ground, yoked to a team of eight ghostly horses with starry voids where their eyes ought to have been and black fire shooting from their red mouths. He climbed onto it from his own chariot, taking up the reins that burned golden white, tugging on it to alert the Stormhorses to his command. They raised their heads, turning to look at him with blank contempt, their nostrils breathing black fire and red smoke. Their teeth were jagged shards. Strange parasites writhed on their purple tongues.

"What rules? If you mean the Krushan rules of war, I have no use for them. I am Dronas. I make my own rules. The first and last rule is that I always win, whatever the odds."

"Guru!"

The shout came from the lips of Dhuryo Krushan, up on the hilltop in his chariot. He leaped out, leaning over the edge to call out to Dronas. "Our armies are on the field! My brothers are on the field!"

Dronas laughed at his former pupil. "Boy, it is time you learned that war is not a game for children. It is the price we pay for power. And the price of war *is* the prize of war."

Others began shouting to Dronas, keenly aware of the destructive power of Warbreaker and the Stormhorses. Dronas ignored them all. He concentrated his attention on directing his will through the reins to the Storm-horses. Their consciousness was dark and frightful, alien minds capable of comprehending only two commands: Destroy. And Halt.

Dronas felt the power of the storm god himself throbbing through the floor of the chariot, through the reins in his hands, surrounding him like a cloud of lightning. He felt powerful, invulnerable, omnipotent. All fear, all doubt, all rational thought fled. He knew only the mindless desire to slay, slaughter, massacre, destroy. He was Inadran himself, put on earth for just this purpose. He was Death Incarnate. He was God.

With a shriek that chilled the bones of soldiers miles away on the field of Beha'al, the Stormhorses plunged forward, their heels striking fire from the air itself, the mighty vehicle building speed and power.

Dronas drove it straight at Krushni.

Arrow

~

Arrow couldn't believe Dronas could be foolish enough to use the chariot of Inadran himself.

Even the stone god had to resorted its use only as a very last resort: at the very end of the First Great Urrkh War. The stone gods were outnumbered and surrounded, their celestial city besieged and beleaguered. The urrkh were infinite in number, and killing them was meaningless because their guru possessed the secret mantra of resurrection. No matter how many urrkh were slain by Inadran and his fellow stone gods, they were resurrected and sent back to the battlefield as fresh as the first day they had taken up their weapons.

For their part, the stone gods, while immortal and near indestructible, were beyond exhausted and losing heart. Already, the battle had raged for half an eon with no end in sight. The urrkh would not cease until the stone gods yielded, no matter how long that took. They were long past the point of diplomacy or peace talks. They could spend all eternity fighting on with neither side losing nor winning, and what use was that as a life?

The other stone gods, led by Vish, had pleaded with Inadran time and time again to bring forth his chariot Warbreaker and end the impasse. Finally, Inadran gave in to their pleas, seeing that there was no other way. He summoned up the dreadful vehicle and climbed aboard. The other stone gods had retreated from the field, stepping back behind the impenetrable walls of Stonehaven, the eternal city. From its protective ramparts, they watched with trepidation as the Stormlord drove the Stormhorses into battle alone against a teeming army of urrkh.

What happened next, none of the scrolls told, nor did any guru claim knowledge of it. They always hinted at the calamity that followed and how even Vish regretted petitioning Inadran to use the chariot, but never spelled out the details. All they would say was that the stone gods won the battle that day, putting an end to the urrkh siege of Stonehaven, and pulling down the curtain on the First Great Urrkh War.

Now Arrow watched with a frozen heart as Dronas, laughing like a maniac, drove the same terrible god weapon directly at Princess Krushni.

Yudi! Arrow sent.

I see it! I don't believe it, but I see it, Yudi replied grimly.

Old man's insane! Brum sent.

Out of his gourd, Saha agreed.

Can he even control that thing? Kula asked.

Arrow didn't need the question answered. The answer was obvious.

Dronas could not. No one could. Once unleashed, nothing and no one could stop Warbreaker, not even its charioteer.

Only Inadran himself could do that.

Krushni

~

WARBREAKER ROARED ACROSS THE battlefield, cutting a wide swath. Everything in its path and for a hundred yards on either side was scorched and blasted by its icy blue-red power. Krushni watched as a dozen Krushan chariots on the slope around and below Dronas were caught in its fury. The charioteers and horses froze, the flesh and clothing on their bodies blazing bright blue before melting off their skeletons. Only their bones remained, still poised in the actions they were engaged in at the moment they were struck. The chariots too were frozen in the blue flames, burning coldly; wisps of red smoke rose from their remains. On the hilltop, the Krushan chariots and the Gwannlander defenders clashing feverishly were blasted as well, suffering the same fate.

Dronas's insane laughter filled the air as the guru drove the celestial chariot at her with a relentless, manic joy.

The use of the God Mantras has unhinged him, Drishya said to her silently. *He used them too liberally in too short a span, deluding him into thinking he too is an immortal. Summoning Warbreaker completed the delusion; he is no longer in the realm of the sane now. He believes himself to be a stone god and everyone else to be urrkh. That is the danger of using a weapon as omnipotent as Warbreaker.*

Krushni had come to the same conclusion. As had others on the field, she knew without being able to read their minds: Vrath, Vessa, the Shvate Five, Jarsun of course, and even the Krushan Hundred, all of them knew their scrolls well enough to see the grave nature of the threat. No mortal had ever used three God Mantras in a row, not merely mantras granting benign boons, but war mantras intended only for the most dire crises. And no mortal, Krushan or stone god, had ever summoned the chariot of Inadran.

Even the Lord of Storms and War himself, the scrolls said, had sworn never to use the chariot again, dismissing it to the Neverever lest it tempt him or his fellow stone gods.

Dronas had sealed his own fate and, with it, the fate of everyone else on the field of Beha'al.

Everyone here will die, she sent back to Drishya.

If we are lucky, he replied, only *everyone here will die.*

What he had not said, but meant, was *If not stopped, Warbreaker will continue until it has killed everyone on Arthaloka.*

And no one could stop it but Inadran himself.

Krushni had a feeling the stone god was unlikely to put in an appearance here today to help them. The stone gods had not been seen on the mortal plane since before the origin of the Krushan and stonefire. She doubted humans' petty conflicts concerned the immortals or that they were even aware of what transpired here.

Even if they are aware that their weapons are being used, Drishya sent, *they cannot intervene in the affairs of mortals. Those were the terms of the peace pact they made with the urrkh at the end of the Last Great Urrkh War. "Neither urrkh nor stone god will intervene in the affairs of —"*

Thank you, brother, Krushni sent, *but the details don't matter. I need to deal with this now before it destroys us all.*

The chariot had burned a wide arc of destruction, leaving smoking skeletons and empty chariots blazing with the same eerie blue flames. It was about to reach Krushni. Even though the entire exchange with Drishya had taken only a moment, Warbreaker had already slain several thousands in that span. If she didn't do something, millions — tens, even hundreds of millions across Arthaloka — would die.

Krushni focused her energies and clapped her palms together with as much force as she could summon.

Arrow

~

KRUSHNI SLAMMED HER HANDS together, creating a thunderclap. The boom deafened ordinary mortals for half a mile, making even Arrow's ears ring. The wave of energy released by the peal manifested as a wall of white light. The wall sizzled and sparkled, its solid form shifting and jittering.

A hundred lightning bolts packed together tightly! Arrow was impressed. That was no ordinary conjuror's trick. It took real power and talent to do something like that.

Krushni pushed her palms outward, throwing the wall of lightning at the oncoming chariot. The blue light of the racing horses, their red smoke and black flames colliding with the blinding whiteness of the wall.

The collision caused a flash and another boom, louder than the first and with rolling after-echoes. Arrow saw a rainbow of colors for an instant, flickering in bursts and dots at the edges of his vision. They forced them away, clearing their eyes.

The chariot struck the lightning wall.

. . . And burst through it.

The packed bolts of lightning were released on impact, flung in every direction like flying splinters from a tree shattered by a mythic axe.

The lightning bolts skittered and danced, some striking the ground dozens or hundreds of yards away, blasting chariots, horses, infantry, even elephants, to bloody bits. Several zigzagged upward, disappearing Stone Father knew where before igniting in the sky. A hundred explosions sounded simultaneously, creating a deafening burst of sound. Body parts of animals and humans rained down and spattered everywhere.

Arrow ignored them, ignored everything else.

They had eyes only for Krushni and Warbreaker.

Even before she flung the lightning wall at the oncoming chariot, Krushni had flown up into the air.

She was now hovering a hundred yards above the ground, staring down at the chariot.

A lightning bolt struck the air near her, knocking her a few dozen yards sideways. She regained control of her flight and found the chariot again.

Warbreaker had passed the spot where she had been standing and was continuing its inexorable journey of destruction.

Arrow could see the frustration and anger on Krushni's face. She didn't know what to do next or how to stop the chariot.

That's because it's unstoppable, Arrow thought, wishing it were possible to speak to her the way the Five spoke to each other. But while Arrow could feel her emotions, her thoughts were still inscrutable. It would take time and intimacy to develop a mental bond strong enough to allow free thought exchange.

Right now, time was one thing they didn't have.

If Warbreaker wasn't stopped, it would destroy everyone on the battlefield, and then the world.

Dronas was still laughing, his manic guffaws counterpointed by the screams of terror that rose from the Krushan and Gwannlanders alike who stood in the path of the racing chariot. Every yard the chariot covered, more died.

There was only one thing to be done. And only Arrow could do it.

Krushni

~

KRUSHNI STARED IN DISMAY as the chariot shattered the wall of lightning, sending lightning bolts rebounding in every direction. One struck very near her, almost toppling her, and she fought to regain her balance. When she was upright again, she saw that Dronas was driving the chariot onward without any loss of speed, laughing maniacally. The guru had been elevated to the point of insanity by the godlike power he now controlled.

The consequences of the lightning wall being shattered were still ricocheting as bolts skittered every which way, causing additional damage and deaths. Krushni moaned as she saw dying or hurt. From up here, she had a bird's-eye view of most of the field of Beha'al. While most of the conflict was centered below her, where all the empowered Krushan and demigods on both sides were concentrated, the entire front was a seething mass of chaos.

The battle was in full swing, and she had no need to assess losses to know who already had the advantage. While the tactics the Gwannlander side had used to open the battle had been extremely effective, they were no match for the sheer numbers and brute force of the Krushan army. Add to that Dronas and the Krushan Hundred's own participation, and the outcome was obvious. It would all be over very soon.

And some of the most powerful players had yet to enter the fray. Vrath and Vessa on her side. Jarsun on the Krushan side. They had their own private vendettas to address and would only intervene to pursue those ends. In a sense, they were above the petty troubles of mere mortals. She didn't know whether to despise them for their power and privilege or to envy them.

The Shvate Five, Mother Jeel bless their kind hearts, were adding their strength to the Gwannland defense, doing a fair bit of damage. Ekluv had joined them, battling alongside his cousins, and between the six of them, they were holding back the enemy valiantly. But they could not be everywhere at once, and the battle for Gwannland was being lost for the most part with every minute that passed.

Her heart sank as she saw Gwannlanders fighting bravely all along the front, only to be overwhelmed by impossible odds. The Krushan chariot regiments alone were wreaking havoc. Gwannland's chariot cadre numbered barely a few thousand, their heavy cavalry about fifteen thousand or so, and they had no elephants at all. The pachyderms, or hasti, as they were known across Arthaloka, were not native to the eastern part of the continent, and were mainly found in the western and central regions, much too far to be brought over that enormous distance.

She had to do something, anything, to stop Dronas. Her people were counting on her. She was the only reason they were here in the first place. Many had tried to convince Vensera of the wisdom of acquiescing to Dronas, acknowledging his claim, spurious though it was, and accepting subjugation. That way, at least they could hope to survive as a race. The fact that Dronas had every intention of erasing them entirely from the face of Arthaloka seemed to escape them.

She understood their desperation: they were caught between extinction now and extinction tomorrow. Who wouldn't want to live another day? She was the one who had spurred them on to fight back, against all odds, convincing them that allies would come, it was only a matter of time.

And they had, at that. The powerful support she had raised here today was unprecedented. In any other circumstances, she had enough to wage war against almost any power in the continent. But looking at the field today, the turn of events, she had to think that maybe she had been on a fool's errand from the start. Had her own quest for vengeance and justice for her slain mother cost the lives of countless Gwannlanders? Was she going to be responsible for precipitating a genocide here today? After all, Dronas had come to the wedding contest to win a bride. If she had let him win, perhaps he might have relented a little, allowing New Gwannland to continue existence in some form, however oppressive, if only out of consideration for his new bride.

That was the traditional Arthalokan way to resolve longstanding feuds between nations, wasn't it? Marry off a prince or princess and transmute the enemy's bloodlust into plain old lust? Perhaps she ought to have sold her body in exchange for her people's survival. Instead, she had spurned Dronas's attempt to win the contest and humiliated him over what he probably saw as an irrelevant technicality designed especially to thwart him.

Of course he would take that personally. She might as well have slapped him and told him what a despicable monster and tyrant he really was. He was that, of course, but as princess, she was obligated to attempt diplomacy. But she had to say to hell with diplomacy, he *is* a monster and tyrant and I don't give a damn if his precious male ego is insulted. And she had provoked this very battle, and with it, the extinction of the entire Gwannland population who had adored, idolized, and supported her so heartfully.

All this passed through her mind in the fleeting moments after Dronas's chariot burst through the lightning wall and continued its destructive rampage across the field.

Now he was on the hilltop, on the Gwannland side, smashing through her ranks and laying waste to valiant soldiers who had no defense against the unstoppable power of the god vehicle. She had to do something, but for the life of her, she could not think *what*. Whatever she did next, it had to be directed only at Dronas, and not cause the destructive fallout that the lightning wall had caused, but if such a counterstrike existed, she could not think of it. As far as she knew, there was no weapon, no move that could defend against Warbreaker. That was the very reason it was called Warbreaker. Once it was deployed, the battle — and the entire war — was over, because it left no survivors.

That outcome was only a short while away now, and there was nothing she could do to stop it.

A lone figure racing contrary to the flow of battle caught her attention.

It was one of the Shvate Five.

Arrow.

The handsome, darkest one of them all.

Arrow was running across the field like an athlete in a sprint race, headed directly into the path of Dronas's chariot.

What did they hope to achieve except their own destruction? Even a Krushan was no match for the chariot of Inadran. As the legends emphasized so clearly, the stone gods themselves had feared and shunned the chariot as being too powerful. They had feared it being used against them someday and had wanted it destroyed — except that it could not be destroyed, only appeased for a while by death on a massive scale. Perhaps that was the very reason Inadran had granted Dronas's wish in whatever arcane deal they had struck: better to let Warbreaker slaughter mortals on the lower plane and satisfy its thirst for blood.

Krushni flew lower, intending to warn Arrow against whatever pointless attempt they were about to make.

Then, with a flash of insight, she remembered that Arrow was the one who had been fathered by the Lord of Storms and War himself.

Arrow was the direct avatar of Inadran.

Arrow

~

ARROW RACED PAST GAPING holes blown out by the lightning bolts, carpeted with bodies, chariots, and horse carcasses, wove through spearmen battling for dominance of the hilltop, leaped over a mangled heap of un-recognizable flesh and bone, closing the distance to the speeding chariot. Warbreaker's wheels struck blue sparks from the ground, leaving little wisps of black flame and red smoke in its wake. Dronas's laughter vied with the snorting and hissing of the steeds.

Now Arrow was alongside the chariot, matching pace to that of the snorting team. "Dronas!" they called out.

The guru paused his laughter long enough to look at Arrow.

"Yield, and I shall let you live," said the child of Karni and Shvate.

Dronas stared for a moment as if Arrow were a crow that had just spo-ken. Then the guru's face relaxed into a look of utter contempt and amuse-ment. He yanked the reins to his right, making Warbreaker swerve into Arrow's path.

The chariot would have struck Arrow had they not leaped up into the air at that exact moment. Instead, Warbreaker merely adjusted course slightly and continued on its frenzied way.

Arrow ascended fifteen feet without any effort and timed their descent so that the chariot was directly below when they landed — in the very char-iot well that had almost smashed into them.

Dronas snarled, eyes flashing with the same shade of scarlet as the flames from the horses' mouths. He drew his sword with one lightning-quick hand, and slashed at Arrow.

Arrow twisted quickly and slipped under the blade, feeling its sharply honed edge slash the first layer of skin on their chest, drawing thin trickles of blood.

They straightened up, working their own sword and rising to eye level once more.

Arrow could see the insanity in Dronas's eyes, blazing cold murderous grey.

"Impudent stripling, you dare challenge Dronas aboard the chariot of Inadran himself? I will cut you into a thousand pieces and feed you to my horses!"

Dronas cut the sword in a smooth but obvious strike at Arrow's neck.

Arrow parried the blow. The sound of clashing steel and a shower of sparks rose from their blades.

Dronas turned his sword sideways in a sharp arc, cutting back inward at Arrow's right side.

Arrow somersaulted over the blade and over Dronas's head, throwing themself forward to land standing on the front edge of the chariot well.

Dronas was already committed to his action and was able to turn it somehow with the ease of a master.

Arrow admired the seemingly impossible action but had no time to dally with a drawn-out sword fight. They had not leaped into the chariot to engage Dronas himself, but to gain control of Warbreaker.

Arrow somersaulted again, corkscrewing in midair to land with both feet on the backs of the front pair of horses. The Stormhorses stared up at him hatefully but did not whinny or rear as ordinary horses might have. They were the horses of the most cruel and despotic stone god of them all; Inadran cared only for his animals as much as he needed to. In battle, he drove them mercilessly. That had made them just as aggressive as Inadran himself. They glared up at Arrow, bucking and tossing their heads to try to throw them off. Arrow resisted, countering their every move by bending their body. From the chariot, Dronas roared angrily, lashing out with the long whip. The leather ends flicked Arrow's back and shoulder with knife-like force, slashing skin and flaying layers of flesh. Arrow ignored the pain.

What are you doing?

It was Krushni. Arrow was surprised to hear her speaking directly inside their head. They could still hear their brothers and sisters, and that meant the others could hear Krushni as well.

She was still hovering above the ground, flying backward to follow the path of Warbreaker. She frowned down at Arrow.

They smiled at her. *Trying to save this battle.*

Dronas lashed out again with the whip, catching Arrow on the neck and face. One of the tips of the lash almost cut their eye but they turned away at the last instant and took it on the cheekbone. Their face burned, and blood dripped freely onto their bare chest. Arrow ignored the pain, but decided that Dronas couldn't be allowed to use the whip a third time.

Reaching down, they took hold of the reins of the forward pair of Stormhorses. Blue lightning crackled and fizzed, stinging their palms. The right-hand Stormhorse turned her head, spitting black fire. The flames were searing hot.

Arrow smiled grimly at her. "Time to return home, Airavat!"

They yanked back hard on the bit, overriding the reins, and pulled upward with all their might. For a long moment, nothing changed. The chariot thundered on over the battlefield, reaping lives like a sickle reaping wheat; humans and animals died; Dronas cursed and ranted and raised his whip a third time; Arrow's siblings watched with growing anxiety; and the sun continued to rise up over the well-bloodied field of Beha'al.

Then, with a shuddering, screaming protest, the Stormhorses tossed their heads in fury and leaped up, drawing sparks from empty air as their hooves pounded emptiness in search of the sky highway, the mythical road of their stone god master.

Arrow felt a flush of relief as the chariot left the battlefield and shot upward, rising with astonishing speed as the Stormhorses regained their natural ground — the empty ether — and flew heavenward.

Showoff! Brum teased good-naturedly.

Look who's talking! Arrow sent back, sending the mental equivalent of a smile.

Arrow, are you sure? That was Yudi being a mother hen again in their mother's absence.

Yes, they answered simply. The Stormhorses took all their strength to control. They were bucking and resisting, unwilling to spare all those mortal lives still there for the taking.

From Krushni's mind came a strong sense of concern for Arrow's well-being and some confusion. *Where are you taking them?*

High enough to do what needs to be done.

And what is that?

Keep everyone alive long enough to fight a fair battle.

From the chariot, Arrow heard Dronas scream with impotent fury as he realized what was happening, even without the benefit of mindspeech. The guru had just been outmatched and outwitted, for the first — and last — time in his life. He began flinging everything within reach at Arrow, starting with his javelins.

Arrow ignored the ripping wound caused by a javelin that sliced their back and right shoulder as it skimmed past, and forced the Stormhorses to fly faster and higher. The sky above them curdled into a stormscape, boiling and seething furiously as if in anticipation of their approach. Lightning lurked within its depths, uncoiling its blades like a gargantuan awakening from an eon's slumber.

"*Stormfather!*" Arrow cried, feeling their skin rippling and glowing as they finally allowed the power within to respond to the stimulating presence of Warbreaker. The Stormhorses whinnied, showing crazed eyes as they saw Arrow for what they truly were. "*Take back your boon!*"

And the sky split open.

Jarsun

~

JARSUN LAUGHED. HIS OWN aides and soldiers turned to stare at him fearfully as he threw back his head and roared his delight. The suddenly monsoon-dark sky boomed and gnashed furious white teeth as the tiny speck flew into the mouth of the gargantuan. The chariot and its occupants were too high up to be visible anymore, but he knew well enough what was happening up there.

Brilliant. That young Krushan — Arrow, was it? — was both gifted and decisive. Definitely one to watch. Jarsun would not have expected a man as soft-hearted and moralistic as Shvate Krushan to sire such a child. Then again, it hadn't been Shvate's loins that had sired the heir; Stone God Inadran himself had accomplished that task. And it showed, in Jarsun's opinion. It took a warlord, the greatest warlord of all time, to sire a champion like Arrow Krushan.

His laughter was lost as the sky exploded with sound and light and fury. Animals and humans screamed and lowered their heads, seeking to immerse themselves in Artha's solid embrace to escape what their senses told them was the world ending.

Sadly, it was not as final as all that. A good world ending would have been fun; Jarsun had seen too few in his journeys through the ways, and they were far more brutal and much less spectacular to watch than this light-and-sound show. No. Arrow Krushan had been sufficiently clever to take the chariot of Inadran high enough that the impact of its destruction would not cause harm on the earth below. All they got was a blinding burst of light the equivalent of a thousand lightning bolts and a sound that resembled a thousand peals of thunder, both unleashed distantly enough that to Krushan senses, they were as thrilling as a fireworks display, and as harmless.

To mortals they were something more, but still not life-threatening.

Still, even his aides cowered in the dirt, physically incapable of overcoming their survival instincts when every fiber of their being told them the world was ending.

"Regain your feet!" Jarsun admonished. "That was naught but the child of Shvate eliminating the god weapon that Dronas foolishly deployed."

Dronas was stupid to have unleashed Warbreaker, Jarsun thought as he grinned up at the curdled sky, boiling with a dense layer of red clouds filled with black flames. If he had not been stopped, he would have killed every living being on the field, if not all Arthaloka, including himself. Jarsun doubted that had been Dronas's intention: the guru was too enamored of the pleasures of the flesh and the rewards of power to kill himself. He had simply grown drunk with his own power and was desperate to achieve victory at any cost. It was a good thing Arrow Krushan had stopped him so decisively. Dronas was stupid, but Jarsun was not done with this world. Not yet.

Nervous heads rose hesitantly, peering cautiously at the boiling sky. Voices rose, shouts broke out, and fingers pointed up.

Jarsun glanced up in time to see a hole opening in the dense cloud mass. Two tiny objects were falling through it.

One fell like deadweight all the way down, like the arrows the contestants had shot skyward during the wedding contest, until it landed with a wet splatter a mile or so away. That would be the corpse of Dronas, whatever remained of it after it had been exposed to the equivalent of a thousand storms.

The second object was also a human figure, but this one was alive and upright and descended at its own, controlled pace. It touched ground at the frontline, on the hilltop near the Gwannlander command. Arrow Krushan looked none the worse, thought Jarsun, as they set down their feet on solid ground again. If anything, they looked quite becoming, glowing with the power of a Krushan multiplied tenfold by the flush of having survived a cataclysmic event.

Yes, that one bore watching. It was a shame they were the child of the man Jarsun had killed with his own hands and that they knew it; Arrow would have proved quite useful for Jarsun in his plans of empire.

Still, Jarsun thought, grinning, there were plenty more players in the game. And the battle was still young.

Krushni

～

KRUSHNI RAN TO ARROW and embraced him. "You risked your life!"

"It was worth it," they said, smiling.

She stepped back and looked them up and down. "You are unharmed."

"I feel good. Very good, in fact!"

Arrow looked it too. There was a glow at the edges of their skin, the power leaking through the pores like light out of a silk-covered lantern.

She nodded, relieved. "I am glad."

Arrow gestured over their shoulder. "There's still a great deal of work left to win this battle."

"Yes, and we must press our advantage now, while they are still reeling from the shock of Dronas's loss."

She pointed to the spot where Dronas's body had fallen. It was thick with Dronas's soldiers. They seemed to be somewhat chaotic. She could see some kind of tussle breaking out in the midst of the crowd. Several similar upheavals started around it.

"Dronas was a tyrant. He controlled his people through force and intimidation. With him gone, many would rather flee the field rather than continue risking their lives without promise of reward."

"That is good," Arrow said. "But Dronas's army was only a fraction of the Krushan forces. We still have a vast host to deal with."

They turned and pointed. "And unlike Dronas's feckless fighters, the Krushan will not be daunted by the loss of one or even all their champions. Once launched, it is a juggernaut that keeps moving until told to halt. The only person who can give that command now is Emperor Adri himself, and he will never yield now that he has begun this campaign."

She nodded as she followed Arrow's arm, which was sweeping the entire panorama. For as far as the eye could see in every direction, the Krushan army was advancing. Even with their losses at the start of battle, it was still a formidable sight.

"We have suffered more grievously than they," she said, nodding back over her own shoulder. "They could afford to lose a tenth or even a fifth of their great numbers. We, on the other hand, have already lost more than two out of every ten. And the sun is a long way from its peak as yet."

Arrow said grimly, "We must break their advance."

"That cannot be done by my soldiers alone."

"True. Infantry is no match for heavy armored cavalry, chariots, and elephants. We will need to use other means."

She smiled without humor. "Are you saying what I am thinking?"

"You know I am, Princess. You are in my mind."

"As you are in mine," she said.

She could indeed sense what Arrow was feeling and thinking; not as readily as she could Drishya's thoughts and emotions, but enough to know that they felt attracted to her just as she felt attracted in return.

And so do their siblings.

They all touched minds, the five of them and Krushni. She saw, in Yudi's mind, the strategy they must adopt now in order to break the Krushan advance. Even as everyone noted their roles in the imminent attack, she could feel their emotions running unchecked.

Brum felt a powerful attraction for her, but also felt an overwhelming bashfulness that prevented her from admitting her feelings in spoken words. After Arrow's, her attraction was the most powerful.

I have much to consider after this battle. If we win this battle.

Moments later, the strategy clear in their six minds, Krushni prepared to enter the fray. This time, it would end only when the Krushan had been pushed back — or the Gwannlander forces were annihilated.

"Shall we?" Arrow asked, offering her a hand as if inviting her to dance at a ball.

She took it. "Let's."

They ran together to the edge of the hill, launching themselves off the top and into midair.

Below, around, and beyond, the great army of the Krushan awaited.

Yudi

~

1

YUDI FELT THE FAMILIAR thrill of combat as his siblings and he engaged the enemy. All his warring thoughts were stilled for the duration as he fought for his life.

Unlike his siblings, he was not empowered apart from the basic strengths that came with being a Krushan. He had neither Brum's prodigious strength and ability to summon the weight and force of the wind, Kula's ability to communicate with and command the cooperation of the animal world, Saha's extraordinary speed, dexterity, and manipulation of the tiniest of objects while in rapid motion, nor Arrow's enormous talent at weapons and combat.

But despite lacking their special physical talents, he was faster, and harder to wound or kill than any of them. He also healed quickly and could survive all the most fatal of injuries. None of those were anything to sniff at when fighting mere mortals.

His true gift was his intellect. It enabled him to think most shrewdly, anticipate moves and tactics, and even read the ebb and flow of events so he could predict exactly who would do what next, where and when it would happen, and how he must act to avoid or take advantage of each circumstance.

In addition, there was his constant connection with his siblings, which meant each of them knew at all times what the others were doing, including when one of them was in need of assistance. Because he was the weakest of them all, comparatively speaking, the others were quicker to come to his aid than to one another's. That felt strangely awkward at times, as he was the eldest and the one in charge, but it was also reassuring to know that when circumstances demanded it, he had four powerful siblings to rush to his side.

And there was an additional gift.

Stonefire.

The Krushan's connection with the alien being and its supernatural, unfathomable consciousness gave all of them an awareness of a large dimension to everything that transpired on this mortal plane. To Yudi, it was like being able to glimpse the hidden workings of a theater beyond the performance. Even as events played out on the visible stage, he was constantly aware of the larger connections, meanings, and implications. He also felt the presence of stonefire around him, in tiny chips buried deep within the ground beneath his feet, little pebbles, rocks, and fragments scattered across distant regions, and even, a whole continent away, the largest stonefire artifact of all, the Burning Throne itself.

The throne watched all that played out on this theater of war and upon the larger theater of the world itself. It surveyed, assessed, weighed, judged, and came to conclusions too arcane for mortal minds to comprehend, but which, to a Krushan, provided deep insights into the interconnectedness of things and how they might relate to one's own ends.

For Yudi, deeply schooled in the theory and practice of warcraft and the governance of empire, this was a powerful tool, giving him a level of understanding that far exceeded the actual events unfolding before his eyes.

Just as a captain understands the motive behind the orders he gave the mindless, obedient soldiers, and the colonel knows more than the captain, and the general more than all the ranks combined, and the emperor sees the larger means and ends, and a stone god the eventual outcome of all those events, so the throne sat in judgment over all life, all actions on the living plane, and judged how best to nudge, deflect, thwart, or abet those events in order to serve its own ends.

These complex levels of interpretation often made Yudi seem closed, remote, and aloof to other people. Even his family teased him or grew exasperated with him for being unable to simply "be in the moment" with them. But he could hardly help it. That was his gift — and his curse — just as being born Krushan was both things at once. And truth be told, he thrived on it. These were as meat and wine to him, and he consumed them with a bottomless hunger.

At times, even he tired of his relentless pursuit of information, knowledge, insight, and understanding. Even he wished he could simply "be" and not constantly be working out the implications and outcomes of even the most trivial of things.

When going into combat, as he was now, he finally got his wish.

This was the only time when the analytical, calculating Yudi retreated to the back of his brain and the active, alive, sensual, and existing physical being came to the forefront. All knowledge and study was forced to seat itself, and only the present moment and what he did or did not do, what was done to him, or what was about to be done mattered.

Life and death.

He was in the moment now, fully present, as the Five met the enemy in a headlong rush.

The Krushan army, seemingly undaunted by the five lone enemies racing downhill at them like suicidal fools, altered their tune when the individual soldiers realized who they were about to face.

"The Shvates!" one of them cried, flinging down his spear and turning to flee — only to be hacked down by his captain's sword.

Others goggled in fear as the Five closed the distance and came within strike range.

"Raise —" shouted the captain of the regiment directly in front of the Five, raising her dripping sword.

She never got to finish her order.

Brum and Kula, who were always the first, smashed into the massed infantry. Soldiers, weapons, and armor flew in all directions as Brum drove into their ranks like a one-woman battering ram.

Yudi felt a fleeting moment of remorse for those poor, outmatched mortal men and women who died without having a chance to even raise their weapons. His remorse was easily quelled by the knowledge that these same men and women would have overrun Gwannland and all of Eastern Arthaloka, slaughtering anyone and everyone their leaders ordered killed, no matter how helpless, frail, infirm, ill, old, or young. And that was before he even factored in the Burnt Empire's despicable attitudes toward enslaving the conquered survivors and using them as free labor to build its outpost cities and forts.

Unfair though this seemed, when viewed on the larger scale of the battle as a whole, it was the only way to break the brute force of the Krushan army. Once unleashed, it was a rampaging elephant in musth, maddened and driven by its own lust, and the only way to stop its rampage and save oneself was to kill it.

Yudi lashed out at a pair of Krushan soldiers, whose eyes glittered beneath their visors as they hacked and hewed at him from both sides. He parried one's sword with his right hand, and cut beneath the other's sword with his left hand, feeling the familiar bite of flesh where his blade met his body. The soldier cried out and turned away to clutch his mortal wound, while Yudi spun around, taking the surviving soldier with both swords at once, all but cutting the poor woman into three parts. Both fell away dying and were instantly replaced by three more, seeking to rush him from all sides and box him in.

He danced away, cutting through by piercing the one circling behind with the point of his sword. The soldier gasped, not expecting such a direct thrust, and doubled over. Yudi kicked him aside, off his sword point, and used the momentum from the kick to somersault over the heads of the other two, raking his sword across their necks and shoulders as he went. They screamed and clutched at their wounds, and then before they could react, he was past them and already engaging with more Krushan.

2

He was aware of his siblings at the periphery of his vision on both sides, as well as through their subliminal connection.

Kula was moving at an impossible speed, almost as fast as a ray of light traversed a great distance, and at that speed, everyone and everything else appeared to cease motion. Time itself seemed to stand still or slow down to the point where he could do anything with ease without anyone being able to see him as anything more than a blur. He snapped necks and arms, crossed soldiers' blades so they were gutting each other, and caused unspeakable damage to dozens before the first one completed the action he or she had begun. He sped through the Krushan army like a dervish of destruction, leaving a swath of mortally wounded, dying, dead, or incapacitated enemies in his wake.

Brum had sacrificed her own speed for power and weight, using her ability to inhale impossible amounts of air to increase her weight several dozenfold. She slammed through entire regiments of Krushan like an elephant smashing through wooden fencing. The enemy soldiers went flying, scattered in all directions in a bloody, splintering mess.

Saha had called on the insects and creatures of the ground and the air and unleashed them upon the hapless Krushan who faced her. Soldiers writhed and twisted, dropping their weapons or unable to defend themselves effectively as they were bitten by ants, bees, millipedes, spiders, scorpions, snakes, birds, even giant swarms of mites, midges, and mosquitoes. Those Krushan soldiers who didn't die of the toxins from the insect bites lay writhing and suffering on the ground, out of the fray.

As for Arrow, they were a sight to see. Yudi always wished he could simply stand and observe Arrow in combat. Of all Yudi's siblings, they were the one who fought like a master artist.

Arrow was working with swords today. Not just the two they carried, but the swords of the enemies unfortunate enough to face them.

They rushed at a regiment of Krushan infantry in a headlong, breakneck motion, seemingly defenseless and unarmed. Yet even as the soldiers slashed, hacked, cut, and swung their blades, Arrow was able to take their weapons from their hands as effortlessly as an athlete snatching up the baton in a relay race. It was as if they were *giving up* their weapons, although Yudi knew that was not the case: the looks of bewilderment on their faces as the weapons left their fists confirmed this. Arrow took these weapons and used them to cut down other soldiers — not holding on to the same swords but releasing them the instant the intended victims were struck, then moving on to deftly pluck more swords out of other hands.

Arrow sprinted, spun, bent, twisted, turned, and engaged in a breathtaking ballet of motions — snatching, cutting, grabbing, hacking, taking, stabbing — like a dancer twirling through an entire company, all of whom were well-rehearsed and knew exactly when to drop and cry out as they were passed by. The only thing amiss about this deadly dance was that their cries were genuine and the blood was real.

Arrow could have dispatched the same number in far less time, from a safe distance, using their incredible skill with the bow. Yudi had seen them take down an entire company of a hundred soldiers once, the vicious mercenaries of a brutal duke in another, distant land, using just three arrows. It had been a marvel of motion, angles, deflection, and an impossible-seeming sequential effect, with each arrow setting off a chain of reactions that drove the soldiers to "accidentally" wound, injure, or kill their comrades. Arrow could use any weapon, under any circumstances, to achieve unbelievable results. But Arrow chose to fight this way today because it was what gave the most satisfaction.

"I like to face my enemy and give them a chance to fight back," Arrow had said to Yudi, who had asked, after the three arrows had taken down the duke's company, why he didn't always use those methods.

Brum had laughed and commented that anyone who faced Arrow never had a chance, no matter how Arrow fought them. She was right, but Arrow was too; there was dignity and honor in facing one's opponent, as opposed to what Dronas had attempted to do: invoke God Mantras and use celestial weapons to massacre from the safety of his chariot.

3

Yudi fought his own fight, taking a nick here and cut there, a blow to the nose that left him dripping blood from one nostril, another bludgeon to the head that he felt even through his helmet and left him disoriented. He shook it off, taking down the taller, bigger woman who had struck him with her sword hilt, moving on to reap more enemies. Moving, always moving, never allowing himself to be completely surrounded because that would be the end of him. As long as he was in motion, he could fight on, or dance away, out of reach of the storm of swords when it grew too frenetic to defend against.

He was no Arrow, nowhere close to his sibling's elegance and grace. Arrow was liquid fire sluicing through sand, leaving a trail of burnt saffron. Yudi felt clumsy as a dromad and heavy-footed as an elephant in comparison, but his lithe physique, strong legwork, and nimble blades kept him alive and his enemies at bay even as he took a steady toll. He worked at it harder than anyone else: what his siblings could accomplish with a flick of effort took him sweat and strain, but he sweated and strained willingly and accomplished more than any ordinary Krushan army regular on the field. Their heavier armor and cumbersome gear, meant to withstand a sustained campaign in enemy territory, made them twice his weight and half as quick, and he took full advantage of those differences, even while artfully dodging their heavier weapons and avoiding their bone-crushing armored studs.

The minutes rolled by quicker than before, the battle now fiercely underway.

The Five had spread out after their first punch through the center and were now scattered across the length of the front. That was the point: to slow the Krushan advance and inflict maximum damage in the shortest time. That was what they did best. Without the numbers and sustenance to fight a drawn-out campaign, they had to rely on strike-and-smash tactics. Quick, deadly, very damaging. Wound as many as possible, kill when you can. Each wounded enemy soldier added chaos and confusion to the Krushan ranks.

Kills sounded more impressive when totaled up, but Yudi knew from his study of war history that wars were won by attrition. Even the Krushan standing order to abandon the wounded could not keep friends, siblings, mates, lovers from stopping to help the fallen. And all that screaming and begging for help wore down the enemy mentally and emotionally, taking its toll as the morning went on and those standing grew exhausted, hungry, thirsty, and less confident despite their superior odds. Yudi estimated that he brought down at least two hundred in the first hour alone. Multiply that number tenfold to a hundredfold for his siblings, and they were inflicting real damage on the enemy.

Brum had smashed through several infantry regiments, costing them dearly and leaving the survivors reeling and shaken, before starting on the elephants. The massive Hastinaga elephants, bred for war over generations, trained and drilled to military perfection, were heavily armored; the spacious platforms on their backs each held five highly skilled spearmen and archers. They were most effectively deployed after the infantry and chariots went in and softened up the enemy frontline. The elephant cadres were then sent thundering across the battlefield to pound all resistance out of the foe.

Whatever remained was then picked off by ones and twos by the armored cavalry.

Most Krushan battles rarely required more than the first two cadres — infantry and chariot — but if and when the elephants were sent in, that almost always signaled the end of the battle, if not the war. No army on Arthaloka, no defensive formation, no fortification could withstand the bone-crushing force of tens of thousands of oversized elephants, each weighing more than two tons with armor and occupants, all charging and bellowing at once. Entire cities had fallen to the might of the elephant cadres alone.

That was when they were charging together, under the momentum of their own great mass, aroused to fever pitch by their mahouts and the awareness of their own great numbers. An elephant charge was more a stampede than an orderly attack, and there was no stopping that juggernaut once it was underway.

But when they were standing still, they were *not* a juggernaut. They were just oversized beasts dreaming of chewing cud and grazing in endless green pastures, rolling in cool, muddy ponds, munching sugarcane happily, and nuzzling trunks with their mates and young ones. "Giant cows," as a guru had once described them.

Brum's attack caught them at their most vulnerable. Fenced in by their own infantry in front and cavalry behind, the elephants could do nothing but sit and wait to be called upon. When Brum came at them, like a Southeastern cyclone out of nowhere, they had no way to attack, avoid, or retreat. All they could do was sit there and watch her with alarm and consternation. Even the archers and spearmen were trained for assault, not defense. How could they defend against a single warrior with the strength of ten elephants and the speed of a typhoon? Closely lined as they were, every spear thrown and arrow shot was more likely to strike their neighbor elephants or fellow soldiers, while Brum simply wove her way between — or *under* — the massed elephants.

It was quite a sight to behold.

Even from a distance, hearing the sounds and glimpsing only flashes of it, Yudi could imagine the rest based on his connection with his sister's mind and her point of view.

Brum first tried to use her ability to suck the air around her to render the elephants unconscious. If possible, she would rather not hurt the beasts. Even though they were trained and bred for war, and had probably killed any number of innocents, they had been forced and brainwashed into doing so; they were not natural killers. But while her ability could produce the desired result in an enclosed space, it was not effective in the open. No matter how much or how quickly she inhaled, new air rushed in to replace it. All she achieved was creating a gust which ruffled hair and blew dirt and grass around. She had no choice but to do what was needed.

Brum held in the enormous quantity of air she had inhaled, using it to increase her weight and mass, as well as to power her attacks. She drove into the ranks of elephants with pile-driver force, sending them careening into each other. The beasts bellowed and screamed, unaccustomed to facing anyone heavier and stronger than themselves. They fell, toppling over onto their sides. The soldiers on their platforms were crushed, the platforms themselves shattered, and chaos descended. Brum continued her rampage, moving through the packed elephants and knocking them over for the several minutes that the inhaled air took to dissipate. As her weight lightened and her pace slowed, she leaped over a fallen bull elephant, his trunk waving in the air as he trumpeted his anger, and took stock of her first assault.

Hundreds of elephants lay on their sides, their spearmen and archers either killed outright or severely injured. Many more were still flailing about, panicked by the tiny human who had wreaked such havoc on their fellows. They ran about wildly, seeking to escape being attacked themselves, while their mahouts tried to restrain them and get them back into ranks. A few stampeded away, turning back to run at — and over — the cavalry behind, others running forward to bring more misery to the already hammered infantry.

Brum nodded, satisfied that the tactic was working. It was also designed to cause maximum harm to the human riders and the least amount to the elephants themselves. Saha thanked her for being considerate and used her own powers to soothe the fallen elephants who had suffered minor injuries.

Brum inhaled even more air, weighing down her body till it was thrice the weight and mass of a war elephant. Then she launched her second assault. At the rate she was going, she would run through a substantial part of the Krushan elephant cadre in another hour.

4

Saha targeted all the human soldiers in the Krushan army at once, across the entire span and breadth of the field of Beha'al. She did this while standing still in one place, on a grassy hummock. Closing her eyes and focusing her mind on the birds of the sky, she summoned them down from hundreds of miles away. They flocked to the battlefield, the sky turning dark as clusters of several hundred thousand birds descended. There were predator birds, their claws and beaks deadly sharp, large carrion birds, even small everyday songbirds. They circled the field, picking their targets on the Krushan side, and fell upon them like the wrath of a vengeful stone god.

Krushan soldiers on horseback, on elephantback, in chariots, and on foot all cried out with horror as shadowy blurs fell upon their faces, pecking and clawing at their eyes, ears, noses, cheeks, throats, even lips and tongues with vicious precision. Tens of thousands were blinded, muted, disfigured in the first assault itself. Those that were not presently dealing with the attacks of the other Shvate siblings tried to raise their swords, spears, axes, maces, bows, to defend themselves. But there were too many birds, perhaps a dozen for each soldier on the field, and it was impossible to avoid them entirely. A few thousand birds fell, injured or killed by a few lucky Krushan, but the humans were quickly struck by other birds as their hands were occupied with the use of their weapons, leaving their faces completely unguarded.

By the time the attack ended, more than half the Krushan army had lost either an eye or both eyes, a tongue, an ear, or chunks of flesh from their faces and were doubled over screaming in pain and terror. A goodly number of the injured had their throats torn out or pecked full of holes, and died within moments.

Saha had done it all without moving a finger herself or using a weapon. Still, she regretted using the birds to fight and mourned the deaths of those that had fallen.

5

Kula was using his extraordinary speed to brilliant effect. As before, he simply continued doing what he had been doing, racing at incredible speed through the Krushan army, moving an arm here, turning a head there, lifting a leg, a finger, a chin, an elbow, a sword, a spear. By the time he passed, the men and women he had manipulated continued what they had been doing, but this time they harmed themselves or their comrades without understanding why or how it was happening. The confusion only added to their panic and chaos, and though he caused few actual injuries and even fewer deaths, it completely dissipated the advance of the Krushan forces.

6

Arrow was splendid to observe, as always.

They focused their energies on the cavalry while the other siblings attacked the infantry and elephant cadres. Like the elephants, the cavalry were sitting targets at this early stage in the battle. They had switched to the bow. Such was Arrow's skill with the weapon that they were able to aim arrows to wound the riders without killing any of them or harming the horses. The wounds were not severe enough to maim them for life but would prevent them from brandishing or using any weapon.

Yudi watched with admiration as a single arrow shot from his sibling's bow clipped all hundred riders in a company before losing power and embedding itself in the dirt. The arrows were guided by Arrow's perfect eye and powered by lightning, striking with precision only the tendons that allowed the men and women to raise their arms. A second shot accomplished the same thing with their other arms, and then Arrow moved on to the next company.

As the cavalry got wind of this attack and tried to take evasive action by dismounting and hiding behind their mounts, Arrow altered the trajectory of the arrows to zigzag among the horses, striking their targets with ruthless precision. The curses and shouts of rage of thousands filled the air as the fabled Krushan Riders, made up mostly of lords, ladies, and other titled gentry, were incapacitated at least for the duration of the battle. They would recover from their wounds in a few weeks and would still be able to ride, but as warriors they were now useless.

It takes a master warrior to win without killing, Yudi sent to his sibling.

Arrow sent the mental equivalent of a bashful smile and a shrug. *Why kill when this does the job as efficiently?*

Wise choice, Yudi replied. *After all, our quarrel is not with these soldiers.*

You said it, big brother, Brum said. *When do we get to lock horns with Jarsun?*

He's next, Yudi sent back.

Krushni

~

KRUSHNI SURVEYED THE FIELD with a deep sense of satisfaction and relief.

The tide had turned. The great Krushan army's advance, which had seemed unstoppable only this morning, had been completely stalled. The sun was close to its noonday zenith, and already a battle that had looked unwinnable now might be anyone's game. The enemy was in shambles. The Five had wreaked havoc on the Krushan army, disabling hundreds of thousands while taking a shockingly low toll of life.

On the Gwannland side too, things had changed. The Krushan chariot advance, led by Dronas's own regiments, was effectively broken.

The reason for this was her brother Drishya and herself.

As she scanned the battlefield, using her Krushan senses to probe where the naked eye could not see, Krushni saw her brother finishing the task he had begun only a few hours before.

Drishya had summoned his chosen weapon again, but this time, he used the power of his mind to wield it. The golden disc spun at blinding speed on the tip of his forefinger before he flung it at the last ragged regiment of Dronas chariots. The disc flew from his fingertip to arc through the air like a golden blur. Like a ray of sunlight, it flashed across the field, severing the heads of the charioteers as it went. A hundred, two hundred ... Krushni knew the disc could continue indefinitely if Drishya willed it. As the heads toppled, the chariots came to a standstill, the well-trained horses sensing the lack of pull on their reins. The last moving chariots halted, effectively ending the advance.

The disc returned to Drishya's finger.

Sister, he sent, *shall I deal with the Krushan army next?*

Krushni was tempted to say yes. Mother Goddess alone knew how much terror and bloodshed that great force had perpetrated. A part of her dearly wanted to punish every last human and animal that wore the Krushan colors and sigil for their part in supporting the cruelest imperial regime in Arthalokan history. But she knew that would itself be a cruel act.

Mother would not want me to do it, she thought. *If she were still here with me today, she would say, "Krush, isn't winning enough?"*

Krushni felt a pang of pain as she thought of her mother, lost to her when Krushni was still a child on the cusp of young womanhood. When she closed her eyes, she could still feel the blasting heat of the Red Desert, smell the deeply embedded odor of stale human sweat and Vanjhani food after more than a decade of traveling with the wagon train, hear the last liquid sounds as Jarsun buried his dagger in Aqreen's body, and see the light go out of those beloved eyes.

Sister?

Krushni snapped back to herself, back in the here and now. *No, Drishya. We have turned the battle. That is enough for now. Stand down, brother.*

She glanced over her shoulder at the command point where her father and mother in this lifetime would be waiting and watching the progress of the battle. She felt a stab of guilt at the thought that she was still mourning her birth mother Aqreen's death of fifteen years ago, when her mother in this lifetime, Vensera, was near death right now, right here. She knew she ought to be with Vensera and Gwann now, to spend the last moments of the queen's life with her. But there was still work to be done.

The advance had been halted. The tables had been turned. The battle might even be won now. But it was not over yet. There was still a giant obstacle and threat that had to be overcome. The main reason for this battle, and for the presence of so many of them on this field.

Jarsun.

Jarsun

⁓

1

JARSUN WATCHED WITH IDLE amusement as Vrath left his position on the far hilltop with Jilana and Vessa, rising up in the air, carried on waves of water vapor. Vrath drew his power from Jeel, the Mother River that sustained the world. Jeel, in a mortal avatar forced upon her by an ancient curse, had birthed him, the last of eight children she had borne during her marriage to Emperor Sha'ant. She had taken Vrath with her when she reverted to her aqueous form, returning him when he was grown to young adulthood. She remained a constant presence in his life, not only as the river that flowed through the heart of Hastinaga city itself, but as a living goddess who appeared and spoke to him when she willed it. All his power came from her, drawn from the particles of water in the air, the ground, the sky, and all forms of it everywhere.

To the humans on the field, it looked like Vrath was flying. Jarsun knew that his fellow Krushan was in fact being carried by minuscule particles of water vapor. His thin lips tightened as he recalled, initially with delight, his one previous battle with Vrath. He had used his powers to attack Vrath, almost killing him.

Then his lips curled with distaste as he recalled how Vrath had overcome that attack by calling down a rain cloud out of a clear blue sky, and had attacked Jarsun with a cold, fierce precision that had come close to ending Jarsun's time on this mortal plane. That was the closest Jarsun had ever come to feeling vulnerable, and he hadn't liked it one bit. He knew that in an all-out battle with Vrath, it was an open question which of them would be left standing.

Thankfully, this time, he wouldn't have to test that argument.

It was time to reveal his secret.

2

"Jarsun," Vrath said. He hovered in midair some three hundred yards above the ground, on the same level as the hilltop on which Jarsun sat upon his horse. "I challenge you to a duel, one-on-one, as per the Krushan Rule of Personal Challenge, as noted in the Imperial Edict of Empress Janasheera issued in Year Seventy-six of Chakra Twelve. Under the terms of the rule, I ask that you withdraw your army to your own lines and order them to refrain from any further violence until our duel is concluded. Under the same rule, in the event of my victory in this duel, your troops will retreat and this conflict will be concluded."

The armies waited, hundreds of thousands watching and listening to hear Jarsun's answer. Both sides had already ceased hostilities, aware of Vrath's intention through the insidious grapevine that passed on information of the Krushan with lightning speed.

Jarsun smiled and said nothing.

Vrath waited patiently. His smooth, flawless features were an expressionless mask; his oversized, magnificently muscled body was a sculpture of ideal masculinity. His glacial grey eyes glittered like ice in morning sunlight on the heights of the Coldheart Mountains, where the River Jeel originated. The only sign of his aging since the Battle of the Rebels decades ago was the whitening of his long, lustrous hair. It had grown out even longer, reaching almost to his waist now, and remained rich and thick, smooth and full-bodied, but where it had been mostly bluish black then, the color of a river's depths, it was now silver, like the dancing fish that leaped up the Jeel in autumn, going upriver to mate and birth their brood.

Finally, Vrath spoke again. "Jarsun, I await your answer."

Jarsun remained silent. His thin lips retained their look of bored amusement. His tongue tips flicked in and out of the corners mockingly. His horse pawed the ground restlessly, then stilled itself, remembering that its master was prone to punishing signs of impatience with pain.

"Speak, Jarsun. Do you or do you not accept my challenge?"

Still Jarsun kept his silence. The sun inched toward its zenith, shining down on a battered but still enormous Krushan host, and a depleted but still determined Gwannlander force as both sides waited.

Finally, Vrath said, "If you refuse to duel me, you will forfeit. Then you must withdraw your army and leave the field, and Gwannland will be declared victorious by default. Speak now, or consider yourself defeated."

It was time.

Jarsun said, "Vrath!"

The armies held their breath, waiting to hear his response.

"The armies of the Burnt Empire are not mine to command, not yet. Their presence here was ordained by your chosen emperor, Adri Krushan. They were sent to support the campaign of Guru Dronas. If you wish them to withdraw, petition Guru Dronas."

Vrath replied, "Guru Dronas appears to have fled the battle and Arthaloka for good."

Jarsun laughed. "A fine choice of words. You always did have a liquid wit. Yes, I noticed Guru Dronas's demise. That leaves you with only one option. Appeal to your own emperor, Adri."

Vrath said, "In Guru Dronas's absence, there remains only one commander on the field. It was my impression that you now command these armies."

"I do not serve the Burnt Empire," Jarsun said cheerfully. "You may recall that you and your stepmother, Jilana, are the reason for that circumstance. You denied my infant daughter her rightful claim to the Burning Throne, despite her passing the Test of Fire."

"I do not wish to rake up old coals with you, Jarsun. Speak to the point. Do you not consider yourself the leader of this campaign after Dronas's demise?"

"That depends."

"Upon what does it depend?"

"Upon what your emperor decides."

"So you insist on appealing to Adri before agreeing to this duel."

Jarsun shook his head, chuckling throatily. It came out as a hissing sneer.

"This duel will not happen, Vrath. I know you are eager to die by my hands. You almost did die on the last occasion we faced each other. But I see no need to kill you, since we are now family."

Vrath showed the slightest trace of disgust on his smooth, sculpted features. "We will never be on the same side. If you refer to your alliance with the armies of Krushan that our emperor granted the use of, then you well know that is merely a military alliance intended to give the Burnt Empire access to and control of the east and south of the continent. The Burnt Empire has many such allies across Arthaloka. That does not make us 'family.' You gave up that privilege when you were excommunicated and cast out of the House of Krushan decades ago. Nothing can change that."

"Is that so?" Jarsun said, mockingly. "I think we should ask Emperor Adri how he feels about that."

Jarsun gestured and reopened the portal to Hastinaga, to the room that housed the Burning Throne.

Krushni

~

THE PORTAL OPENED TO reveal Emperor Adri seated upon the Burning Throne. Jarsun did something using his urrkh sorcery to expand the portal manifold times until Adri loomed over the battlefield, as large as a mountain.

He wants the emperor to be visible to everyone on the battlefield. He wants them all to know what he's about to say.

"Nephew," Jarsun said with a tone that mimicked affection, "it is time to enlighten your uncle Vrath on my new status within the House of Krushan."

Adri considered Jarsun from the distant throne room.

The emperor of the Burnt Empire sat dwarfed by the great black rock, roughly hewn by unknown forces into the semblance of a seat. Its jagged shards extended on all sides. The deep black surface was darker than any natural substance upon this world, darker even than ebony, darker than the blackest night. In that darkness was a sense of aliveness, of motion, of sentience. It oozed and swam, swirled and crept, like a swarm of scorpions unearthed on a moonless night. The supernatural flames, blackish red, fluttered and sprang out in unpredictable patterns, constant and eternal. The flames rose and fell to indicate the intensity of stonefire's own responses to stimuli, as well as to the moods and temper of the one occupying it.

Within its black claw, Adri's sightless eyes were gouged-out tunnels to the afterlife, his long, lean face hardened by decades of solitary brooding. He and the throne complemented each other as perhaps no other Krushan since the First of the Race. In that moment, he was truly the Burnt Emperor.

When he spoke, his words carried fire and ice both, echoed in the cavernous chamber, deserted except for himself and stonefire.

"Tell him yourself."

Krushni saw her father in her previous life blink, his nictitating eyelids flickering shut and open. He was taken aback by the blunt command.

Jarsun recovered quickly. By his own choice, he had made the dialogue as public as could possibly be, to a vast multitude who feared and respected, however reluctantly, the power and authority of the man he was addressing. He had no alternative but to accede gracefully.

"Certainly, Your Highness," he said, attempting an imitation of a smile.

Jarsun turned to Vrath, who was still hovering in midair above the battleground.

"It is time to correct a misimpression that the elders of House Krushan, and the world at large, harbor about the line of succession."

Vrath stared back at Jarsun impassively. "Continue."

Krushni saw Jarsun smile, this time more genuinely, a sly, foxy show of teeth that expressed the delight he felt for what he was about to reveal.

"You believe that Crown Prince Dhuryo and his brethren were born of Adri's seed, fathered upon Empress Geldry," Jarsun said pompously, unable to restrain a sneer. "Your belief is false. They are indeed born of Geldry, but their sire was not Emperor Adri."

Vrath waited silently until it was evident that Jarsun expected him to react, saying finally, "You claim it was someone other than Adri?"

Jarsun laughed. "I do not claim. I state it as a fact. The Krushan Hundred were fathered by none other than myself, which makes them my children under Krushan law, and therefore makes me the emperor of the Burning Throne. In short, it establishes my legitimacy and authority as liege of the Burnt Empire and patriarch of the House of Krushan. Take note of this, Prince Regent Vrath and Dowager Empress Jilana."

There was stony silence for a long moment after Jarsun finished. Across the battleground, there were occasional murmurs and restless chatter, punctuated by the usual battlefield sounds of wounded and dying soldiers and animals. From Vrath himself, hovering above the hill, and Jilana, a mile away but still part of the dialogue, there was no visible or audible response.

Krushni saw Jarsun's eyes flicker again, and a line as thin as a delicate knife-cut creased his forehead vertically. His tongue tips flickered in and out numerous times. *He doesn't like this. It's not the reaction he expected,* she thought with satisfaction.

I guess this isn't going as well as Big Bully thought it would, Brum sent in her droll way.

No, it certainly is not, Yudi sent, sounding very pleased.

Jarsun looked around, sensing that something had gone awry, but unable to pinpoint what, how, or where.

With no response forthcoming from anyone else, he finally said, "Do you not have anything to say to that, Vrath?"

Vrath allowed several minutes to pass before saying, in his unshakeable calm tones, "It is an interesting delusion. It seems you have the makings of a bard. That is quite unlike most Krushan. Perhaps you inherited this trait from your urrkh father's side."

Jarsun's tongue lashed out, his pointed fangs showing clearly, eyes flashing. "How dare you impugn —"

He broke off abruptly, remembering where they were and the audience listening and watching the exchange. He visibly regained his composure.

"Of course you would not wish to take my word for it. It is in your nature to distrust and disbelieve anything I say. Because to accept my words as truth would be to acknowledge that your own power and stature within House Krushan is now diminished and that you must bow and show respect to me, as the true emperor."

He laughed and spread his hands, turning around to show the world that he was unaffected by Vrath's rejection.

And by doing so, he proves how much he is affected, Arrow sent.

Precisely, Yudi sent. *In contrast, witness Great-Uncle Vrath's calm composure and measured tones, without any trace of emotion. That is how an elder Krushan should behave, no matter what the circumstances.*

Jarsun broke off his laughter abruptly, turning back to the portal.

"Good nephew," he said to Adri. "Pray, enlighten your ignorant elders, Vrath and Jilana, on the veracity of my statements."

A continent away, Adri remained shrouded in darkness, his features glimpsed only in the glow of stonefire flames.

Jarsun said again, sounding piqued now, "Nephew? Pray, speak. Explain to them how it was that I came to sire the princes that the world considers your heirs."

Adri remained motionless. "Explain it yourself."

Jarsun stared at the portal. Krushni sensed his growing rage, curbed only by his need for Adri's public support and most of all, the throne's support. Unlike other kingdoms and empires, the ruler of the Burnt Empire could not simply be assassinated, overthrown, or forced into submission. The throne itself protected its occupant from all aggression. Even the slightest hint of animosity or conflict against the emperor would make the throne lash out with deadly force.

After a lifetime of intimidating, bullying, badgering, murdering, torturing, and having his way, Jarsun now faced the one being on Arthaloka whom he could not bend to his will, the one being he could not attack or kill. It was not enough to eliminate the current occupant of the throne; one had to pass the Test of Fire and be accepted by stonefire itself. Nor could one bypass stonefire and simply declare oneself ruler of the Burnt Empire. Only the One Who Sat upon the Burning Throne could be the ruler of the empire. Whether Jarsun liked it or not, he had to accept whatever Adri said without argument or dissent.

"Very well," Jarsun said, pretending to show good humor. "For the enlightenment of lesser minds, let me expound. There are other worlds than this one, infinite variations on our Arthaloka. In some, there are no mortals at all, only beasts of the wild. In others, there is constant war, famine, disaster. Some have only one moon, unlike our world, which is munificent in satellite bodies. Others have two suns. As a Krushan of special talents, I possess the ability to walk the ways, traveling between these alternate versions of Arthaloka and returning at will. In one such world, I found Geldry, and she was attracted to me of her own volition—"

Jilana spoke forcefully from the hilltop, not far from where Krushni stood. "You transformed your appearance to that of Adri, lured her there, making her believe it was a waking dream. You seduced her and bedded her in that world, impregnating her with your demon seed. When you had finished using her — raping her, I should say, for it could not be deemed consensual if she was not fully aware of what was happening — you returned her to our world."

Jarsun turned to seek out Jilana on the hilltop. "I did nothing to her that she did not desire herself."

"Justify it any way you wish," Jilana said. "You deceived, lured, raped, and impregnated her. That is the truth of the matter."

Jarsun seemed about to reply with more force and anger, but checked himself.

He smiled, tongue tips snaking out.

"However it happened, I *did* father the Krushan Hundred upon her that night. Which makes me their true sire and, under law, the rightful emperor of the Burnt Empire. I revealed the truth to my nephew Adri some time ago, along with several other facts of particular interest to him. At the time, I made it clear to him that I respected his position as occupant of the Burning Throne and assured him that I would not attempt to unseat him during his lifetime."

Because you know that only the throne can decide that, you scum from the river bottom, Brum sent furiously.

"I am content to let Adri rule as long as he lives. I am content to remain as patriarch of House Krushan and regent of the empire until then. After his demise, which I trust will be at a ripe old age, I will see my eldest son, Dhuryo Krushan, installed upon the throne and continue to protect and support him until my own time is at an end."

Jarsun spread his arms. "All will be as it is now. There will be no strife or dissonance within House Krushan or the empire. The only difference is that the world, and you of House Krushan, must accept me, publicly and permanently, as the patriarch and senior-most Krushan, and accord me the respect, honor, and privilege that is mine by right and under Krushan law."

Jilana laughed harshly.

"Now you are deluding yourself, Jarsun! What you desire will never come to pass."

Jarsun regarded Jilana coldly. Then he shrugged.

"It is not up to you to decide. Once Adri acknowledges my legitimate claim and accepts my blessings to continue as emperor under my patronage, it will be official. It will be law."

Vrath spoke unsolicited for the first time. "What does Emperor Adri say to that?"

All eyes were on the portal, and on the shadowy figure in the throne room a continent away. Adri leaned forward, bringing his hard face and blank eyes into the firelight. In response to his change of mood, the throne blazed hotter and fiercer, its flames turning deep orange and crimson. He spoke a single word.

"Nay."

Now things get really *interesting,* Brum sent happily.

Jarsun

~

NAY?

Had Adri just said *nay*?

No, it could not possibly be. Jarsun had prepared Adri for this very moment, groomed him for *years*, feeding his insecurities, harping on his fears and doubts, nurturing his inherent distrust of his own family, feeding his rage against his enemies, both real and perceived . . . Jarsun had invested so much time, effort, and manipulation in grooming Adri for his part in this great game.

How could Adri now say . . . *nay*?

Impossible.

"My good nephew," he said, struggling to maintain his smile and appearance of good humor, "surely you are denying Vrath, are you not?"

Adri regarded him across the thirty thousand miles that separated them. "I am denying you, Jarsun."

Jarsun blinked, feeling his patience and unflappability evaporate rapidly. "You *cannot* deny me. I am the father of the heirs to the empire. You remain upon the Burning Throne solely at my pleasure. That is law, and none can deny the law, at peril of their lives."

Adri smiled. It was an eerie smile, his face lit by the ghostly flames of the throne in the dark shadowy chamber. There was not a trace of warmth in that smile. "You are only the father of Geldry's children. Dhuryo and the rest of the Krushan Hundred. That is all you are."

Jarsun frowned. What manner of bedevilment was this? "You have failed to produce an heir. Your time is not long in this world. I am the patriarch of House Krushan. I decide who deserves to sit upon the throne!"

"You are wrong on all counts, Jarsun," Adri said. "You are no patriarch except in your own deluded mind. You decide nothing. As for whether or not I live a long life — as you yourself prayed I would only a short while ago — or am not long for this world — as you now say — that is not for you to decide either. I am the lawful liege of stonefire, and stonefire sustains me and enlivens me. Stonefire says that I shall live many decades more, possibly even longer. Even you cannot dispute stonefire."

"Stonefire is a *thing*," Jarsun said, hearing his tone become less controlled, his pitch ragged. "It lies to you. It lies constantly. I am your family. I am the lawful patriarch of the Burnt Empire. You would do well to heed my words."

With a suddenness that startled even the Krushan watching, a spear of red flame shot from the depths of the throne, through the portal, and struck Jarsun on his forehead. He cried out, and dug his spurs into his mount. The horse, taken by surprise and sensitive to the presence of sorcery, bucked and threw its occupant to the ground. Jarsun fell hard, landing on his shoulder. The horse screamed with panic and, fearing it would now be punished for its transgression, sped away down the hillside, eager to put as much distance as possible between itself and its master-tormentor, as well as the supernatural force that had come close to singeing it.

Jarsun regained his feet more easily than he recovered his dignity. He stood, nursing his shoulder, trembling with anger. The spot on his forehead where the flame had struck was marked by a blackish red oblong that still smoldered and smoked. It felt as if he had been stabbed with a red-hot needle. His free hand stole toward the spot, but he forced himself to stop short of touching it. Every Krushan knew the power — and cruelty — of stonefire, and respected it enough not to question its power. He dared not aggravate the wound further.

Adri leaned back slowly upon the throne. "The Burning Throne lives, hears, and sees all. Only the foolish dare to challenge One Who Sits upon It."

The impudence of the boy! How dare he?

Jarsun's eyes darted from side to side, as he sought a way out of this situation. How could things have gone so wrong so quickly?

He saw Vrath, still hovering in midair, and Jilana on the far hilltop, watching with a tight smile on her lined face.

He swallowed his hatred for both of them and suppressed the memory of how they had humiliated him the day he had approached them with his newborn daughter, who was entitled to the Test of Fire.

"Vrath. Jilana." He forced his voice to remain level. "As elders of the House Krushan, it's your responsibility to uphold the law. Do you not acknowledge my claim?"

Vrath turned to look back at Jilana, who answered for both of them. That was a bad sign. There was no love lost between Jarsun and Vrath, but Jilana positively loathed Jarsun.

"Your claim is rejected."

Jarsun could not believe his ears. "You question the legitimacy of my statements? I can prove to you that the Krushan Hundred are my offspring through Geldry! The throne itself can confirm it, even if Adri will not. All I have to do is —"

Jilana raised a hand. "Enough. Let us waste no more time on this pointless debate. For clarity, let me state that no one is questioning that the Krushan Hundred are your offspring."

Finally, a spark of reason! Jarsun leaped at it.

"Then you must accept my claim as patriarch! You cannot accept one thing without the other. As the next heir to the throne, Dhuryo Krushan, is my son, therefore —"

"Again, Jarsun," Jilana said with a world-weary tone, "I say to you, Dhuryo is indeed your son, but he is not the next heir to the throne. That privilege belongs to someone else."

Jarsun stared at her, then at Vrath, whose perfect features remained as inscrutable as stone. What was she talking about? Had everyone gone insane all of a sudden? Was this some conspiracy against him? No, as elders, they could not deny or defy Krushan law. To do so would undermine their own authority and legitimacy and invite censure from the throne itself. Yet it was he, Jarsun, that the throne had just struck. That could only mean that — that . . . What did it mean, exactly? His head was reeling, and not solely because of his fall from the horse or the blow from stonefire. Everything was going very, very wrong, and he could not understand why or how, for the first time in his entire life.

"Let me enlighten you," Adri's voice said.

Jarsun spun around to look at the portal. His hand rose instinctively, as if to ward off another possible strike from stonefire.

Adri smiled at him, sensing his fear. *The throne speaks to him and through him now,* Jarsun realized. Adri was fully in his element, in the prime of his power as occupant of the Burning Throne and emperor of the Burnt Empire.

"The next heir to the throne is my son."

And without Jarsun willing it or using his urrkh powers, the portal widened, irising open to reveal not just Adri upon the throne, but the entire raised and terraced dais upon which the throne sat in the center of the vast chamber.

Contrary to what Jarsun had assumed, Adri was not alone in the throne room. There were several others with him.

And Jarsun recognized them.

Krushni

─

AND NOW WE COME to the nub.

Krushni watched with grim satisfaction as Jarsun's grand plan dissolved before his eyes. She took no pleasure in watching another person's distress, but this was war, and this man, her father in another life, was the murderer of her mother, a genocidal tyrant, and the cruelest being alive. His distress was only the fruit of his own poisonous tree being fed back to him by karma. Let him choke on it now!

"Daughter."

She turned to see her father approaching, supporting her mother.

"Mother! Father!" She ran to Vensera and Gwann, taking her mother's shoulder and supporting her. "You should not be exerting yourself."

Vensera smiled at her wanly. "What good will it do for me to rest? I know that your powers purchased a little more time for me, but I fear that time is coming to an end. I would spend my last moments with you, dear one."

Krushni's throat caught. Another life, another mother lost too soon. *Is this how it will always be for me? Life after life?*

No. She pushed the thought away firmly. It would not always be thus. A better time was coming. For her. For everyone in Arthaloka. The events unfolding this very moment on the field of Beha'al were bringing about that brighter, more peaceful future. And she had played her part in that remaking.

"Every moment you spend with me is a gift, Mother," she said quietly. "Come. Watch us change the world now."

She guided Vensera to a boulder large enough for the three of them to sit upon. The queen of Gwannland breathed out a soft sigh as she rested her weight. Then they all watched.

Jarsun

～

1

"YOUR SON?" JARSUN SAID, incredulously. "You have no son, Adri. The children you believe to be yours are *mine*. Dhuryo is my son, not yours."

"I do not speak of Dhuryo or his brothers," Adri said imperiously. "I speak of my firstborn, who was birthed before Dhuryo and the Krushan Hundred, who were conceived through your despicable deception."

Jarsun looked around wildly. What madness was this? Were they all deluded? "Geldry had no other children before Dhuryo!"

"Nor do I speak of Geldry," Adri said. He gestured to one of the figures standing in the shadows below the throne, upon the large, irregularly shaped dais. The figure climbed the steps up to Adri. She hesitated briefly, fearful of stonefire, but Adri's outstretched hand gave her confidence enough to ascend the last step. She took Adri's hand. The flames of the throne turned a softer, warmer golden-sienna hue.

"I speak of my true love, my companion Sauvali, mother of my firstborn child."

Jarsun stared at the woman standing beside Adri, her dark face altered and thickened in middle age but still recognizable even after all these years. It was the face and the person he had sought for years, searching through the ways.

Sauvali, the maid. Adri's lover. The mother of his unborn child whom Jarsun had targeted in that attack at the picnic. His mercenaries had kidnapped her, taking her downriver on a boat, to be brought and held at a

383

remote location awaiting further orders from Jarsun. But when he had reached the spot, the mercenaries were unaccompanied. Vessa had waylaid them en route and taken the woman from them by force. Jarsun had punished their mistake with death, painful and torturous, before setting off in search of Vessa and the woman. He had never found them, even after years of questing. And now, out of the blue, here she was, alive and seemingly whole and well.

That damned sage!

Jarsun struggled to regain his composure. "It is a miracle! I am so pleased for you, Adri. Your long-lost love has returned to you."

"Yes," Adri said coldly, "which is strange, don't you think? Considering that you yourself fed me a pack of lies about my sister-in-law and wife colluding to have us attacked and Sauvali abducted. You also said at the time that Sauvali had been killed, along with my unborn son. And I was stupid and confused enough to actually believe you for all these years!"

Jarsun spread his hands, feigning innocence. "That is what I believed! I only told you in your best interests, Adri. I am happy to be proven wrong. Delighted that you have been reunited!"

Adri snorted dismissively. "You mean you are shocked and angry to see that she survived your assassins. I only recently learned the truth, and met her only this very day. I wanted to strike out at you at once, to punish you for your vile acts and for deceiving me and preying on my vulnerability. But mostly for your unforgivable crimes. It was you who tried to slay my beloved and my unborn child. You murdered your own father-in-law, Aqron, and your wife, Aqreen, because they did not support your plan to exploit your own daughter, Krushita, for your ambitions. But above all, you committed one crime that I personally will never forgive you for, Jarsun. You slew my brother Shvate. A great warrior and fine king, the best Krushan that ever lived, and you murdered him in cold blood, duping him into trusting you by taking on the appearance of Great Father Vessa and entering his forest hut. And then, to serve your own vile plan, you lied to me that it was Vessa himself who committed that crime."

Jarsun shook his head, not trusting himself to speak. How had Adri learned everything? The answer was obvious, he realized suddenly. He had just said it himself: Vessa. Only the old guru could have put the whole thing together and unearthed the truth. He turned to seek out the white-bearded figure on the far hilltop, but Vessa was no longer standing there beside Jilana.

"I am here, Jarsun," said Vessa's voice. "And I am not alone."

2

Jarsun turned to look at the portal.

Vessa had also stepped out of the shadows on the dais. With him was a young man with strangely familiar features.

"This is Ekluv, son of Sauvali and Adri, and the eldest heir to the Burning Throne. It is he, not Dhuryo or his brothers, who will succeed Adri. The elders of the House Krushan have acknowledged his claim, and he has been anointed crown prince this very day. I am pleased to inform you that your plan to abduct and kill him and his mother backfired. Adri's love for Sauvali and the fruit of their loving union has produced this true heir. Thus love triumphs over deception and falsity. And thus shall it ever be. That may not be Krushan law, but it is the law of karma."

Vessa indicated the fourth and last person on the dais, who also stepped forward now to join Vessa and Ekluv.

"You already know Karni, widow of Shvate, whom you cruelly murdered in her presence and the presence of her five little children that day in that hut in the forest."

Karni stared at Jarsun through the portal with a look that would have killed if it were possible.

Jarsun flinched. He struggled to find a way out of this predicament. Why had he made this exchange public? That had been his only mistake. The rest of it did not matter one whit. So what if he was what they said he was; he had never claimed to be a knight of righteous justice. He was Jarsun Krushan. It was his destiny to rule the world. His right. His entitlement. Nobody would deny him that god-given privilege.

"You are all fools!" he shouted. "I am Jarsun Krushan. I am a god in mortal form. You will all be my slaves. I will destroy everyone who stands in my way."

He gestured, uttering the command to shut the portal.

Nothing happened.

Vessa raised his hand. "Your power is useless here, Jarsun. Stonefire itself has turned against you. The Burning Throne has made its decision clear. Earlier, it only struck you as a warning. Beware that it does not strike you dead where you stand."

Jarsun took a step back. He could still feel the heat of the tiny smidgen of fire smoldering in his forehead. As if sensing his fear, it grew hotter, the flame flicking out of the oblong hole. He could see at the edge of his vision and hear it crackling. He smelled his own flesh and skin burning, his blood bubbling in the wound. He knew then that he dared not attempt another sorcerous attack on Vessa, Adri, or anyone else whom the throne would protect.

Adri spoke. "Jarsun, your great game is done. Your crimes are revealed. Your deceptions, your lies, your manipulations, everything is known to the world. There is no corner of Arthaloka where you can flee. You have only two choices now. I grant you these not out of the goodness of my heart, but because I would see an end to this conflict. The first choice is to go into exile in the ways, to a place of Great Father Vessa's choosing. He will open a one-way portal and permit you to enter that world, an alternate Arthaloka. There you will remain till the end of your natural time."

Jarsun snorted. "I can imagine. He will send me to a hell on earth. You may as well call it a prison world."

Adri inclined his head, not denying Jarsun's rebuttal. "Alternatively, you can choose to duel here and now on the field of Beha'al. If you live, you will be allowed to go to a world of your own choosing, and Guru Vessa will close the way permanently behind you, aided by the power of stonefire. The throne will not permit one such as you to remain alive upon this plane. If you refuse or defy me, or attempt to flee, then the throne will seek you out and strike you dead, no matter where you go."

Jarsun stared at Adri with hatred brimming in his heart. He wanted to lash out with all his fury, but the instant his anger began to rise, the color of the flames changed to deeper reds and darker orange. Stonefire made a sound very much like a rumbling growl. Jarsun swallowed and backed down at once. He knew when he was outmatched.

He still could not believe it had come to this. He had been outwitted and outmaneuvered.

He laughed then, long and low and bitter. "I see you have learned well, nephew. Perhaps you will make a good emperor yet."

"I *am* a good emperor," Adri replied harshly. "I will become a great one. I have asked my sister-in-law Karni to advise me from today onward. She will speak on behalf of my brother Shvate. We were ordained to rule together, jointly. Shvate is no more, abdicated by his own choice. But Karni will continue his legacy and honor his memory. From this day forth, the Burnt Empire will be remade anew. I have decided to end our campaign of endless war and conquest, to rule no longer by force and intimidation but to usher in a new reign of peace, prosperity, and inclusivity. I intend to take many lessons in that regard from my distant cousin and ally, Princess Krushni of Gwannland, which I now reinstate to its former borders and entrust with the governance and peacekeeping of all Eastern Arthaloka, while retaining each individual kingdom's sovereign independence."

Jarsun shook his head. "So you mean to take my territories from me as well? What is that if not conquering by other means?"

"I will conquer nothing. They will be free to govern themselves, with only the choice of calling upon the Burnt Empire for help should any future tyrants or conquerors rise in your wake. I mean to encourage them as well as all the kingdoms of the Burnt Empire to become republics and allow the will of the people to prevail."

Jarsun hawked and spat. "It will fail. These grandiose plans are too rich for peasant stomachs."

"Only time will show," Adri said. "Now, my patience is at an end. I ask you again, make your choice at once. Exile? Or duel?"

3

Jarsun turned to look at Vrath. So. He was to face his old antagonist once again. So be it. It was a better option than just being packed off to a prison world with his tail between his legs. At least he would get to kill one more Krushan before he left, going to a place of his own choosing. He would build his own Burnt Empire there, undo this foolish plan of peace and prosperity. The mortal world only understood the language of war. He would give them eternal war, eternal conflict, and rule them all with an iron fist.

"Duel," he said.

Krushni

～

1

"I MUST LEAVE YOU now, Mother," Krushni said, rising from the rock.

Vensera looked at her with eyes that betrayed the pain she was in. Krushni had repaired her wounds but could not spare her the pain they'd inflicted. There were limits to all sorcery, however powerful.

"Do us proud," her mother said. "Finish what you started."

Krushni embraced her, wondering if Vensera would still be alive by the time she returned. She hugged her mother like it was the last time, glad that at least in this life, she had been given the chance to embrace her mother one last time, and to tell her —

"I love you," she said, dabbing away the tears from her eye.

"I love you too," Vensera said. "May Mother Jeel go with you, my child."

Krushni nodded to her father, Gwann, who acknowledged her and said, "End it, Krushni. End it."

She turned and flew away from them, not daring to look back one last time.

She flew toward Jarsun.

2

Jarsun stared at her as she approached.

"*You?*" he said.

She ignored him and turned to Vrath.

The elder looked at her with a kindly expression in his grey eyes. "You are certain?"

"I have never been more certain of anything in my life," she said.

He accepted that and flew back to the hilltop to join Jilana.

Now Krushni was alone with Jarsun. She descended, landing within yards of where he stood. He stared at her with hateful eyes. But there was something else in his expression, something that might have been . . . shame? Fear? Fury? All of the above?

"I am to duel *you*?" he said. "You, a mere chit of a girl? This is ridiculous!"

Jarsun turned to the portal. "I will not lower myself to fighting a mere child! At least give me a worthy opponent."

Adri said nothing. The throne spoke for him, spitting a ball of fire at Jarsun's feet. The fire caught the grass on the hilltop, scorching it instantly, burning into the ground itself. Jarsun stepped back quickly.

"Hello, father from another life," Krushni said.

Jarsun turned back to look at her. There was that look again. She didn't know what it meant, but she was past caring. She had waited too long and felt too much to want to prolong this moment. All she wanted was to be done with this and move on with her life.

A world awaited.

"Enough talking, then. Fight me," she said.

Jarsun glanced back at the portal, then at her again. He was boxed in, she knew. It was the only way to force the hand of someone as wily and slippery as he. Like all bullies, however powerful and ensorcelled, Jarsun feared one thing above all: a fair fight. He was about to get one, whether he liked it or not.

He shook himself, shrugging his shoulders. "Very well, then. I will take great pleasure in killing you, child. I should have put you down along with your mother in the Red Desert, like a bitch and her whelps. I will correct that lapse now."

He came at her without further warning, stretching his body into an impossibly long, undulating length of muscled flesh, striking at her throat with his fangs.

Krushni was prepared. She grasped him with lightning speed, gripping him by *his* throat with both hands. He writhed and hissed and spat at her furiously, unaccustomed to being restrained.

"I made a great mistake that day in the desert, Father," she said. "I was stupid enough to think that because you were my patriarch, I owed you one more chance. It was I who convinced Mother to meet with you one last time to hear you out. That was my mistake. I thought I owed you that right. But now I know better. Being a patriarch didn't give you the right to tyrannize us. That day I lost the one person who loved me the most and whom I loved the most in the world. But now I have a chance to avenge her and save countless mothers from suffering the same fate. It's time to end your reign of evil, Father. And it falls to me to do it today."

She held him up for all to see. "Because, you see, Father, I know that while you seem to be indestructible, you have a weakness and I have learned it. I was given that secret by another mother, one who has hunted you for decades and has given me the privilege to fulfill the mission that was entrusted to her."

Jarsun hissed furiously, his serpent eyes flicking as he writhed and struggled to break free of her grip.

Krushni said to him, "Ladislew sends her farewell."

He stopped writhing for a moment, staring at her.

3

Krushni did exactly as Ladislew had instructed her. She grasped Jarsun by the throat in one hand and used the other to pry him open at the almost invisible seam that ran along the length of his body.

Jarsun is actually two beings in one body, Ladislew had said. *He can separate both by his own will and rejoin them at will. He cannot be slain by any means known to human or Krushan. Even if torn apart, the two halves remain powerful and deadly, though not as powerful as the single body conjoined. It is at that time he is most vulnerable, when he is separated. You must tear him asunder, then keep each part separate and make sure they can never be joined back together. That is the only way. I cannot do it alone, but you could, given help.*

Now Krushni prayed to Mother Jeel that Ladislew had been right.

Reaching into her belly, she pulled a weapon that she had contained within her for the longest time. It emerged, dripping with Krushni's own blood, an old dagger made of iron and bone, stained with the remnants of its last victim.

The dagger tipped with the same venom Jarsun had used to murder Krushni's mother.

She found the seam in Jarsun's head and used the dagger to pry it open. It took tremendous strength, the amount she would have needed to cut through a mountain. But she did it. The dagger snapped halfway, but she persevered with the broken blade, forcing it in as Jarsun howled an unearthly, hair-raising scream.

The two halves of Jarsun came apart with a sucking, liquid sound that turned her stomach. Both halves writhed and fought desperately, lashing out at her with their tails. They cut her face and neck and body in a hundred places, like a cat-o'-nine-tails worked by a madman. She ignored the pain and bleeding cuts and held on with all her might.

"Guru!" she called. "It is time!"

Vessa gestured. Two separate portals opened, one to either side of Krushni.

One led to a dark, smoking wilderness seething with clawed monstrosities. The other led to a desolate, frozen world teeming with gigantic tentacled shapes.

The two halves of Jarsun lashed around Krushni, taking hold of her arms, her throat, any part they could attach themselves to, holding on with the suction of a deep sea beast. She resisted them, ignored the agony of the venom they injected into her body, and gripped one half tightly enough to choke its shrieking head.

She threw the other half into the smoking world, through the portal.

It flew, writhing and snapping. At the very last instant, its tail caught hold of the edge of the portal, trying to drag itself back.

"Guru!" she shouted.

But Vessa had already given the command.

The portal irised shut, severing the tail that had poked into this world. It fell dead and bleeding onto the hillside and tumbled down in the tall grass. The rest of that half of Jarsun was gone with the closing of the portal.

Krushni turned to throw the other half through the second portal. A freezing wind howled through the opening, and a towering creature uncoiled its tentacles and probed at the portal.

"Now, child!" Vessa shouted.

Krushni threw the rest of Jarsun into the frozen world, just as the first tentacles were about to come through the opening.

The portal irised shut.

Vessa chanted the Ashcrit mantras that would shut off both portals for all time.

Now, even if Jarsun somehow found a way to use his powers in either world, he could never conjoin again to form the being that was himself, nor could he return to this world of Arthaloka.

Krushni slumped down on her knees, exhausted and bleeding all over. Every muscle in her body ached, but in her heart a great stone had been raised and flung aside, revealing a bounty of joy.

4

"You have done well, cousin," Adri said through the portal to Hastinaga. "I ask Great Father Vessa to now open another portal to return my armies home. I regret the loss of life already caused. I was too strongly influenced by Jarsun's lies and power games. I should never have supported that arrogant fool Dronas and served his agenda, even to further the interests of the Burnt Empire. And once I had indulged him and, by extension, Jarsun, had I rebuffed him, I would have risked his wrath against the empire's outlying territories, perhaps even Hastinaga itself. That is why I was compelled to wait for this battle, and the death of Dronas, to act. You can now rely on my support unconditionally. You have my word that Gwannland and Eastern Arthaloka will never see another Krushan soldier again."

Krushni nodded. "Thank you, cousin. The time for empires is past. It is time to let the people live as people."

He inclined his head. "Wise words. Rule well, cousin. Rule well, and live long, and love deeply."

Adri looked at Sauvali. "Empress Sauvali and I, along with my sister-in-law, Queen Karni, will help me correct the mistakes I have made in the past."

"And we, the elders, will be there to guide you through this brave new age," Jilana said.

"Goodbye, cousin Krushni," Adri said.

The portal winked shut.

So this is the end of the Burnt Empire, Krushni thought as she forced herself back to her feet.

And the beginning of a new world.

Our world.

Acknowledgments

Once again, John Joseph Adams, without whom the book you hold in your hands and its predecessor would not exist. He believed in me, in this story and these amazing characters, and has been a pillar of support. By far the finest editor I have had the pleasure of working with over a long career. Looking forward to many more books together, John!

The rest of the team at HMH has been awesome. It takes a publishing village to raise a book as beautiful as this one, and I can't thank them enough for their support and enthusiasm.

Hubris is what it takes to attempt a series this ambitious and complex.

Humility is what's required to carry it from idea to final publication.

Everything I do, alone at a computer for long hours over long days and even longer months and years, is only the beginning of the process by which a book goes from my hands to yours. There are literally hundreds of people involved along the way, and every single one of you deserves my thanks. This is the best job in the world, and it wouldn't be possible without you. Thank you for doing what you do to make books reach their readers. You are special, you matter, you are wonderful. Please keep doing what you doing!

My family is the foundation of my life, and I am only one small part of that matrix of love and solidarity. Unlike the cruel, often barbaric world of the Burnt Empire and its power-greedy demagogues, we are not supporters of patriarchal structures. I'd like to think that Krushita — or Krushni, or even simply Krush — better represents my true self, the self that lives with my wonderful, endlessly supportive, and giving family. They are my real world, my reality. The only reason I can vanish into the secondary world of an epic fantasy series for hours each day for decades is because I have them to return home to at the end. They make it all possible by making me possible.

Thank you, Biki, Yashka, Yoda, Helene, and the littlest one of us all, Leia. Love and only love forever. We go on.

Ashok Kumar Banker